D0285735

MOONLIGHTER

MOONLIGHTER

sarina bowen

TUXBURY PUBLISHING LLC

Copyright © 2019 by Sarina Bowen

All rights reserved.

No part of this book may be reproduced in any form or by any electronic or mechanical means, including information storage and retrieval systems, without written permission from the author, except for the use of brief quotations in a book review.

Cover design by: Hang Le

EARLY JULY

ERIC

REPORTING for a lunch date at my family's security firm is always trippy.

At first glance, the converted old factory building on West 18th Street might belong to any company. The lobby—with its sleek, industrial furnishings and employee turnstiles— is carefully nondescript. There's no sign, though. That's your first clue. No logo. No name.

My brother likes secrets. So much so that I don't actually know the legal name of this place. To outsiders—such as me—Max refers to it as The Company. The family joke is that I'll learn the name in his will after he dies.

"But what if I die first?" I always ask.

"You won't," is his reply. "Your line of work is safer than mine."

And that's saying something, since I'm a professional hockey player. My workdays are spent facing down a dozen guys with big sticks who are trying to crush me like a bug.

I approach the receptionist behind the imposing reception desk. She looks normal enough. She's pretty hot, honestly. Although she's probably trained in a dozen ways to kill me. My brother likes to hire sweet young things with a military background and serious skills at the firing range.

"Hi there," I say as she waves me forward. I happen to know that the desk itself is bulletproof. And there's an armored cabinet at the receptionist's feet, should she wish to make herself scarce. And those are just the security features that I know about. "I'm Eric Bayer, and I have a lunch date with the assholes who run this place."

The young woman blinks. And then her eyes light up with recognition. After all, I look a lot like a scruffier, less intense version of her boss. She gives me a big, flirtatious smile. "Nice to meet you, Eric Bayer."

I hold my breath, because what comes next is crucial for her job security.

There's a beat of hesitation on her side of the desk. But then she does exactly the right thing. "Can I see some ID?"

"Of course." I slide my driver's license across the granite countertop, happy that she got it right. Even if she recognizes me from TV—and my team got a whole lot of publicity this past month—the poor thing would have been fired if she didn't verify my identity.

My brother is a ruthless employer. And kind of a dick. But he can't afford to make mistakes. His clients' lives are on the line.

The receptionist scans my ID. Then she pretends to scrutinize it. But we both know that a computer is currently checking my driver's license number against a database of known undesirables. And because there are approximately seventeen cameras focused on me at the moment, a human is also watching somewhere, and weighing in on whether or not I'll be allowed upstairs.

There's a soft chime, after which a little green light on her desk winks on.

I grin. "You know what that means."

"Congratulations on not being an imposter. Here's your pass and your ID." She takes another appreciative glance at my photo before handing it back. She looks me dead in the eye and drops her voice to a sultry whisper that makes "Have a nice lunch" sound dirty.

"You know it." I throw in a wink to amuse whomever is manning the control room right now. Maybe I'll ask for her number on my way out.

But first, lunch. I move my ass toward the elevators. The doors part as I arrive. I step inside, and they close again.

A sensor has already scanned the chip on my visitor's pass, so the moment the doors close, the car begins to rise toward the sixth floor. The elevator buttons wouldn't even work if I pressed one. Only employees can choose a destination, and only if they're approved to go there.

It's like an even more paranoid version of the Death Star. Although, I've been promised tacos, and I don't think the dark lord eats Mexican.

Buying me lunch is no strain, because my brother and my dad have made several billion dollars together. And they did it by being the two most paranoid men in Manhattan.

I glide slowly higher, past five floors I've never visited. But presumably they're filled with busy employees. My father started this company when I was eleven years old. Before that, he had a couple of successful decades as a naval intelligence officer, and then as a police chief on Long Island, where I grew up.

In my father's hands, The Company was an ordinary private security firm. Back then it even had a name — Bayer Security. If you had some money and needed to keep your family safe, you could call Carl Bayer to set up a discreet security detail.

But then, about ten years ago, my brother left his government job. Although he was never allowed to say so, I'm pretty sure he used to be a CIA analyst specializing in cyber security.

So Max joined Dad's firm, offering to help Dad branch out into e-security as well as physical security. I thought their partnership wouldn't last the week. It's generous to say that Dad and Max both have strong personalities. The less generous version is that Dad's kind of a cheerful tyrant and Max is a broody asshole.

Besides — Dad's gumshoe security work and Max's hacker skills didn't seem to have much in common.

But what do I know? The firm took off like a rocket and never looked back. They made their billions by chaining Max's genius brain to Dad's New York connections.

Not only did my brother accurately predict the importance of cybersecurity, he was one of the first geniuses on the scene. As security evolved from muscles and guns to a cyber arms race, he and Dad — plus Max's college roommate — began writing the code and designing the tools that keep captains of industry safe and their data secure. They also license a few of their toys to other security companies and probably the government.

It's the most successful company that you've never heard of.

In contrast, I've been a professional athlete for fifteen years. I make seven million dollars a year, and I'm basically the family slacker.

The elevator doors part on the sixth floor. I step out into a vast open space. This is no typical C-suite of plush offices. It looks more like a Silicon Valley startup, with brightly colored furniture and a big kitchen along one wall. There are offices up here, but the majority of the floor space remains open for collaboration and for testing whatever The Company needs to test. Weapons, maybe. Or detection devices. Facial recognition software imbedded in sunglasses. Tiny drones disguised as dragonflies. A phone signal jammer that looks like an ordinary pencil eraser.

Fun times on the sixth floor. I'm just here for the tacos.

My brother is sitting in his office, talking a mile a minute into his earpiece, his hands typing furiously at the same time. The office window looks normal until you happen to glance at the computer screen. Its display looks black, but that's only a trick. The glass in his office window blocks light waves from his monitor so that nobody passing by can read what's on his screen.

The first time he showed me that glass in action, I thought it was amazing. "Jesus, really?" I'd said, ducking in and out of the office to see the difference. "You're getting a patent for that, right?"

"No fucking way!" Max had looked appalled. "Only losers get patents. You have to disclose too much information. Patents are for suckers."

If we didn't look vaguely alike, it would be hard to guess we share a gene pool.

Dad's office door is open, but he's not inside. So I scan the wide-open areas, looking for his silver hair.

But it's busy up here. Two young women are perched on an indescribable piece of furniture. It's a bright salmon-colored sofa that's shaped like a cresting wave. They're having a discussion which involves wild gesticulation and frequent references to a laptop on the table in front of them.

Then there's the two guys who are testing some kind of electronic device over against the wall. One of them is standing with his arms and legs spread, while the other one waves a hand-held gizmo at his body. I can't make any sense of it. But there's a ringing sound, and the two guys let out a whoop and high-five each other in an obvious nerdgasm.

And people think my job is weird.

I finally spot my father at the other end of the space, inside a conference room resembling a glassed-in tank. Dad's assistant — Shelby — spots me approaching and opens the door. "Come in, Eric!" she says. "He's in a feisty mood today, though. Careful."

My father has been in a feisty mood for seventy-six years, and we both know it. "Hey, pops. What's happening?"

"Eric." He stands up and gives me a bear hug. My dad is an affectionate man. Part of the reason his firm grew so fast (even before my genius brother got involved) is that he's such a magnetic person. He knows everyone in New York City, and he's not afraid to hug 'em all. "Great to see ya. Shame about game seven."

"Isn't it?" I try to keep my expression neutral, but it's going to be a while until I feel okay about it. We lost in the last game of the final round. We were literally one goal away from the Stanley Cup. I played on an aching knee, with a barely healed shoulder. I gave it everything I had, and my everything wasn't quite enough.

"Sit, sit, sit!" Dad offers me a conference room chair like it's a royal throne. Although, given the money they throw around, it might cost as much.

I sit down and lean back into the leather seat. "Where's this taco joint, anyway? Is it in the neighborhood?"

"Listen," Dad says. "I need you to do something for me."

"Hmm?" I'm busy sizing him up, because I haven't seen him in a while, and he's getting on in years. He was forty when Max was born, and forty-two when I came along.

But I have to admit he looks as heathy as ever. He's dressed in khaki pants and a button down, but there's a very fit body under the starched fabric. He has a closet full of the same J. Press blue oxfords, which the housekeeper irons each week and rehangs in his closet.

The scent of Niagara shirt starch—the kind in the spray can? It's the scent of my childhood.

"You look good, Dad. You still working out?" Ten years ago I set him up with a personal trainer for his birthday. I was twenty-five and making seven figures a year and it still seemed to both of us like an extravagant gift. But now he and Max could buy and sell me ten times over.

"Twice a week!" Dad crows. "But listen—this favor…"

"I'm on vacation," I say preemptively. "Our season lasted as long as a season can last, so I only get a few more weeks off. I plan to enjoy them."

"A few weeks," my dad says slowly. "We only need one. Two, tops."

"For what?" Now I'm alarmed. "I'm just here for lunch."

In truth, my schedule is flexible. When it became clear that we'd finally make the playoffs, not one guy on the team wanted to pick the date for his vacation getaway. We didn't want to jinx ourselves.

It didn't help. Now we're home again, with no parade to plan and no cup to carry down the Brooklyn Promenade.

But that doesn't mean I'm not a busy man. I need to work out like a beast this summer. I've already drawn up my cardio and gym schedules. I need to reach peak performance just as training camp starts again in August.

My dad is still talking, though. "This client is a lovely young woman," he's saying. "Her only crime was to date a man who isn't as nice as he seemed."

"Bummer," I say carefully. "But that doesn't have anything to do with me."

"She broke up with him, and he didn't take it well."

"That's a dick move," I empathize. "But I'm sure you guys can keep her safe."

"No, you will," says Max from the doorway. And when I look up, he's smirking at me.

"No, I won't," I push back from the table. "Let's go, okay? I'm starved."

"We're staying right here," Dad says. "Scout is bringing in the food from some food cart she loves. She says the flavors are outta this world."

Something tells me they'd need to be the best tacos in the galaxy to make up for whatever Max and my father are trying to railroad me into right now. "I'm just here for lunch. You guys know that, right?"

"Ah, there's our client now."

I look up to see a beautiful woman striding toward the conference room in shiny high heels. For a second I get a little stuck staring at the lower half of her, because there are legs for *days*. But because I've learned to be subtle in my thirty-four years, I lift my gaze—past the mango-colored designer suit, and the sweep of long shiny hair—to take in her pristine face.

Oh, hell. It's a familiar face. A very beautiful one, but not one I wanted to see today. Alex Engels and I have history—but not the simple, sexual kind.

Nothing about Alex is simple, in fact. She's the most successful female CEO in America. Her father was one of my dad's first corporate clients. The first time I met her, I was thirteen and she was eleven. We were friends. Briefly, anyway.

It was the summer just after my mother left the family for good. My father was trying to get his private security business off the ground. He was scrambling for childcare, so he brought me to stay at the Engels mansion on Martha's Vineyard, while my father flew around the world protecting Alex's father.

I was a very angry boy back then. Not the best company. But Alex was lonely, too. She was an only child who'd also lost her mother. So she put up with me. We became the kind of reluctant friends that lonely middle-schoolers can still be when their hormones haven't kicked in yet.

Which is to say that she badgered me into all kinds of activities that summer, and I let her. We biked. We swam. We spied on the entire staff of the Engels estate, and invented secret machinations for everyone coming and going. We eluded our fathers, her summertime nanny, the tennis instructor and anyone else who might have tried to rein us in.

It was probably just what my wounded little soul needed.

But after that, I didn't see her for years. Twenty-one years, to be exact. I found myself doing this math just three months ago when a chance event brought us face to face at a black tie party in Bal Harbor, Florida.

That moment went poorly. And now I am inwardly cringing as Alex draws near. My father gallantly sweeps open the door to the conference room and beckons her inside. "Alex! You lovely thing. It's a pleasure to see you again."

"Hey, Alex," Max says, reaching out to shake her hand. "Thanks for coming downtown."

"No, thank *you* for handling my crisis on short notice," she says in that silky voice of hers. This lady was born with poise. I've only seen her flustered once in my life.

Unfortunately, that one instance was last time we met.

"…And you remember my younger son, Eric," my father says.

I see Alex stiffen. Then her gaze swings toward me, where I'm staying out of the way in the corner, trying to guess how to play this.

"Eric," she says quietly. "Of *course* I remember Eric." But then two bright spots appear on her cheekbones. And if this were a Disney movie, her nose would start to grow right now from that lie she just told. Because when Alex and I saw each other in April, she did not, in fact, remember me.

Kids, it was awkward.

2
————

ALEX

OH BOY. This is all my fault. I deserve Eric Bayer's scowl. And I owe him an apology.

Unfortunately, that's been a theme this year. I've made so many mistakes that I've lost count.

One of those errors is leaning back in his chair, his handsome face lifted toward mine, hesitation in his intelligent gray eyes. Eric Bayer is one of the more attractive men I've ever had the pleasure to meet. Too bad all that raw, masculine beauty addled me so badly this spring that I failed to recognize him.

"How've you been, Alex?" he asks calmly.

"Um…" That useless non-word just sort of hangs over the gleaming conference table. I never say *um*. I'm an industry leader. I'm as comfortable at a lectern in front of a full auditorium as I am in my own living room. And I've been responding politely to small talk since I was a toddler.

But today? All I've got is *um*.

Carl Bayer chuckles. "Alex needs our help, or she wouldn't be here right now," he says, stepping in to smooth things over. "But Eric doesn't know your story. I promised you complete discretion. So I needed to get both of you in a room before I said a word about it. How long has it been since you two saw each other? Twenty years?"

"Twenty-one," I blurt out before I can think better of it. "Except…"

"…We saw each other in April," he says smoothly. "But only for a split second."

"Only for a split second," I echo. "And I'm ashamed to say that I didn't recognize Eric."

"Really?" His brother Max laughs.

"Really," I say with a sigh, hoping Eric believes me. And now I'm even more embarrassed, because when the two are side by side, the resemblance is obvious. I've known Max for a few years, since I hired him to handle my corporate security.

And I'd known in a vague way that Eric had become a professional athlete. But I didn't anticipate seeing him at that Brooklyn Bruisers benefit in Florida.

"It was no big deal," Eric says quietly.

I shoot him a grateful glance. I'll have to find a moment to finally apologize. It's not clear to me why he's here, anyway. Unless he's just a big fan of tacos and visiting his family while he's on vacation?

"Sorry I'm late!"

We all turn at the sound of a female voice. Scout enters the room carrying a big box with a popular taco truck's label on the side. "Hey Alex! I hope you're hungry. I bought some of everything they had."

My stomach growls at the first whiff of spicy pork. Lately I'm starving all the time. And the scent of cumin and chilis is almost more than I can bear.

"Excellent work, as always," Max says.

Scout isn't his assistant, though. She's his lead investigator. "Here, Max. Make yourself useful." She tosses him a stack of plates to distribute. "Alex, chicken, pork or steak?"

"Yes."

Scout laughs. "Fair enough." She pulls three wrapped tacos from the box and hands them over to me. "And Eric? Shame about game seven."

He sighs. "I'll take whatever you've got."

"See that, guys? Eric is pleasant and biddable. Everyone be more like Eric."

"He's pleasant to *you* maybe," Max chuckles. "He ignores me."

"So do I, though," Scout says.

While the others continue to bicker and dole out the lunch, I take my plate and move around the table to sit next to Eric. "Hi," I say lightly, giving him a friendly smile. As if it could make up for the obnoxious thing I said to him in April.

As if.

"Hi yourself," he rumbles. Then he unwraps a taco and ignores me.

Ah, well. I guess three or four months isn't enough time to get over a bruised ego. I was the host of a beautiful party on a beautiful beach. But I was distraught that night. I'd recently learned that I was pregnant, which should have been joyous news. Except —and this still shames me—I wasn't sure who the father was.

That's been settled now. But in April I was a total wreck. It was the first time in my life that I'd made such a serious error of judgment and planning. And instead of curling up in a ball like I'd wanted to, I'd had to smile my way through a black tie party for charity.

By the end of the night I was exhausted and brittle. And that's when I came face to face with a certain gorgeous hockey player. We'd been accidentally trading stares earlier in the evening. Or, rather, I'd *assumed* it was accidental. Every time I looked up he was gazing at me. I thought it was awfully forward of him.

And then he approached.

"Hey, Alex. I've been waiting all night to speak to you." He gave me a panty-melting smile. "I was hoping we could finally sit down together for a drink. Maybe go somewhere quieter?"

His approach was so familiar. So *slick*, or so I thought. In retrospect, it was just what you might say to someone who was supposed to remember that the two of you spent an entire month of your childhood together on the beach at Martha's Vineyard.

But I didn't understand. I thought he was a handsome stranger trying to get under my Dior gown. "Look, I'm flattered," I'd said. "And I'm sure you're *really* good company in private." I even gave him a wink of understanding that now makes me want to die. "But I am *not* in the market tonight. I'm whatever the opposite of being in the market is."

He'd opened his mouth to argue, but then shut it again. Twice. Then an expression I know too well overtook his rugged face.

Embarrassment. A guy like that doesn't get shot down.

"Right," he'd said eventually, letting out an awkward chuckle. "Never mind, then. Nice party. Thank you for doing all this for children's charities."

He'd given me a polite head bow, plunked his drink onto the tray of a passing waiter, and made his escape. He left the party so fast I could almost see contrails behind him.

It wasn't until the following day when I learned of my mistake. At breakfast, my assistant, Rolf, asked me if Eric Bayer had found a minute to talk with me. "I sent him over to you at one point, but someone grabbed you before he got there."

"Eric Bayer?" Of course I recognized the name. "He was at the party?"

Rolf gave me a crooked smile. "You didn't *see* him? Hot hockey player? Defenseman? Pretty gray eyes? He left a note at the front desk before the party, asking if the two of you could catch up. It's in your itinerary folder. And I assumed you knew each other."

"A note?" I hadn't found it.

But then it all clicked, and that's when the shame set in. Twelve hours too late, I realized I'd blown off an old friend after failing to recognize him.

I was *mortified*. As the head of a multinational corporation, remembering names and faces was half the job. I could pick out tech CEOs from across a crowded room. I knew their wives names and their assistants' quirks. I took pride in remembering everyone I met.

Except Eric Bayer.

Here's the thing about making a faux pax: you *must* apologize immediately. If you don't, it just gets worse when you see that person again. But I didn't do it. I didn't have his address, and I couldn't think what to say to this man that I'd known when we were both in middle school. Besides—I thought the chances of bumping into him again were low.

Yet here we are.

I'm still embarrassed. But not too embarrassed to eat all three tacos in rapid succession.

"Have another?" Scout offers. "There's more."

When I glance around, I see that everyone else has barely begun eating. Max looks at my plate, and then his lips twitch.

"No, thank you," I say primly.

"Mexican soda?" Scout offers.

"Sure, why not?" I say. "Maybe my tape worm will like that, too."

There are polite chuckles. But my face flames.

"Now Alex," Carl says, pushing his plate aside. "Let's go over your security concerns for this upcoming trip."

Oh, goody. Another awkward thing to navigate. "Well, I'm probably being overly cautious."

"I wouldn't say that," Carl argues. "A man put his hands on you in anger. That's serious business."

I take a breath in through my nose and focus all my attention on the older man. I know it's not my fault that my ex turned out to be a first rate creep. But I still feel ashamed. Even though everyone in this room is here to help me.

Except Eric. I really wish he wasn't about to hear any of this.

"Okay, thank you," I say softly.

Carl gives me a kind smile. He's still a handsome fella. It's easy to see where the Bayer brothers got their good looks. Maybe Carl's hair has thinned, but his shoulders are square and his posture is commanding. "You're headed to an unfamiliar location, to a high stress event. We won't let you face that alone."

"Thank you," I say again, my eyes hot. People at work sometimes describe me as having ice in my veins. But it's not true today. Carl's kind words make my eyes sting. And here's something I didn't know about being pregnant—it makes you more emotional. I don't know if I've ever felt as vulnerable as I do right now.

Carl takes a small remote control device out of his pocket, and points it at the clear glass wall. "Is this our guy?" When he presses a button, an image resolves on the surface of the glass, seemingly out of thin air.

I would be very impressed by this slick technology if I weren't looking at a life-size photo of Jared Tatum, my ex. Honestly, "ex" is even a stretch. It doesn't take too long to realize a man is a liar and a weasel.

It doesn't take long to get pregnant, either. But that's on me.

So maybe I'm having a petulant loser's baby. But at thirty-two, with no soulmate in sight, to raise the child myself was an easy decision. I always wanted a family, though I assumed I'd have a nice husband first.

But the talent pool of men my age just keeps getting thinner. The nice guys are already married. And the few who aren't don't date. Or they date women younger than I am.

Besides, I'm so used to my independence that I'm beginning to think I'm not marriage material. I don't like to take help from others. Or advice. You don't get to be a CEO without trusting your own gut above all others.

And, either way, I'll have a baby at New Year's, in less than six months. Becoming a single mom is my choice to make, and I've made it.

"Who is this guy?" Eric asks beside me. If I'm not mistaken, there's a note of disdain in his voice.

I force myself to look up at the screen again. "My ex," I say curtly. "We dated in March and April, until I realized he was only interested in my father's venture capital fund."

"Jared Tatum, thirty-three years old," Carl supplies. "Founder and CEO of Fitband International."

"That better be him," Max says. "Otherwise I've hacked into an unrelated man's email and bank accounts."

"You hacked him? Is that legal?" I hear myself ask. And then I realize that's a stupid question. Of course it's not legal. The reason I pay this security firm so well is that they're willing and able to do things that ordinary people can't. "Never mind, I retract the question."

Max clicks his pen. "There's actually no law against this particular hack. But my methods are a trade secret."

"I understand completely." Max knows all my secrets, too. I trust him with my life and my corporation.

He nods. "So, I'm going to explain what I did, because it's instructive, not just for this moment, but for your own protection."

"Okay."

"First we determined that your ex likes pork buns, specifically the ones from this place around the corner from his building."

"Ben's Buns," I say.

"That's the place. So I built a little app that offers fifty percent off pork buns. We papered your ex's car and apartment with flyers until we convinced him to download the app and try it out."

"Excuse me," Scout says with a mouth full of taco. "*Who* convinced him to try it out?"

Max chuckles. "Okay, fine. Scout was the brains of this part of the operation." Their eyes meet, and there's a moment of tension.

Hmm. Interesting.

"So…" Max turns to me again. "Your ex probably makes more than most people will ever have, but the man likes to save money on pork buns. He clicked through the Terms of Service on this app and ordered some pork."

"Oh." I think I know where this story is going.

"The TOS gave me the right to any and all data from his phone."

"No shit?" Eric says. "You evil bastard."

Max grins. "Yup. He's ordered twenty-eight dollars worth of buns. So I purchased his digital footprint for fourteen bucks."

"But how is *that* legal?" Eric asks.

Max shrugs. "If I used the data for, say, embezzlement or insider trading, *then* I'll have broken the law. All I've done so far is to overstep the app store terms of service. I wrote an evil piece of software, but it passed their shitty quality review. That's on them."

"That's…amazing," I whisper.

"No." Max shakes his head. "It's really not. But this is the world we live in, Alex. Some of us understand how it actually works, and some of us don't."

Now there's a sobering thought.

Carl Bayer clears his throat and then steers us all back to the topic at hand. "What is our comfort level with Mr. Tatum attending the Big Island Conference?"

"Very high," Max responds. "His decision to attend was sudden. But now he holds a nonrefundable plane ticket. And just this morning he bought a new golf club for the trip."

"What a party animal," Eric mumbles. And if I weren't so stressed out about seeing my ex at the conference, I'd laugh.

"Has he stopped trying to contact you?" Carl asks me.

I shake my head. "The last message was two days ago—the one I forwarded to you." Carl nods. "None since then. But, of course, he mentioned the conference—and wanting to get back together." I fight off a shudder.

"Right," the older man says. "So that's why we're going to keep him away from you in Hawaii. Our goal is simple—minimal contact with Mr. Tatum. He'll get no access. No extended verbal contact—nothing beyond a passing 'hello,' and no closer than ten feet. Not until he's back in New York, anyway. That's when we'll approach him for further negotiations."

"Negotiations?" Eric asks.

"That part is on a need-to-know basis," his father says.

My face burns again. Nobody knows I'm pregnant. Jared Tatum has no idea. I'm going to eventually have to tell him, and convince him to sign away his custodial rights. There will probably be a great deal of money involved in this negotiation.

Carl Bayer and a lawyer are going to handle the whole thing. But I already feel dirty.

"There are a few ways we can work this at the conference," Max Bayer says. "But one idea in particular stands out."

"That I should just stay home?" I ask, looking away from the screen. The idea of trying to avoid Jared for a week straight exhausts me.

"You can if you wish," Max says gently.

"No, I really can't. I've bet my entire career on this product launch." That's not an exaggeration. "So, hit me with your second-best solution." Although nothing short of time travel can fix the hideous mistake I made by trusting Jared Tatum.

"If Tatum thinks you've moved on, he'll be less likely to bother you," Carl says. "So your bodyguard for the week will play the part of your new boyfriend."

"Your big, strong, grumpy, possessive boyfriend," Max says with obvious glee.

"Oh, jeez." I laugh, but it's not a horrible idea. "So who's playing the role of my…" I break off, because it hits me. Now I know exactly why Eric is at this meeting.

But when I glance at him, he's staring intently at the top of his water bottle, as if something fascinating were printed there.

And just when I thought it couldn't get any more awkward.

3

ERIC

"MAX, you're such an asshole. A first rate, manipulating, stinking pile of shit."

"Tell me how you really feel." My brother actually laughs.

To my credit, I sat through the rest of the meeting in total silence. I only made one noise, the moment my brother happened to mention when Alex was leaving for Hawaii. I made an honest-to-god choking sound when he said that the conference starts in forty-eight hours.

I've been railroaded into traveling five thousand miles. And now that Alex has left the building—escorted by my father and Scout—I can finally tell my brother exactly what I think of his plan. "Of all the asshole maneuvers you've ever pulled, this is the assholiest."

He snickers. "Come with me. Upstairs."

"Why?" I snarl. "It's not enough that you're sending me to Hawaii against my will? You have to march me around your office, too?"

He rolls his eyes. "I thought you might want to play some ping-pong, that's all."

I make an angry noise. But the truth is that smashing a ball into my brother sounds pretty good right about now.

The jerk calmly tosses a few bottles into the recycling bin and then holds open the conference room door for me. It's a brilliant move on his part because out here in the center of the suite, I can't yell at him without sounding like a dick.

"Hey, Eric!" Shelby greets me as we emerge. "How were the tacos?"

"Great," I say because none of this is Shelby's fault. "But now I have heartburn," I mumble.

My brother walks me past the main elevators to a smaller one just beyond. He presses his palm against a metal plate on the wall. There's no call button here. This elevator only responds to Max and a few of his closest associates, and it's the only way to get to his apartment on the penthouse floor above us.

The door opens immediately, and we both get in. As soon as the doors close again, I'm back to giving him the business. "I can't even tell you how uncomfortable this is. *So* awkward. So obnoxious. This is heavy handed, even for you."

"A little," he admits as the doors open again. "Dad said you'd be mad. But there wasn't time to find someone else. Come on. Let's play."

I follow him into his ridiculous apartment where everything is brick and leather and ten times larger than necessary. The ping-pong table is in the center of the space, between the dining table and the living room furniture. I choose a paddle and take up a position at one end.

"A thousand dollars a point," Max says. "But I serve first."

"Sure." Ping-pong is perhaps the only interest we've ever had in common. From birth, the two of us could not be more different. Which is why I'm continuously baffled by the fact that he and my father keep trying to pull me into the family business.

Max serves, and I return it, kicking off a fierce volley. We slam the ball back and forth seven or eight times in a row before I'm able to put one out of his reach near the corner of the table.

He pauses before serving again. "It's a week in Hawaii," he says. "You don't have any better plans." Then he serves, the bastard.

"You don't *know* that," I snap, my eyes focused on the ball. "And why blindside me?"

"Because it works," the infuriating pissant says.

I will kill you with my bare hands. But first I'm going to destroy him at ping-pong. Our volley lasts twice as long this time, but after a dozen returns, I've lulled him into a false sense of security. *Bam.* I sear his backhand again. He gets the paddle on the ball, but his return misses the table.

I chase flying objects for a living, after all.

"Nice one," he says calmly. "You *are* going to help Alex, right?"

"Of *course* I'll help Alex. And then I'll never accept another lunch invitation from you again. Why would I, when you manipulate me? You could have just explained the situation, and then asked for my help."

He leans against the table. "Because every other time I've explained a situation and asked for your help you turn me down."

"Those other times it wasn't Alex." Even if she doesn't remember me, I remember her, and her family's kindness. They housed me at their beach mansion for eight weeks at a difficult time in my life.

Besides—only an asshole would let a predator menace an old friend. Maybe I'm self-centered, but I'm not an animal. Alex and I used to be friends. She was eleven that summer, going on thirty-one. She was fierce and clever and completely entertaining.

So this won't be a boring week. And—not that I'm admitting this to Max—I can probably work out as hard in Hawaii as I can at home. With better scenery.

But there are a few details that don't add up. "What's the deal with this ex of hers? He was violent?"

"He's a dickweasel," Max says. "There are other complications, too."

"Like what?"

"She'll explain. What else are you going to talk about on the twelve-hour flight? You'd better go home and pack."

"You're just trying to get rid of me before I score on you again. You got what you wanted, and now you have other people to manipulate."

He shrugs. "Your flight leaves at six p.m."

"Six...*today?* The conference doesn't start until Thursday!"

"Sure, but she took meetings for Wednesday, and there's a six-hour time difference. Alex needs to acclimate."

I make a noise of rage. "You arrogant, controlling, manipulative motherfucker."

Max's eyes go to his smart watch, where I'm sure he gets an incoming message every seven seconds. Ignoring the insults, he asks, "She honestly didn't recognize you?"

"No!" I bellow.

He glances up and smiles. "Ouch."

I want to choke him. I really do. It might be the end of me, though. This fucking apartment is probably equipped with a mechanism that senses danger. If I lunge for him, the ping-pong table would probably swallow me whole and digest me slowly. Like a high-tech Venus Flytrap.

"Just tell me why," I say. "Why me? Anyone could stand next to Alex and ward off her ex-boyfriend."

"Because you're real," Max says, simultaneously typing about ninety-eight words per minute into his watch. "Your story checks out. Professional athlete. Friend of Alex's family from way back. You don't have to fake anything. Even your ill-fated meeting this spring fits with the story. Old friends who reconnected."

Or failed to. When I roll my eyes, I catch a glimpse at the clock on the wall. It's titanium, and probably doubles as a grenade launcher. In this place, nothing is exactly what it seems. Except for the time, which is pushing three o'clock. "Fuck me. I really do have to go home and pack."

And here I thought I was going to spend the evening watching violent movies in my underwear and eating take-out. As one does. But now I'm getting on a twelve-hour flight?

How do I get myself into these situations?

"Safe travels," my brother grunts. He taps the screen, oblivious to my irritation. "I just deposited two grand into your bank account. Good game. And don't let that fucker near Alex."

"I won't. Jesus." Just because I don't want this job doesn't mean I won't do it well. This ex of hers *hits* women? If he so much as blinks in our direction, I'll crack him in half. And I'll enjoy it.

"Later, then." There's no chance Max wants a hug or to walk me out, so I just turn and head for the exit.

"One more thing?" he says.

I pause on my way to the elevator. "What now?"

"Don't fuck her. She's vulnerable right now."

"Oh, please," I mutter, remembering how quickly she shut me down in Florida.

Then I get the hell out of there.

I'M BARELY OUT of the building by the time Max's travel coordinator starts sending me texts. *Check your email for a packing list. Car arrives in 2 hours, 7 minutes.*

I read the email on the train back to Brooklyn.

Pack the following clothing:

White dress shirt

Business suit in gray or navy blue

Silk tie

Dress shoes

Casual shoes

Resort wear for a 5-day stay. (Laundry service available)

Bathing suit, beach wear

Socks, underwear, toiletries

Technology and Identification:

Personal electronics and chargers

Passport

Weaponry and tech equipment:

K-Tech phone

Await further instructions and hardware.

I'm on the road with my team eighty nights a year. It's a hard way to live, and probably goes a long way toward explaining why I'm single.

But the upside? Packing a suitcase is as easy as breathing. Within thirty minutes of stepping into my apartment, I'm done. Then I ask the front desk to hold my mail. That takes three more minutes.

Then? I search my brain for anyone else who might need to hear that I'll be gone for five days, and I come up mostly empty. My calendar has me out to dinner with my teammates on Thursday night. But that happens seventy nights a year. I'm not sure they'll even miss me.

Max is just lucky that I'm aggressively single.

The black sedan that Max's travel team sends to pick me up is right on time. "I'm heading to the private air terminal at LaGuardia," I tell the driver.

"Yessir. It's been handled."

Of course it has. This car was probably hired before I even turned up for lunch today.

What a dick my brother is.

Sometimes, my conscience adds. Max is a good man. A loyal man. In a foxhole, there's nobody I'd rather have at my side. But he doesn't do emotions like normal people.

He used to, I guess. When we were kids, he was pretty normal. We cried in the same Disney movies. He smiled as often as anyone else.

Something changed, though, after he went to work in Washington, DC. My brother was a spy, even if he never admitted it. "Intelligence analyst" is as much as he would ever say. And that job wears on a guy, I guess. He spent several years in Washington before leaving whichever agency had crushed his spirit.

I don't know the whole story. And he'll never tell me, anyway.

When we reach the airport, my sedan pulls up behind an identical black sedan, whose driver pulls a mango-colored suitcase from the trunk.

Alex waits on the curb, looking both impatient and ridiculously attractive. She's changed into a more casual dress, but her long, shapely legs are still there, taunting me. If she were even a little bit more receptive, I'd already be plotting to have those legs wrapped around my naked body later.

I'm not in the market, she'd snapped. Apparently scrawny assholes are her type, though.

Women confuse me. They really do.

I jump out and get my bag, thanking the driver. I pick up my suitcase, and then I pick up Alex's, too.

"Eric," she says sharply by way of a greeting. "You don't have to carry my things."

"Don't I?" I grumble. "Wouldn't your boyfriend do that? Be kind of a dick move not to, honestly." With both bags in hand, I turn toward the doors, which slide open for me. I walk into the terminal without checking to see if she's followed me.

Which, for the record, is also a dick move. But nobody's perfect.

"Look," she says, tapping along behind me in a pair of impractical shoes. "Can I just get my apology out of the way?"

"Sure, go for it." If the lady wants to apologize for wounding my ego at a party, who am I to say no?

"I didn't recognize you."

"Yeah, I got that."

She puts a smooth hand on my wrist, stopping my progress. "I *really* didn't recognize you. And I want to show you why."

"Show me?" I snort. "Was I wearing a disguise?"

"Well—"

That's when our conversation is interrupted by a well-dressed woman who asks for our IDs. Alex hands hers over, and I do the same. This is luxury travel—you don't wait in line. There isn't even a desk, just this fashionably dressed person who spends ten seconds verifying our identities before waving us over to a private waiting room.

"It will just be five minutes," we're promised.

We sit side by side on a leather sofa, and I try not to notice that Alex is wearing a sexy, floral perfume. She extracts a phone from her pocketbook, tapping the screen a few times, pulling up a photograph.

The moment I see it, I let out a bark of laughter. "Holy shit." I take her phone. It's a photo of the two of us, taken more than twenty years ago. We're standing in front of the Vineyard Tennis Club, where her father was a member. "Jesus Christ. We are hilarious." The disgruntled expression on both of our faces is priceless.

"Aren't we?"

"Yeah, but—" I laugh again. And it's not because of eleven-year-old Alex. She looks more or less the same, with piercing blue eyes and shiny hair falling onto her shoulders. I'd know her anywhere.

But holy cannoli—I am unrecognizable. This photo must have been taken about ten minutes before I hit puberty. I'm not just skinny but *scrawny*, with pointy elbows and knobby knees sticking out of my white tennis shorts.

"So I was really a looker, is what you're saying?"

She smirks. "You were twelve."

"Thirteen."

"Still. I hadn't seen you since you were just a kid. I had this vague idea that you played a sport. But I had no idea you were on Nate Kattenberger's hockey team. He never mentioned the connection between one of his players and our mutual security company."

"How do you know Nate?" I ask.

"College. He was one of my best friends. We were in all the same computer programming classes."

I make a noncommittal grunt, even though the whole thing makes sense. I don't talk much about The Company, either. It's an invasive presence in my teammates' lives. Useful, but intrusive. I don't advertise the fact that my father and brother run the place.

"And hockey?" she adds. "Really?"

"What's wrong with hockey? It's the best sport there is. I never saw you as a computer nerd, either."

"No?" She raises a perfect eyebrow at me. "What did you think I'd become when I grew up?"

That's easy. "Dictator of a small but warlike country."

Alex laughs. "To be fair, I don't write code anymore. I'm the head of a warlike cable and internet company."

"See? My guesses are better than your guesses."

"That's ridiculous."

A new voice breaks into our argument. "Ms. Engels? Your plane is ready."

"Excellent," she says. But she doesn't stand up. "Just give us two minutes."

"Yes, ma'am."

"What, you like this sofa?" I ask. "Who lingers at the airport when they don't need to?"

Alex gives me a withering look. "I just have to ask you a question before we go."

"What, Engels? Hit me."

She folds her hands primly. "Why did you volunteer for this trip? Was it to get even with me for humiliating you?"

"Fuck no." What a stupid question. "In the first place, it takes a hell of a lot more to humiliate a man than a quick brushoff at a party. And secondly, I didn't volunteer for this trip at all."

Her head jerks backward. "What? Then why are you here?"

"Because my father has a soft spot for you, and my brother is a scheming asshole." She might as well know the truth. "I didn't know about your conference until I'd eaten two of my three tacos."

Alex's blue eyes bulge. "You didn't *know?* And yet you packed your bags anyway?"

"Don't be too impressed." I shrug. "I haven't been to the beach in a long time. And running in the sand is good cardio."

She blinks. "Okay, back up. You really want to go to Hawaii? It's going to be a boring week of accompanying me to parties and meetings."

"That does sound dreadful," I admit. But I'm going out of duty more than for the scenery. It's not her fault that my family are thoughtless freaks. "But it's fine. Let's board your gas-guzzling private jet and get on with it."

I stand, but she holds up a hand. "No. Wait."

"What do you mean, *wait?* I thought people chartered jets so they didn't have to wait!"

"Listen," she begs. "If you're not into playing this role, then it will never work. I'll ask Max to send somebody else."

"If Max had someone else to send, he would have. Trust me."

She winces.

"Besides, I can play the role, Alex. It's not like it's hard."

"You'd think." She scowls. "But don't forget—you'll have to pretend to like me."

"Huh," I say, scratching my chin. "So, like, I shouldn't ogle other women? Or pick up some chick at the bar, and take her back to my room?"

"Of *course* not." A look of pure horror crosses Alex's face.

"But *baby*," I complain. "Maybe your new boyfriend is a swinger. How do you feel about threesomes?"

"Eric!" Her eyes bug out.

That's when I crack up. "Do they let gullible people run companies? I'm surprised."

"You're *not* funny!" Alex tips her head back and glares at the ceiling. "Please, just go home. I don't need a fake boyfriend. I changed my mind."

"Alex, calm down." Although I'm still snickering inside. "You know how some people learn a trade at the dinner table? Like, how to run a pharmacy, or how to rope cattle?"

"Or how to license cable channels for fun and profit? I know how that works. And *The Journal* still thinks my father secretly runs my company."

"Well, what I learned at the dinner table was how to be a bodyguard. How to punch someone to inflict maximum pain. How to neutralize an opponent without making any noise. How to blend in with my surroundings. And—since I'm me—the whole attractive arm candy thing comes naturally."

She rolls her pretty eyes. "So you're saying you're like Jason Bourne, but more egotistical?"

"And more athletic. Honestly? That guy is a punter. He draws way too much attention to himself. And I call bullshit on some of those car chases."

"Excuse me, Ms. Engels?"

We look up to find another obsequious airport employee waiting there with a smile on her face. "Your takeoff window depends on a timely departure."

Alex springs off the sofa. "All right. I'm ready to go."

"Of course, baby. Let's do this."

She shoots me a glare as I bend down to grab our baggage. "You can still stay home, you know."

"Darling, I wouldn't dream of it." I give her a sleazy smile, which only makes her roll her eyes.

The airport employee is glancing between us, looking unsettled, so I leave the waiting room and carry our bags outside, where a chauffeured golf cart drives us a couple of hundred yards to a waiting Gulf Stream.

"Last chance," Alex says as we reach the steps leading up to the plane.

But I follow her aboard. If she thinks I can't play this role, she's got another think coming.

Inside Alex's jet, everything is leather and wood. It's like my brother's apartment but with wings. The passenger cabin sports two huge reclining chairs on opposite sides of the center aisle. Beyond those, I spot a dining table with two bench seats. In the very back there's a door marked *bedroom*.

I give a low whistle. "Nice digs, lady."

"What, this old thing?" she gives me a tight smile. "It's a little ridiculous. But I travel a lot."

A male flight attendant joins us. "Alex! Welcome aboard."

"Thank you, Manny. This is Eric Bayer, my—" Her hesitation lasts only a micromoment. But I realize that it's just occurring to her that we're going to have to pretend to be a couple. "Old friend."

"Did you just call me *old*?"

"Well, you're *much* older than in that photo I just showed you. Didn't we just go over this?"

I laugh in spite of myself. I'd forgotten that Alex was sharp-tongued, even as a child.

"Welcome, Eric," the flight attendant says. "Make yourself at home. Let's get those bags stowed." He opens a closet to indicate where our suitcases go.

Alex makes a move to stow her own, but I take it from her again. "I've got this, sweet cheeks."

"Thank you. *Dear*," she says, shooting me an angry look. But a guy's got to have his fun.

Manny is well trained enough to ignore the whole thing. "Please be seated for takeoff at your earliest convenience. With your seatbelts fastened."

"Thank you," Alex says.

I wait for her to choose a seat before I claim the other one. The chair is broad and comfortable, the leather cool beneath my fingers. I'd still rather be eating guacamole on my sofa right now, but we don't always get everything we want.

Manny does his safety checks and closes the cockpit door before disappearing into the little kitchen up front. I hear the engines change tone, and we eventually push back toward the taxiway.

"Listen. About that night in April," Alex says suddenly. "I was having a horrible moment. I was rude to several people that night, which is not in my nature. I was exhausted and disappointed with myself."

"You already apologized to me," I remind her. "It's no big deal."

"By the time you and I spoke, I was just out of gas. And I thought you were just some guy looking around the party at the end of the night for…" She clears her throat. "I was wrong, and I'm sorry."

"Thank you," I say.

Except now I'm the asshole. Because she wasn't wrong. Alex looked fucking *great* at that party. I'd wanted to talk to her, sure. But I wouldn't have said no to unzipping that dress, either. Sue me.

"The thing is?" she adds. "Sitting down in a quiet corner some-where and remembering that summer on the Vineyard was prob-ably exactly what I needed that night. So I really blew it."

"Well, it's a long flight," I point out. "Got nothing but time now."

She glances over at me again. "I apologize for that, too. I don't normally kidnap people to Hawaii."

I shrug. "My brother loves to withhold details. He is the worst kind of tyrant. He knew that if he asked me to work this week for him that I would say no."

"So, he laid the damsel in distress thing on pretty heavily didn't he?"

"Yeah, I guess. Not that I got the whole story." I turn in my seat and give her an appraising look. And I like what I see. Full lips that I shouldn't be admiring. Long, kissable neck…

"There's a reason my ex needs to stay clear of me," she says. "I am not ready for him to know that I'm three months pregnant."

Wait, what?

I do a terrible job of covering my shock. "You're —*sorry?*"

Her smile turns rueful. "That was my original reaction, too."

"Oh. Uh…" I swallow hard, and realize I'm staring at her. "Congratulations."

"Thank you," she laughs. "When I saw you in April, I was freaking out about this turn of events, and trying to host a black-tie party. I absolutely want children, but it wasn't a goal of mine to have them with someone who hit me."

"Okay…" I swallow hard as all the details continue to fall into place. "So you need to keep him in the dark about this development?"

"For now," she agrees. "He only wanted capital from me, anyway. And he's going to get plenty of it when he signs the agreement to forgo custody."

"But first you have to get through this business trip? Without him suspecting?"

She nods. "I just hit the three-month mark. It was too soon to have that conversation. And now I have a crucial product launch to get through before the baby arrives in December. I can't skip this conference. And I can't let that man get close to me."

"Wow." Now I understand why Alex needs someone at her side this week. It's almost enough to make me feel less grumpy.

Almost. Not quite.

And now I have a new problem. I'm traveling with a pregnant lady? Good lord. I know nothing of pregnant women. In fact, I've gone to great lengths to avoid being near them. What the fuck do you even say? "Do you, uh, feel okay?"

"Most of the time. The random barfing has finally stopped."

"Well, hallelujah." This whole conversation makes me want to triple check the expiration date on my current box of condoms.

"It's not as bad as it sounds," she says with a shrug. "I feel pretty great most days. And as soon as this trip is over, I can start to get excited. I spent the first three months kicking myself for being so stupid. And the doctor told me not to count my blessings before the twelve-week mark. So it hasn't really sunk in yet. But I want this child."

"Then, congratulations, Alex. Your fake boyfriend is happy for you."

"Thank you," she replies. "I'll try not to barf when I smell our food cooking."

"Good plan."

What have I got myself into?

4

ALEX

I TRY to settle in for the flight, but it's not easy to let down my guard around Mr. Hot-but-Grumpy. As the jet climbs toward a cruising altitude, I keep sneaking looks across the aisle, trying to imagine six nights and seven days with this man I barely know.

Come to think of it, he was kind of broody at thirteen, too. Not that I let him get away with it. I had no playmates on the Vineyard, so I adopted him as my friend for the summer.

I'll admit he was a good sport, though. I don't remember asking him if he wanted to ride horses, fish, or play tennis. I just sort of shoved different kinds of sports equipment into his hands and demanded that he accompany me. And he did.

Now I've inadvertently stolen another week of his life? He should have run while he had the chance.

I pull out my phone and wake it up. "Bingley," I prompt.

"Yes, my queen?" the phone replies.

Eric gives a snort. "Please tell me that's not a real assistant who calls you that."

Bingley answers for himself. "I am very real, sir. I am not, however, human."

"Well, that clears that up." He quirks an eyebrow at me over the cover of his *Sports Illustrated*.

"Bingley is an AI version of a virtual assistant. Nate Kattenberger developed him."

"Cool." Eric shrugs.

"I need you to greet him, though. He's part of my security detail, so he needs to recognize your voice. Bingley, please meet Mr. Eric Bayer."

Eric scowls. "Hello, computer. 'Sup?"

"It's a pleasure to make your acquaintance!" Bingley replies in his crisp British accent. "Should you need my assistance, feel free to call me by name. If your request does not conflict with my queen's best interests, I shall endeavor to obey!"

"I'm flattered," Eric grunts.

"Thank you, Eric," I say. "Bingley, fill me in on the evening's itinerary."

"Certainly, my liege! When we reach a cruising altitude of thirty-thousand feet, Manny will serve you a sesame chicken salad on a bed of noodles, with gelato for dessert. For our guest, we have a choice of steak tips in wine sauce or Lobster mac and cheese."

God I'm hungry again already. "Please ask Manny to bring out both."

"Of course, madame. What would Eric like to drink? We have a selection of beer and wine, and several sodas."

"Sparkling water, please," my guest says. "Does the robot serve drinks? That would be fun to watch."

Bingley answers the question himself. "I may have a silver tongue, sire, but no hands. Your meal will be served by a human. This flight will land once at LAX for a quick refueling. Our estimated arrival time in Hawaii is nine-fifty-two p.m. local time. The time difference is six hours."

"Thank you."

"You just thanked a computer," Eric says from inside his magazine.

He's right. And it is a little weird. But Bingley is a big part of my new product launch, so I've been conversing with him as much as I can. Besides, I don't like Eric's attitude. "It's never wrong to be polite," I point out.

"Uh huh. The big tech companies have already taught us to clutch our phones all day. Now we need to chat them up, too?"

"Yours probably wouldn't want to talk to you anyway," I chirp.

"Maybe I should find you a surly virtual assistant to match your demeanor. You could ignore each other."

"Sounds perfect," he says with a smirk.

That smirk shouldn't turn me on, should it? I must be hungrier than I thought.

I sit back and wait for dinner. And I don't steal glances at Eric.

Not many, anyway.

O══▪

"ALEX. WAKE UP." A hand pats my upper arm.

Someone is trying to wake me, but I'm not having it. I screw my eyes more tightly closed and press my face into the pillow.

"Alex, we've landed. You need to get up."

"No." Whatever the man is saying, I really don't care. My bed is comfortable, and my body knows it's not time to wake up.

"The car is on the tarmac. And Manny can't clock out until you're out of here."

I'm too tired to care, though. Oh, well.

Somebody grumbles. And then two strong arms lift me right off the bed. There's cool air where my pillow should be. That's inconvenient. But then the pillow is replaced by the firm warmth of a man's chest. I press my cheek against it. He smells like clean shirts and spicy cologne.

"I'm assuming you had shoes on at some point, Engels?" The question rumbles against my face.

Shoes. Man. Rock-solid chest. And nobody calls me Engels, except...

I wake suddenly to find that I'm in Eric Bayer's arms. And he's carrying me down the aisle of the jet. And I startle so violently that my head smacks into his unshaven jaw.

"Ow!" he growls.

"Put me down!" I yelp. "What the hell?" I can't get off the plane like this. CEOs are not carried off jets like children.

Eric sets me on my feet in a hurry. But I'm wobbly from sleep, so I end up grabbing his firm torso with two hands to steady myself. Good lord, the man is like sun-warmed concrete. Hot and unyielding.

He looks down at me, one eyebrow cocked. "You weren't listening."

"I couldn't hear you!" I holler. "I was sleeping! What time is it?"

"Eleven p.m., Hawaii time."

"Which is…" I do the math. "Four in the morning New York time." No wonder I'm so out of it. "Sorry, um, about whacking you in the chin. Let's roll."

He chuckles, and then rubs his jaw. "Sure, Sleepmonster. Let's roll."

"Hey! *You're* the Sleepmonster." That's what I used to call him that summer on the Vineyard. I always woke up first. Then I'd pace the second-floor hallway, making noise and generally being a pain in the ass until he finally crawled out of bed.

"Not anymore, apparently." He turns and exits the plane.

I need a minute to step back into my shoes and grab my carryon. I haven't thought about that summer in a long time. After he finally got up, I used to instruct him on what we were doing that day. It might be horseback riding, or tennis, or collecting shells on the beach. Or playing board games or asking the Magic 8 Ball stupid questions.

Good lord, I was a bossy little girl. I wonder if he hated it and I didn't notice.

When I'm ready, I walk carefully down the aisle of the jet, past the seat where Eric slept. I felt a little guilty crawling into the bed while he was snoozing in the chair.

But not guilty enough not to do it.

All our bags have been loaded into the car already, which means Eric took care of everything while I was sleeping.

I wonder if I'll ever stop embarrassing myself in front of Eric Bayer.

SIGNS POINT TO NO, as my old Magic 8 Ball would have said.

Because I pass out in the car, too. I don't wake up until it stops. And then I discover I'm sleeping with my face propped against Eric's muscular shoulder.

"Oh god, I'm so sorry." I sit up straight, as if that might help him forget. There's a little spot of drool near the collar of his polo.

Shoot me.

"It's fine," he grumbles. "Just another part of the job description nobody ever gave me. Bodyguard, and pillow to the rich and famous."

He slides out of the car, and I follow, finding myself blinking up at the entrance to one of Hawaii's chicest spa resorts. I'm too tired to appreciate the asymmetrical stone facade and the carefully lit water features. But it will be promising tomorrow in the daylight.

Eric already has our two suitcases in hand and it's all I can do to grab my own carry-on bag and follow him inside the lobby. Luckily, there's no wait at the check in desk, and all I have to do is hand over my credit card and remain vertical while the desk agent makes two key cards and small talk with Eric.

"There are three pools on the property. The dolphin experience is located down in the cove."

"Great. Can you tell me where to find the gym?" he asks.

"On the lower level, sir. We have personal trainers, as well. Touch two on your in-room phone to schedule an appointment or a spa treatment."

"Thank you."

"Can I show you to your suite?" the woman asks.

"We'd rather just go on up ourselves," Eric says, holding out a hand for the key cards.

"Certainly. Your suitcases are already on their way."

"Thank you," I whisper as soon as the elevator doors close on us. "I can't handle people right now."

"I noticed that," he chuckles.

"Usually I'm a great traveler. Another symptom of pregnancy is extreme exhaustion. Apparently growing an entire human takes a lot of extra energy."

"Ah," he says. "Yeah, I've never tried that myself, so…" He runs a hand through his hair.

I don't know why I feel the need to explain myself. It's the middle of the night back at home. I'm asleep on my feet right now, but anyone would be

Luckily, moments later Eric opens the door to a plush suite. I drag myself inside. And because this is a very nice hotel, our luggage is already waiting for us. I unzip my suitcase and pull out a nightgown along with my toiletry bag. Then I disappear into the marble clad bathroom ahead of Eric. But somebody has to go first, right?

After I've changed and brushed my teeth, I take a look in the mirror. My eyes are red, and my hair is messed. I look like a disaster. And when I turn my head, I catch sight of a red indentation on my jaw. Good lord. There's a Lacoste alligator molded into my face from sleeping on Eric.

There is really no end to today's mortifications.

After brushing my hair forward to hide the mark, I put on a brave face and leave the bathroom. Eric is in the bedroom, hanging his suit jacket in the closet. My sleep addled brain spends a few seconds remembering how fabulous he looks in a tux. In Florida, when I was trying to figure out why he kept glancing at me, I allowed myself a few glances of my own.

My old friend is seriously hot. As fake boyfriends go, he's an A-lister.

"You should get some sleep," he says with a glance over his shoulder. I'm obviously not the only one who thinks I look like a zombie right now.

"So should you," I point out. Then I turn around and count the beds.

There's only one.

Oh, dear. I should have seen this wrinkle coming.

But Eric isn't the only one caught off guard today by Max Bayer's security arrangements. I expected The Company would send a bodyguard with me to Hawaii. But I didn't anticipate the ruse of a pretend boyfriend, so it hadn't occurred to me to ask my assistant to change my travel accommodations. She always books a one-bedroom suite.

Oops.

Eric watches me with a smirk. "Maybe the living room couch folds out."

I pad back into that room to check. The couch is a sleek, modern thing that's low to the floor. I try to lift a cushion, but you can't. The sofa is a monolith.

Well, this is awkward.

"It doesn't fold," I say when I return to the bedroom. "But it's okay. We'll share the bed." And suddenly I don't know where to put my eyes. I meant platonically, of course. But sharing a bed with Eric—under different circumstances, of course—isn't the worst idea I've ever heard. "It's large enough," I mumble.

We both turn to glance at it at the same time. If possible, even more awkwardness sets in.

"I could call downstairs and ask them to send us up a cot," he says, closing the closet door.

"That will never work," I argue. "Because you would feel like a heel making the pregnant lady take the cot. And I would feel like a diva asking the six-foot-tall athlete to sleep there."

"Six-two," he corrects me.

"We'll share the bed," I repeat. I'm so tired right now I just need a tiny fractional part of the bed and I'll be gone from this world.

"Fine. If I can pretend to be your boyfriend outside of this room, I suppose I can pretend to be a gentleman inside it."

"Is it that much of a stretch?" I walk over to the nearest side, lift the covers and slide in.

"I guess you'll find out," he says.

I throw four throw pillows overboard and wiggle down in the sheets. I sigh as my head hits the pillow. I don't even dignify his taunt with a response. I feel perfectly safe with Eric. He might not like this arrangement. But he's not going to hurt me.

My eyelids feel heavy when I close them.

Footsteps cross the rug, and the lamp beside my head goes out. He says two words so quietly that I almost miss them. "Goodnight, Sleepmonster."

I would answer him, but I'm already asleep.

5

ERIC

WHEN I OPEN my sticky eyes the next morning, the clock beside me says 5:23.

Ouch. Jetlag.

Although maybe it's not just the jet lag that woke me. It's too warm in this bed. And all that heat is coming from a sleeping woman who's curled up against my back, her nose in the nape of my neck. She's thrown a smooth leg over mine, and her hand is wrapped around my waist.

Holy hell. Not only does she throw off as much heat as a campfire, my subconscious hasn't missed those soft curves molded to my back, or that hand that's only a few inches north of my erection.

Christ. I close my eyes, and—for the briefest moment—I allow myself to imagine what it would be like to just roll over and pull her warm, sweet body underneath mine. It's been way too long since I saw any action. I'm due.

Then I open my eyes and remember how sharply she turned me down that night in Florida. There was no ambiguity there.

That cruddy memory wakes me up and settles me down at the same time. I need to get out of this bed. Slowly, I ease myself away from her body. Alex doesn't move. I am pure stealth as I slide my feet over the side of the bed and sit up. Having accomplished that, I rise and make my way into the living room of the suite, where it's cooler.

The sky outside our floor-to-ceiling windows shows only a streak of light on the horizon. But it's enough to see the ocean shining back at me. I unlock the sliding glass door and push it open. A fresh, salty breeze rises to meet me.

When I step outside, I see how large the terrace of this suite really is. It wraps to the side, past a table and two chairs, lush flower boxes, and... Is that a private lap pool? It's rectangular, and maybe fifteen feet long by four feet wide.

Okay. Maybe an unexpected week in Hawaii isn't pure torture.

After I give myself a tour of the fancy private patio, I return inside to find the in-room coffee maker. I pop an espresso pod inside. Two minutes later I'm sipping coffee when I hear Alex stirring in the bedroom. She makes a phone call, and then I hear water splashing in the bathroom.

I'm contemplating a second cup of coffee when I hear a knock on the door of the suite.

"Alex? Are you expecting anyone?" I call toward the bedroom.

"I ordered food. Let them in." There's a beat of silence. "Please."

I'm still wearing boxers only. But who cares, right? The delivery guy has probably seen worse. And I tip well. So I cross to the door and pull it open.

Hell, there are five hotel employees outside, bearing two carts, a room service table, and God knows what else. "Are you sure you have the right room?"

"Delivery for Alex Engels."

I step aside but watch them with growing suspicion. Maybe I do share my brother's genome after all. Why five people? And what's all this stuff?

It becomes clear a moment later as the employees unload a disturbing amount of food from those carts into the suite's kitchenette. There's a case of bottled water, plus several other beverages and mixers. There's fruit piled in a basket. Boxes of crackers. Various cheeses and yogurts are tucked into the refrigerator, along with pate and other charcuterie items. There's cereal, milk, various teas, cookies, and biscuits.

"My God," I grumble.

"Sorry to take so long, sir," someone says. "Your breakfast is still hot."

I notice another employee setting out the room service items on the dining table. There's two big plates with omelets, bacon, potatoes, toast and fruit. There's a pot of coffee, for which I'm grateful.

"Sign here." A bill wallet is thrust against my chest.

"Um, gratuity…"

"Already added," the young man says.

Of course it is. I scribble my signature.

"Oh, and here's your package." The guy hands me a box and then follows his coworkers out into the hallway.

I look down at the box I'm holding against my bare belly. It weighs hardly anything at all, and it's addressed to me, not Alex. The sender is listed as MAX YOUR ASSHOLE BROTHER.

Huh. At least it's honest. But the postmark is from three days ago, which really hacks me off. And I have no idea what Max has sent us.

As it happens, I don't find out for another few minutes because whoever packed the darned thing assumed this box would need to survive a battlefield assault. I've never seen so much tape in my life. Picking at it with a fingernail gets me nowhere.

So I pour myself a cup of room service coffee and then dig up a knife from a drawer in the kitchenette. When I finally cut all the tape off the box, I find…a throw pillow? What the fuck? It's small, done up in white and black dots on one side, with stripes on the other.

My brother has obviously lost his mind. Neither one of us has the least bit of interest in home furnishings. I toss the pillow onto a dining chair and pluck a handwritten note out of the box.

Hey, Eric—whatever you do, don't toss the pillow around. There's a very sensitive camera inside.

Well, fuck.

Locate the camera by feeling both sides to identify the hard spot. Then put this on a piece of furniture which faces the door *to the suite. When you and Alex aren't at home, we'll watch the door for you. Please check your texts just before you reenter the hotel room each time, in case we've picked anything up.*

After you position the pillow, text "sight check" to 35763. You should get a response within five minutes. If you don't, I need to hear about it. —M

That's all he wrote. No *please*. No *thank you*.

Whatever. I adjust the pillow on the sofa as he asked, and then find my phone to send the text.

I'm annoyed, but not too annoyed to sit down at the table and pick up my fork. The first bite of omelet is just what I need in this life. "Alex!" I call. "Your breakfast is getting cold."

She emerges a moment later wearing a resort robe and a towel over her hair. I am not going to admire her legs. Nope. Even though she rubbed them against mine all night while I was trying to sleep.

"Morning." She blinks at me. Specifically at my abs, I think. "Where are your pajamas?"

"Don't own any." I glance down at my boxers. All the important bits are covered. "Does it matter? I could put on my bathing suit instead. It's more or less the same thing in a brighter color."

"Right." She clears her throat. But I don't miss her eyes making another quick sweep of my body. And I have to hold back a laugh. Could Alex be having a moment of regret? "Um…" She shakes her head once. "Thank you for dealing with the delivery."

"No problem." I lift a hand to my chest and stroke a palm down my bare skin.

And, yup, her eyes lock onto my fingers, and she follows my movements like a hungry dog eyes a piece of meat.

How funny is this? Now I'm definitely not putting on a shirt this morning. Not until I absolutely have to. Why ruin the fun?

She finally drags her gaze off my body, picks up a coffee urn and pours herself a cup. Then she takes a moment to examine both coffee urns. "I think you have the decaf."

"What?" I yelp. "Who orders decaf?"

"Pregnant women." She takes the cup out of my hand and swaps it with hers. "I am allowed to drink a single cup of real coffee each day, but I try to wait until the moment when I need it most." She picks up the urn of regular coffee and tops up the cup of decaf. "Although, jet lag calls for cheating. Just a harmless amount."

"No judgment here." Unlike my brother, I'm not in the business of telling anyone what to do.

Speaking of my brother, my phone vibrates with a text. I shove a strip of bacon in my mouth, wipe my hands, and then get up to read it.

Max: Camera works!

Eric: Okay. Whatever. Why does Alex need this level of spy fuckery in her life?

Max: Because she's worth a couple billion, and people are assholes? It's not that complicated.

Eric: It's just so invasive.

Max: So turn the pillow around when you're in. Just don't forget to reverse it when you leave. Alex knows the drill. She won't forget. Nice underwear. Where are your pajamas?

I don't even bother to reply. Why is everyone so obsessed with pajamas?

By the time I get back to the table, the food from Alex's plate is missing. I actually scan my surroundings. "Where did it go?"

"Where did what go?"

"Your breakfast. There's no way you ate that so fast. It was the size of a football."

Her eyes flare. "That is a dickish thing to point out. I was hungry." She picks a strawberry out of the fruit salad and nibbles it daintily.

"I didn't mean it as an insult." I stab my own omelet. "I genuinely did not believe you could... Never mind." One does not win an argument with a woman. One simply survives it.

"Look." She throws down the napkin. "Pregnancy has given me the appetite of a teenage boy. Ergo, my ass has doubled in size. But if you want to keep breathing, don't make any cracks about that."

"I would never. There's nothing wrong with your ass. Not one thing." I refill my coffee. "Not that I looked," I add quickly.

But I totally did.

Her eyes narrow as she gets up from the table. "You don't have to flatter me, either."

"I don't do flattery. Now, what's on your agenda for today?"

"Sunning myself at the pool, mostly. I'll look over my speech and return some emails. The conference doesn't get going until tomorrow."

"Okay." I guess I'm sitting by the pool, then. "After you've had enough sun, I need to get a workout in. So you'll need to come back to the room, or else head to the gym with me."

"I could stand to get some exercise. It's good for jet lag. How long do you spend in the gym?"

"Two to three, depending on how good the equipment is."

She blinks. "Two to three…hours?"

"Give or take. Depends how far I run after lifting."

"That's impossible. I can't spend three hours holed up in the room waiting for you. I was going to get a massage and a pedicure."

"Two then," I concede. "That's my bare minimum. You have to do your job, right? I also have to do mine."

"And your job is working out like a mad man?"

"Working out like a *beast*," I correct her. "I'm thirty-four years old, Alex. In four weeks I'll be at training camp, fighting to dominate guys who are wet behind the ears at twenty-two. They want to take my place on the team. I can't let 'em. I don't work out, I get soft."

"I see. Okay." She folds her hands. "I think I know a way to compromise."

I DON'T LIKE COMPROMISE.

Alex's solution is that she gets her early afternoon spa treatments while I finish my workout. That ought to make sense, except for a couple of crucial details.

She has the hotel staff bring a treadmill up to the private patio, so that I can run ten miles while looking out at the ocean. The treadmill is cranking at a brisk pace, and I'm sweating out of every pore as the waves lap the beach.

But I'm not looking at the ocean as often as I should be, because Alex is also getting a massage on a portable table a couple of meters away from me. Face down, she's oiled up and naked on that table, her skin glinting in the Hawaiian sun.

Sure, there's a towel covering her ass. So all I can see is her back and her oil-slicked limbs. And a kissable stretch of her neck. But my imagination is top notch. Worse, another guy—and he's a young, twenty-something Hawaiian stud—has his hands sliding up and down all of Alex's bare skin.

I can't stop glancing over there. I'm probably going to stumble and kill myself. It will be all Alex's fault, too. She even moans once in a while, especially when he works on her feet.

It's the moans that really kill me.

Note to self: it's not easy to run with a semi. This is not relaxing. My body temperature is climbing to an unreasonable level, and I don't know whether to blame all the weight training I did earlier, the Hawaiian sun, or the luscious woman on the massage table.

At the nine mile mark I slap the stop button on the treadmill and let it slow to a stop. I can't take it any more.

"Quitting early?" Alex asks from the massage table.

I don't even answer that insulting question. "Avert your eyes."

"Why?"

I march over to the edge of that pool, my back to Alex and the masseuse, my front to the Hawaiian surf. I strip off my sweaty running shorts and jump into the narrow pool.

Ahhhhh. Cool water is just what I need.

"Where is your bathing suit?" Alex yelps. "It's not *that* private a terrace."

"Where is yours?" I fire back.

The massage therapist laughs. "We're done out here, anyway. I can't do a pedicure in the sun; it makes the polish sticky. Here's your robe."

"It's just as well," Alex says. "There are snacks inside."

"I thought we were having a late lunch?" I need a real meal after that workout.

"Oh, we are," Alex assures me. "The snacks are just a warmup."

She sits up, clutching a sheet to her luscious bosom while I suffer. It's going to be a long week in Hawaii.

Max isn't getting a Christmas present this year. Or ever again.

6

ALEX

AT FIRST I thought I was imagining it. But no—I called this. Eric Bayer is taunting me with his hot body. He wants me to feel bad about turning him down that time in April.

He wants revenge. And even worse? It's working.

No man has ever had such an unruly effect on my hormones. Maybe it's the pregnancy. Or the jet lag. Or the sunshine. But I can't stop looking at the hunk of male glory that is Eric Bayer. Two-hundred-odd pounds of muscle and smirking.

I shouldn't even be attracted to him. But I am. And it's bad. Really bad. For example, I never thought much about a man's gluteus maximus before now. But I've been treated to over an hour of those sculpted buns on the treadmill. They're going to be jogging through my dreams forever. I can just tell.

Also, I never knew that a man's back muscles could be so sexy. Or his calves...

This is going to be the longest week in paradise *ever*.

After my spa treatments, I take a cool shower and wash my hair. When I come out, Eric is seated on the sofa in nothing but a fresh pair of shorts and two days worth of scruff on his rugged jaw.

He's sitting on his butt, thankfully. So I can't ogle it. But, hell! That hard chest and that glorious set of abs? It's killing me. Seriously? Does the man even own a shirt?

Pregnancy has turned me into a woman with a voracious

appetite. And not just for food. I want to climb him like one of the trees we used to scale on the Vineyard.

Maybe I'll have to order up that cot after all. Or change rooms? We could have adjacent rooms with an open door between them. And separate beds. That should do the trick.

Eric's cool gray eyes flick up at me. "Hey. Lunch time?" He looks back down at his phone, but not before giving me a head to toe once-over.

I'm wearing my slinkiest sundress, just in case I'm not the only one who feels a stirring sensation down below. Why should I be the only one to suffer? I straighten my spine and lift my chin, which has the advantage of emphasizing my bust.

As it happens, my boobs are in a tight race with my ass for which body part can most quickly expand. I'm busting out of all my bras, and should probably shop for new ones. So let's just say I'm filling out this dress a lot better than my preteen self would have dreamt possible.

"Lunch would be nice," I murmur, and somehow it comes out sounding like a proposition. As if I'd said, *sex on the terrace sounds wonderful.*

His eyes go hot and then cool again so fast that I may have imagined it. "The restaurant is probably air conditioned. You might need a sweater."

"Pregnant women run hot," I say, and that sounds kinky, too. They do, though. "Although I'm pretty sure they'd frown on a shirtless customer."

He makes a grumpy noise and stands up. "One second. I'll find a shirt."

Point to Alex! I love competition. And if Eric wants to make our time together into some kind of libido battle, then I'm here for that.

Up to a point, anyway. I pull out my phone while he's changing his clothes, and dial the hotel's reception desk.

"Yes, Ms. Engels," the receptionist says. "How can I assist you?"

"This suite is lovely," I say quietly, moving toward the terrace door for a little privacy. "But perhaps I've booked the wrong room for my needs. Could you possibly relocate us to two adjacent king rooms instead?"

"I'm sorry to say that we're fully booked," the receptionist says. "I could call around to other hotels…"

"Oh, no." Of course they're booked. The tech conference draws executives from all over Asia and North America. "Thank you. I should probably stay put."

"If you need a cot sent to your room, I could try to find availability."

Someone clears his throat behind me, and I whirl around to see Eric waiting for me in a tight Brooklyn Bruisers T-shirt. Every ripple of muscle is visible where the cotton stretches to accommodate him. And the short sleeves don't cover those powerful arms…

"Ms. Engels?" the receptionist asks. "The cot?"

"Oh! Thank you," I say quickly. "That won't be necessary. Thanks for your help," I babble, and then quickly end the call.

"Problem?" Eric asks. And is he flexing his pecs at me? "Did I spill something on my shirt?"

My face burns as I drag my gaze up to meet his. "No spills. But I'm not sure that fits you. Consider sizing up."

"No way." He gives me a slow smile. "This shirt is lucky."

"Oh." All the athletes I know are superstitious. "You mean you win games after you wear it?"

"No, I mean it's lucky to be wrapped so tightly around me. I wouldn't want to deprive this shirt of that privilege. Wouldn't you agree?"

"The ego on you," I scoff. "Time for lunch." I grab my clutch purse off a table, checking to make sure that my key card is there. "Do we need to turn the cushion around? Which side has the camera?"

"Oh, fuck." He sighs. "I hate that thing." He walks over to the couch and faces the spotted side toward the door. "Okay, let's roll." He beckons me toward the door of the suite.

We step outside together. And as we head for the elevator, Eric puts his big hand at the center of my back. It's just a light touch, but his thumb finds the divot of my spine. And his light caress sends shivers down my bare arms. I stiffen and skitter away.

"Alex, look." He stops in front of the elevator. "We need to get a few rules straight."

"Rules?" I blink up at him, not really hearing. I still have goose bumps from his touch.

"Focus." He snaps his fingers. "I'm supposed to pretend to be your jealous boyfriend."

"Right." I force my gaze up to his face where it belongs.

"According to my brother, your ex's flight landed…" He looks at the watch on his thick wrist. "…Two hours ago. So tell me right now what's allowed. I don't want to make you uncomfortable. But I have to touch you occasionally to sell this. How about an arm around your shoulders? Or maybe I should hold your hand? You didn't like it when I touched your back."

"It's f-fine," I stutter. "My back is…yup."

He squints at me, as if evaluating me for signs of a stroke. "You okay?"

"Sure!" I chirp like a crazy person. "Carry on." The truth is that I need Eric as my smokescreen. It's a perfectly good plan.

I just didn't expect to experience a hormone spike every time he got near me.

We're silent in the elevator until Eric says, "Whenever you spot him, I want you to nudge me. I'm positive I can keep this prick away from you. But the first time he approaches you, I may not be subtle."

"Okay," I agree as some long-dormant portion of my heart flutters. I've never wanted to be anyone's damsel in distress. But the idea of Eric getting into Jared's face is pretty hot.

"What's he like, anyway?" Eric asks. "Is he the kind of guy who'll beat on his chest and make a big scene?"

"No," I say as the elevator doors open into the lobby. "I take him for a coward. He's the kind to choose his fights very carefully."

"And this man hit you?" he asks under his breath. We're crossing the lobby toward the doors to the beach restaurant.

"Only once," I confirm, and Eric growls immediately. "I think he scared himself." But he scared me even more. The menace on his face was actually more terrifying than the blow itself.

"Even once is too often," Eric says darkly.

I don't disagree. "I can't see him taking a swing at *you*, though. He's cunning. He won't start a fight he can't win."

Eric glowers, and my attitude toward him softens even more. But then he ruins it by opening his mouth. "After lunch can we go to the beach? After the conference starts, I'll be trapped in boring meeting rooms with you for hours on end."

"Right," I agree with a sigh. The beach is probably just another excuse for him to take off his shirt again. I mentally catalogue my bikini choices. I'm definitely wearing the smallest one, while I still have the body for it. This might be my bikini collection's last hurrah.

The hotel restaurant is a sleek Asian fusion place that's half inside, half outside. "Where would you like to sit?" the hostess asks us.

"Outside," I say at the exact moment Eric says, "Inside."

The hostess freezes, glancing from one of us to the other.

"The lady has chosen," Eric says tightly. "Outside it is."

"Afraid to mess up your hair?" I ask after she leaves us at a lovely table near the railing, with an unobstructed view of the ocean.

"Not at all," he says, opening the menu. "But outside tables always leave one person in the shade, and one facing into the sun. And chivalry demands that I'm the one who squints."

I look him up and down. "You're not squinting at all."

"Not yet," he says with a sigh.

"Are you always such a grump?" I ask him. "Or are you usually a pleasant, happy-go-lucky guy who just hates his life this week?"

"Little of both," he says. "My buddies are hiking in Vermont right now."

"I'm sorry. You'll just have to have freshly caught seafood and a tropical drink instead. The horror."

He gives me a smirk, and then lifts his sunglasses from the collar of his too-tight tee and slips them on.

Sure enough, not more than ten minutes later, I notice that the angle of the sun has shifted. A beam of sunlight is now hitting him square in the forehead. "Oh, dear."

"Right. One hundred percent predictable." He lifts his iced tea and sighs.

"I never noticed that before. I guess I don't eat outside very often."

"Maybe the men you're dining with always give you the shady side," he suggests.

"There aren't a lot of men. Well, there hadn't been in a long time. But after I turned thirty, I realized that I was married to my job. And I think I went a little crazy. Such a cliché, but..." I let the sentence die. "You're still single, though. So I guess you understand."

"Yeah, sure. I'm married to my job, too. But I like it that way. When I was in college I had this semester where I got all bent out of shape over a girl And that's when a coach gave me the best advice I've ever gotten in my life." He sips his tea slowly.

Very slowly. And then it occurs to me that he might not actually finish that thought. "*Well?*" What an infuriating man.

He levels me with one of those sexy smirks that I am starting to hate. "He said, Eric, you can do anything. But you can't do everything."

"Really?" I yelp. "What a cliché. I saw that printed on a notebook just last week."

He shrugs. "So I have it hanging on my wall at home, too. Because it's true. To compete at the highest level you need to commit. And once I really owned that idea, everything got easier for me."

The waiter picks this moment to deposit our lunches in front of us. I thank him, but my mind is still chewing over Eric's words.

"You know, women are told that they can have it all," I point out. "A fulfilling career. A husband and children. And the message is that maybe there's something wrong with us if we don't at least try."

He shrugs. "I don't believe that at all. Life is all about hard choices. I made my peace with that a long time ago."

Well, I haven't. Although it's hard to argue that Eric's viewpoint is wrong. My quest for a partner ended badly. Although sometimes

I just wonder if I'm not to blame. I'm so used to calling the shots for myself that I don't really want someone else to do it for me.

"You gotta do you, though," he says, taking a big bite of his fish. "Besides, I'm sure you can have any guy you want."

"You'd be wrong," I reply quickly. "The men who date me are usually looking for money or prestige. The men who don't need those things all seem to want wives who are willing to stay at home and throw dinner parties and make them look good. They don't want someone who travels ninety days a year and earns more than they do."

He stares at me for a moment, and I wish those sunglasses weren't hiding his intelligent gray eyes. "Those men are doofuses. They're probably just afraid of you."

"Some of them," I concede, lifting my fork. "But I'm not easy to date. And it doesn't matter anymore, because I've given it up."

"That's not very considerate," he says, eating a french fry that looks perfectly salted and absolutely delicious. "What about your fake boyfriend's needs? In fact..." He gets up from his place at the table, then nudges his plate next to mine. "Scoot over, would you?"

"Why? *Oh.*" He means to sit next to me on the same side of the table. So I move over to make room on the padded bench.

Then his solid bulk lands beside me, his left arm around my shoulder. "Okay, honey bunch. Eat up," he says in a voice that's loud enough to carry a couple of tables in either direction. "You need to keep up your strength for me. No passing out early like you did last night."

"Eric!" I hiss.

He laughs. "I'm committed to playing this role. I'm all in. The good news is that you can steal my fries if you want. I see you eyeing them."

Oh, dear. I wonder what else he's noticed me eyeing?

But yay, fries! I take one and dip it in his ketchup. "Thank you, lover." My boob manages to press against his arm just before I lift the french fry to my mouth. I give him a glance that says, *two can play at this.*

He gives me a slow, conspiratorial smile, and it confuses me.

Are we joking, here? Or are we flirting for real? Those cool gray eyes aren't always easy to read.

Fine. It's probably all in my head. Who looks at a hormonal, stressed out woman—pregnant with another man's baby—and says, *I need to hit that.* And let's not forget I insulted him a couple of months ago.

"You're a pretty good sport, Eric," I say quietly.

"Thank you, babycakes. More water?" He lifts the carafe the waiter brought us and offers it to me.

"Sure, hunk-muffin."

He snorts, and I laugh. The tension I was feeling slides blissfully away. We can do this. We can be friends again under tricky circumstances, like we were so many years before.

But then I happen to glance up, and the smile slides right off my face. Because Jared Tatum is taking a seat about twenty feet away from our table.

And just like that I'm stressed out all over again.

7

ERIC

THE FIRST TWO times Alex moves her smooth knee against mine, I think it's a come-on. In fact, I can't resist sliding a hand beneath the table and smoothing her skirt over her leg.

She promptly kicks me.

And that's when I finally realize that the knee maneuver was meant to be a nudge, telling me her ex is in view.

Whoops. My bad.

I sit up straighter and scan the room. And there he is, only two tables away. As adversaries go, he's not that interesting. Khaki pants. Blue polo shirt. Closely cropped brown hair and wire-rimmed glasses. He's perusing the menu, his feet crossed at the ankles.

Eh. I could crush him in the palm of my hand. And it would be very satisfying.

"You're making a face," Alex whispers beside me.

"So?"

"That's not good acting. No Academy Award for you."

"I call bullshit. My job description is simply to be your very convincing jealous boyfriend." I put an arm around her again and pull Alex close. *Oh, the hardship.* She smells like flowers and sunshine. And just to show her what a good actor I am, I turn and press a soft kiss to her temple. And then another. Acting is good work if you can get it. Her skin is so soft against my lips...

She clears her throat.

I release her. "Now who isn't playing her role?"

"Not true." She lifts her chin and turns to sear me with a look. "I don't do PDA. Ever."

"Not even for your big, grumpy, jealous boyfriend?"

"Not at a business conference." She gives her head a shake. "There are other ways to act like a couple without pawing each other."

I laugh out loud. "Pawing? I kissed you on your stubborn, bossy head. If there were pawing, you'd know. I could demonstrate later, if you want. No pressure."

Her cheeks pink up. "You're teasing me."

"Just a little," I admit. "Not that it doesn't sound like fun. But I would never embarrass you, Engels. I know you're surrounded by colleagues."

"And competitors," she adds. "Half the people at this conference would like nothing better than to take me down. The other half want to kiss my ass."

"Mmm." I waggle my eyebrows at her. "Your boyfriend would be in that latter category, then. I love a shapely ass."

"God, tone it down a notch."

"You can take the guy out of the locker room, but you can't take the locker room out of the guy. And why would you even want to?" I glance over and find that her ex has spotted us. "Lean against me a second. I need to make a point."

Her eyes widen just slightly. But then she moves in, resting her head on my shoulder.

I run a hand down her bare arm, then give her a peck on the forehead. "Good girl," I say, and it comes out sounding rough. "He's getting the message, I think." In my peripheral vision, I can tell he's watching us.

"Why can't he just crawl back into his hole and die?" Alex whispers.

"Such strong words from my love bunny." Turning her face into my shoulder, she giggles. And just for a second she sounds like her eleven-year-old self. And the familiarity gives me goose bumps.

We laughed a lot, I realize. A long-dormant memory of chasing her down the beach washes over me.

That was another lifetime ago. I give myself a mental shake. "Should I get the check? As soon as you're finished, we can leave. Oh, wait. You're already done." The way this woman can put away food is truly astonishing.

"But…" She straightens up. "No dessert? It's a long time until dinner."

I laugh, because a pregnant Alex is a hilarious Alex. "I think I saw an ice cream shop on the resort map. We could walk there on the beach."

"Really?" Her expression brightens, and I feel my reality slip a little. In real life, I'll never be the married guy with the pregnant wife craving ice cream and pickles. But right this second I understand that guy. He's in over his head. But the trusting eyes of a hungry woman are blinking up at him, and he'll do whatever it takes to keep her happy.

I'm deep into my role, I guess. That must be why I lean down and give Alex a single kiss—the kind that even CEOs permit. Just a lip touch, really. But it's enough to make my body flash with unexpected heat.

And with something else, too. Possessiveness. I don't understand it at all. But right this second I would sink my claws into anyone who tried to harm her, and my adversary would not even be able to *crawl* away from the fight.

"We should get the check," Alex whispers, holding my gaze. We're having a staring contest. I don't know how it started, and I don't know how to stop.

Jesus. I must be better at this acting thing than I thought. Or maybe it's the jet lag messing with me. That must be it.

I finally look away and take a slow breath. Only to find Jared Tatum—her asshole ex—staring back at me with murder in his close-set eyes.

So I glare right back. *Not today, Satan. You can fuck right off.*

He scowls and looks away. Now he's got the message. Alex is here with me, whether he likes it or not.

OUR WALK on the sand is a nice diversion. I don't know what I'm doing in Hawaii, but it sure is a beautiful spot in the world. The beach sand is white. And there's a view of Diamond Head in the distance.

Also, there's a nice view of Alex in a pink bikini so small that I wonder how it was manufactured. Child labor? Robot bees? The rounded swells of her breasts are right there, torturing me.

I have to keep reminding myself that she's off-limits. But it's not easy. I'm supposed to *pretend* to be the guy who puts his hands all over her. But I'm not supposed to *think* about putting my hands all over her?

Straight up, this was my brother's worst idea ever. I'm sure of it because parts of me want to be, well, straight up.

At least this isn't a long walk. The high-end resort and spa where we're staying is connected to the conference hotel by two routes: you can either walk down the trellised path that connects the properties, or walk down the beach.

We've taken the beach route. It's shorter and more beautiful.

"All the meetings are down here at this bigger hotel," Alex says. "I wanted to stay in the quieter resort, and I don't mind the walk."

"Uh huh. How many meetings are we talking about?"

"Twelve? Fifteen, tops."

Holy crap. "I'm gonna get rigor mortis."

"We'll get the hotel to send a treadmill," Alex teases me. "You can sweat it up in the corner of the room while I'm making deals at the conference table."

She's kidding, but if that weren't wildly impractical I'd probably take her up on it. "I'll find a book to read."

"Actually, I don't see why you need to sit through these meetings," she says. "You can just step out."

"It's tempting. But I promised my brother I wouldn't leave you alone. What would your usual bodyguard do?"

"He'd wait in the hall."

"But I can't do that. It would look ridiculous for your boyfriend to lurk in the hallway. Max has made this weird, right?"

"A little," she admits.

Yup. I'm totally calling him later to complain.

Meanwhile, when we reach the ice cream stand, Alex orders a sundae the size of a lifeboat. "Aren't you having anything?" she yelps when I sit down at a table instead of placing a second order.

"Maybe later," I say, because it's more diplomatic than pointing out that I'm full from lunch, and probably will be for three more hours. "I don't need more food. What I need is a nap." Or, in a perfect world, sex and *then* a nap. I need to burn off some tension.

My surroundings aren't helping, either. The beach is decorated with miles of scantily clad women. None of them hold a candle to the bombshell eating ice cream across from me, though.

Whenever Alex licks that spoon, it makes me crazy. I wish she'd stop.

"Bite?" she offers, which means I'm staring. She digs the spoon into the vanilla ice cream, sweeping it through a bit of caramel sauce, and catching a chunk of fresh mango. Then she offers it to me.

I open my mouth like a bird, just to see what she'll do.

Alex rises from her chair and leans over the table to feed me. As I sweep a cold spoonful of wonder into my mouth, her cleavage is right at eye level. That's where I'd rather put my tongue, damn it. Forget the ice cream.

This is going to be the longest week of my life.

"TENNIS COURTS!" Alex says on the walk back. "I'll call the concierge and see if we can get a slot. You still play, right? And tennis works with your fitness goals."

"Sure," I say, because why not? A couple of hours watching Alex's sleek legs maneuver, just out of reach, a few yards in front of me? What's a little more torture between friends? "Here's what we should do—hire a tennis pro, and then hide from him in the shrubberies."

"Why would—" She breaks off as she remembers how we used to pull this very trick on Martha's Vineyard. "Oh my God. I was *such* a brat." She puts a hand in front of her mouth and laughs. "My poor father. I don't think I did one thing he asked for that entire year."

"Not like he was around to notice." That just slips out. I was such a bitter kid that summer. Our fathers basically abandoned us to the help so they could fly around the world and do whatever it was they did.

"That was the summer of the telecom merger," she says as we pace across the sand. "We didn't see much of them, did we?"

"Nope." Alex's father was still running the cable empire that Alex now commands. And mine was trying to get his fledgling security business off the ground.

"Guess they didn't have much choice," Alex points out.

I only make a grunt of acknowledgment. This period of my life isn't something I talk about. Alex's mother had passed away when she was seven. By the time I met her in Massachusetts, she was used to being the only child of a single dad. It was familiar.

But I was still raw.

My mother had left the previous September, just after Max and I headed back to school. I don't know why, but I'd spent the year convinced she'd turn up again by summer. To my mind, surviving the school year without her was a personal test. If I passed, the reward would be her reappearance.

I have no idea where I got that idea. But I was crushed when it didn't happen.

"Do you get along with your dad?" Alex asks now.

"Sure. I guess. He and Max are really tight, because they work together. But dad and I are solid enough." Except when he tries to get me to talk about my future. And then I'm only annoyed.

"What about your mother?" she presses.

"What about her?" I grumble. "Is this an interview?"

"Sorry," she says quickly. "I just wondered when you saw her again after that summer."

"The answer is never."

"Oh." And now Alex is clearly wishing she hadn't asked. "Sorry."

"Thanks, but I've had twenty more years to get over it."

"Still." Alex shrugs. "You never really get over that. I didn't, anyway."

It surprises me that she's willing to say so. Max and I never mention our mother. *Never.* Max would no sooner say her name aloud than he'd admit to being afraid of snakes. And he *hates* snakes. Come to think of it, I know more about how my brother feels about snakes than about how he feels about Mom.

And I'm exactly the same. I don't speak her name because it gives her too much power. But the wound is still deep. She left us and never looked back. Not only was it hurtful, it's shameful. Who does that?

Once in a while, my dad brings it up. He says he blames the age difference between them. He didn't start a family until he was forty, and she was twenty-five. As a young man, he was a military intelligence officer for the US Navy. After that, he became the chief of police in the New Jersey town where I grew up. So by the time he met and married my mom, he was ready to settle down.

"She wasn't in the same place," he once said, in a dramatic understatement.

I remember my mother as someone who was always dissatisfied. With me. With dad. With the house where we lived. Still, it took me by complete surprise when she walked out.

It was a Sunday. There was football on TV. Dad got a call and announced he had to make an unexpected trip into town. That happens a lot when you're the chief of police, and none of us was surprised.

But mom lost it, throwing one of her fits. "You're never home! You don't care about me!" I sat on the couch and pretended she wasn't screaming and crying. I never knew what to do when my mom was upset.

Only it didn't end in the usual way—with the slam of the bedroom door. This time she packed a bag and walked right out the front door, barely even saying goodbye. "I'll be at my sisters," she said to Max, who followed her outside.

I stared at the football game, barely seeing it. They fought all the time, but she never walked out before.

Even then, I didn't really think it was permanent. Who leaves without saying goodbye to her kids? I didn't cry, or plead with her.

Not because I wouldn't have bothered. Just because I didn't believe she meant to stay away.

For a month I watched the front door, thinking she'd walk back through it. Then one day dad took me out for ice cream after school—just me, not Max. "She's not coming back, son," he said as the spoon halted on its way to my mouth. "It's not your fault, either."

"Then whose fault is it?" I'd spat.

"Nobody's," my dad grumbled. "Your mom expects her life to be one long party. But nobody's is. She'll figure that out eventually. I'm just sorry for you and your brother that she couldn't be the mother you need. I guess that's what I get for marrying someone fifteen years younger than I am."

And remind me why I'm thinking about this? The Hawaiian sand is warm under my feet. I'm carrying my shoes and watching children run into and out of the surf. I'm full of good food, and the sun is shining. My bossy companion in the tiny bikini is whistling an off-key tune.

"Where shall we have dinner?" Alex asks as our hotel comes into view.

"Dinner? Aren't you too full of ice cream to care?"

"Eventually I will, though, and so will you." Alex gives me a glare that dares me to argue. "I'm going to look for a nice restaurant off the property. I'd rather not run into *him* again before I have to."

"Yeah, okay." If Alex wants to dine somewhere special, I won't argue. Much.

We're just heading up the carefully manicured path to the hotel when my phone makes a sound I've never heard before. It's a buzz, like an angry wasp.

Worse, Alex's phone does the same. She halts in her tracks. "That can't be good. My phone only makes that sound when theres a security breach."

"Does that happen a lot?"

"No."

I lift my head and scan our surroundings. The resort's generous lawn is lightly occupied by sunbathers in hammocks. Four teenagers are playing chess with giant pieces on a black-and-white tiled patio.

It's not exactly a threatening environment, but I take a step closer to Alex anyway, and then I pull out my phone. There's a message from an unidentified number. ***Return to the room, but do not touch anything until cleared by our team***.

"Well, that's ominous," Alex grumbles, looking over my shoulder. She pulls out her phone. "I have the same message."

We ride the elevator in silence. And when we reach the suite, the door is already ajar. Inside I spot an unfamiliar man. He turns immediately to flash me his ID. There's no name on it, of course. The Company doesn't do that. There is, however, a holographic picture of a skeleton key. That's my brother's symbol.

I nod. "I'm Eric. Nice to meet you—?"

"Pieter. Sorry for the intrusion."

"What happened here?"

Before he gets a chance to answer, another man appears in the bedroom doorway, and I'm startled to see that it's Gunnar, my brother's second-in-command. "Hey, Eric. Alex. You guys had a break-in."

"By who?" Alex asks, her voice tight.

"Pieter, please close the door," he says instead of answering.

As the other man does his bidding, I feel a flash of anger at whichever asshole is responsible for putting that scared look on Alex's face. But also at my brother Max, for making me a part of this drama. And Gunnar is in Hawaii? They obviously have a cast of thousands here to protect Alex. This shouldn't be my problem.

Except it is, because Alex looks pale right now, and I feel like a heel for wishing myself away from here.

"All right," Gunnar says, plunking a tablet on the table. "Sit down, and I'll show you what we saw on the feed."

I sit down beside Alex on the sofa while Gunnar brings up the video shot by the pillow cam. The same one currently parked behind my left butt cheek.

And I have to admit that the gear Max and Gunnar have perfected over the years is pretty damn impressive. Gunnar waves his hand in front of the screen to start the silent video playing. On it, our hotel room appears in perfect resolution. The door swings open, admitting a man who is already shoving a key card into his pocket. He's wearing a fishing hat with a wide brim that dips over his features. If you passed him in the lobby, it would only look a little sloppy. But it does a remarkable job concealing the top half of his face.

"Shit," I curse as he moves through the frame without showing his eyes. I can barely make out his jawline.

"Please tell me you recognize him?" Gunnar asks. "Because that doesn't look like Jared Tatum to me. His shoulders are too broad."

Alex just shakes her head. The intruder does a quick circuit of the room, pulling on gloves then stopping in front of Alex's laptop on the desk. He opens the lid, and the screen blinks to life. I hear Alex's sharp intake of breath as he pulls out his phone and snaps a picture of the login screen.

Then he closes it again and walks away, circling behind the camera.

"Now he's offscreen for seventy seconds," Gunnar says.

Alex groans. "I left my prenatal vitamins in the bedroom. And there's a pregnancy book in my luggage. I should have been more careful."

"You think this guy is working for your ex?" I ask. "That was fast."

"It *was* fast," Gunnar says. "Can I ask you a question, Alex? Tatum registered for the conference at the last minute, right? Does he have any real business here, besides asking you to get back together?"

"Well, sure," she says slowly. "He needs to do another round of funding for his startup. There are people here who could help him."

Okay. I'm still in the dark, though. "Who else would stalk Alex?" I ask.

Gunnar's forehead wrinkles. "When you run a big company, you make enemies. On any given day, there are a dozen people mad at Alex."

"Sad but true," she murmurs.

In my peripheral vision, I see Pieter wave his hands. We all look up at once, and he beckons to Gunnar.

"So let's not leap to conclusions yet," Gunnar says in a normal voice. But he's already on his feet and walking toward the bedroom. "I'm just going to use the bathroom before I head out."

"Um, okay?" Alex says, clearly confused.

Gunnar holds up a hand that's meant to keep us where we're seated. But I'm not in the mood to obey. I kick off my flip flops and then pace across the rug to see what the hell they found.

In the bedroom, Pieter is standing beside a framed painting on the wall. He points, and I see it—something small on the top of the frame. It's no bigger than a coat button.

I hear water running behind the bathroom door. And then Gunnar opens the bathroom door, holding three fingers to Pieter. On a count of three, he flushes the toilet.

At the same moment as the loud flush, Pieter reaches up and plucks the device off the picture frame. He places it on his palm, and then cups his hand over it, the same way you would a real bug. He walks by me, heading for the door to the suite, while Gunnar rushes to open it for him.

Pieter leaves with that thing in his hand. And when I turn around again, Alex is heading out onto the terrace, looking white as a sheet.

Gunnar is still poking around the suite with some kind of sensing device in his hand, scanning every baseboard. As I watch, he picks up the hotel's phone and examines it. Then he sets it down again. Then he heads over to the bed and starts tossing pillows onto the floor.

I follow Alex outside. She's sitting on one of the outdoor sofas, her knees tucked in tight to her chest as if making herself as small as possible. This posture of fear hits me right in the solar plexus.

The Alex I remember is bossy and forthright. She doesn't curl up into a ball. Ever.

"Hey," I say, sitting down right beside her. Then I drag the footstool closer. I stretch out my legs and nudge her to do the same. "You're going to be okay."

"I know that," she snaps. And then she puts her head in her hands and cries.

8

ALEX

WELL, this is both terrifying and mortifying.

"I'm sorry," I gasp. "I'm not a crier." It's true, but pretty difficult to prove with all these tears streaming down my face. I swipe at them hastily. "It's the hormones."

Eric makes a small noise of concern then puts an arm around me, pulling me closer, until my unhappy head meets his shoulder.

The pregnancy hormones are wreaking havoc on my fortitude, because nothing has ever felt better to me than Eric's solid bulk under my cheek. I've never been the sort of woman who needs a man to tell her that everything is all right. But my burdens are extra heavy today.

"Tell me why you're so freaked," he whispers. "Gunnar will get to the bottom of it."

"He's stripping the bed right now, isn't he?"

"Yeah," he admits.

"A bug in the *bedroom*. This is such a disaster. And it's all my fault. Of all the men I could have..." I swallow hard and sit up straight again. "What if Jared won't sign the papers just to spite me? What if he won't give me custody?" My anxieties bound around like the white-tailed deer on Martha's Vineyard.

"Slow down there. Breaking and entering won't sound good to a judge," he points out. "The crazier he acts, the worse it will be for him."

I actually shiver. That's how terrified I am of Jared. Before now, I'd wondered if I'd just built him up in my mind—if he wasn't really as big a creep as I'd made him out to be.

And then someone put a bug in my hotel room.

Eric's strong arm tightens around me. "Deep breaths. I mean that literally. Do you do yoga?"

"Sometimes." I take a very long inhale. When I can't possibly bring in any more air, I let it out slowly through my mouth.

"There you go. Bedrooms are where they put bugs, anyway."

"Who does?" I gasp.

"Breathe," he chides. "Anyone who bugs a home hits the kitchen and bedroom first, because that's where most serious conversations happen. Those are the places where people forget to be on their guard. My brother and father yap about this shit all the time. I could write a manual on how to invade people's privacy."

I laugh. "Fun times at the Bayer Family dinner table."

"You know it. My dad taught me to hot-wire a car when I was sixteen."

"Just for fun?" I ask, perking up a little. The distraction of hearing about Eric's family is even better than deep breathing.

"We were out fishing at a quiet lake in the middle of New Jersey. And I dropped the keys out of the boat. Plunk. Right into the lake. So we had to hot-wire our own car just to get home."

"Oh, man." I laugh. "Was your father pissed off?"

"That's putting it mildly. He made me pay for the replacement key. Fifty bucks. I had to mow three extra lawns just to cover the cost."

"Both our dads are hard-asses," I realize. And I'm breathing easier now. I shouldn't stay right here, plastered to Eric as tightly as a bumper sticker, letting him console me. His role as my fake boyfriend doesn't really extend to this.

But I like it, okay? Sue me.

And now my adrenaline rush is turning into an adrenaline crash. I'm suddenly so tired. I put my head back down on his shoulder and close my eyes. Just for a minute.

That was the idea, anyway. But the next thing I know, I hear

Gunnar's voice. My eyes fly open, and both Pieter and Gunnar are standing there in front of us.

I sit up straight just in time to hear Gunnar say that they didn't find anything else in the suite. "He only had enough time to drop the one device. And he didn't come out on the terrace, or we would have seen it in the video."

"True," I say, blinking to clear my vision.

"We're leaving you a metal rod to secure this sliding door—" Gunnar gestures at the terrace door. "—And an alarm to hang on your hotel room door when you turn in for the night. It's a simple device. Lock up and then hang it on the door handle before you turn it on. If it's jostled, it screams."

"Got it," Eric says.

"We'll put a tail on Tatum. You won't notice our guy, but he'll follow Tatum any time the man is outside his hotel room."

"But how will you know when he leaves his room?" I try to picture a security agent standing around on Jared's hotel floor, trying to look inconspicuous.

Gunnar grins. "Don't ask, don't tell."

"Okay."

"Do me a favor, though? Email me or Max with the list of meetings you're taking. We need to take a second look at those business connections. Oh, and if you turned down any requests for meetings, we want those, too."

"Sure." Although it won't be easy to remember who had asked me for a meeting. "I'll check with my assistant. I'm sure we rebuffed a few suppliers who weren't up for consideration."

"Consideration for what?" Eric asks.

"Making the new hardware for my product launch. It's a sophisticated home network system—both a router and a smart speaker rolled together."

"With Bingley?" he asks.

"Exactly. We're buying a lot of components for delivery in October. Chips. Motherboards. Housing. High-end speakers."

"Your wallet is open," Gunnar points out. "That makes you interesting to half the people at the conference."

"Interesting enough for industrial espionage?" Eric asks.

"Absolutely," Gunnar agrees cheerfully. "Industrial espionage is as common as brushing and flossing at these things."

It's true, but I never used to worry very much. It's weird how my pregnancy has shifted my focus. I'm more afraid of everything right now. Although I'm more afraid of Jared than I am of corporate spies.

"Tomorrow is the cocktail party, right?" Pieter asks.

"I could skip it," I offer.

Gunnar shakes his head. "You carry on with whatever you had planned. Nobody's going to get into your room again. And nobody is going to hurt you. You'll have lots of coverage, okay?"

Pieter pulls two key cards out of his pocket. There are initials written on them in Sharpie: an *A* and an *E*. "Take these. We had the lock recoded. The housekeepers' key cards won't work on that door any longer. The hotel won't send anyone to your room without your express permission."

"I don't need housekeeping, anyway."

"Fine. And now we'll receive an automated text anytime your room door is opened with a key card. If it's either of your key cards, we'll match the location of your phones to the room. If it's not your key card, we'll come running."

"Okay," I say, feeling a little sturdier already. There are three strapping, intelligent men here to protect me, after all. "That ought to cover it."

"We tried moving you to a different room, but the hotel is full."

I could have told them that. "I'll be fine. He won't come back, right? He'll realize that his bug failed immediately, and that we're stepping up the security."

"That's right," Gunnar says. "Chin up. And text me or call me at any moment."

"Will do." I give him a calm smile. Putting others at ease is something I learned to do at an early age. Some days it's more useful than my double masters degrees.

Then he and Pieter depart, leaving Eric and I on the terrace together. "Now what?" Eric asks. "Want me to make a dinner reservation? Or would you rather have room service and television?"

"I like the second option. I'm still jet-lagged," I say by way of an excuse. But the truth is that I just don't feel like making myself visible right now. That video shook me up more than I care to admit. The sight of a stranger so casually breaking in to snoop gives me the willies.

"Fine. A nap sounds good to me right now. Will it bum you out if I fall asleep? We could put the alarm on the door."

"I'll be fine," I lie. "But let's look at that alarm anyway."

Back inside the room, we hang the alarm by its strap over the hotel room door. The device is plastic, and bright orange. It looks like a child's toy. I press its only button, and a light winks on.

Then, as a test, Eric turns the door handle to open the door.

An ear splitting shriek rends my ears, and I push that button again as fast as I can get to it. The return of silence is a huge relief.

"Jesus Christ. I guess it works," Eric grumbles.

"It's a laugh a minute with me, isn't it?" I lock the door again and then carefully press the button to arm the device.

When I stand up, Eric pulls me into a quick hug. I get a whiff of his coconut-scented shampoo before he releases me again. "Chin up, Engels. There's nothing to be afraid of."

"I know," I mumble. "Take your nap, already. I have work to do."

He gives me a smile that says he knows I'm all bluster. Then he ambles his big self into the bedroom and disappears.

Alone on the sofa, I open my email. The first message is bad news—my assistant Rolf will be a day late. *Grandma needs me in New York*, is all he wrote. *See you Thursday*.

Great. More chaos. He's going to miss a day of meetings?

Now I'm both jumpy and blue.

From the bedroom I hear the gentle sound of Eric's deep, sleeping breaths, and I last no more than five minutes on the sofa alone. I'm weary and a little freaked out. So I tiptoe into the bedroom, lie down on my own side of the bed, and close my eyes.

The sound of Eric's slow breathing is more relaxing than any reassurances from my expensive security team. Finally calm, I fall asleep, too.

9

ERIC

"PILLOW" is apparently part of my job description.

The next morning I wake up with Alex asleep on my chest, her hair splayed decadently across my skin. Not one part of her—not even a toe—is on her own side of the bed.

Carefully, I slide her off my body, her hair tickling my sensitive skin.

"Sorry," she mumbles, rolling over.

She should be. Cuddling without sex? It's just wrong.

In the living room, I disarm our front door, as one does. Then I order room service for both of us. After a day with Alex, I already know her order: plenty of everything, plus decaf.

While I wait for the food, I check my messages.

Change of plans, my brother has written. ***Pieter and another guard will escort Alex to all her meetings today. You won't be needed until the cocktail party.***

Wait, what?

After yesterday's break-in, The Company has obviously closed ranks. Is it weird that I'm a little insulted? Fired from a job I didn't even want. Now, that's flattering. At least I can get a good workout in.

I DO USE my time wisely. I spend two hours in the weight room, plus an hour of stretching. Then I have a healthy lunch alone, where I don't need to pretend to be anyone's boyfriend.

It's great, if a little solitary.

My phone rings while I'm drinking coffee on a chaise on the beach. I answer it right away, in case Alex needs me. But it's only my asshole brother. "How's it going?" he asks.

"Great. Why? Done with me?"

"Not hardly. What gave you that idea?"

"You have a cast of thousands. I'm just not sure I'm needed."

"Little brother, are you feeling ignored? The gigolo at odds between dates…"

"Shut up. This was your idea. I could just come home."

He laughs. "Don't get any ideas. It's true that I didn't expect to fly in more staff for this event. But Alex is not the only tech executive I'm protecting in Hawaii this week."

"Oh."

"Yeah, I pulled agents off other work. But she's the only one who's having security issues. And we haven't identified the guy in the break-in video. Yet."

"It wasn't the ex-boyfriend," I offer. "I saw that guy at lunch yesterday."

"And?" Max asks. "What did you think?"

"He doesn't work out."

Max laughs. "Your measure of a man's worth."

"Hey!" Although he is partly right. "I couldn't exactly see into his soul from across a crowded restaurant. But he isn't a grave physical threat. He looked angry, though."

"At you?"

"Yeah. He wasn't expecting to see Alex with a guy."

"And you rubbed it in, I guess?"

"A little. I sent a message."

He's quiet for a second. "And the break-in happened an hour later."

"Right. Which seems ridiculously aggressive for a rich guy with a romantic grudge."

"I think so, too," Max chuckles.

"Which means someone else broke in," I conclude. "Who?"

"Not sure," Max grunts. "I'm working on a couple theories."

"Care to share?"

"Not at this time."

I groan. "So let me get this straight. Either her ex has socio-pathic tendencies, or some other character is stalking Alex. But you won't tell me anything more."

"That sums it up pretty well. But Eric—this is normal. All my clients are at risk, pretty much all the time. Worrying about them is what I do. Alex's break-in is just another day at the office. Let me go do my job, and when I have actionable advice, you'll know it."

"And you wonder why I'm eager to work with you. I don't even know the *name* of your company."

"Because you don't need to. It's not a secret because I'm an asshole. It's a secret because it makes an important point. Anyone who works for me needs to understand that secrets are currency. If they can't accept that, they aren't a good fit."

Then I'm not a good fit. I don't say it aloud, because I don't wish to prolong this conversation. And ultimately, I don't need to know the name of a company I'll never work for. "Whatever."

"Stay the course, Eric. It's either the boyfriend or it's not."

"*Ex*-boyfriend," I grunt. "Alex is more afraid of him than anything else."

"Agreed. Which is why you're so important to this equation. Your job is twofold—to keep Jared Tatum away from Alex, and to make Alex feel safe. You keep an eye on Alex so that we can keep an eye on everything else."

"Fine," I agree. "I have to get off the phone now, or I'll have an uneven tan on my face."

Max belly laughs. "It's good to hear your priorities are in line."

"As always. Later, killjoy."

"Later, dumbass."

And people say I'm not very cuddly.

I set my phone to wake me up in twenty minutes, and then I take a catnap on the beach.

MY DAY of leisure ends abruptly at six, when Alex tries to remove my copy of *Sports Illustrated* from my hands.

But I have fast reflexes. I catch her manicured hand just as it closes around the pages. "No way," I argue. "I'm right in the middle of this article."

"The cocktail party is already starting, and I want to be there in half an hour."

"So?" I hold tightly to my magazine. "It's a ten minute walk to the other hotel. That means I still have fifteen minutes to sit here."

"You're not dressed. You need a blazer and tie for this."

"Yeah, I allocated five minutes for getting dressed." I close the magazine and look up. And that's a mistake, because I almost swallow my tongue. Alex is wearing a halter dress that seems to offer her breasts to me like gourmet treats on a buffet table.

"What?" she says, and I realize I'm staring. "Is it too much?"

"No!" I say quickly, because I'm not an idiot.

"Really—am I bursting out of here?" She lifts her hands and *cups her breasts*. "Nothing quite fits me right now. But this dress has a fit-and-flare shape, so it covers up my expanding ass."

My mouth is suddenly dry. The sight of Alex touching herself—however briefly—is going to live on in my dirtiest dreams, I just know it. "You look great," I rasp. "'Scuse me. I better…" I get up from the sofa and head into the bedroom.

I have got to get a hold of myself.

Putting on a suit ought to do the trick, though. Who wants to wear a tie in Hawaii? In fact, fuck the tie. If I'm supposed to be her bad boy arm candy, I can buck convention. I'm skipping the tie. And I'm not shaving, either. Three days worth of scruff is a good look on me.

I put on a linen jacket over dark jeans and a white shirt, open at the neck. When I check the mirror, I see a guy looking sharp, and a little more dangerous than a tech executive. I grin at my reflection. Who knew acting could be so fun?

When I walk into the living room, I find Alex standing in front of a full-length mirror, fussing with her hair. She turns around, and my pulse kicks up a notch.

"You're staring," she whispers. "You're going to make me self-conscious."

"Why? You look hot in that dress." It's just the truth.

She looks down. "I'm not the same shape as I was a few months ago. Jared might notice and wonder why."

"No way. That's not how men work," I point out. "When he looks at you, there's no chance his brain says"—I deliver this next part in a weird, nerdy voice—"she looks curvier, in a way that indicates early pregnancy."

"No?" She smiles.

"Not a chance. He'll take one look at you, and his brain will start melting. Ask me how I know."

She rolls her eyes. "Thank you, Mr. Flattery."

"It's not flattery if it's true. Now, let's go. If I'm wearing a suit jacket, I deserve a drink."

"Fine." She takes one more glance at herself in the mirror. "I'll grab my bag."

THE WALK to the other hotel takes longer than it should because Alex is wearing heels and the flagstone path between the properties is somewhat uneven.

"If I were a dick, I'd challenge you to a race. First one there gets a cookie."

Alex stops in her tracks. "That sounds familiar."

"It should. You pulled that same stunt on me on the Vineyard."

"What a pain in the ass I was," she says as we continue along the path. "I cheated, too, right? I would only throw down that challenge when I was standing up and ready to go but you were still sitting on your beach towel."

I laugh because it's true. "You'd better hope that nobody ever wants to interview me about you. *What was Alex Engels like as a child? Were there signs she'd become a CEO?* Absolutely! She got up early, never sat down, and cheated every chance she got."

"Shhh!" Alex hisses. "I have a reputation to uphold. And I won *some* of those races honestly."

"Maybe *once*," I scoff. "But not in silly shoes like those."

"No kidding. I didn't learn to wear heels until after college. Now they're a necessity. Not only do they make my legs look longer, they bring me closer to eye level with all the men I have to deal with."

I don't think her legs could possibly look any longer, but I keep that to myself.

"WHAT ARE YOU DRINKING?" I ask when we finally arrive at the party. It's on another terrace overlooking the beach. Torches are lit at the boundary of the space, and the light makes Alex's skin look even more golden than usual.

"Well, my usual drink is a gin and tonic, so I guess I'm drinking tonic water and lime," she says, surveying the crowd.

"I can't leave you alone, though. You'll need to accompany me to the bar," I say. "We're like characters in a comedy, trying not to reveal that we're handcuffed together."

"Oh, don't worry." She sighs. "I just spotted the ex. He's in the far corner, kissing up to the CFO of Verizon."

"Good time to grab a drink, then." I put an arm around her shoulder and tuck her against me. Then I guide her over to the bar. "Evening," I say to the young bartender when he gives me a glance. "Two tonic waters with lime, please. No hurry."

"Eric," she whispers. "You can have a real drink."

"Later," I promise her. My gut says I'll be handling her ex tonight, and I will do so with a clear head. "What's your play, anyway?"

"Sorry?"

"Your play. Your goal. Your mission for this party. Unless you just love a good cash bar and some boring small talk."

"Not particularly." Alex's smile lights up her whole face. "I'm here to give a piece of my mind to the conference organizer. Then I'm out of here, out of these shoes, and out of this dress."

Yes, please. I give her a slow once-over, because that declaration makes me imagine her naked. "Can I watch that last part?"

"Eric!" she smacks my arm.

The bartender chimes in. "Can't blame a guy for asking." He sets two glasses down on the bar in front of us. "Four bucks."

"Thanks, dude." I drop a ten on the bar and hand her a drink. "Your fake boyfriend bought you a fake cocktail. Drink up."

She gives me a wary smile. "You're good for my ego."

"I don't think he was faking," the young bartender says, already pouring the next customer's drinks. He may be young, but he's already wise. They must teach that at bartending school.

"So let's find this guy you need to speak to," I prompt.

"He's over there," Alex says, pointing at a cluster of gray-haired men near the dance floor.

Unfortunately, we don't get very far. As soon as Alex and I venture further into the party, I see her ex excuse himself from a conversation and make a beeline for Alex.

"Oh, shit," she squeaks.

"Easy," I say quietly. "We can't ignore him for six days. It's better if he states his case and then I send him away."

"Ugh. I hope you can make your point quickly."

"Alexandra," the twit says as he approaches. "Long time no see."

"That was intentional," she says, taking a sip of her drink.

I manage not to laugh, but it isn't easy.

Tatum frowns. "Look, I'm sorry things ended badly. I've been thinking about you. I have something to give you, and—"

"I accept your apology," she says quickly. "Now, if you'll excuse us…"

He reaches for her hand. "Can I speak to you a moment?"

"No," I say, stepping between the two of them, my intention impossible to miss. "Not happening."

Her ex has to lift his chin to look me in the eye. "Alex can speak for herself."

"Normally, yes. But you haven't shown a lot of patience for her viewpoint in the past. Or am I wrong about that? Maybe I'm a dick, but I'd never *hit* her."

"Jesus," he hisses as heads begin to turn. "That was a fluke."

"A *fluke*?" Alex yips from behind me. "That's just insulting. Did your hand find my face by accident?"

"Why don't you just fluke off right now?" I say, taking a step closer to him, which forces him to take a step backward. "Did you know I hit guys for a living?"

His lip curls, and for a moment, I wonder if he's dumb enough to punch me. But Alex was right. He's here to impress, and there are too many people watching. After another beat of enraged silence, he turns his back and strides away from us and then right out of the party.

"Well. " I dust my hands against each other. "That's taken care of. Now let's handle your thing."

"Right. In a second." Alex takes a sip of her drink, and I notice her hand is shaking.

"Hey!" I pull her against me. "Everything is fine. That went exactly like I expected."

"I'm usually good in a fight, I swear." She presses her face against my lapel. "But that man makes me so nervous."

"We could just bail on this party," I point out.

"No way." She stands up straighter. Then she takes my glass out of my hand and maneuvers toward the bar. "Could you pour some gin into his drink?" she asks the bartender. "I think he deserves it."

The guy grabs a bottle of Plymouth off the top shelf and tips it over my glass. "Well done, man. You won't be hearing from him again. Drink's on the house."

"Thanks." I grab a straw and stir up my cocktail. "I did fly five thousand miles to tell that guy off."

Alex just shakes her head. "Ridiculous, right?"

"Nah, it was kind of fun. Now, who did you need to see?"

"He's over there." She takes my hand and squeezes it.

As her fingers close around mine, just for a second I feel like that kid on Martha's Vineyard again—ready for trouble, and ready to follow Alex to the next adventure.

10

ALEX

I HAVE to admit that Eric's caveman routine was kind of hot. If anyone finds out how much I enjoyed the sight of a man defending me, I'll have to turn in my lady-boss card.

I'm blaming that on the pregnancy hormones, too, I decide as we maneuver through the crowd. There's a dance floor in the center of the action, where quite a few couples move together to the music of a four-piece band.

"I thought this would be a sausage fest," Eric says, his hand still in mine. "Do all tech conferences have dancing?"

"No," I tell him with a glance over my shoulder. "But most tech conferences are in Vegas. This one is special. The wives and husbands like to come along to this one."

"Ah. So I'm not the only arm candy here?" He frees his hand from mine, only to place it on the small of my back.

"Nope." *But you're the hottest*, I privately add. My hormones are dancing the foxtrot even before that hand slides to my waist.

"Alex Engels! So nice to see you."

The executive's voice lifts me out of my reverie and reminds me that I'm here to network. I stop and turn. It would be rude not to greet the CFO of a gaming company and his golfing buddy, the venture capitalist.

I put on my Corporate Leader face and greet these men by

name. "Arnie! Roger. Great to see you." Names and faces have always come easily to me. "This is my boyfriend, Eric Bayer."

It's funny how the lie just rolls off my tongue.

"Are you in tech, Eric?" the head of SumoChip asks him.

"Not a chance," he says easily. "I'm a forward for the Brooklyn Bruisers hockey team."

It's almost ridiculous how quickly their faces light up. "Great season!" Arnie gushes. "Shame about game seven."

"Wasn't it, though?" Eric says with a sigh.

Then the three of them pick apart the hockey playoffs season while I sip my drink and plot out what I want to say to the head of this convention.

"We're boring Alex with this sports talk," Roger says eventually.

"I do own a basketball team," I remind him. "But hockey was never my favorite sport."

Eric grabs his chest in a mock expression of horror.

"Until now, Honeybunch," I add, to the amusement of the tech executives.

Eric gives me a wry grin and slips his arm around my waist. "Thin ice, cutie."

The other men think that's hilarious. But finally, we're free of them. "You play the boyfriend role well," I whisper as I lead him across the space.

"Nothing to it," he says. "You'd almost think I'd been somebody's boyfriend before."

"I'm sure you have been."

He gives his head a single shake. "Not often. Nobody wants a guy who travels as much as I do. Even if they say they do, they don't."

"I'm familiar with that problem myself."

"I'll bet you are."

"Now who are we homing in on, here?" he asks quietly.

I glance at the group of men against the windows. Unfortunately, one of my own executives has joined the group. "The guy in the green tie is Trent Trainor. He runs this event, and I have some feedback that will be unwelcome."

"Oh, brother. Will I need hazard pay for this?"

I pat his arm. "Nope. This time I get to do all the talking. The shorter man standing next to him is Peter Whitbread. He works for me." He's the general counsel and an old contemporary of my dad's. Unfortunately, Peter is still pissed off that I'm CEO and he's not.

"But you don't like him," Eric guesses.

"Is it that obvious? The feeling is mutual, too. Let's get this over with."

"Yes, ma'am."

I make my approach. "Evening, gentlemen."

Four executives—all in their fifties—turn to me with polite smiles, each one a multi-millionaire, but each one slightly over the hill. These are the people who run tech conferences—the aging B team. Because the very sharpest minds in tech don't have the time.

And now I've interrupted whatever boys' club conversation they were enjoying—favorite golf courses or favorite titty bars. Take your pick.

"Good evening, Alexandra," Trainor says. "We can't wait to hear your speech on Friday night."

"She's going to knock your socks off, Trent," Peter Whitbread says. "Such a smart girl."

Girl! He couldn't be more condescending even if he pinched me on the cheek. Even worse—it's all intentional. He hates me, and never misses a chance to demean me.

At least once a week I fantasize about pushing him off the board of my company. But I never follow through because he is, unfortunately, useful. He's been at Engels Cable Media for so long that he knows where all the bodies are buried.

"The speech is shipshape," I say, holding my smile. I make eye contact with all the stuffed shirts in the circle. "I do have one question, however."

"What's that?" Trainor takes a deep drink of his scotch.

I pass my own glass to Eric, who takes it without comment, and I pull a sheet of paper out of my bag. "I was looking over the program you put together. Sixteen panels, with fifty experts in total."

"All the greatest minds in tech," another man says.

"Don't worry, I won't miss your panel," I say brightly. "But I do wonder how you've managed this."

"Many calls, much begging," Trainor says with a jowly grin.

"So, I guess all the women turned you down, then?" I pretend to scan the sheet. "All but two. Your panels are four percent women and six percent people of color. Lots of white guys made themselves available, though."

Eric snorts beside me, but he doesn't say a word.

Once again, heads are starting to turn. I guess it's the night for making scenes. "Mr. Trainor, I've been coming to this conference for five years. But my firm won't commit a single sponsorship dollar next year until I've read the panel lineup. Peter here won't be available for your golf foursome unless at least twenty percent of the speakers are women."

"*Twenty* percent?" Whitbread gasps.

"Now, Alex," Trainor chuckles. "That's a big number."

"No, it isn't." Even though I've rehearsed this speech, my heart still races. "Twenty percent is laughably low. Once you realize that not all experts look exactly like you, I promise you'll start spotting them everywhere."

"But, Alex," he sputters. "What about *you?* Your picture is on the front of the pamphlet!"

"I saw that. And I'm sure you remembered that I complained last year. You swore you were listening. So you invited me to give one of the keynotes. I get it. That's a nice job of coopting your loudest critic. But it isn't enough."

People are staring now, but I keep my chin high. "Until you actually *change* the things that need changing, this will be my last visit to Hawaii. And Peter's, by the way. I'll stay home next year and celebrate your event by writing an Op Ed about your conference in the *Wall Street Journal*. You gentleman have a fun night."

My pulse pounds in my ears as I turn. Eric pivots at exactly the same time I do, taking my arm and stepping casually away. I suppose professional athletes all have excellent timing. You'd have to.

It isn't until we're several paces away that I see he's trying not to laugh.

"Shh," I coach. "It's not funny."

"But *you* are quite funny." He chuckles. "Kicking ass and taking names." He puts both our empty glasses down on a high table and leads me a little further away from the men I just savaged.

"They had it coming."

"I have no doubt."

"I'm sorry I didn't introduce you, but—"

"You were too busy swinging." Eric halts, and I realize we're right in the middle of the dance floor. Couples move slowly around us to the band's Hawaiian-tinged jazz.

Smooth as silk, he takes my hand and slips it onto his shoulder. Then he tucks his hand onto my waist. He turns me slowly, stepping in time to the music.

"I'm not really a dancer," I stammer, the adrenaline still coursing through my body.

"Well, I'm good enough for both of us," he says in that smug tone that makes me either want to kill him or kiss him. "Besides, there were a couple of dudes making a beeline for you. To your left."

My eyes dart to the side, and I see exactly who he means. They're Jared Tatum's two golf buddies. "Ugh. No. Those are the ex's friends."

"They didn't look like fun to me either," Eric says, his low voice vibrating in my chest as he turns me around. "So I took evasive maneuvers."

"You are too slick for your own good." I'm so close to him now. There was no alcohol in my drink, but I'm high on a blend of my own bravery and Eric's clean, masculine scent. It's a potent brew.

"Your ex's pals are watching," Eric whispers. He steps in closer and brushes a kiss across my cheek.

"What was that for?"

"So they won't cut in. I'm not allowed to leave you alone. And three people slow-dancing together is just awkward."

I laugh suddenly, picturing Eric wrapping his arms around me and another guy.

His response is to kiss me again with soft lips on my cheekbone. But this time, the kiss lingers.

My laughter dies in my throat, and goose bumps rise up on both arms. My bra suddenly feels too tight.

Good lord. My response to a kiss on the cheek is pretty extreme. If he kissed me for real, I'd probably combust.

Eric straightens again, piercing me with those gray eyes. Then they darken, as if he can read my reaction from my face.

I look away. But it's too late. My cheeks are flushed, and my heart is galloping. Anyone who looks at me right now would know why. "Did they go away?" I croak, as if Jared's friends are even the least bit interesting to me right now.

Eric doesn't answer. I can feel the weight of his stare as he turns me in another slow circle. I'm terribly aware of his hands on my body. His thumb is stroking my palm, and the sensation makes my whole arm tingle. And his other hand rides low at the small of my back, his pinky finger sliding down onto my bottom.

And I am made of shivers.

"Alex," he whispers under his breath.

"Mmm, what?" I breathe.

The next kiss starts at my forehead, makes a brief touchdown on the bridge of my nose, and then slides confidently onto my mouth for a split second.

I whimper like a fool.

He chuckles, which is when I realize I'm being teased.

"What are you doing?" I whisper harshly.

"Experimenting," he rumbles.

"No, you're teasing me."

He shakes his head. "Teasing is when you won't follow through. Which I totally will. And you liked it."

I did. I liked it very much. But that doesn't mean it's a good idea. "You should stop," I say in a shaky voice.

"Should I?" he tilts his head. "I don't mean to split hairs. But saying I *should* isn't the same thing as asking me to stop."

"No, I suppose it isn't."

"Tell you what. One kiss. One real one. And then you can decide, once and for all."

"One more kiss?" I repeat like a ninny.

The music stops, and I'm vaguely aware that the people around us are applauding the four-piece band. But I can barely hear it as Eric takes my face in both hands, tilting my chin up to meet his.

I try to brace myself, but it's no good. His mouth is there before I'm ready. The kiss is slow—first, a gentle slide, but then his lips part mine as he tastes me softly. It's the gentleness that's so shocking. Like he's holding himself back. Like he's savoring this.

I'm savoring it, too.

But just when I lean forward for more, he pulls back. Those firm lips are just *gone*. "I don't like you," I say immediately.

"Yeah, you do," he insists. "You'll like me even better when I'm unzipping that dress upstairs."

My body flashes cold and then hot. We can't possibly do that. This trip is already so weird. "But then what happens?"

"Well, I'd have to remove your bra. And I'd want to spend some quality time with the breasts that have been torturing me since we arrived here. I'll suck on your tits until you're begging me to—"

I reach up and put a hand over his mouth. "That is *not* what I meant." Although, I sure liked the sound of it. "You can't just say things like that in a crowded room."

His eyebrows lift, and his expression says, *I think I just did*.

I drop my hand. "What I meant was—what happens after the fun part is over?"

"More fun parts?"

"Awkwardness always follows fun," I point out.

His grin is knowing. "Like it isn't awkward already? We share a bed, and you're not very good at staying on your side."

I wince.

"And it's awkward that you're pretending not to shiver every time I touch you."

"That's…a hormone thing. Just chemistry," I babble.

"No kidding. But why waste it? Four nights, Engels. If you want, we can keep pretending that we don't both need the same thing. But I've got better uses for your time. Naked uses." He holds out a hand, waiting for me to take it, so he can lead me off the dance floor.

"You're serious about this."

"Absofuckinglutely."

I hesitate for a half second, tops. Then I put my hand in his.

"Smart girl," he says under his breath as we stride forward together toward the lobby, hand in hand.

Before we're clear of the party, a couple of acquaintances try to flag me down. "Hey, Tim!" I call out. But I don't slow down. In fact, I accelerate, instead, which makes Eric chuckle.

He slaps the elevator button the moment we reach it.

That's when the first bit of awkwardness sets in. We're just standing there holding hands. And by the time the elevator arrives, there's an elderly couple also heading upstairs. They press the button for the third floor. The ride ought to feel short, but it doesn't.

"I didn't cheat!" the man crows as the doors close.

"I saw you!"

"It's a misunderstanding," he says.

"There was an ace in your shirt pocket! And a king under your butt on the chair."

"I have no idea where those cards came from!"

The elevator doors part, thank God. The couple moves slowly out of the elevator. "You have a good night," Eric calls after them. He's probably coming to his senses already. Who would want to hook up with a hormonal pregnant lady?

The doors begin to slide closed again, and before we continue our ascent, Eric's rough hand is cupping my face. Before I can even make sense of it, he's taking my mouth in a hot kiss.

I whimper against his lips. And I guess he hasn't come to his senses after all. I'm definitely losing mine. Eric's bossy kisses leave me no time to think. As soon as one kiss ends, another one has already begun.

The elevator doors part again, and my fingers clutch instinctively at the lapels of his jacket, because I don't want him to stop.

Eric solves this problem by reaching behind me, sliding a thick forearm beneath my bum and lifting me up into the air. We're still lip-locked as we leave the elevator. The man is seriously coordinated.

Just…wow.

The next thing I hear is the beep of a hotel door lock disengaging. I wrap my arms around his neck for what I assume will be a quick trip to the bedroom. But when the door clicks shut, he turns and leans me against it.

Our kiss breaks momentarily, and he looks down at me with lust-filled eyes. "I would never pressure you. Tell me that you're a hundred percent down for this."

Is he kidding right now? My face is flushed. My lips are swollen from his kisses. My panties are damp. But the sexiest thing of all is the way he's looking at me as if he can't *wait* to get my dress off. If he calls this off, I will be seriously disappointed. And also mortified. "No second thoughts, Bayer. Or I'm going to think you're all talk."

Those dark eyes flare. "You won't think so in a minute."

"So you say…"

He thrusts his hips forward, and I gasp happily. I'm basically straddling the most ambitious erection that's come my way in a long time. "Here's what's going to happen. I'm going to drop you on the bed in a minute. You get thirty seconds to remove this dress. And then I get to do the rest."

"Thirty seconds?" I squeak. "There's a zipper down the back."

He actually rolls his eyes. "I'll handle the zipper, then."

"Fine. Let's go. Time's a'wasting."

About a quarter second after I issue this little challenge, I'm flying through the air again. This time his hot mouth roams my neck while he carries me through the suite. My body lights up like a circuit board, flashing everywhere at once with heat and awareness. And when he drops me on the bed as promised, I turn my back so he can free me of this dress.

He unzips me the smart way—by holding the fabric at the top in one hand and easing the zipper down with the other.

This bothers me a little. He's obviously unzipped so many dresses that he knows exactly what to do. As the fabric slides down my bare back, I worry that my newly chubby body will disappoint.

I slip off the bed and then step out of the dress. Then I turn slowly around to face him, wearing nothing but a skimpy lace bra and tiny panties.

"Oh, *hell* yes," he says.

I guess I'm not a disappointment after all.

11

ERIC

I'M NOT REALLY PREPARED for the sight of Alex in a see-through bra and panties. It's barely fair that a woman could be smarter than ninety-nine percent of the population, richer than God, and also look so ravishing.

"You're staring," she complains.

"Of course I am. Because you're mouth-watering." I toss my jacket at a chair. "Lie down on the bed."

She lifts one foot, reaching for the strap that secures her high-heeled shoe.

"No," I say sharply. "Leave that on."

"Why?"

"Because."

"Because—?"

She only gets the one word out before I unzip my fly, reach inside, and pull my erection out. "Because I like that view," I say roughly.

"Oh." Her cheeks redden, and her gaze is latched to my cock. "It appears that you do."

"You think?" I give myself a slow stroke, just because she's watching.

She swallows roughly.

"You're still standing there," I point out.

"Take off your shirt."

"That is not how this works." I cross my hands in front of my chest and wait.

She swallows roughly. And then she finally backs up a step, sits on the edge of the bed, and scoots onto the white duvet.

Finally. As a reward, I begin to unbutton my shirt. "I like the lace," I tell her.

"You can have it," she says. "This bra is too small. I can't wait to get it off."

"It's boobaliscious," I agree.

She laughs immediately. "What are you, still thirteen?"

"Only for jokes." I throw my shirt aside, and I don't miss Alex's hot gaze on my chest. It only takes me a couple more moments to divest myself of the rest of my clothes. I kneel on the bed, naked, a moment later. "Remember when I said you look exactly the same as when we met twenty-one years ago?"

She gives me a small, distracted nod.

"Well, I lied." She's magnificent, and definitely all woman now. I drop my lips to lick her nipple through the transparent lace of her bra.

"Yessss," she sighs, her hands already threading into my hair.

I'm in heaven, tonguing the valley of her breasts, licking and teasing her nipples through the lace. She's already squeezing her legs together in anticipation. But I take my time. If I'm lucky, we'll have three or four nights together before we go back to our separate lives.

Four nights used to sound like forever to me. Maybe I'm getting old, but I already know they'll fly by in a blink.

After I torture her heavy breasts for a while, I nose my way down her smooth stomach. One at a time, I lift her legs onto my shoulders. The heels of her shoes lie against my back, and I think I like it. Leaning in, I part her legs and use the flat of my tongue to moisten the lace of her panties.

"Oh please, oh please," she pants.

Chuckling, I ease my thumb over the dampened fabric. "Not yet, bossy. I'm just warming up."

"Warm up faster," she breathes.

So naturally I do the opposite—torturing her with slow licks and nibbles on her silky thighs. I take my time, leaving that scrap of lace firmly in place until she's digging those heels into my back and cursing my name.

I'm hard as nails and torturing both of us now. So I ease the panties out of my way and kiss her pussy. Finally. She tastes like heaven, and the sounds she makes are music to my ears.

And, fine, my ego. She's loving everything I do. "More," she pants. "Please."

"Please, what?"

"Please, oh great one? Sir? Whatever the hell you want to be called." She locks her thighs around my head. "Just hurry up and fuck me."

And I'm dead. I have never laughed with my face between someone's legs before. But there's a first for everything.

She doesn't even care. She just lifts her hips and takes advantage of the friction.

"You are a good time, Alex," I say, easing her beautiful legs off my body and straightening up. "I need to find a condom."

"Oh, wait!" She raises herself up on both elbows. Her face is flushed and her hair is mussed. "Condoms are full of chemicals. I can't do that."

"Wait, what?"

She shakes her head. "Spermicide. I don't know what's in that stuff."

"Well…" I don't, either, of course. "We don't have to have sex."

She sits up quickly. "Oh, yes, we do. I mean—if you know you're healthy. Nate is always bragging about the healthcare he gives your team. And I can't get any more pregnant than I already am."

I sit my naked ass down on the bed and try to think. "I'm very careful, and I've been tested very recently." She's right about the healthcare. Our team doctor cheerfully calls us in for frequent testing. He has all the single guys on a rotation.

It's just that I never do this. I never go bare. That's far more intimacy than I'm used to.

"Eric," she whispers. "I probably won't have sex again for five years. Don't make me wait."

"Five years?" My head swings toward her in disbelief.

"I'm exaggerating, maybe. But single moms don't see a lot of action." She shakes her head. "Never mind. That's not even relevant. I just really want to."

As do I. But… "Five years?" I repeat. "No pressure, though."

She laughs. And then she reaches around behind her body and unhooks that lace bra. She tosses it aside, and now all I can see are heavy breasts begging to be stroked and kissed. She puts her palms underneath them, cupping herself, offering them to me. "No pressure," she echoes.

Holy hell. I suddenly like Hawaii a whole lot better than I did a few hours ago.

With a groan, I climb farther onto the bed, laying her out as I go. We're skin to skin, and my arms are full of a curvy goddess. My mouth sinks onto hers, and our kiss is deep and serious. She tastes like desire, and she smells like heaven.

I lose myself in her mouth for a few glorious minutes. We kiss and clutch and tease. When I can't wait any longer, I work a hand between our bodies and grip myself. She lifts her hips to brace for me.

Then there's nothing left to keep me from heaven except my nagging conscience. Logically, I know this is okay. She wants this. I want this. Owing to excellent health care and my recent dry spell, there is no reason at all why I can't do this.

Still. Crossing this line isn't easy. I've followed the same rules my whole adult life. Wrap it up. Keep your distance. Don't take advantage, and don't get attached.

Alex's trust in me isn't misplaced. But that doesn't mean it's easy to accept.

Slowly, I drag my cock head along her sweet, slick pussy. There's nothing like it, and I feel like a hedonist. Alex's eyes squeeze shut with pleasure. But when she opens them again, they beg me for more.

And I can't help myself for one more minute. I lift her knee and thrust my hips forward, entering her in one sweet slide. We moan in stereo, gazes locked, faces flushed, hearts beating in sync. Exhaling slowly, I ease back to repeat the motion.

It's heaven. So hot. So wet. So unlike any other time. I'm speechless as I find a rhythm, slow at first, and then faster.

Soon I'm flying. Her nails dig into my back a little more deeply with every thrust. Each movement brings her another sob or moan of pleasure.

"Alex," I murmur. I have no other coherent words. But none are needed. We're communicating on a primal level now. I've had a lot of sex, but I've never felt so joined to anyone.

Maybe the whole fake boyfriend role is screwing with my head. Because sex with Alex suddenly feels…inevitable. Like I'm meant to be here and nowhere else.

Closing my eyes, I brace my arms on the mattress. Composure is part of my personality. I pride myself on my self-control. But even I have my limits. I'm drowning in pleasure. And when I drop down to kiss her again, it's almost too much. There is no part of me untouched by her warmth and softness. Her tongue is in my mouth. Her scent is in my lungs.

It's perfect. Too perfect. "Alex," I growl against her lips. "Come, honey."

She only whimpers in response, her arms tightening around me.

I capture one silky knee in my hand, and slow my pace, grinding down for her. "Come on, baby. You know you want to." I grit my teeth as she moans in my mouth.

And then I feel it. A clench and a shudder. A gasp and a moan.

"Fuck yes," I grunt. She makes the most beautiful, high-pitched keen of pleasure. And I'm just done. I thrust forward once more in slow motion and let myself go. It's pure pleasure and aching relief. My groan is low and long as I empty my soul into her beautiful body.

"Oh my god," Alex breathes when we're finally both still.

My thoughts exactly. If I had thoughts.

We're still tangled up together, her knees clenched around my sides. Those high heels are gone, though, flung off at some point during the frenzy.

"You okay?" I pant, knowing that I should roll over. But I'm too spent to move yet. I feel a little stunned.

She takes a deep breath and lets it out. "I'm…wow."

I guess that's not a complaint. With a final groan, I roll off of her and then collapse onto the bed beside her. But it feels wrong to be separated from her just yet, so I gather her into my arms. Her face rests against my shoulder, and I can feel the wild rhythm of her heartbeat against mine as I close my eyes.

"Obviously, I've been spending time with the wrong men," she babbles. "That was educational."

"Educational," I murmur. I guess it was. Although my brain has melted, and I'm not tracking the conversation very well. I honestly never expected this to happen. I didn't even want to come to Hawaii.

But it's been a long time since I've felt such a powerful attraction to anyone. I am shook.

"Now the awkwardness sets in," Alex murmurs. "Right?"

I run a hand down the smooth skin of her rib cage. "I think it can wait until at least tomorrow." Sex never makes me feel awkward. Life is too short, and I'm too full of dopamine or whatever natural drug it is that makes me feel like I've won the national championship of sex. There isn't even a condom to throw away. I'm living my best life right now.

We lie together for a long time, and it's nice. My occasional hookups are never this cozy. Alex is stroking the arch of my foot with her own foot. My nose is buried in her hair.

It's…sweet. Or something. And I don't have to wonder how soon I can leave. I only have to wonder how soon we can do it again.

Because we are definitely doing that again.

Eventually she stirs and rolls over, and I sit up reluctantly. "Do you want anything from the fridge?"

She smiles at me. "A sip of your beer. I stocked it for you."

"That was nice." I can't resist running a hand through her hair.

"Someone should be able to drink beer. And I can have a sip."

"Just a sip? Want me to pour you a little bit?"

She shakes her head. "I'm willing to make all kinds of bad decisions for me. But none for the baby. I'll take a can of seltzer water."

"Sure thing." I swing my legs off the side of the bed, then walk naked toward the bedroom door.

"Eric!" Alex's voice is full of alarm.

"Yes?" I pause at the doorway.

She tugs the sheet up to cover her boobs. "Put on some shorts."

"Why?" I look down. My body rocks. It's just the truth. "Why would I cover up all this awesomeness?"

She looks pained. "Because of the pillow cam."

"Oh, fuck."

"Right. We already did. And when you carried me through the living room while I mauled you, that was the fairly obvious outcome."

"Huh." I pause in the doorway. "Maybe I shouldn't appear on camera for another half an hour, just to impress the security team with my stamina."

"Eric!" Alex grabs one of the bed pillows and hurls it at me.

I catch it, laughing. "Relax, okay? Nobody noticed. There's just some agent in a room full of monitors somewhere. They probably only check the video if there's an issue."

"Just put on some shorts."

"Women are usually trying to get me to take *off* my clothes. Do you really want to be the one exception?"

"It's not like I don't appreciate the view." Unless I'm crazy, her cheeks turn pink.

God, that blush. Unbelievably, I feel my blood stir again. And the urge to kiss her is strong.

I don't, though. I duck into the bathroom for a very fast shower and then find some boxers to wear. Once I'm suitably covered, I go into the living room, turn that fucking pillow around, arm the door alarm, and then pour two drinks.

By the time I'm back, Alex is sitting up in bed, wearing a night-gown and flipping through channels on the TV.

As she settles on a cooking show, I climb into bed beside her and hand her a glass of seltzer.

"Thank you," she says sweetly.

"You're very welcome." The domesticity of this moment feels entirely unfamiliar to me. I offer my glass to Alex. "You wanted a sip?"

She takes it in hand and inhales the yeasty scent of my ale. "I miss grownup drinks. I really do." She takes the world's daintiest sip and hands it back to me.

"How many more months?"

"My due date is in January. But if I breastfeed, I won't really drink, then, either."

"Oh." I know *nothing* about babies or childbirth. "Is it too soon to name this baby? I'd like to put in an early vote for Eric."

"You are such an egomaniac." She gives me a little poke on my bare belly.

"It's a good name! We can't all be named Alexandra."

"Sure we can. There's always Alexander if it's a boy."

"You know…" I take a sip of beer. "I'm not at all surprised that you're named after a great conquerer."

"Why? Should I take that as a compliment?"

"Maybe. You've been bossing me around since the day I met you."

I get another poke. "What does Eric mean? Is it…German?"

"Norse."

"Does it mean 'man with great big hockey stick?'"

I snort with laughter. "Yeah, baby."

"What does Eric really mean?"

"It means *alone*. The first syllable, anyway. But together it's supposed to mean sole ruler. Or autocrat."

"Of course it does. Now who's bossy?"

"Are you going to let me check the baseball game?"

She holds on tightly to the remote. "Maybe. Does *check* imply an hour of baseball watching?"

"Depends on if it's a close game."

"Then, no. There's always your phone."

Yeah, there's the bossy personality I remember so well. I never once controlled the TV channel on the Vineyard, either. "You know, you're the reason I watched *Dirty Dancing* about thirty times."

"I'll make it thirty-one if you keep complaining."

I get up again and locate my phone. When I pick it up, the edges are glowing yellow, which indicates that someone has sent me an urgent text.

It's from my brother. All it says is *I told you not to fuck her*.

"Uh oh."

"Problem?" Alex asks.

"No," I lie. "This was just, uh, a team message." I'm not about to embarrass Alex.

My reply to my brother is short, too. *Should have sent a different guy to Hawaii, then*.

There are a hundred other things I could add. *We're adults, and it's none of your business*, is at the top of my list.

Beside me Alex flips the channels, her hair tousled, her cheeks pink.

Everyone in this bed is having a great night. Max can go fuck himself.

12

ALEX

PLAYING it cool is a particular skill of mine. Even from a young age, I knew how to pull on a mask. How to pretend to be calm even when I'm all stirred up inside.

But tonight is a serious test of my skills. I can't hold the thread of this TV show, because my cunning mind—the one that can spot a trend from two years away and make million-dollar decisions in the blink of an eye? It's blown. To bits.

No man has ever overwhelmed me like Hurricane Eric. That was a Category 5 experience. Even *before* we made it into the bedroom, it was already the most passionate night of my life. The man carried me into the hotel suite, pressed me up against the door, and kissed the daylights out of me.

I honestly thought that only happened in films. Passion isn't something I dwell upon. I've been more focused on finding my Forever Guy.

But tonight that seems like a mistake. Every man I dated was either A) looking only for fun or B) ultimately a bore. Or he was Jared Tatum, world's biggest asshole.

I kept searching until this year, when I began to feel desperate and depressed. That led to some bad decision making. First, I got drunk and had sex with my old friend, Nate. It was awkward from start to finish. There's nothing like endangering a really good friendship to make you see your own desperation for what it is.

And then—in an effort to move on from that disaster—I dated Jared Tatum. I'd met him before and dismissed him already. I knew in my gut that he wasn't The One. He wasn't even in the top fifty. But I let the charade drag on because I was in despair. Bad choice after bad choice.

But tonight, Eric Bayer demonstrated what I've been missing all along. Let's hear it for incredible sex without expectations.

The TV flickers in front of me, but I'm too stuck inside my head to watch. I hand the remote control to Eric. "Here. Watch your game if you want."

"No way, really?" He puts an arm around me as he begins to flip the channels. "I knew you were a fun date, Engels."

When he smiles, I feel it everywhere.

AFTER MIDNIGHT, I finally fall asleep. But then I have dirty dreams. My subconscious has rediscovered sex, and it wants more.

The dream begins like a replay. Eric carries me into the suite and kisses me against the door. But this time we don't stop. He lifts up my dress and just goes for it.

And then—because dreams don't have to make sense—we're on the bed again. We have sex in several different positions, without any kind of pause or end. Several times during the night, my eyes snap open in the dark. Each time I find the real Eric sleeping soundly beside me. I listen to his deep breathing and fall asleep again, still overheated and restless.

Eventually, I wake in the morning light to find that I'm wrapped around him. Honestly, I don't know why this keeps happening. I've been sleeping alone for the vast majority of my life.

Note to self—I never once woke up wrapped around Jared Tatum. Maybe that should have been a sign.

Eric feels so good, though. A big solid hunk of man. I love the scrape of the rough hair on his legs against mine. And the tight abs beneath my palm are not to be believed.

Later, I'll blame my dreams for making me so bold. But it seems perfectly natural to coast my palm down his bare skin until I meet the waistband of his boxers. Crisp cotton greets my fingers, and it's covering a proud erection that's trying to break free of those shorts.

Well, *good morning*. I slide my hand down his length. Just the heat against my palm turns me on. I'm already embarrassingly wet.

But I've always been a go-getter, so I run my hand lightly over the cotton. And when Eric gives a grunt of pleasure, I slip my hand beneath the waistband and close my fingers around his cock.

He groans happily. And after a minute or two, he rolls onto his back, reaches down and shoves his boxers off his body. "If you're going to do a thing, do it right," he says, opening his eyes. "Take that off." He points at my nightgown.

Well, heck. I thought a sleepy Eric would be easier to control. Apparently, I was wrong, because I find myself lifting my silk gown over my head and throwing it onto the rug.

"Good morning to me," he whispers. "Come give me a kiss."

But I don't remember handing him the reins. So I lean down and lick his cock from root to tip instead.

"Oh. Fuck. Wow. Yeah," he sputters. He gathers my hair in one big hand. "Do that again."

Part of me wants to argue. But most of me wants to do exactly what he says. I nuzzle his cock, letting the head bump against my nose. He smells salty and clean. I take a soft, teasing lick and hear myself moan. When I open my mouth and take him in, he's weighty on my tongue.

"Yeah. More. Suck me." His hips shift with eagerness.

But I take my time, of course. There's no reason to let on that I had a fitful night's sleep. That his naked body starred in my dreams and probably will again.

I'm winning at life right now, anyway. Who knew I'd get a last, sexual hurrah before I became a mother? And who could guess that I'd have it with a fine specimen like Eric Bayer? Seriously, pinch me.

And he might just do that. He has a firm grip on my hair, and he's trying his best to fuck my mouth, twisting his hips for more.

I pop off him, just because I can.

"Fuuuuuck," he moans. "Engels."

"Yes?" I whisper playfully.

"Suck my cock, honey. You know you love it."

My body tightens deliciously because he's right. So I dip my head and take him as deeply as I dare. I give a solid suck and look up at him for approval. And—wow. He's propped up on those incredible arms. His hair is wild, and his face is flushed. As he breathes, those abs ripple.

"You see something you like?" he asks with a grin.

I drop my gaze and close my eyes, laving my tongue along his shaft. My skin flashes hot, and I squeeze my legs together against the emptiness. I hate the easy way he makes me feel so unhinged.

But I go to town with all the enthusiasm of a sex-starved woman who had dirty dreams all night and is living another one right now.

"Come here," he says after a few amazing minutes.

"Kind of busy here," I gasp before taking him into my mouth again.

"Yeah, well, I can't take much more of your wicked tongue. If you want to ride me, you better do it soon."

Oh, wow. I really do want that. As I glance up again at his sex-flushed face, I'm unable to hide how much.

"I know what you need," he says softly.

"You do, do you?" I argue out of reflex, but it's clear that I'm not fooling anyone.

Smirking, he sits up and crooks a finger at me. That smug gesture should annoy me, but I'm blinded by his perfect body. Maybe you're allowed to be smug if you've got those washboard abs and that V of muscle swooping down on either side of your flat stomach.

I'm all too willing to crawl toward him, naked, and climb into his lap.

"That's a girl," he says, lifting one hand to my breast, giving my nipple a quick pinch, and then coasting his palm down my body. His touch is appraising, like I'm a racehorse he's inspecting, and I have no idea why I like it.

I hate myself a little for wanting him to do it again.

"You woke me up for a reason," he murmurs. "Don't make me wait."

Still, I hesitate. Hopefully he takes it as a tease, because I don't want him to know that I'm a little intimidated. My inner nerd girl doesn't have a lot of experience initiating sex with god-shaped men in broad daylight.

He reaches around and caresses my ass. That gets me moving. I lift myself onto my knees while I grip his shoulders.

"There you go." He lines himself up beneath me.

Inspired, I sink slowly down onto every delicious inch of him. And we both groan at the same time as I bottom out, so full of him that I can't help but pause and catch my breath.

"I fucking love Hawaii," he grunts, rolling his hips toward mine. "Come on, now. Give it to me. You know you want to."

I really do. I rise up with delicious slowness and then sink happily down. It's so good that I immediately do it again.

"Yeah," he rasps. Pushy hands grip my hips. "Faster."

His commanding voice makes me want to please him. It's as if this were my only job—making those grey eyes darken with lust, making his face even more flushed. I lean into it, picking up the pace until it's quicker than I need it to be.

But it's so, so dirty to be pistoning his cock into my body. This is bad girl stuff right here. It's…freeing. It's making Eric's breath come in irregular gusts.

"Fuck," he pants, jacking his hips beneath me. "Yeah, Alex. Look at you go. So hot when you do that."

The orgasm comes out of nowhere, zinging through my core, shimmering through my whole being. The startled gasp I let out quickly turns into a low, sultry moan.

"Jesus," he gasps. "Aw, yeah." He braces his hands on the bed and lifts me clear off the mattress on his next thrust. I grip his shoulders, insensible, just trying to stay on board as I shudder through my climax.

Eric makes a hot noise, throws his head back and locks all his muscles at once. I watch his pulse pound in his neck as he spills inside me.

After a long moment and another low groan, he lowers his ass to the bed in a hurry, catching me around the waist again with his hands. "Holy shit. That's a much better wake up call than my phone alarm playing some Fall Out Boy."

"I don't…know what that is," I wheeze, trying to take in enough oxygen that I can slow my breathing to something like normal.

"Never mind." He laughs, burying his face in my neck and kissing me. "It doesn't matter."

I'm still planted on him, which is going to get awkward in a minute. But I am afraid to break this connection. I have a feeling I'll be embarrassed about this later. I've never woken a man out of a sound sleep to have sex before. I just *mauled* him.

He doesn't seem to mind, though. His hand is heavy on the back of my head, his fingers in my hair. For several minutes we just stay like this—sweaty and loose-limbed—while our heart rates slowly even out to a sleepy, quiet state.

"Alex," he whispers, running a hand down my back.

"Mmm?"

"I don't mean to sound ungrateful, but don't you have an eight-thirty meeting?"

"Yeah." I pick my head up. "What time is it?"

"Not sure. But it's awfully light outside."

I roll off of him, which I'm loathe to do. He feels so good. But I have to nudge my phone, which is sitting on the table. "Bingley, what time is it?"

"Good morning your highness! It is nine minutes past eight. Your first meeting begins in twenty-one minutes at—?"

"Bingley!" I squeak. "Why didn't you wake me up?"

"You didn't ask me to. I did not hear from you last night…"

"Oh, but I did," Eric says with a chuckle.

"Be grateful," I snap, hopping out of bed.

"Apologies, my queen!" Bingley says. "We are in an unfamiliar time zone. And my instructions are such that—"

"I know. Later, Bingley." This is entirely my fault. I dart into the bathroom without another word.

As I pass the giant mirror on the way to the shower, I see a pink-faced woman with sex-mussed hair. It's going to take more than twenty-one minutes to fix this disaster.

Bingley's right—I am a queen. The queen of wrecking all my own plans.

13

ERIC

FOR A MOMENT I just lie there in the bed, my body heavy with extreme sexual gratification. I feel a little stunned, like a bird who has just flown into a window pane. I've been flattened by something I didn't see coming.

Also, Alex has stolen the bathroom, which just figures. She's sexy, delicious, and occasionally infuriating.

I heave myself up out of the bed and wander into the living room. There's another bathroom here, with a shower, too. Of course there is. The super rich never wait for anything. I turn on the spray and help myself to the luxury bath products on offer.

When I emerge a few minutes later, I smell like coconuts. I feel a little nutty so that's only fair. In my towel, I wander over to the house phone and contemplate a room service order. Alex probably doesn't have time to wait for it. Then again, the woman really likes her food…

I'm just reaching for the phone when there's a very brisk knock on the door. It's enough to set off that shrieking alarm, so my eardrums nearly split before I get to the door and hit the off button. My towel lands around my ankles, damn it.

"Okay, thanks for that," I grumble, grabbing my towel and opening the door.

I was expecting Gunnar or Pieter, but a startled stranger blinks back at me. "Wait. Is this Alex's room?" demands a young man dressed in a pink button-down shirt and khakis.

"That depends," I tell this harmless creature. "On who you are."

"Who am *I*?" he sniffs. "Who are *you*?" His eyes travel down my mostly naked body, taking in the towel I'm holding closed with one hand. "Not that I mind the view. But what are you doing in Alex's room?"

"I'm Eric, her big jealous boyfriend."

"Like hell," he snorts. "I'm Rolf, her all-knowing assistant. I've never seen you before. And you're not her type."

"She's making some changes." I lean menacingly against the door frame. "Let's see some ID."

"Oh, for fuck's sake." He pulls out his wallet. "It's you who's the suspicious one."

Someone laughs in the hallway, and it sounds like Gunnar. That fucker is just enjoying the drama.

Rolf flashes me a corporate ID with his name on it and then pushes past. "Seriously, who are you?"

"I told you already."

He shakes his head. "Alex doesn't have a boyfriend. Not since that turd Jared."

At least Rolf and I are on the same page about something. "You'll have to take up your questions with her." I don't need to argue with this kid. She can tell him whatever version of the truth she wants.

Speaking of Alex—she comes flying out of the bedroom in a flowered dress and sandals. Her hair is smooth, and she's wearing lipstick.

"Holy hell. That's a goddamn magic trick. Not fifteen minutes ago you were—"

She cuts me off with a warning glare. "Do not finish that sentence."

"Alex," Rolf says. "Who is this dude?"

"Long story," she says.

"Quite long indeed," I say just to be an ass. "Massive."

That gets me an eye roll from Alex. "Rolf, please tell me that bag you're carrying has coffee in it."

"A half-decaf coffee with two percent milk and an almond croissant. But I haven't decided yet if I'm giving it to you. I don't like to be out of the loop."

She stops in front of him. "Rolf, you're a genius, a lifesaver, and I treasure you. I will fill you in as soon as possible."

"That's better." He hands her the bag.

"How's your grandmother?" Alex asks.

"The same. They say she needs nursing care. I shouldn't even be in Hawaii right now."

There's a tap on the door, and then Gunnar steps in. "Ready? We'd better head down."

I look down at my towel. "Guys, I need a minute."

"You're not coming," Gunnar says. "We're keeping the threat level high, so I'm escorting her today. It looks less weird to have the bodyguard sit through the meetings. We don't want to blow your cover." He turns toward the door. "You're on for dinner, though."

"Oh. Well," I say uselessly.

"Later, boyfriend," Alex says

Within five seconds, they're all gone. I get one more curious look from Rolf before the door clicks shut, leaving me standing mostly naked in a hotel room I never planned to visit. I feel a little slutty, if I'm honest. Like a high-priced escort.

Then again, slutty looks good on me. So I go back to the house phone and order a light breakfast and a pot of coffee.

I DO a nice long workout in the hotel gym. My only interruption is when my bad knee begins to throb, and I have to take a break to rewrap it. I first tore my ACL back in college. The reconstruction surgery went really well and didn't interfere with my career. That was almost fifteen years ago, though, and I've been warned that arthritis is a common long-term result.

Last season I had some pain, so we've been monitoring the situation. They tell me I might need another surgery, but I'll put that off as long as I can.

I'd meant to go running on the beach after the gym. But my knee is still acting up, and I call it quits after only two miles. New plan: lunch and then a swim in the lap pool on the terrace. There's more than one way to get a cardio workout.

In the hotel restaurant, I take a seat indoors at the bar and order lunch. I'm just finishing an excellent blackened fish sandwich when someone takes the barstool right beside me. "A coke, please, and put it on this guy's tab."

I look up and find it's Gunnar, and he's alone. And I almost choke on my last bite of fish. "If you're here, and I'm here, then who's with Alex?"

"Easy," he says quietly. "She's in the world's dullest lunch meeting with Pieter, Rolf, and a content provider from L.A. The reason I'm here right now is that Tatum is seated about ten barstools down from you."

"Oh." I know better than to look around for Gunnar's target, so I push my plate away and keep my focus on him. "Then you're not here to deliver a lecture from my brother?"

"Not a chance." Gunnar chuckles. "But forgetting about the security camera was a rookie move."

"Yeah. I know." Thank goodness I didn't peel Alex out of her clothes until after we moved to the bedroom.

"Besides, your brother is one to talk. It would be hypocritical of him to lecture you for hooking up with Alex."

"Wait, what?" I stiffen. "My brother and—?" I can't even finish the sentence because the idea of my brother and Alex together makes me irrationally angry.

"No! That's not what I meant." He laughs. "Good thing, though. You look like you're about to slug someone."

Do I? My fist is clenched, which is weird because jealousy isn't my style. I don't know what's wrong with me.

"I just meant that he's no saint."

That's interesting. So much of my brother's life is a mystery to me. But I don't want to pump Gunnar for details, so change the subject. "What's the plan for tomorrow night? Alex is giving some kind of speech?"

"Right. We'll cover her when she's at the podium, and you'll stay close to her at the table. There's no need for anything more drastic than that."

"Got it. Any other news?"

Gunnar shakes his head. "We still don't know who that is in the break-in video if that's what you're asking. We may never know. In fact, it's better if we never hear from him again."

"I suppose that's true."

But what a frustrating job Gunnar has. My job always has an endpoint—you either win the game, or you lose. You advance, or you get knocked out. I like knowing where I stand.

"My boy is on the move," Gunnar mutters. "I'll be shoving off in a moment. Thanks for the drink."

"Don't mention it. But are you usually stuck on surveillance duty?" He's my brother's number two. I always assumed he spent his time in the background, keeping tabs on everyone else.

"This job is different every day." He shrugs. "And that's a good thing." At that, he slides off the barstool and makes his way casually out of the restaurant, checking his watch like a man without a care in the world.

AN HOUR LATER, I learn that swimming against a steady current is surprisingly difficult. Unlike swimming real laps, there's no break every fifty meters. And after an hour, I'm wheezing like an old polar bear. Every stroke is harder than the last.

I'm trying to decide if I can last for another ten minutes when a pair of smooth and shapely legs appears in the water in front of me.

Alex is back. It's the perfect excuse to give up.

I stand to greet her. Or at least I try, but the force of the current pushes me off my feet, and I end up struggling like a fool until I locate the off button.

Finally the current dies, leaving me standing chest deep in water, breathing hard. "Hi," I wheeze.

She grins. "Hi, fake boyfriend. How was your day?"

"The usual. A nice long workout until my arms and legs felt like falling off. Then a healthy lunch, a little sunbathing naked on the terrace. And now a swim. About the same as yours, I guess."

"I hope you didn't burn anything important."

"Don't you worry." I take a step closer and notice that she's eyeing my abs. "And how was your day?"

"Oh, just the usual. Back-to-back meetings, negotiations, and brain-to-brain combat. One supplier tried to convince me that I should buy his batteries because they were especially *proton neutral*." She tips her head back and laughs. "It's like they can't fathom that I have a brain."

"Unbelievable," I say, creeping closer to the hottie in the sundress. "I think that guy has the same degree as I do, though."

She cocks her perfect head. "In what, exactly?"

"In bullshit and shenanigans." Even as I say it, I dart forward, grab her by the hips, and pull her into the pool with me.

The shriek is deafening—louder than the door alarm, but much more fun. "Eric!" she howls.

"All this talk about your big brain," I tease, holding her in my arms. "And yet you're just sitting there on the edge of the pool, vulnerable as a kitten."

"My dress!"

"What? Is it the kind that melts?"

She slaps my chest, but I don't let go of her. "I was going to wear this out to dinner! We have a reservation."

"Oh, shit. Well, if I'd known we had a reservation," I deadpan, "I woulda done it, anyway. Hold your breath."

"What? Oh!"

I lift us both a little higher in the water as if preparing to dive. Alex is a smart girl, so she catches on fast and holds her breath.

But what do I do? I kiss her instead.

Her surprise lasts, oh, half a second. But then her slippery arms wrap around my neck, and she kisses the hell out of me. Her ankles squeeze my ass, and her tongue slips into my mouth.

Holy cow. That escalated quickly.

Just when I'm settling into the idea of missing our dinner date for an energetic bedroom workout, she jerks back again. "We have a *reservation*. In half an hour," she clarifies breathlessly.

"Oh, well," I say quietly. There are drops of water clinging to her cleavage, and I want to lick them off. "I'd hate to keep the hostess at some restaurant waiting."

When she smiles, I kiss her again. And again. I thought about her entirely too much today. A man's mind wanders when he's bench-pressing almost twice his weight and sweating like an ox.

Our kisses are deep and hungry. And I'm guessing Alex had some inappropriate thoughts of her own between meetings. Or during. This bodes well for my evening, but I pull back, anyway, giving her a grin that I've been told is slightly obnoxious. "Better change your dress, then."

She blinks. "You are such a jerk."

"Am not."

"Are so."

I just smile because I've made everything more fun. Tonight we'll be dining on fine Hawaiian cuisine with a side of potent antic-ipation. And when the payoff comes, it will be twice as sweet.

"Go on now," I say, setting her onto the side of the pool. "You'd better go do whatever it is you do with all those products on the bathroom counter."

She gives me an arch look but doesn't complain. Rising to her feet, she moves with dignity even while dripping wet.

"I'm a gentleman, so you can use my dry towel," I add, just to be an ass.

"*Such* a gentleman," she grumbles, grabbing the towel and doing her best to stop her dress from dripping everywhere.

I climb out of the pool, and she tosses me the wet towel before heading inside to get dibs on the master bathroom. But do I get a parting glare that makes me chuckle.

I'm still smiling as I head inside myself a few minutes later. But I stop short of the bedroom because I hear a knock on the hotel suite door.

"Yeah?" I call out. But there's no answer, except for another knock.

Alex peers out of the bedroom, her face wary, and I wave her back. Then I step over to the peephole and take a look into the hallway. And he's standing right there—Tatum, her ex. He doesn't look any more appealing through the fisheye lens than he did last time I saw him.

I yank the door open all the way but block it with my body. "And here I thought you and I didn't really hit it off last night. Now you want to be friends?"

He scowls. "I need to speak with Alex for a moment."

"She's in the shower."

"I'll wait."

I sigh. "No, you won't."

"That's not your decision."

It is, but I don't argue the point. "Seriously, have you met Alex? If she wanted to speak with you, it wouldn't matter what I think. She'd be returning your calls."

His jaw tenses, and I can see that I've made my point. "Still, I just need to give her something."

"What is it?"

"A *gift*, asshole." He shows me a small gift bag in his hand. "It's a fitness band—the kind that my company makes. Alex told me once that my product wasn't designed well for women. And I told her she was wrong."

I manage to withhold my surprise.

With his free hand, Mr. Douchewaffle scrubs his forehead. "But after I thought it over some more, I hired a female designer who said all the same things that Alex did." He offers me the bag. "Here. I want her to know that I listened."

"Too late, though?" I press.

He flinches. "Just give her the bag. And of course I hope she'll call me. But even if she doesn't, I want her to have this."

"All right," I agree cheerfully. "Will do." And then I shut the door on him, which feels pretty good.

When I carry the little bag into the bedroom, Alex is waiting just out of sight. Wearing only a hotel bathrobe, she looks about as nervous as a long-tailed cat in a room full of rocking chairs.

"Did you hear any of that?"

"All of it," she nods. "Thank you for playing Bad Cop."

I slap my chest. "I think it comes naturally to me."

But my joke doesn't seem to put her at ease. In fact, she looks pale. "Hey, sit down. Are you shaking?" I guide her toward the edge of the bed.

"I know it's silly."

"Not silly," I argue. "But I'll admit that I'm a little mystified. I heard you give a tongue lashing to a trio of sexist executives last night. But this needle-dick frightens you? He's not worth it."

"I *know* that, but he could seriously complicate my life. And..." She sighs. "Nobody has ever hit me before. It's like he burst the bubble I was living in, where my wits were always enough to keep me safe."

That makes me pause. I forget, sometimes, that not everybody feels physically capable of physically defending themselves. "I know he scares you, but you're going to be okay. You have the resources to defeat him."

"I do," she agrees. "And isn't that just plain lucky?" She takes the bag and holds it up in the air. "He needs money to make more of these. So I'm going to bribe him. That's all he ever wanted from me anyway." She makes a face. "And now he's going to get millions just for leaving me alone—"

She breaks off at another knock on the door. "I think I know who that is," I tell her. I pick up the gift bag and take it into the living room. When I look through the peephole, I see Gunnar.

I open the door and give him the bag without a word.

Then I go back to Alex, wrapping an arm around her. "They have to check that bag for bugs."

"Yikes. I was too wound up to think of that."

"I got you. Can I ask a stupid question?"

"Sure."

"Have you thought about just keeping Tatum in the dark? What if you just never told him about the baby?"

"Believe me, I've had this fantasy many times. But I can't disappear to a convent for six months. During my third trimester, I'll meet with dozens of industry executives. It would get back to him." She shivers. "I don't want to spend the next year wondering when he's gonna turn up asking questions. I have too much on my plate already for that kind of uncertainty."

"Yeah, okay." I notice she has a hand spread out on her stomach. I reach down and cover it. "If you want to keep your secret a little longer, don't make this a habit just yet."

"You're right." She pulls both our hands away.

"What does it feel like anyway?"

"Well, nothing much. At the beginning, I threw up all the time. Now I'm just hungry. But pretty soon I'll be able to feel the baby move. They say it's like a little flutter at first."

"Wow." Maybe I'm just slow, but up until now, it didn't really sink in. There aren't two of us sitting here right now. There are three.

Until Alex stands up suddenly. "We should go to dinner. I just need to put on clothes."

Not for my sake. The joke is on the tip of my tongue, but for some reason, I hold back my snark. "All right. Let's go," I say instead. "I'll be ready in five minutes."

She gives me a weak smile and disappears into the closet.

14

ERIC

WE DINE on a terrace at a restaurant just a couple of miles down the beach from our hotel. I order the freshest sushi I've ever had in my life. Alex orders seared salmon because pregnant women aren't allowed to eat raw fish. But she seems happy, anyway.

Especially when Gunnar texts us both to say that the gift from Tatum is clean. It's just a fitness band. It doesn't have evil superpowers.

"I feel like celebrating. What if we walked back?" she asks as I sign the check. "It's such a nice night, and I spent the day holed up in conference rooms."

"Sure. Let's do it." I don't think my knee will complain. Much. And I love the beach.

Alex cancels the car that's waiting for us, and we head down to the shore. The sun is setting, and the tide is going out, so the beach looks like a photo in a travel magazine.

And, fine, it's the most romantic place I've ever been. I'm not the kind of guy who thinks much about romance, but I'd have to be dead not to notice the rosy pink sky and the way the breeze ruffles Alex's skirt around her bare knees.

She bends down and removes her sandals, dangling them off one finger so she can walk barefoot in the sand. I stop to remove my shoes, as well, and just when I've got the first one off, she's says: "Last one to that funny palm tree is a stink monster."

Then she takes off running.

Aw, hell. I haven't lost a race to Alex in twenty-one years, and I don't plan to start now. I take off after her with one shoe on and one off. My knee complains immediately, but I'm a very competitive man. And, let's face it, a hell of an athlete. I can outrun a girl even while taking it easy on my knee.

Alex squeaks as I gain on her. The leaning palm tree is within reach, so I dive for it like I'm sliding into home plate. "Yes!" I shout from the still-warm sand. "Guess who's a stink monster?"

With a grumpy noise, Alex kicks some sand onto my bare foot. "Maybe this wasn't the tree I was referring to."

"Maybe you should be a better loser." I remove my other shoe and then climb to my feet. "You still cheat, huh?"

She gives me a cheeky smile. "You're still smug, huh?"

It's the smile that does me in, I think. I step close and, dropping my shoes into the sand, I take her chin. My kiss is aggressive, but she's ready for me. As my lips find her softer ones, she doesn't hesitate. She wraps a smooth hand around the back of my neck, tugging me down, giving as good as she gets.

"Fair warning," I say, pulling away. "When the joking is done and the races are run, we are going to end up naked on one of the many surfaces of our hotel suite."

"Do I get to pick which one?" she asks, lifting the chin that's still trapped by my hand.

"Only if you don't give me any more of your sass," I whisper.

"Probably not, then," she says with a shrug.

Yeah. It's her attitude that makes me so crazy. "I might need two surfaces."

"Smack talker." She takes my hand in hers, and we start down the beach.

"Hey, I can deliver. I'm very competent. You don't know."

"Uh huh." Her eyes dart to mine. "You're so competent you just left your shoes behind in the sand."

"Aw, shit!" I say, dropping her hand. "Be right back."

She laughs the entire time it takes me to collect them.

IT'S all fun and games until we encounter a fence that partitions the beach. It's well camouflaged as a rock wall, so we don't even realize the problem until we're upon it.

"Uh oh," Alex says. "Private property?"

I stand up on my toes and peer over the top. "Yup. Someone's mansion."

"I guess we'll have to go around?" she asks, peering toward the road. We can't even see it from here, though.

"No way. Seriously? What would eleven-year-old Alex have done?"

She laughs. "I don't know. Scale the wall?"

"Duh."

Alex looks dubious. "Trespassing is cute when you're eleven. I don't know if it's a good look on me now."

"We're not going to break into the actual mansion, Allie. We're just going to walk on their sand."

"There could be guards. Or a big, slobbery dog."

"Slobbery dogs aren't so bad." Maybe it's all this talk of our youth, but my inner thirteen-year-old leans over and licks the side of Alex's face.

She shrieks and pushes me away.

Ouch, my ears. "Climb the rocks, wild one. Here, I'll start." I find a toe hold and lift myself up to peer over the wall. "This mansion is dark. Nobody will notice if we run across."

"Can't we just go around?" she asks. "The tide is out."

"You would say that. You're not the one wearing long pants." I jump back down, taking care with my knee. But I follow Alex to the water's edge, anyway. She's right—the water is only a foot deep in between waves. She hikes her skirt up a little and wades around the rocks.

I roll up my khakis as best I can, then wade in. A wave soaks my shins immediately. "Shit."

"Thirteen-year-old Eric wouldn't care about some wet cuffs," Alex scoffs. "And since you threw me into the pool earlier, I don't see how you can complain."

She's right, damn it. We wade onto the shore on the other side of the wall. By silent, mutual agreement, we don't speak as we trespass across somebody's private stretch of sand. The waves break with a soft rhythm, sending foamy water across our toes.

Alex is on the ocean side, so the next wave hits her first, and she checks her balance for a wobbly second. I grab her hand, even though there's no danger. When a dog barks in the distance, our eyes meet. "I think he sounds extra slobbery, don't you?"

"Shut up," she retorts. Still, she picks up the pace.

I chuckle, wet but giddy. It's been years since we snuck around on the beach, trespassing without a second thought. Back then, Alex hadn't cared what anyone else thought. In fact, the first time we ditched the tennis instructor to dig up clams and sell them for ice cream money, I was the worrier. "Are we going to get in trouble?"

"No way," she'd said. "The nanny isn't paying attention, and the tennis pro already got paid. As long as I turn up for dinner in a clean shirt, no one will ask any questions."

Nobody is paying attention now, either. We reach the barrier on the far side of the private beach without incident, and this time it's a low wall of flat stones. "It's like they're not even trying to keep us out," Alex says.

"Right?" We climb over then hop down onto the sand at the same moment. Our hotel is now in view. "Should we get a drink at the outdoor bar?"

"Yes!" she says. "Unless…"

She doesn't have to finish—I know that she's worried about running into Jared. "Let me ask Gunnar where he is."

I have an answer thirty seconds later. "Jared is at a cabaret show in Honolulu. We're free to go to the bar."

"Sweet! I wonder if they'll make me a virgin strawberry margarita."

"But that's just…a cup of strawberries and some lime juice?"

"Don't judge. Look, there's two open barstools. Oh, heck." Alex takes off like a shot because another couple is heading for the bar from the opposite direction.

Lord, never get between this woman and a fruity drink. She gets there faster than Usain Bolt, and I jog up a few seconds later.

"Hang on, are you limping?" she asks, patting the stool beside her.

"No," I lie. "My knee is a little tender, but it's nothing."

"*Eric.*" Her face falls. "Is this my fault?"

"What?" I sit down. "Why would you even think that?"

"Because of…" She looks over both shoulders to make sure nobody is listening. "The door."

"What?" I'm not following.

"The *door*. To the suite. Last night, when we came in, you *picked me up* and…"

I burst out laughing.

"What? I'm a good girl. We don't finish our sentences when we're talking about…" She clears her throat.

I die.

"Oh, stop." She waves down the bartender. "Could you please make me a virgin strawberry margarita?"

"Sure, but…" He frowns. "That's just, like, a strawberry smoothie."

"I'll take it. And he'll have whatever arrogant people who lose footraces drink."

I wipe my eyes. "A Big Swell IPA, please."

"Coming right up." The bartender grabs his blender and gets busy making Alex's drink.

"Listen, Engels. You're not the cause of my knee pain. I've been squatting three-fifteen this week because the hotel doesn't have enough plates for me to go heavier."

"Three *hundred* and fifteen? *Pounds*?" She gapes.

"You know it. So unless you weigh more than that, a little sex up against the hotel room door isn't going to hurt me."

"Omigod, lower your *voice*," she hisses.

I laugh.

"Excuse me, Ms. Engels?"

We look up to find a tall man in an expensive suit standing beside Alex. He's about thirty, I guess. East Asian by heritage, or at least partly. He's a good looking guy, and well dressed. But there's something slick about him that puts me on my guard. "Can we help you?"

"I'm Xian Smith." His tone says I should know who that is.

"Hello, Mr. Smith," Alex says. "It's a pleasure to meet you." Although I know her well enough by now to know from her tone that it isn't, actually, much of a pleasure.

"You're a busy woman," he says with a smile. "But I'm still hoping to sit down with you before you leave Hawaii. I only require twenty minutes of your time."

My phone buzzes in my pocket. Twice. And something about the timing makes me pull it out and check the message. *Take the meeting*, it says.

I glance up and spot Gunnar at the end of the bar. He nods once.

"Mr. Smith," Alex says. "I'm sure you understand my time constraints. There are only so many hours in the day."

Naturally, the bartender picks that moment to set down our drinks. Alex's is a red confection that screams *leisure time!*

She scowls.

"Um, Alex?" I say, putting a hand on her shoulder. "You do have a free half-hour on Saturday."

Alex's chin whips in my direction. "Excuse me?"

"We had that *cancellation*," I hint. And I casually move my phone where she can see it but Mr. Xian Smith cannot. "See?"

Her eyes dart to the screen and then widen. Then her scowl deepens. "Well, I suppose I could make the time. If I shuffle a couple of things."

"It would mean a lot to me," Smith says with a sly smile. "I know you're scrambling to make your new toy, and I'm a hundred percent sure I can help you meet your deadlines." He lays a business card on the bar in front of her.

Alex blinks. "All right. We'll email a time and a place."

"Excellent," he says. "We'll speak soon." Then, like a man who knows when to make an exit, he slips into the darkness.

Alex lifts her strawberry smoothie and takes a long drink from the straw while the man puts more distance between us. "What the hell?" she hisses after he's gone. "Did you write that?"

"No! I don't give a fuck who you meet. That was Gunnar. He was seated at the end of the bar."

Alex looks up, but he's gone already, so I receive the glare meant for him. "Why would Gunnar interfere in my schedule? What does Max want from me?"

"Lady, I was singing that same tune a few days ago. But now I don't care so much. Come upstairs with me."

She gives me an arch look. "Why?"

"Why do you think? My knee needs a workout." I wave at the bartender. "I'll take the check when you're ready. There's somewhere I need to be." Then I lean very close to Alex's ear. "Inside you," I whisper.

When I pull back, she's sipping her drink, eyes wide.

"Well?" I ask as the bill lands in front of me.

"What about finishing your beer?" she asks.

"There are other things I need to finish." I give her a wink as I scribble a tip onto the bill, along with our room number. "If you think a cold beer is enough to slow me down, you haven't figured me out yet." I slip a hand under the bar and palm her bare knee.

Her knee moves imperceptibly closer to my hand. "I don't usually do this."

"Do what?"

"Have a fling that can't lead anywhere."

"I have them all the time," I admit. "I never hear complaints. And I feel no shame."

Alex gets quiet. She's watching me, and I can almost hear the gears turning in her head. Last night I led her somewhere she wasn't planning to go. She likes it, but she's wary.

I, however, am not. So I slide my fingers up her thigh, and I smile when she shivers. "Don't overthink it."

"That's easy for you to say. A little more thinking this past year would have served me well."

"I understand," I tell her. "But with me, there won't be repercussions. I can't change your life, and I am not going to suddenly turn into an asshole you'll regret."

Her expression softens. "I know that. I hope we stay friends."

"Count on it," I tell her. Then I lean in and give her a soft kiss. Just a quick one. "Now, finish your smoothie and take me upstairs.

Quick, before some other mysterious gentleman shows up to claim your time. I get very jealous, you see. I'm needy."

She laughs. "Oh, please. You're ridiculous."

"Uh huh. But part of me is needy. The part in my pants."

"Quiet! What did we just talk about?" She lifts her drink and drains it thoroughly.

"How can you do that without getting an ice-cream headache?"

"It's my special superpower. We can't all lift three hundred and fifteen pounds."

"Usually I'm up in the four hundreds. But the gym here sucks." I slide off the barstool, take one last gulp of beer, and abandon the rest. I take Alex's hand and lead her away from the bar.

"Tonight feels like a vacation," she says. "Thank you for that. I often travel to beautiful destinations but see nothing beyond the hotel and the boardroom."

"I'm familiar with the problem." I squeeze her hand. "I visit thirty cities a year and see only the rink and the hotel." We reach the elevator, and it opens immediately. "You know what else feels like a vacation?"

"Fruity drinks?"

"Hotel sex." I back her up against the elevator wall as the doors slide shut. "Lots and lots of hotel sex." My kiss doesn't ask permission. My tongue is in her mouth before the elevator begins to rise. She tastes like cool strawberries and good times.

"Eric," she whispers beneath me.

"Mmm?"

"You really are a fun date. You make me feel like I'm borrowing someone else's life for a few days. Some fun person's."

I chuckle against her mouth. "Baby, it's all you." The doors open behind me, and I take her hand, marching her out and toward the suite. I flash my key, and the door opens easily.

Once inside, I lift my middle finger and aim it right at the pillow camera.

Alex laughs. "Arm the doors, would you?"

"Yes, ma'am."

By the time I'm done locking us in for the night, Alex is finished brushing her teeth in the bathroom. I help myself to the zipper on her dress, easing it down and off her body. Then I kiss the back of her neck.

She makes a happy sound that tells me she likes that, so I unhook her bra, too. Then I reach around, cupping her breasts. Our eyes lock in the mirror, and I give her nipples twin pinches. "L-lets go to bed?" she asks quietly.

"What if we stayed here?" I run my hands down her sides, then I slide a palm across her belly and downward, claiming her mound, fitting my hand between her legs in an unmistakably possessive maneuver. "Don't you want to watch me fuck you?"

Her eyes are saucers. "I…guess?"

"She guesses." I laugh then turn her around. "Sit up here." I boost her onto the counter. "Now, unbutton my shirt."

She immediately does as I ask. And while she's busy, I kiss her neck, and her jaw. "Did you think about me today?" I whisper against her skin.

"Y-yes," she whispers, her fingers stumbling.

"Did your pussy get wet right in the middle of your meeting?"

She moans.

"It's going to be worse tomorrow," I mutter, kissing the corner of her mouth. "You're going to be sitting there talking about super-conductors—"

"Semiconductors," she corrects in a breathy voice.

"Whatever. The point is it doesn't matter what you're supposed to be talking about because you're going to picture me bending you over this countertop." I straighten up and remove my shirt. "Now, unzip me and take out my cock."

Alex makes a shocked noise but then gets right to work. I dive in for a real kiss, and it doesn't even slow her down. A moment later, smooth hands greet my cockhead, which is already engorged, and grip my shaft. I groan into her mouth. "Good girl."

I kick off my shorts and underwear with her help. My shoes, too, for good measure. That's all our clothes, except for Alex's sandals and her panties. The sandals I scoop off her feet. That's easy. But the panties are in my way.

As I drop to my knees and kiss open her thighs, I see only one solution. A quick two-handed tug on the strip of fabric at her hip brings me the sound of tearing seams.

"Eric!" she squeaks.

"You'll thank me in a minute."

At least I hope she will, because I need another taste. Alex wasn't the only one who couldn't get through the day without flashbacks. I nose along the smooth skin of her thigh and inhale deeply of her feminine scent. She's perfect. Dinner was perfect. The walk on the beach was perfect. This moment is perfect.

It's unlike me to be so invested in anyone. I'm enjoying myself way too much.

And three more nights in Hawaii doesn't seem like enough.

15

ALEX

I AM DEFINITELY LIVING someone else's life tonight, and that lucky woman has it good. We walked into the suite no more than five minutes ago, and already Eric's tongue is... *Ohhh.*

My fingers find their way into his hair as he begins to worship me with his mouth and his lips. He is easily the most sexually attuned man that I've ever had the pleasure to encounter.

He's ruining me for other men, and I don't even care.

"Mmm," he says as he slowly tastes me, and I have to close my eyes and take it all in. I don't want to miss a single sensation. I like it all—not just the naughty tongue, but the scrape of his whiskers against my thighs and the roughness of his fingertips on my knees.

He's devouring me, and it's almost too good. I love this, but I also crave him inside me. "Eric, stop. Come here."

Ignoring me, he gives another long lick and a gentle suck.

"Ah!" I gasp, trying to hold back my pleasure. "Please. Now."

"Please, what?"

"Eric!"

He grins up at me from the floor. "The lady boss wants something?"

"You know I do."

He chuckles, but finally stands up. One hand grasps his cock, and he gives himself an easy stroke. I can't tear my gaze away.

"You can look if I can look," he says, calling me on it. "Spread your legs for me."

The command makes me self-conscious, though, and I close them instead.

"Alex," he chuckles. "Fair's fair. Besides—that woman whose life you're borrowing? I think she likes it dirty."

I glance up into his smiling eyes and wonder how he knew exactly the right thing to say to me. Slowly, I spread my knees as wide as I can.

Eric makes an appreciative noise. And then he steps into the space I've created, bringing us close together. I can feel the heat radiating off his skin as he kisses my cheekbone while slowly penetrating me.

We both groan happily.

He wraps his arms around me and rocks sweetly inside me. "Perfect," he whispers against my face. "Perfectly addictive." Then he lifts my chin and kisses me.

I brace my hands behind me on the counter so he can move. Then I just lean back and let myself feel everything he's giving me. All I know are the twin sensations of heated skin and deep kisses.

Until he stops, breaking both our kiss and our connection. I look up, bewildered, as he scoops me off the counter.

"Turn around," he says, and then does it for me, rotating my body with his hands on my bare hips. "I want you to watch. I've been the only one enjoying this perfect view."

Eric grabs a towel off the rack and tosses it onto the counter. "Rest your arms on here."

I let him bend me over like a Barbie doll. In the mirror, I see why. He steps up behind me, arm flexing, erection in hand. He nudges my legs apart with one of his muscular knees. Then, with a brow furrowed by desire, he pushes inside.

Oh, wow. I take a deep breath and blow it out as my body welcomes him in again.

"Open your eyes," he grunts.

I hadn't realized I'd closed them. But in a moment, I'm grateful for the reminder. Because the sight of Eric gripping my hips and slowly pumping his body into mine is not to be missed.

I am mesmerized by the undulating flex of his chest and the warm light bathing our skin.

So this is what it feels like to truly let go and live in the moment. I can't look away.

"That's right," he groans. "Don't miss it."

I will, though. I'll miss this the second we're through.

BUT FIRST, sleep. I spend another glorious night curled up around Eric in our luxurious bed, until Bingley wakes me with: "Rise and shine my queen! It is time to go forth and conquer the kingdom of technology!"

"Oh, stuff it," Eric murmurs into his pillow.

"Someone sounds grumpy!" Bingley says cheerfully. "Shall I order coffee?"

Eric's head pops off the pillow. "You can do that?"

"It would be an honor and a privilege! Would you like me to list the room service entrees?"

"Not necessary," he grunts. "Two pots of coffee. One regular, one decaf. A western omelet and a fruit and granola plate."

"I want an omelet, too," I pipe up.

"The omelet is for you," Eric says. "I'm having the granola."

"Oh. Well. Carry on."

Bingley reads the order back to us and then puts it through to the hotel.

Before getting out of bed, I nudge Eric's naked hip. "I thought you said you didn't ever want to converse with your phone?"

"Don't gloat," he says. "I didn't realize he could feed me."

I head for the shower, smiling.

AFTER MY OMELET, though, I find myself sitting down for a video chat with Eric's brother. I'm dressed in a prim little suit and ready for the day. But when he appears on screen, I feel a flash of embarrassment, anyway.

This man recruited his brother to protect me in Hawaii. He did it as a favor to help me through my time of need. And then I jumped on his brother like a cat in heat. Several times. I wonder if blushing shows up on a video chat.

"Good morning," Max says. "I need to talk to you for a quick second about Xian Smith."

"Right," I say with a sigh. "Really, Max? *Take the meeting?* Which of my long-time suppliers shall I cut from my docket in order to accommodate your curiosity?"

"I don't care. Pick one." His grin is as infuriating as his brother's. It must be a family trait. "You're doing this as a favor to me, but also for yourself."

"He's a components broker, right? I don't need a middleman when I can deal directly with Chinese manufacturers."

"I understand," Max says with a nod. "But I'm working on a theory about Smith, and the more I learn about him, the better I can protect your company. What do you know about him?"

"Not much." I try to remember what people have said. "And only gossip."

"Let's hear it."

"He showed up at a Vegas conference two years ago, brokering cellular modems from small factories in Zhengzhou. People said his prices were unbeatable."

"Go on." Max scribbles something down on a legal pad.

"After that I heard he was trying to make connections in Taiwan and Vietnam. He was working the multi-source angle, helping manufacturers avoid Chinese imports during the tariff wars."

"Okay." Max adds to his notes. "So when you meet with him, please try to remember everything he asks you. What's his angle? How is he offering to help you? Is he trying to compete on price, or on something else?"

"Fine." I grumble. "He seemed to know that I'm scrambling to source my new device. 'Your new toy,' he called it."

"That's an open secret, though? You've been talking to suppliers for weeks already. And he's well connected."

"Obviously. It's going to be a short meeting, though. This launch is too important for me to try a new supplier."

"I know. But do me a favor? Play dumb. Pump him for information about what he can offer."

"Fine. Whatever. I'll do your dirty work. Is there anything else I can do for you Max? Spy on anyone else? Bring you a sandwich?"

He laughs. "Thanks, but I have people for that. And I'm very particular about my sandwiches."

"Of course you are."

"Oh—there is one small thing you can do for me. Tell my brother to stop mooning the pillow cam whenever he's alone in the suite."

"He *didn't*." I clap a hand over my mouth.

"Oh, he does. Frequently." Max shakes his head. "Tell him middle school is over. Find a new joke."

"It's *my* ass!" Eric yells from the other room. "I can shake it wherever I want."

Max shakes his head. "Later, Alex. Good luck today."

"Thanks, Max." I give him a wave and disconnect our call.

IT'S another long day of meetings, including a business lunch. Eight hours pass before I'm escorted back to the suite by Pieter and my assistant, Rolf, who's yapping at my heels like a frustrated chihuahua. "We never called Pam in London. And I still need you to open DocuSign and authorize the quarterlies."

"Later," I say as the lock clicks to green and I push into the suite. "I need a snack, and then I have to get ready." And I'm just so tired, suddenly. What I really need is a nap. But that's not going to happen.

"Well, fine," Rolf says from the hallway. "You don't call, you don't text. You don't send flowers!"

"I love you Rolf. Now go away."

"That's what they all say." He sighs heavily as I shut the door.

When I turn around, it's as if I've stumbled into a fraternity house. The TV is on, tuned to sports news. There are dirty plates on the coffee table beside an empty protein drink container. And there's rock music blaring from a speaker somewhere.

I locate Eric on the rug, wearing nothing but a bathing suit. He's doing push-ups.

"Hi, honey I'm home," I say to his very well-formed backside.

"Thirty-four. Thirty-five. Thirty-six…"

"The dinner starts in an hour."

"Thirty-seven…" There's a grunt and a pause. "Thirty-eight…"

"What? Only thirty-eight? I could beat that with one hand tied behind my back."

Eric laughs. I see his back shaking. Then he collapses onto the rug. "You wrecked my set!"

"Oh, sure, blame the pregnant lady." I step over his body and proceed to the kitchenette. "Is there any yogurt left?"

He rolls over. "I thought you said dinner was soon."

"It is. But when you're the speaker, you can't eat. Too risky."

"Risky? Like you might choke and die before your speech?"

"No, like you might get sauce on your dress."

"Heavens!" He eyes me from the floor. "This audience is mostly men, right?"

"Sure."

"A spill on your dress won't be the thing they notice first. For better or for worse, those eyes will be on whichever parts of you the dress doesn't cover."

Yikes. I pull a cup of yogurt out of the fridge. "Thanks for making me self-conscious."

"I'm sorry." He sits up. "I shouldn't be flip about your big talk."

Twenty-one years later and it's still true—Eric is the nicest grouch I've ever met. "The problem is you're right. But I still want to look good and speak well."

"Is this speech hard?"

I shake my head. "Not really. I'm revealing a project I've been developing for two years. So it's not like I'll forget what to say. But I still have to get up there and say it, knowing that half the audience thinks I'm only in charge because daddy gave me the job."

Oops. That old fear just slid right out.

"Fuck them," Eric says with a flip of his hand. "You don't need their validation."

My spoon hovers above the surface of my yogurt. *You don't need their validation*. Such a simple idea. But it's one that doesn't occur to me nearly often enough. "You are very useful. Even outside the bedroom."

His laugh is sharp and sudden. "I'm honored that you noticed. Can I have the first shower?"

"Sure, but leave the bathroom door open."

"What, you need a show?" He jumps to his feet and flexes his biceps.

"Nice," I say. "But I need you to avoid steaming up the mirror."

He throws his head back and laughs. "God, you are hard on my ego."

"I am not hard on your ego, Mr. Hot Bod. Well, unless we're counting the night I didn't recognize you and shot you down when you weren't even hitting on me."

"Oh, we're counting it." He walks slowly toward the pillow cam, drops his shorts, and shakes his butt in front of it.

I almost choke on the yogurt.

"But—full disclosure?" He pulls up his shorts again and walks toward me in the kitchen area. "If you *had* recognized me, and we did pull off a conversation in some quiet corner, I would have totally hit on you. It was only a matter of time."

Again, my spoon stops midair, and my mouth hangs open.

But Eric is already halfway to the master bathroom, humming to himself.

And he leaves the door open like I asked.

16

ERIC

IT'S NOT until I'm wearing my suit and escorting Alex into the ballroom that I understand what a big deal Alex is. I mean—she's already a big deal to me. And she looks ravishing in a sleek black dress that hugs her bust and then sweeps into billows of fabric, artfully concealing the rest of her body from prying eyes.

But I admit to being taken aback by the flurry of whispers that her entrance causes. "Engels, people are pointing and staring," I whisper as we parade past a million other tables toward the front of the room. "It's like if Taylor Swift entered a middle school cafeteria."

"That would cause screaming, not whispers."

"Still."

An organizer in a severely tight bun leads us to table #1. "Let me know if there's anything I can get you. Anything at all."

"Thank you. This looks lovely," Alex says as I pull out her chair. I take the seat on her right, and Rolf takes the one on her left.

"Please let there be wine," Rolf says.

"You can't drink until after our presentation goes off without a hitch."

"Well, goddamnit. I'm eating, though. You can't stop me."

"You two are like an old married couple," I point out.

"We get that a lot," Alex says.

The food isn't half bad, either, although Alex doesn't eat anything.

"There has to be something here that doesn't stain," I point out. "These rolls are pretty good." I offer her the basket.

She shakes her head. "It's okay. I feel a little off, anyway."

"Bet you'll feel better when the speech is done," Rolf says. "She gets nervous," he stage-whispers to me.

"I do *not*." She chews her lip. "You're sure the prototype is working?"

"Working great," Rolf assures her. "Bingley and I had a whole conversation about gifts I could get my grandma for her birthday."

"Good."

The gentleman in charge of this event—the same one Alex reamed the other night—is up on stage. "Tonight, we welcome a special guest. Alexandra Engels is the President and CEO of Engels Media Communications. At the age of twenty-nine, Alex became the youngest female CEO of a Fortune 500 company. Before that, she earned a B.S. at Harkness College, followed by double Master's Degrees in Business and Computer Programming at MIT.

"Now she's busy proving to the world that cable companies are no longer boring little utilities, but innovative tech companies in their own right. We're honored that Alex chose to make a major product announcement at the Oahu Conference…"

I lean over and give her a kiss on the cheek. "Knock 'em dead, hot stuff. I'm pulling for you."

She gives me a soft look. "Thank you." Then she pushes back her chair and prepares to stand up at the right moment.

"Please welcome to the podium Ms. Alexandra Engels."

The applause is loud. Alex rises, making her way up a few steps to the stage. She takes the microphone in hand with the confidence of a pop star.

"Ladies and gentlemen, it's my pleasure to be here in Hawaii. And I've brought a friend—someone I've been waiting two years to introduce. Please say hello to my Butler. His name is Bingley."

There's more applause while Alex steps out from behind the podium, microphone in hand, and over to a cart draped with a black cloth. She lifts it to reveal a metallic orb. It's titanium, with a fine mesh surface. "Hello, Bingley," she says. "Apologies for the blanket."

"I don't mind the dark, but I do feel somewhat emasculated," he explains.

The audience roars.

"I'm truly sorry," Alex says. "Can we talk?"

"Absolutely," the virtual butler says smoothly. "But if you don't mind, please verify your identity first."

"Don't you recognize my voice?" Alex asks.

"Naturally! But there are *quite* a few people in this room, and I need to know who I'm serving."

Alex places her palm on top of the orb for a moment.

"Thank you, Miss Alex! How may I serve you?"

"Well, everyone else is eating dinner, but I didn't get a chance. What are the most highly rated restaurants on Oahu? Could you look that up for me?"

"One moment, my queen."

The audience roars again. I glance around the room at all the tech geeks, and every face is turned toward Alex. My gaze snags on her ex, sitting a few tables away from me. He looks enthralled.

But who wouldn't be? Alex and Bingley go on together like a two-man act. He recommends some restaurants and offers to call them. It's clear that everyone is charmed. "That will be all, Bingley," she says while they're still chuckling. "I'll call you if I need you."

"Certainly, my liege! Just don't cover me with —"

She drops the black cloth over him again.

"Blast it!"

As the laughter dies down, she takes her place behind the podium. "Charming fellow, isn't he? Bingley's AI brain was developed by my friend Nate Kattenberger at K-Tech. The Butler contains terrific technology, well executed. He's the best smart speaker to come to the market and a joy to have around. Although,

I wonder how many executives in this audience would tell me that the market for smart speakers is crowded. Am I right?"

The audience gets quiet.

"The Butler's price tag will be well over three hundred dollars. Whereas you can get a cheap smart speaker for fifty bucks right now. So, you might ask yourself why I went to all the trouble. The answer—I promise you—is much bigger than Bingley's hunky British accent."

There's a murmur of uncomfortable chuckling.

"The Butler is a very different product than others on the market. It's what Bingley *won't* do that's truly innovative." She holds up two fingers in turn. "He won't let you down—not without a fight—and he won't tell anyone your personal information, your search history, or your thoughts and dreams."

She taps thoughtfully on the podium. "We are at a crossroads in consumer tastes and preference. Gone are the days when consumers blindly put their trust in the latest slick app or gadget. The world is covered over with shiny apps. And the tech industry has widely abused its customers' trust in the name of data mining and advertising.

"The next wave of consumer tech will be driven by two very important ideas—excellence and privacy.

"Excellence means creating a product that people will brag about owning. That's the only kind of product I'm going to make. But excellence also means *privacy*. Our customers haven't always valued their privacy highly enough. It's partly their fault for choosing convenience over safety. But it's mostly our fault for not disclosing the risks.

"Meanwhile, some of our colleagues have made woeful apps and products. Our failure to ask the big questions has led, for example, to a globally insecure banking system, hacked electrical grids, and misused facial recognition software. If we're not careful, our societal legacy will be global chaos, wrongful arrests, and surveillance by abusive exes."

I nearly choke on my sip of wine. She slipped that line right in there, smooth as silk. I can't help myself. My eyes dart to Jared

Tatum, just to see his reaction. But his face is as placid as it was before.

Hmm.

"All in the name of a fun time and a good bargain," Alex is saying. "But everyone in this room has the power to build better tools. I'm here to tell you that privacy is sexy. And our customers are not stupid. They *will* pay more for products that aren't peddling their private information to the highest bidder. They will reward you for your thoughtful innovation. They are slowly learning that there's no such thing as free."

Alex glances toward her new device. "The Butler does all his own offline processing. The owner's voice is never transmitted to our servers unless the customer approves it in real time. And all information is completely encrypted."

She glances around the room, making eye contact with people at dozens of tables. "This project took me two years. Building a truly private product wasn't easy. But neither was it impossible.

"Privacy is not a party trick. It's not cute or funny. But it's important to our future as a civilization. Tonight, I challenge all of you to look at your work and consider your business models. What will you add to the future of personal electronics? What will your legacy be? Thank you and good night."

The applause is thunderous.

ON HER WAY back to the table, several people flag Alex down. So it takes several minutes for Alex to reappear at my side.

"That was amazing," I tell her when she finally sits down again.

"Remarkable," the gray-haired men at our table agree. "Well done."

"Thank you." Her smile is tight. Honestly, she looks awfully tense for somebody who's just finished giving a terrific speech. But I don't ask her why, because the MC is introducing someone else now. A lifetime achievement award is about to be granted, and the audience listens politely.

I hope the speeches end soon. I've already heard the best one, and I can't wait to take off this bowtie. The night is still young, too. If we got out of here, I could have a glass of scotch or a walk on the beach.

Not two minutes later, though, Alex clamps her hand onto my wrist. "Ladies room," she gasps. Then she pushes back her chair and stands up.

Well, fine. I guess I'm getting my wish. It's my job to stay close to Alex, so as Alex walks away, I casually place my napkin on the table, nod to the others, and ease out of my chair.

Something is wrong, though. It's not like Alex to storm out of the room during a quiet moment like this. As I wind between the tables, following her out, it's clear that we're interrupting the action onstage.

And she's really moving. Even my longer stride can't keep up with the beautiful woman in the cocktail dress and three-inch heels. She's leaving the way you'd evacuate from a fire.

When I reach the lobby, she's still moving fast—a human streak heading for the bathrooms. My only guess is that she ate something earlier that doesn't agree with her. So I let her escape to the sanctity of the women's room, and I park myself right outside to wait.

It's not really like me to worry. But the minutes tick by with no sign from her. Gunnar appears eventually, crossing the empty lobby with a casual stride. "Everything okay?" he asks when he reaches me.

"I really don't know," I admit. "All she said was that she needed the ladies' room."

"Did you see anyone else go in there?" he asks. "I need to check on her."

"I haven't seen a soul," I admit. "You know what? Let me do it."

Gunnar shrugs, and I push open the door, hearing only silence inside. "Alex, are you in here?" I step further into the quiet bathroom. Only one of the stall doors is closed. "Alex, you're scaring me."

"I'm…I'm bleeding," she gasps.

"What?" My heart rate doubles. "You're hurt?"

"No. I...don't know what's happening. I might be having a miscarriage."

Oh Jesus. I hear the toilet flush. And a moment later, the stall door opens, and a very pale Alex comes out. "I need to go to a hospital."

"Okay, all right." I hold out a hand, and she grips it, teetering briefly on those heels. That's when instinct takes over. I just pluck her off the floor carry her toward the door of the restroom. "Gunnar," I bark as I approach the door, and he opens it. I carry Alex out. "We are going to the E.R."

"Oh hell. Need company?"

"What we need is a car."

"On it." He taps his watch, then starts speaking while he jogs across the lobby toward the main entrance.

"This is bad," Alex says as I carry her toward the doors.

"You don't know that for sure," I say. But who the fuck am I to say so? I'm just a dumb jock who hates the look of fear on Alex's face. "Let's find a doctor who can help you out."

She bites her lip and doesn't say another word. By the time I get all the way outside, Gunnar has a black passenger sedan and a driver waiting. I place Alex on the back seat and slide in beside her. "We need..."

"The emergency room," Gunnar finishes for me. "The driver knows." He shuts the door and raps twice on the glass.

And off we go.

○━━👎

"DO you need me to step out?" I ask the tech who wheels the sonogram machine into the exam room where Alex is reclined.

"Not if you'd rather stay," the man says. He has a cheerful round face and wears crisp blue scrubs. "I'm going to need you in a robe," he says to Alex. "Open at the front, okay? You can leave your bra on. I just need to get at that belly. I'll be right back."

Alex nods. She's tense and silent.

When we drove up fifteen minutes ago, I'd remarked that this hospital is kind of small. "It probably doesn't matter," Alex had said. "It's so early in my pregnancy, if I am miscarrying, there's nothing anyone can do."

So here we are. And I guess rural Oahu is the place to be if you're in need of an emergency evaluation on a Friday night. This place is clean and cheerful, and quieter than any New York City E.R. could ever be.

"Need help with that zipper?" I offer as the technician slips away.

"Thank you," she says quietly, twisting to show me her back. "I'm sorry for this."

"No, I'm sorry." It's just dawning on me that this is all my fault. What was I even thinking, taking a pregnant woman to bed? I wasn't rough with her. But I wasn't careful, either. "Slip your arms out of those straps." I say gruffly, lifting the hospital gown and hold it behind her.

"This part really wasn't in your job description," she murmurs as she sheds the top half of the dress and then dons the hospital gown.

I pull the halves together for her. "Honestly, hospitals don't bother me much. I'm a frequent flier."

"Why?"

"Knee surgery. Shoulder surgery. That *is* part of my job description."

"Better you than me," she grumbles. "I hate hospitals. So much." She lifts her hips and I slide the dress out from under her. My gut goes a little sideways when I see blood on it. Not just a little bit, either. Quickly, I sweep the dress out of sight behind me. But of course she knows it's there.

Oh Alex. I'm so sorry.

And now I feel like punching something. So much for my chipper small talk.

"Knock knock," the sonogram guy says. "Now let's have a look at that baby." He enters the room and snaps on the monitor. I move to the head of the bed to get out of the way as the technician grabs a tube of goo and squirts it on Alex's exposed stomach.

Alex's face creases with tension, and she clutches my fingers more tightly. I doubt she even knows she's doing it. The tech puts the wand on her belly and slides it around for a moment. Then he actually smiles. "Well, hi there! Look at you, moving around!"

And, whoa. There's a baby on that screen. It's shaped like a peanut. Or a lima bean. But that's a baby, and it's lifting its tiny hand. "Is it sucking its thumb?"

"Yep!" the tech says.

"That's good, right?" Alex lifts her chin as if getting closer to the screen will tell her what she needs to know.

"Very good. See that nice strong heartbeat?" He hits a button and then we can hear it. A rapid, rhythmic whoosh.

And I am speechless.

But not Alex. "Can you tell if anything is wrong?"

"Someone from OB will be down to speak to you," he says. "But all I see is a healthy fetus that's positioned correctly. With bleeding, we always need to rule out an ectopic pregnancy. But that's not an issue for you. Hang in there, Ms. Engels. There are no guarantees. But I don't think you're having your heart broken tonight."

Her face relaxes for the first time since we got here.

"Before I go, do you already know the sex of your baby?"

"No!" Alex says. "I thought I didn't want to know. But now I think I do. Tell me."

"Are you sure?"

"Yes!"

He chuckles. "It's a girl. I'm ninety percent sure."

"A little girl," Alex whispers, awe in her voice.

"I'll make an extra print for you. Just try to relax okay?"

She sets her head back and lets out a deep breath. Then she remembers to unclench my hand.

THE NEXT VISITOR is a curt female obstetrician. "I'm Dr. Patel," she says crisply. "Tell me about the bleeding you're experiencing."

"Bright red blood everywhere. It came on very suddenly."

"Significant cramping?"

"No, just a twinge."

"And have you experienced bleeding earlier in your pregnancy? Spotting? Red or brown in color?"

"Not a bit. That's why I panicked."

"Okay…" The doctor makes a thoughtful face. "I don't believe you're miscarrying. The suddenness of your symptoms is a little odd. Most women aren't aware, though, that twenty-five percent of healthy full-term pregnancies experience some unexplained bleeding during the first trimester."

"Twenty five percent?" Alex sounds so hopeful.

"That's right. It's a very common symptom of early pregnancy and often signifies nothing. Now, your pregnancy is a couple of weeks more advanced than we typically see this, and the sudden onset is a little unusual. But there's still no reason to panic."

"Then what should I do?"

"I think we'll keep you here overnight, but I'm fairly certain there's no real cause for alarm. When you get home, your doctor will keep an eye out for placenta previa, for example. But that's not the end of the world either.

"What's that?" I hear myself ask.

"In early pregnancy, the placenta rides low. Then it's supposed to shift higher. Otherwise bleeding can occur, and a c-section may be necessary."

I still have no idea what she's saying, but it doesn't sound that bad.

"You'll move up to the second floor," the doctor says, scribbling something on a chart. "Your husband can stay with you."

Your husband. Under different circumstances, we might have a laugh over that mistake. But the doctor is about to make her escape. And I have a pressing question. So I follow her into the hallway.

"Excuse me. Doctor Patel?"

She turns around.

"Can I ask you a question?"

"Of course."

I drop my voice because I don't want anyone to overhear. "Look, is there any way I caused this?"

She blinks. "Well, first, we don't know if there's a problem. Everything might be fine."

"I know that, but…" Words fail me. And I don't even know if I'm ready to hear the answer to the question I can't spit out.

"Look, Mr.…"

"Bayer."

"Mr. Bayer, I'm going to assume you're asking about sexual intercourse?"

"Um, yup." And this is officially the most awkward conversation I've ever had.

"Pregnant couples are encouraged to enjoy a normal sex life. If sex caused miscarriages, the human species would already be extinct."

I feel my shoulder muscles begin to unknit about two seconds after her words sink in. "Oh. Okay."

"Like I said, there's no evidence that this pregnancy will end in miscarriage. But even if it does, please know that most miscarriages are caused by genetic abnormalities, or underlying health problems, such as food poisoning or other pathogens. They are not caused by sex, or stress, or spicy food, or exercise."

"Right. Good."

"Your job is to just breathe through the next twenty-four hours, and to support your partner no matter what happens."

"Yes. Absolutely," I say, willing the conversation to end. "Thank you."

She hugs her clipboard a little more tightly and turns away, her shoes squeaking on the hospital's shiny floor.

THEY MOVE ALEX UPSTAIRS, as promised. An hour later, I'm dozing in a reclining chair in her new hospital room. Or I'm trying to, anyway. The lights are off, and I'm hoping that Alex can fall asleep, giving herself a break from all the anxiety she's still feeling.

But after ten minutes of silence, I hear her let out a sigh.

"What are you thinking about over there in your big brain?" I whisper.

"Paint colors."

"Wait, what?" I chuckle.

"I want to go home and choose colors for the baby's room. Girly colors."

"Were you really going to wait and be surprised?"

"Yep. I didn't want to get attached. Not until I'd dealt with Jared and whether or not he'd sign away his rights. I felt like I didn't deserve her until I knew I could keep her safe."

"Hey." I lift my head. "Safe is a done deal, Alex. We'll get this done." After the words come out, I realize I put myself into that sentence. "Max knows a lot of tricks," I hedge.

"I know. But I want this baby. *This* baby. I'm done beating myself up for past mistakes. I'm ready for her now."

"That's right. You've got this."

She's quiet for a moment. "You're a good friend, Eric."

"I know."

She chuckles. "But not a modest one."

"Nope. You want modest, you need another friend." I smile into the dark, because it's all true.

"You can go back to the hotel, you know. You don't have to stay here and wait in that chair."

The thought hadn't even crossed my mind. "We're friends, right? Friends don't leave friends alone in strange hospitals." I get up out of the chair, walk over, lean down and kiss her cheek. "Try to sleep. Is there anything I can do for you?"

"No. But if they clear me to leave in the morning, you can call Rolf and get him to pack up our hotel room. I just want to get on the plane and go."

"Okay. Sure."

"In fact, if you want to warn the security team and Rolf, that would be helpful. Rolf can put the plane on standby for eight a.m."

"Good idea. Is there anyone else I can call for you? Your dad?"

She shakes her head. "Nah. Let the man sleep. There isn't any news, anyway."

"Right. Okay. I'll make sure we can go home when you're

ready." I stroke a hand over her hair, then take my weary self out into the tropical night to find a place where I'm allowed to make some calls.

And just like that our strange little tropical fling is ending early. I'd never wanted to come to Hawaii. And now I feel sick about leaving early.

It doesn't make a lick of sense. But some things never do.

17

ALEX

"ALEX. TIME TO WAKE UP." A hand pats my upper arm.

Someone is trying to wake me, but I'm not having it. I screw my eyes more tightly closed and press my face into the pillow.

"Alex, we've landed."

"No." Whatever the man is saying, I really don't care. My bed is comfortable, and my body is heavy with exhaustion.

"The car is on the tarmac."

Tell someone who cares.

"Alex." Soft lips meet my cheek. And then a big, solid body fills in all the empty spaces around me. His knees tuck against mine, his arm reaches around to hug me. "Come on, honey. It's time to move. And I know you don't like it when I pick you up and carry you."

Sometimes I do, my subconscious prods. *I like it a lot. Especially against the door…*

That thought brings me suddenly to wakefulness. And to my crushing disappointment, we're not in the hotel suite bed. We're not even in Hawaii. The jet has landed in New York. I may or may not still be bleeding. And my life is just as messy as it was when I got onto this plane a few days ago.

Probably even more.

With a groan, I brace a hand on the bed and push myself into a vertical position.

Eric sits up as well, giving me a smug look. "Good nap?"

"Yes," I admit. "Don't smirk." Although I like that smirk, damn it. I like it too much. And it's no longer mine to admire.

Eric helps me to my feet. We're alone on the jet, and the door is already open. I glance around for my luggage. "It's already in the car," Eric says.

"Oh." I blink, disoriented. "So this is it." I feel like I'm still caught in a dream state. Hawaii was like one long, tropical dream. And the tarmac at La Guardia is what you get when you wake up.

"You okay?" He runs a hand over my hair, which is probably a mess.

"Absolutely," I lie. "Let's go."

Eric doesn't let go of my hand as we walk slowly down the stairs, leaving the jet behind. But I feel a little more awake with each step. The summer heat and the smell of asphalt hit me with a slap of reality.

"Look," Eric says when we reach the ground. "Can I come by tomorrow to see how you're doing?"

I look up, catching the warmth in his gray eyes, and noticing the way his thick hair is tousled by the wind. And more of Eric's company sounds fantastic.

Except it really wouldn't be. We're not a couple. We're never going to be a couple. And I need to own that fact right now, while I still can. "Tomorrow isn't a great idea. I…" I clear my throat. "It's been fun, but now it's back to real life. For both of us, no?"

"We're home early." He frowns. "And I'm still on vacation for another couple weeks."

"Well, I'm not." I hate the cold sound of my own voice. But I know what will happen if he comes over tomorrow. Either I'll end up in his arms. Or I'll wish I were there. Either way, it's not what either of us needs. "Eric, the truth is that I have a few precious months to launch a project, bribe or blackmail my sperm donor, and gestate a baby. I can't afford distractions."

"Of the naked variety," he clarifies.

"Of any variety." I can see the driver of my car tapping the steering wheel impatiently. "It was fun, but it was only a few days. You said so yourself."

"Yeah," he says slowly. "But you have to let me know that you and the baby are okay. And we said we'd stay friends."

My heart crumples. "I don't think I can do that." I mean it literally, but it comes out cold, as if I have somewhere more important to be.

His eyes narrow, he opens his mouth to argue with me. Then he shuts it again and takes both my hands instead. "Well, if that's how you want it to go, you take care of yourself." His voice is gruff.

"You, too." I give him a weak smile, hoping he'll release me.

Instead, he leans in and gives me a single soft kiss. Just a peck, really. And it's over way too soon.

18

MID AUGUST

ERIC

THERE'S one minute left in the scrimmage, and I just won the faceoff.

One minute is plenty of time if you have A) the puck B) Trevi on one side and C) Campeau on the other.

A rookie with crazy eyes launches my way, hell bent on stripping me. So I drag the puck away on the edge of my stick, like a worm on a fishhook. Trevi is *nearly* open. I wait as long as I possibly can and then flick the puck right past Crazy Eyes' stick.

And, *bam*. Right onto the shooting surface of Trevi's.

My muscles scream, and my knee whimpers as I accelerate out of Crazy Eyes' way. But it's worth it. I get open again. I push my stick forward as if waiting for the pass.

But it's all for show. Because Campeau is also open, and I already know Trevi will pass to him instead.

He does. And then anyone who blinked probably missed Campeau's wrister toward the net. Including the goalie. Because the puck goes in and Campeau laughs out loud as the lamp lights.

"Fucking beautiful!" I bellow as the buzzer sounds. Nothing is better than the last period of a hockey game when my teammates and I are on fire. Nothing.

Our defeated opponents put their hands on their knees, breathing hard. They're only rookies, anyway. This is the week when twenty guys from our affiliate teams in the minor leagues are invited to a training camp skate.

It's always a brutal scrimmage. Management likes to see how we stack up against the young punks they're grooming to take over our spots. But we won, damn it. Even if I'll need an ice bath, a massage, and a double cheeseburger just to feel human again.

We line up to shake hands with the youngsters. And then finally we make our way toward the overcrowded dressing room.

Lord, with twice as many players, it's the crush of humanity in here. Beside me, my teammate Castro shakes his head. "I feel like such a geezer right now."

"Stop," I grunt. "If you're a geezer, then I'm prehistoric." Castro isn't the one whose knee is taped up so completely that it might as well be mummified. "At least we could have some fun with the rookies."

"What do you mean?"

"Hey rookie!" I shout into the melee.

Seven or eight heads turn in our direction at once.

"I was just checking to see who was paying attention."

My other teammates crack up. "Yo!" Leo Trevi calls. "Someone here is going to end up answering to that name all year, though," Leo muses. "Who's it gonna be?"

The minor league guys all grin, but nobody raises his hand. They know better than to boast before our next scrimmage. We'd flatten whomever dared to claim the title before proving himself worthy.

I fucking love it in this room. They're gonna have to carry me out of here feet first.

"Okay, listen up, kids!" Leo's wife hops up onto a bench. "I'm Georgia Trevi, co-head of publicity. The veterans already know the drill. But history has shown that everyone can use a reminder. And you'll answer to me if you get this wrong."

The room is silent, with all the youngsters listening as if their lives depended on it.

"So long as you're here in Brooklyn you're representing the Bruisers organization. I expect you to take care with your actions outside the rink as well as inside. I don't want to see any bar brawls. No photos of you guys acting crazy. No public drunkenness. You want to blow off steam tonight, you do it responsibly. Also? Twenty minutes, boys. Then Coach wants you in the video room." She hops off the bench.

"Good speech, you badass," Leo says to his wife.

"That all goes for you, too, hot stuff." She gives him a smile. "But right now, I have some business with Bayer."

"What did I do?"

Georgia puts her hands on her hips. "What's with the vacation pictures in Hawaii? You and Alex Engels? How did I not hear this gossip?"

Pictures? *Uh oh.* "Don't believe everything you read, Georgia."

"Are you saying this isn't you?" She pulls out her phone and scrolls through a gossip blog I've never heard of. "Here."

As she thrusts the phone at me, I have a moment of dread. What the hell am I about to see? And how much trouble will it cause for Alex?

Naturally, Leo and Castro crowd me on either side.

But my first glimpse of the photo fills me with relief. It's a simple snap of Alex and I walking down the beach together. She's laughing, and I'm grinning. We look deliriously happy, but we're not even holding hands. This is not a scandalous photo. *Not today, Satan.*

"Whoa!" Castro says. "Look at you with the secret billionaire romance."

"Nah," I say, handing Georgia back her phone. "We're just old friends."

"Really?" Trevi says. "Old friends who vacation together in Hawaii?"

"Sometimes," I say mildly.

"Because *that* happens all the time." Georgia's eyes glimmer with questions.

"Hey—aren't you the publicist? You're supposed to hate gossip about the players."

"Oh, I hate it in the press. But I like it for myself. So, Romeo, how do you explain *this*..." She opens a folder she's carrying and pulls out a cream-colored envelope addressed to me at the team headquarters. And the return address is Alex's company's office tower in Manhattan.

"Easily. It's probably a thank you note."

"Thank you for *what*, exactly?" Castro snickers.

"She needed a date to this thing in Hawaii, so I went. Big sacrifice, right? A quick trip on her private jet." I slide my thumb beneath the envelope flap and then pull out the card.

When I open it, there's an immediate peal of laughter. Because Alex has included a copy of that photo from twenty-one years ago, with her looking preternaturally mature and beautiful, and me looking like an escapee from the Lil' Rascals movie.

"You weren't kidding about the old friends thing," Georgia giggles. "That photo makes me want to go out and buy you a sandwich."

"I'll take a sandwich. Anytime, anywhere."

"Let me see that." Jason reaches over and grabs the picture, probably with the hopes of passing it around the locker room. Whatever. But then he freezes. "Oh, shit. Bayer, man. *Wow.*" I look down at the card and see a second photo there as well.

It's a sonogram image of a fetus.

"*Whoa!*" Yell Georgia and Leo simultaneously.

I snap the card closed. "Jesus. Lower your voices."

"What did I miss?" calls Silas from a few yards away.

"Nothing!" Then I look at my three friends, their mouths gaping open in front of me. "It's not *at all* what you think," I say quietly. "She is an old friend who finds herself in a tight spot. That's why she needed a friend to go with her to a business thing in Hawaii. This—" I tap the card, "—Doesn't have anything to do with me. But it's still confidential."

Leo looks deflated. "Not yours, huh? Because that would be some first-class gossip right there. Mr. Single man takes a walk on the not-so-wild side."

"You wish," I tease him. "You smug married people are always trying to flip me."

"Ah, well." He shakes his head. "Someday, though."

As if. "Guys, please don't say anything about Alex to anyone. It isn't public yet."

"Fine!" Georgia throws her hands up in the air. "That was almost really exciting. But I guess I'll have to go back to watching Love Island if I want gossip."

"I guess you will."

"There's one more thing I needed to ask you about. Who is Anton Bayer? He was just added to an AHL roster in Colorado."

"Oh, that's my cousin. Well, my cousin's kid. Good guy, I guess. I don't know him that well."

Georgia makes a note on her legal pad. "Okay. If he's in town when we travel to Denver, can I schedule a photo op? The press loves that stuff. Families in hockey."

"Sure," I say with a shrug. Georgia can spin it that way if she wants, even if my actual family gives zero fucks about hockey.

"Thanks!" She pats me on the arm and then moves away.

"Fifteen minutes, boys!" calls O'Doul, the team captain.

Fifteen minutes is just enough time. After my shower, I slip Alex's note out of my gym bag and read it.

Listen, Stinkmonster:

This is the note I should have written to you after that debacle in Florida. The I'm-sorry-I-behaved-badly note. So here goes:

I'm sorry I was so abrupt with you when we got off the jet. I was really scared and not thinking straight. Not that it's any excuse. You were nothing but wonderful to me in Hawaii. I don't think I'll forget that trip anytime soon.

The baby and I are both fine. My symptoms stopped within forty-eight hours, and I haven't had any more trouble. My doctor here in New York shrugged and said, "it happens."

So I'm back at work, getting ready for my big launch and calling my lawyer every few days to see if they've made their move on the paperwork that I need signed. They haven't approached him yet, though. I think your brother is trying to dig up some more dirt first.

They don't tell me the details, either because it's quasi illegal or they think I'm a fragile flower. But I hope to know more soon.

I hope you're doing great and enjoying the start of the season.

Best,

Alex

I read it twice. It's a nice note, but it doesn't say, "Swing by and visit later." Not that I have her home address, or even her phone number. I never asked for it in Hawaii. I didn't need to. The security team handled everything.

My brother has her number, of course. I could ask him. But that's a crap idea. He didn't like my behavior in Hawaii. He might not even give it to me.

Instead, I do an internet search for Alex's corporate headquarters. I dial the main number and ask to be connected to Alex's office. I wait on hold for a while, and then a man's voice eventually picks up. "You've reached the CEO's office, how can I help you?"

His voice is familiar. "Rolf?"

"Speaking."

"It's Eric Bayer calling. Can I speak to Alex?"

"She's in a meeting."

Of course she is. "Look, Rolf. I got a letter from her today, and I don't have her cell number. I need to reach her."

"I *knew* you weren't really the boyfriend."

"It's complicated. Can you give me her number so that I can speak with her later?"

"No way," he sputters. "I'd have to fire myself immediately for giving out her personal information."

I was afraid of that. "But you can give her mine, right?" I rattle it off, hoping she gets the message. And, more than that, hoping she returns my call. I know I'm supposed to be just a friend. I can live with that. But I'd really like to see her.

When I hang up, Castro is sitting beside me. "So, what's the real story?"

"I told you. It's confidential."

My teammate's eyebrows lift. "I meant with you, blockhead. She's having a confidential baby with some other guy. But you're the one on the beach." He hands me the old photo from Martha's Vineyard. I guess it's made the rounds. I take a good look at it. I see two kids turned loose for the summer to entertain themselves. We thought we were so naughty, but we reek of innocence.

"There's no big story," I repeat. "I've known Alex a long time. I have a soft spot for her, I guess."

"Oh man." Castro shakes his head.

"What?"

"You got that look."

"What look?"

"The one Leo gets whenever Georgia walks into the room. The one that O'Doul—who claimed he'd be single forever—got when he started seeing Ariana. The *look*."

"You're drunk," I grumble. "I'm going to be single until the end of time. Just like your grumpy ass."

He laughs. "Fair enough."

"Let's go!" O'Doul calls out just then. "Let's watch some tape, kids!"

I head for the video theater in a hurry because there are more hockey players here today than there are seats.

But just as I'm trucking down the hallway, someone calls out. "Bayer—can I talk to you for a second?" It's Doc Herberts.

"We're supposed to watch tape."

"I know," he says with a grin. This will only take a minute." He beckons me into his office.

"Hey, Doulie!" I call to our captain. "Save me a seat?" My teammate nods, and I follow Herberts into his office. I sit down, taking care to hide my wince.

"How's the knee?" he asks immediately.

"Sore," I admit. Doc is no fool. "But I'm wrapping it well, icing it frequently, and I'm careful to warm up."

He nods, because this is stuff that every decent athlete does, anyway. "We've been discussing your MRI," he says. "How many years has it been since your ACL reconstruction?"

"Almost fifteen."

"You know that most ACL patients eventually develop arthritis."

"Yeah, you've said." That means pain and stiffness. But an arthritic knee is still functional.

"Your scans show some meniscal wear, too. The unevenness of the cartilage may be your major source of pain. So, it's possible that a meniscal repair could make you more comfortable. The problem is that we don't know until we try it."

"Because it might be the arthritis?" I guess.

"Exactly."

I think that over. "How big a surgery is meniscal repair? How long would I be out?"

"Well…" The doctor hedges. "It depends on what they see when they get in there. The more cartilage they remove, the longer the recovery time. But you'd be off the roster for at least two months. Potentially longer."

Shit.

"So, it's something to watch. We have to stay on top of it."

"Right. Okay."

"If your pain changes or gets worse, speak up."

"I will," I say, even as my heart drops. I can't afford time off the ice. My team is positioned to go all the way this year, and I won't let them down without a fight. Then there's the issue of my contract extension. I can't even think about that right now.

"Now go kick a rookie out of your seat and watch some tape."

Two minutes later I'm back in the tape room, sliding into a seat between O'Doul and Castro.

"We're hitting the tavern later," Castro says under his breath. "Gonna get into some trouble. Start the season off right."

"You know it," I say as the screen in front of us blinks to life. It's going to be a great season. We have some teams to beat and some things to prove, though. And I intend to be there when it happens.

19

ALEX

ONE OF MY life skills is fooling people into thinking they have my attention. Peter Whitbread—the blowhard who serves as my general counsel—is sitting across from me with a to-do list as long as my arm. And I'm nodding in all the right places.

Or at least I hope I am. Because my baby was kicking a moment ago, and I'm far enough along now that I could feel it—a little whisper of sensation in my belly.

Kick again, sweetie. I'm listening.

She's being coy, now. Figures.

I've made it to week nineteen. Bingley tells me that my daughter is the size of a cucumber.

"...contracts which alter our exposure to libel as interpreted by the seventh district court." The CFO takes a breath.

"Excellent, Peter," I interrupt. This man could go on all day. "Is there anything pressing, though? I have to be across town in an hour."

Frowning, he flips his notebook closed. "Well, I was looking over your charts in preparation for the board meeting. I see that the pre-orders for the Butler aren't really sufficient to cover such a large marketing budget."

My blood pressure doubles immediately, because Whitbread has been the most vocal opponent of The Butler, and he shows no signs of shutting up. "The pre-orders are irrelevant, because there aren't any reviews for the product. Once the tech bloggers start to test it, that's when the buzz begins. We shouldn't even look at pre-orders for another month."

Then he asks the question that's guaranteed to make me insane. "What does your father think?"

"I have no idea," I snap. "And it's completely irrelevant." My father spends the bulk of his time on his VC firm in California. He's still on the board of ECM, but that's his entire involvement.

Whitbread doesn't believe it, though. He thinks my father still calls the shots. Either that, or he just says these things to irritate me.

"Look," I demand. "Do you have a *legal* issue with The Butler? Because that's where your expertise starts and stops. There are a dozen people on my staff more qualified to weigh in on the financials, thanks."

At first he only blinks, because I don't usually clap back so directly. Then his expression darkens. "I've been at this company a long time, little miss. The reason we're still here is that we don't bet more on a new product than we can afford to lose."

"The reason we're still here," I say quietly, "is because I've stopped the bleeding." Every cable company saw a slump as streaming became more popular. But I've turned the ship around. "Furthermore, pet names are an inappropriate form of address."

"Oh, please." He actually rolls his eyes. "I've known you since you had pigtails and braces." Which is factually untrue. "It's a term of endearment."

"Then save it for someone who finds it endearing." My voice is ice cold. But I am *done* with this man second guessing me in meetings. No matter that he's a good lawyer who keeps us out of trouble. I will not be treated like a pre-teen by this entitled ass.

"Well." Whitbread pushes back his chair and stands suddenly. "Don't let me keep you." He marches out of the room and flings the door shut behind himself.

I put my head in my hands the moment he's gone. Lashing out at him was probably stupid. Not that he doesn't deserve it. But I shouldn't give his criticism so much weight.

He doesn't matter, I remind myself. He's just bitter that I'm sitting in the CEO's office instead of him. There's not one person on the board who thinks he has the vision to run this company.

I'm out on a limb with The Butler, though. And he knows it. This product has to be a success. If it's not, the company will lose a pile of money. But worse than that, my credibility will suffer. My next big idea will be harder to launch. And I'll have nobody to blame but myself.

Sixty seconds later, Rolf rushes into my office. "Got a minute before you go? There are messages. First of all, it's raining hockey players…"

"Hockey players?" I sit up straighter.

He places a message on my desk. "Eric Bayer called. He doesn't have your cell number, apparently. And I wouldn't give it to him."

"Oh." I feel my pulse quicken. *He called*. That makes me feel like a teenager waiting for a prom date. And that's ridiculous, because we were never going to be a couple.

"So, here's his number." Rolf slides the paper toward me. "And then—this afternoon is hockey themed, apparently—Nate Kattenberger's assistant called to invite you to the Hamptons benefit that they throw every year. Hockey players at a cocktail party. And some kind of golf thing. I wrote the website address down right here." He slides another paper toward me.

"Thank you. Now, who's this visitor?"

"That's the weird part." Rolf braces both hands on my desk. "He just got off the elevator and asked to see you. His name is Xian Smith, and he said it was urgent."

"Seriously?" I'd missed my meeting with him in Hawaii, by virtue of my early departure. And he's called twice to ask for other meetings. But I just haven't found the time. And *urgent* implies that we have business together. Which we do not. "How did he get in the building?"

Rolf shrugs. "No idea. He has a visitor's badge, too."

"Bring him in. And then take a seat as well."

Rolf disappears, and for a moment I wonder if I've made the right call. It takes balls to talk your way into the CEO's office. And now I'm rewarding that behavior.

But I *had* agreed to meet with him under other circumstances. So asking security to escort him out would be over the top?

"Ms. Engels." I look up to see him framed in my doorway. He's so imposing, and I'm not sure why. He's a tall man, but slim. His expression is flinty, though. I have no idea why I find it unsettling. "Thank you so much for allowing me to impose like this."

"I have five minutes," I say, just to remind him that I know I've been manipulated. But it sounds bitchy, so I stand up to shake his hand. "I'm sorry I was unable to keep our meeting in Hawaii. I left the conference earlier than I'd planned."

"That is perfectly all right. Medical problem, I heard?"

A tingle of unease runs down my spine. But I keep my face impassive. "Turned out to be nothing. Have a seat."

He sits down opposite me, and Rolf casually takes the other chair, a pad of paper in his lap.

"I'll get right to the point, Alex. I was impressed by your keynote in Hawaii. But not everyone can be trusted to manufacture The Butler. And I think you'll be making a grave error if we don't work together."

Oh please. It's the classic hard sell. "What sort of grave error?" I ask, just to hear what he'll say.

"Change is coming to Shenzhen—both political and social. The older players will no longer be reliable." He says all of this in a voice that's slow and serious. Like the sound of someone predicting the end of the world. "And their new rivals will be overrun with demand. I can help you navigate this shift and bring your Butler to market without delay."

Sure you can, pal. He makes it sound like I'm Goldilocks, skipping through the forest alone. I've been working closely with overseas manufacturers for a decade, though. And he's not the first dude to underestimate me.

"That's very kind, but I'm already set for suppliers. Delivery begins in two months. Surely you realize that my manufacturing needs are already met?"

"Are they, though?" he asks slowly, his brown eyes boring into mine. "Needs change. Loyalties shift. You may find that you need the assistance of someone new."

I feel like I've been threatened, and I can't even explain why. "Mr. Smith," I say with as much bravado as I can muster. "I hope we will get a chance to work together. Perhaps next year, or the following one. The Butler will not be my last product launch. And you are a very interesting man." That's putting it nicely.

"How kind of you to say so. But I believe we shall work together sooner than that. Do not hesitate to phone me if you are in need of assistance." At that, he stands gracefully, drops a business card on my desk, and then calmly exits the room.

Rolf and I blink at each other for a moment. "What was that?" I whisper as soon as I'm sure he's really gone.

"No idea," he whispers back. "He's flashy. But a little creepy, too."

No kidding.

"Shall I summon your car?" Rolf looks at his watch.

"Yes, please. And do me a favor? Call downstairs and ask security who authorized Smith's pass."

"Will do."

When I'm alone in my office again, I confront the two phone messages. It's so tempting to call Eric back. I'd love to hear his voice, and I'd love to see him, too.

But we're finished as a couple, so I'm not sure what good it would do.

Then there's Nate Kattenberger's invitation to the Hamptons. I should probably say yes. Nate has been one of my best friends for over a decade, but I've been dodging him lately. I'm still embarrassed about our hookup. Neither of us ever wants to be reminded of that again.

But—and this is the truly embarrassing part—during my darkest time this past spring, I was terribly rude to his new fiancée, Rebecca. I apologized profusely afterward. But I'm still embarrassed.

Let's just say I've given the two of them a wide berth these past few months, in spite of the fact that they've both been very gracious about the whole disaster.

At some point I have to show my face again, though. Nate and

Rebecca are planning their wedding, and I intend to cheer the loudest when they are pronounced man and wife.

So now I type in the URL for Nate's charity event, just to see if I'd like to go. *Raise money for the Boys' and Girls' Clubs of Brooklyn!* There's a slideshow of last year's event, showing hockey players on ice and on the golf course.

When the third photo slides onto my screen, though, it makes my heart drop. It's a photo of Eric Bayer in a suit and tie, with a beautiful young woman on his arm.

The photo is a year old, of course. But it drives home the point that I don't want to run into Eric socially. I have absolutely no interest in watching him pick up another lucky woman to take back to his hotel room.

I'll send a check instead.

I fold Nate's message in two and drop it into the recycling bin. Eric's message, though. I can't bring myself to throw it away. Instead, I open my top desk drawer and slide it inside. I'm not quite ready to be his friend, I guess. The memory of his hot kisses and his sexy smile is still too vivid.

It will probably be vivid until I'm eighty-five years old. It really was that hot.

"Your car is downstairs!" Rolf calls.

"Thanks!"

I close the drawer on the message, get my bag and go.

20

LATE NOVEMBER

ERIC

I SIT on the bench in the practice facility while skaters whiz past me. It's loud in here. The sound of pucks smacking the boards is the soundtrack of my life.

It's supposed to be, anyway. But I'm sitting on the bench with three ice packs on my knee.

My left knee. The one formerly known as my *good* knee.

And I'm trying not to panic.

Last night—during the overtime period—I took a hit and went down hard. But there was no big *pop*. No excruciating pain. I got right up again, but I could tell that something wasn't quite right.

Afterward, I was in some pain. There was swelling, and it was no better in the morning. So they sent me for an MRI.

Doc Herberts prohibited me from practice today. He wouldn't even let me take the morning yoga class. So I'm sitting here like a bump on a log while he talks to an orthopedist on the phone.

"Yeah, okay. Good stuff," Doc says. "Bye."

Good stuff. That has to be good news, right?

He hangs up and turns to me. "He agrees that it's a minor ACL tear. Not a complete blowout. But you need a surgical repair."

Fuck. "Soon?"

"That's right. You'll be back at physical therapy immediately. And off crutches in a week, probably."

The sounds of the rink grow dim in my ears as I try to wrap my head around this. After three months of increased pain in my right knee, I was already scheduled for another round of scans and appointments with the specialist.

Now none of that matters, because I've torn my *other* ACL.

"Is there anyone who'd say I don't need this surgery?" I croak.

Slowly, Herberts shakes his head. "Not unless we wander up Atlantic Avenue and ask random Bruisers fans we meet in the street."

"Well, let's try that." But the joke falls flat, because somewhere in my thick head I know that Doc is right. Not only that, he's sugarcoating it, too. Because after I go through surgery and several weeks of rehab, I'll still have *another* problem knee.

Unless I'm very lucky. But I'm often very lucky.

"So when can we do this?" I grunt.

"Does tomorrow work for you? Grizzaffi will pull some strings to get you into the midtown clinic in the morning. ACL repair is an outpatient procedure these days. You'll need someone to sign you out afterward. But you can sleep in your own bed tomorrow night."

"Great." As if that really matters. I know I should feel grateful that professional athletes don't wait in line. But I only feel grim.

Doc gives me a wry smile. "Hang in there, Eric. I know this is all happening fast. But it could be so much worse. You want me to go over the procedure with you?"

"Nope. Thanks." It won't change the facts.

"Then sleep well. Don't eat breakfast, and check your email before you go to bed. The surgical clinic will send you instructions. And call me tomorrow night when you're home, okay? I need to hear how you're doing."

"I will. Thanks." I get up and head for the locker room, feeling a little stunned. I thought I was going to play Chicago tomorrow. But while my whole team boards the team jet, I'll be headed to the hospital instead.

In the dressing room, I rip off my practice jersey and throw it at the bench. It slides off and onto the floor. Useless. Just like I am right now.

THE BEST THING about family is that they still have to acknowledge you even when you're in a shitty mood.

On Thursday evenings, my father and brother can usually be found in the gaming lounge at the Harkness Club in midtown. I have a standing invitation to join them. But usually I'm too busy playing hockey. Which they seem to take personally.

Tonight I'm free, though. Yay me. And it's just dawning on me that I need to recruit someone to pick me up at the hospital tomorrow.

So I take a cab into Manhattan and limp into the club. It's the kind of place where the doorman wears white gloves and calls you "sir."

"Evening sir," he asks me as he opens the door. "Are you here to join a member?"

"Two of them: Max and Carl Bayer. My name is on file. Hang on…" The Harkness Club is yet another place where I have to dig out my ID just to visit my own family.

That's totally normal, right?

Once management is satisfied that I'm welcome on the premises, I take the elevator upstairs to the gaming parlor. It's a low, paneled room in back. The walls are lined with books, and the furniture is cognac-colored leather. It's not difficult to find Max seated at a backgammon table, rolling the dice with a gleeful look on his smug face.

Get this—my brother thinks backgammon is a real game, but hockey is a waste of time. Chew on that one.

"Hey guys. You're pretty easy to find," I say by way of a greeting.

"Eric! So nice to see you."

The first man to call out a greeting is Max's opponent, who happens to be Chet Engels, Alex's father. I haven't seen him in years, but he looks as spry as ever. I walk (slowly) over and shake his hand.

And now I'm thinking about Alex again, which is something I've been trying not to do.

"Hey, look what the cat dragged in!" my own father cries from a sofa nearby. He's holding a glass of scotch in one hand and a New York Magazine in the other. He tosses the magazine aside. "What's the problem, kid? You don't walk in here for no reason."

So I guess I'm predictable, too. "No problem really," I lie. "What are you two up to tomorrow?"

"Flying to Palm Springs with Chet." He points at Alex's dad. "He's hosting a golf tournament."

"That sounds fun." Let's face it. Anything is more fun than surgery, followed by rehab.

"And I'm going to D.C. for a meeting," Max says, his eyes on the board. "Why?"

"Oh, no big deal. I have to have my knee tweaked tomorrow and somebody has to sign me out of the surgical clinic."

Max looks up from the dice. "Another surgery? How bad?"

"Outpatient," I say. "A small repair to my ACL."

"The same one that tore in college?" Dad asks. They're all staring at me now, worry on their faces.

"Nope!" I say with a plastic smile. "My other knee has decided to join the party."

Nobody laughs.

"I'll call off my trip," Dad says.

"Absolutely!" Mr. Engels agrees. "There will be other tournaments."

"Not necessary," I argue immediately. And now I'm sorry I came. "Honestly. I'll ask a friend. It's really no big thing."

Except I can't ask a friend. They're all going to Chicago in the morning for a game. Literally everyone I know is a hockey player or works for the team. I'll think of something. Or—worst case scenario—I can just talk my way out of the hospital. I've done it before.

"If you're sure," my father says as I sit down beside him. "But what are you going to do about that loft of yours? Can't imagine you're allowed to climb stairs."

He has a point. My studio apartment has double-height ceilings and a sleeping loft. It's pretty slick unless you're on crutches. "I have a pull-out sofa," I remind him.

"When that gets old, come stay in my guest room," Dad offers. "There's always a place for you. And Maisy will spoil you with cookies and milk."

"Thanks, Dad." I guess my weird family isn't so bad. "I might take you up on that." And Dad's housekeeper does make excellent cookies.

"Double you," Mr. Engels says suddenly. He pushes the doubling cube toward my brother.

"*Excellent*," Max says with another smirk.

"Dangnabbit! So it's a terrible idea?" Mr. Engels says, and Max laughs.

A waiter in a black suit approaches me. "What will you have to drink, sir?"

"Uh, ginger ale. Thanks." I'd love to order whiskey, but alcohol the night before surgery is a terrible idea. "And some of those warm cheddar crackers, if they're still on the menu."

"Certainly, sir."

"I love the crackers," my father sighs.

"Me too. And they're going on your tab, so I love 'em even more."

Dad grins.

The crackers are probably twelve bucks or some equally ridiculous price. But they're not even the point of this place. Neither are the fine furnishings. The club's real luxury is the company of other people. In this room, it's against the rules to use your phone. There's no Wi-Fi, either.

Dad and Max probably pay fifty grand a year *each* for the sole purpose of rolling back technology for a few hours a week. Max plays backgammon, and Dad plays poker. There's a masseuse on staff. You can get your shoes shined or your hair cut without an appointment. There are billiards tables, dart boards, and even air hockey. There are racquetball courts in the basement.

But it's all about the camaraderie—rich guys want other rich guys to talk to after a long day making money. These are the same American titans who earn their billions getting everyone addicted to technology. They come here to play chess on a real board with a real opponent.

Tech used to be the luxury. Now it's the *lack* of it that rich people really crave.

My snack arrives, and I dig in while watching my brother clean up the backgammon board with Mr. Engels.

"I should know better than to double down with you," the older man complains. Then he looks quickly over both shoulders, like a naughty schoolboy. He needs to be sure that none of the stewards are nearby to catch him using his phone.

When the coast is clear, he whips it out and opens a payment app.

I glance at the die. The eight is facing up. Club rules say that no money changes hands, during games, but playing just for fun goes against their nature. They play for a hundred dollars a point. They'd like to play for more, but the payment apps would be obligated to investigate all those chunky transactions for money laundering.

Mr. Engels finishes his transfer and pockets the phone. "Well, Carl. I'm finished getting slaughtered by your firstborn. Let's eat before we head to the airport?"

Dad jumps up.

I rise, too, but slowly. "Have a good trip. Dinner soon?"

"Yes!" I get a bear hug. "Take care of yourself, son. Let me know how it goes tomorrow."

"No problem. The surgery is no big thing. It's all about the recovery time."

"Then I hope the physical therapy gods are feeling beneficent." Dad gives me one more slap on the back before he goes.

After the older men leave, I sit down across from Max, offering him a cracker.

"Play a game?" he asks.

"Nah. We already know how that would turn out." My childhood was spent trying to get Max to shoot hoops or kick the soccer ball around, while he tried to get me to lose at Monopoly or poker. We never liked the same things. Never.

"Is it a long surgery?"

"No, it's only a long recovery."

Max grimaces. "Sounds like a blast."

"Oh, it's super fun."

"You could ask Alex," Max says.

"Ask her what?"

"To sign you out of the hospital," he says. "Fair's fair. You got her out of a jam once, right?"

I did, and I don't regret it. But there's no way I'm asking her. She still hasn't returned my call, and I don't make a habit of being pathetic.

Still, it doesn't mean I'm not curious about her. "How's she doing, anyway? Did she get her paperwork signed?" I do the math. If her baby is coming around New Years, that's less than two months away. She must have a big round belly by now.

I shouldn't be sitting here wondering how that looks on her. But I am.

"Not yet." Max shakes his head. "Soon, though. It's taken longer than we'd hoped."

"Shit, why?"

"Tatum hasn't been approached." Max picks up the dice and drops them back in the velvet cup, where they make a satisfying click. "I had trouble getting dirt on him. None of his ex-girlfriends would admit to any abuse. One of them looked terrified when I first said his name, but she wouldn't tell her story. She said they broke up because he left blobs of toothpaste in the sink."

"*Seriously?* Do you think he paid them off?"

Max shrugs. "Not necessarily. Women learn fast not to speak up against a rich guy with a mean streak. And then the cycle is self-perpetuating, because the asshole gets away with it again."

Jesus Christ. "What happens if he can't be pressured into signing?"

"Oh, he will be. The reason we waited so long is that he's launching a road show for his next round of funding. He's desperate for cash, and he's lying to potential investors in his disclosure materials. Now we'll get 'im. Either he signs, or we embarrass the hell out of him."

"But…" That doesn't sound like enough leverage to me. "Isn't every business presentation full of half-truths?"

Max gives me another of his maddening shrugs. "It doesn't

matter. He's bet everything on this startup. He can't afford to lose it."

I shift in my chair, unsatisfied with this scenario. Although nobody asked me.

My brother smirks. "You still have a thing for Alex, don't you?"

"No," I grunt. Of course I do. But every guy knows better than to give his big brother more ammunition. "I just know how worried she must be."

"You shouldn't have gone there with her."

"She's a big girl," I grumble. "Didn't need your permission."

"No kidding. But it's just so messy. Her dad is one of our dad's oldest friends. She's my client. I'm legally prohibited from saying a word about her to anyone. And my mopey brother is sitting here pestering me for details."

"I'm not mopey," I mope.

He grins.

"I'm just having a shitty week."

"I can tell. Why don't you let me send one of my guys to pick you up at the hospital tomorrow?"

"Nah. I got it covered." Sort of. My new plan is to ask the Bruisers intern to do it.

"Hang in there, Eric."

"Thanks." But I wish people would stop saying that to me. I get up slowly from the chair, while my knee screams.

"Want to have breakfast before I leave tomorrow?"

"Can't eat before surgery, Max."

"Ah." He makes a face. "Sorry."

"Yeah. Night."

I go home alone.

"WOW, THERE'S A VIP ELEVATOR?" asks Duff, my newest driver and bodyguard.

"You bet."

The doors swing open. "After you, Miss Alex." He holds out a hand to allow me to step in first. Duff is twenty-two years old and cute in the same way that way that puppies are cute—with lots of tireless enthusiasm.

"Just wait until you see the owner's suite. It will blow your doors right off."

"Awesome!" His tongue is practically hanging out at the prospect of watching a Brooklyn game from a box hanging over center ice. Tonight, Brooklyn is hosting Pittsburgh. It should be a terrific game.

Duff is the only one who knows what a big hockey fan I've become this season. Usually I watch at home, camped out on the sofa in my den, shouting at the TV whenever Eric Bayer takes the ice.

Since I own a cable TV company, I have an eighty-five inch flat screen. It's almost like being there. I can watch beads of sweat roll down Eric's larger-than-life, lickable face in complete privacy.

Except once I screamed so loudly that Duff—who's usually stationed outside my apartment in the hallway—came running in. "Miss Alex? Is everything okay?"

Everything was *not* okay. "That was a terrible call!" I'd shrieked. "Get that ref some glasses. I think he must be blind."

"No way." He'd watched the replay in horror. "So who's on the first line tonight?"

That's how we became hockey pals. And now—when he's on duty and I'm not traveling—we watch the game together. It's basically my whole social life. I work like a dog for ten or twelve hours a day, then I make popcorn to watch hockey with my man-child security guard. I'm too busy and too pregnant to make new friends. Also, I've been avoiding my old friends.

Until tonight.

We emerge from the elevator on the VIP level. I waddle down the hallway, belly first.

"You know which way to go?" he asks.

"Sure thing. Last season I came to a couple of games." It was just a social event for me, though. I wasn't invested in the game. I didn't have a favorite player.

"Why'd you stop?" he asks.

"Just busy." It's only partly true. I've been avoiding my friends for too long now. But here I am, ready to show my face again.

And tonight is the night because I'm a nervous wreck. My legal team *finally* met with Jared Tatum today. Mere hours ago he was informed of my pregnancy and asked to relinquish custody.

So I spent the afternoon checking my phone for messages. And when my lawyers finally called, they told me that the meeting went as well as it could be expected. But that my stunned ex had asked for a few days to read the documents and to get back to them.

"He'll sign, Alex," my lawyer said. "Give him a little while to get his head around it."

But waiting is hard.

Tonight—when I was just home from work and contemplating Nate's emailed invitation to the game—my phone rang. It was Jared Tatum.

I didn't answer it, of course. My lawyers have urged me not to communicate with him directly. But I took it as a sign to get out of the house. I'd opened the door to the hallway where Duff sat.

"Hey, how about a change of plans? Let's watch hockey from the rink this time."

He'd leapt out of his chair. "Seriously Miss Alex? Me, too?"

"Of course. But we have to leave soon. There will be traffic to Brooklyn."

"I'm ready *any* time."

And now here we are, walking down the VIP concourse toward Nate's box. "It's that door," I say, pointing.

"Cool," the kid says. "This is so awesome. And maybe we can ask someone when Eric Bayer is gonna play again?"

"Sure." I feel my face heat, though. Because I don't want anyone to guess my other reason for coming to Brooklyn tonight. My favorite hockey player has been missing for three games. Last week, when I tuned in to watch Brooklyn play Chicago, Eric wasn't on the roster. And when I asked Bingley where he was, he informed me that Bayer was out with "a lower body injury."

I'm familiar with his lower body. And it's a shame if any part of it is injured. So I guess a subtle inquiry wouldn't be out of place. "If it comes up, I'll ask Nate."

"Miss Alex," Duff says with a chuckle. "It's okay to be a fan girl. Everyone has a favorite player. Your secret is safe with me."

But fan girl doesn't even scratch the surface. I haven't been able to stop thinking about Eric. It's been four months since that trip to Hawaii, and not a single day goes by where I don't wonder where he is, or what he's doing.

But I never returned his call to my office, because I don't trust myself. If he came over to visit me, I'm pretty sure I know what would happen. Or worse—I know how bad I'll feel if it didn't.

"Do we have, like, tickets?" Duff asks as we approach the door. "Or do we knock?"

"The pass code is on my phone. Hang on." I pull it out, and discover a message from Eric's brother, Max. **Call me**. "Oh, geez. I have to make a call."

"Right now?" Duff whines.

"Yup. Your boss wants to talk to me." I step to the side, because the game is about to start. It would be rude to take a call in the suite. But if Max has news for me, I need to hear it.

"Alex," Max answers on the second ring. "How'd it go with the lawyers?"

"No news yet. I was hoping you had some."

"No, sorry," he says quickly. "I'm calling about your other problem."

"Oh." I deflate. It hasn't been a good month at work, to put it mildly. There was a fire at the factory in China where we manufacture motherboards for The Butler. My launch had been going well until our supply chain was abruptly threatened. "What's the news?"

"I've come across some evidence of sabotage."

"You're *kidding* me. Who'd want to sabotage the Butler?" The board will lose their minds. They already are. I've spent the week fielding calls about our sudden halt to production. "Are you *sure*?"

"I'm confident. And I'm working on a theory about who did it. Have you found another source for the hardware?"

"Several. I haven't chosen one."

"Is Xian Smith one of the potential distributors?"

"He did call."

"Take the meeting," Max urges me. "Ten bucks says he offers you better terms than anyone else, on more units than anyone else can give you before Christmas. But then you have to turn him down."

"Wait, what?" My head spins. "Max, if he really can bail me out, I'll have to do what's best for the shareholders."

"Let's talk more about this in person," Max says. "Soon."

"You sound very paranoid right now, even for you."

Max laughs. "You pay me a lot of money to be paranoid. Can I see your list of potential new manufacturers? I'll tell you why soon."

"Sure. I have to go."

"Enjoy the game," he says.

I hang up, realizing I never told him I was going to the game. Then again, it's Max's job to know where I am at all times.

His man Duff is already doing a tap dance outside the door. So I quickly key in the entry code and pull open the door.

As I enter the suite, several people turn to face me at once. "Hi, stranger!" Nate calls out. "Come on in."

Rebecca—that kind soul—also finds the will to smile at me. "So glad you made it." She pops a potato chip into her mouth. "Let me take your coat."

"Thank you," I say, feeling sheepish. "Your sweater! It's adorable."

"Thanks!" she glances down. It's purple cashmere and the Bruisers logo is stitched right in. "Nate had it made for me."

"I love it."

I remove my coat, and Becca lets out a little squeak as she takes it from me. "Well! Hello, baby!"

My hand goes instinctively to my belly. "Can't really hide it anymore, can I?"

"Not so much. But you look great! Can I grab you a soda and a snack?"

"I'll get it, Becca. Don't miss the game on my account."

She turns to hang up my jacket, and I actually follow her toward the quiet corner where the coat tree stands. "Hey, Becca?"

"Hmm?" She turns around.

"Thank you for inviting me tonight."

"Oh! We're happy you could come."

"I almost didn't," I admit. "I still feel bad that I was a jerk to you."

"Buddy, no." Becca laughs as she drapes my coat over a hook. "I don't think you cornered the market on bad moments. And anyway, it's all forgotten. Go eat some cheese puffs. The faceoff is in five minutes. Who's the young stud?"

I glance at Duff, who's smiling like he just won the Super Lotto. "My bodyguard. He's a Brooklyn fan, so I brought him with me."

"Excellent. Let's get this party started."

I tell Duff to make himself at home. And when I head over to the drinks table, Nate is there, handing me a glass. "What's new? I feel like I haven't seen you in ages."

"Oh, you know. Running an empire keeps me off the streets." There is a lovely cluelessness to Nate that makes this all easier. He probably doesn't have any idea that I've been avoiding him out of embarrassment.

"Feeling okay?" he asks, grabbing a Diet Coke, his drink of choice.

"I feel great. But *fat*. And maternity clothes are a drag. All those shapeless waistlines. On the positive side, people always offer me a chair when I walk into a room."

He cackles. Then he gestures toward the plush seats at the end of the room, open to the rink. "Take your pick. We're going to win tonight."

"Is that so?"

"It's going to happen."

"Then I'd better find a seat." Smiling, I glance around the familiar room to see who else is here tonight. Georgia—the team publicist—is chatting with Hugh, the general manager. And seated down in front are several men in suits. I spot Stew, Nate's right-hand man at Kattenberger Tech. He's accompanied by their CFO. I should probably say hello.

One man is sitting alone, though. And just as I'm admiring his broad shoulders in his suit jacket, he turns his head.

Grey eyes are the first thing I see. And they're set in the same rugged face that stars in my best dreams. Okay, *all* my recent dreams. I have no idea why Eric Bayer is right here in the box, instead of down on the ice. But I do probably know why he's giving me a look that's one part surprise, one part irritation, and one part hot.

"Wowzers!" Duff says. "There's our guy right there!"

Oh dear. I've made another small miscalculation. Go figure.

I give Eric a startled smile, and then turn back to Nate before he realizes that his hockey player is giving me a hormone rush.

"Hey—I heard about the factory fire." Nate says. "That's frustrating. Can you get more components before Christmas?"

"I'm covered through the holidays. But after that, things get hairy. It's going to cost me." I hold Nate's gaze, but I can feel Eric's presence just a few yards away. I still feel the pull.

Over the public address system, the M.C. announces a ceremonial puck drop. "Here we go!" Nate says cheerfully. "Better grab a seat."

He takes his soda and goes to sit down beside Becca. I fill two small plates with snacks, handing one of them to Duff. "This is for you. Grab a soda whenever you wish."

"This is super fun Miss Alex. Best night on the job, ever."

"Glad to hear it." I take a ginger ale and then head toward the chairs. There's a free one right beside Eric. "Is this seat taken?"

Slowly, he stands up. Then he puts both hands on my shoulders and kisses me on the cheek.

"Jeez!" Duff shouts, taking a seat behind us. "Plot twist."

"*Duff.*" I give him a warning glare.

"Don't you want to sit with your date?" Eric asks me, eyebrows raised.

"I'm the bodyguard!" Duff says with obvious glee. "I'm good right here where I can see all the action. But maybe you can tell us why you're missing games? We've been wondering."

"Have you now?" Eric eyes me with growing amusement. "Maybe if you ever called me back, you'd know."

"Whoa!" yelps Duff.

Kill me already. I sit down primly beside Eric and crack open my soda. "I'm sorry I didn't call you."

"Uh huh," he says. "Busy running the world, I guess. You didn't expect to see me here tonight, did you?"

"No, that's just lucky." I meet his gray eyes with mine, hoping he believes me.

Our gazes lock for a long moment. His is cool. And after a moment he turns back to the ice, where the game is about to begin. "What brings you to Brooklyn?"

"I needed to get out of the house."

"Why?"

"I'm waiting for the lawyers to tell me how it went with Tatum."

His head whips around. "Today was the day?"

"So I'm told."

"How you feeling about your chances?"

I shrug. "The lawyer seemed confident. But then Jared tried to call me tonight."

"You didn't answer, right?"

I shake my head. "I'm not that stupid. But I'm pretty curious to know what he would have said." I pull the phone out of my pocket and peek at it. "He didn't leave a message."

"Maybe he decided he's not that stupid, either."

"What do you mean?"

"Max would find some way to use it against him. That man could find a way to blackmail a nun."

My heart rate doubles. I'd rather not blackmail anybody. "Dare I ask why you're watching from the box tonight?"

"I had to get out of the house."

"*Eric.*"

He laughs. And then he turns slightly to address Duff as well as me. "I had knee surgery last week."

"Oh shit!" Duff says. "Sorry, man."

"So am I," I add, looking down at his knee as a reflex. But all I can see is a slight bulge in his trouser leg where the bandage must be. "How long is that going to set you back?"

"Hard to say," he grunts.

"That's all I get? I promise not to call ESPN." The puck has dropped, so we both lean forward to watch the first line do battle for the puck.

"It's not my favorite topic, Engels."

"Sorry," I say quickly. "Bingley would only tell me that you were out with a lower body injury."

"You asked Bingley about me?"

Whoops. "I was upset about the loss to Ottawa."

"Huh. I don't think you mentioned you were a Brooklyn fan. In fact, I could swear you said you didn't like hockey all that much."

My shrug has as much nonchalance as I can summon. "I watch a game now and then."

"Do you now?"

Duff snickers.

"I was upset about that loss, too," Eric admits.

"Devastating," I quickly agree. "That missed opportunity in the first minute of overtime? Atrocious."

He laughs. "I don't get it."

"Don't get what? The net was wide open!"

He drops his voice so that only I can hear it. "I don't get why you never returned my call. After you sent that card."

"Oh." I'm not really prepared for this question. "I wanted to call."

"And?" He gives me an arch look. "You broke your thumb and couldn't dial? Oh, wait. You have Bingley for that."

"*Eric*." Down on the ice, Brooklyn makes a series of aggressive passes. "I didn't call, because I didn't think it was a good idea."

His gaze is focused on the play below us. "It's okay. I'm used to being everybody's bad idea."

Ouch.

"You look great, by the way," he says, without glancing in my direction.

"You're just being nice. I look like I swallowed a soccer ball."

Still watching his buddies down on the ice, he gives his head a little shake. "It looks good on you. All of it."

"Well, thanks. You don't look so bad yourself."

He rubs his unshaven chin. "I get it."

"You get what?"

"The bad ideas." he whispers. "I have those too when I look at you."

Heat blooms across my face, and I make a concerted effort to keep my gaze on the game below. Although I have no idea how it's going. Because my concentration is shot.

I pick up a cheese puff and take a bite. I try to settle in and watch some hockey. But it won't be easy. I'm sitting next to the hottest man I know, and every night when I close my eyes, his naked body rides through my dreams.

It was four months ago. But the memories are still fresh. Eric bucking against me in the bathroom. Eric hovering over me in bed. Eric kissing me inside the elevator.

"Cheese puff?" I offer in a strangled voice.

He gives me a single head shake, and a glance that tells me he can see right to the heart of me and read all my dirty thoughts.

NATE WASN'T WRONG. Brooklyn looks solid tonight. Near the end of the second period we're up two-zero. But then our defense bobbles a little, and Pittsburgh gets lucky with a goal right between Silas Kelly's legs.

"Jesus fucking Christ," Eric mutters beside me. His hands are white knuckled on the armrests. And when Leo Trevi draws a penalty a minute later, Eric's jaw locks up.

The period ends while we're trying to fight our way through the power play, and Eric looks like a bomb about to blow.

I stand up. "We can rebuild it," I insist, getting to my feet. The fact that pregnant ladies always have to pee is one cliché that's one hundred percent true. "Need anything?" I ask Eric before I go. "Drink? Snacks? Valium?"

He shakes his grumpy head. "No thanks."

"All right then. You hang in there."

I head for the ladies' room, Duff at my heels. "You never let on that you know Eric Bayer," he says. "You think it's okay if I ask for his autograph?"

"Sure. Why not."

I ditch Duff at the door to the ladies' room. But Rebecca is inside, reapplying her lipstick. "How's he doing?" she asks me.

"Who?"

She rolls her eyes. "Eric. He's been a bear this month. I think he'd dive out of the box headfirst if it meant he could play."

"He didn't share much," I admit. "I got the macho brush off when I asked about his knee."

"Men." She blots her lipstick. "They won't give him a timetable for returning to practice, yet. He's frustrated."

As a matter of fact, he did seem awfully brittle. "Was it a big surgery?"

"Not at all. But he was already having trouble with his right knee. So when his left ACL tore, it doubled his troubles."

"Oh no!" I gasp. "His *other* knee? Not the one that was giving him trouble this summer?"

Becca's eyes twinkle. "Did you have a summer fling with my hockey player, Alex? How did I not know this?"

"Well—" God, I don't even know how to answer that. "Just a brief one?" I squeak.

"*Fabulous!*" Becca laughs. "You two would make a cute couple."

"Not hardly." I pat my belly. "This pretty much means I won't be dating anyone for years."

"I don't know." Becca caps her lipstick. "I've heard stranger stories."

Well, I haven't. And anyway, I have to pee. "I hope Eric gets some good news soon," I say, hoping to shift the topic off of me and back onto him.

"These guys are used to a certain amount of pain and uncertainty," Becca says. "But I'm worried about him. The doctor asked him to think about retirement, but he won't have that conversation."

"*Retirement?*" I freeze on the way into a stall. "Really?"

Becca blots her lips. "He might need a surgery on the other knee, too."

"Oh."

Oh.

"Retirement happens to every athlete at some point," Rebecca says. "Either they get cut because they're not performing. Or—like Eric—they're terrific players but an injury compromises their ability. It's never easy."

Of course I know she's right. But I also know how much Eric must hate this. Hockey is everything to him.

Poor Eric.

22

ERIC

I WATCH Alex leave the suite, because I can't help myself. Her body is rounded in the middle. But it only makes her look more lush. She's all curves and shiny hair. And the scent of her perfume is addling my brain.

The bodyguard gallops after her, holding the door, and then they disappear.

Fuck. I wish she hadn't come tonight. While I'm sitting on my ass in a chair instead of down on that ice where I belong? It's literally adding insult to my injury. I'm just off my crutches. There's a cane on the floor beneath my seat. I can't stand the sight of it.

Doc Herberts won't even make a guess about when I can return to practice. And he still wants to talk about a second surgery on the other knee. But that one might be much worse. A month on crutches instead of a week. I'd lose the whole season.

Herberts hinted that I might want to consider retirement. I told him I'd retire when I was dead.

He didn't laugh.

Alone now, I drop a hand to my right knee, which aches all the time. I grab the bottle of ibuprofen out of my pocket and dry swallow two of them.

When Alex returns, Nate buttonholes her. He asks her a question about a factory fire, and then asks her to sit with him.

Nobody distracts me during the third period. We eke out a win, which ought to make me happy. But I'm a grumpy bastard anyway, and not in the mood to celebrate with my teammates.

I wait in my seat as Alex and Nate leave the suite together. Can you blame me for not wanting to limp past Alex? When I finally walk out, the VIP mezzanine is mostly empty.

I've almost made it to the elevator when I hear the tapping of high heels coming my way. "Next time I come to the game, I'm sure you'll be on skates."

"You bet," I mutter, hitting the elevator button.

We get into the elevator together. "Can I drop you somewhere?" Alex asks. "I could ask the driver to take the Manhattan bridge after we swing past your place."

The truth is I don't have a car lined up. And even if the circumstances suck, I don't mind more time with Alex. "Can I hitch a ride to Manhattan?" I ask her. "I'm staying at my dad's place for a few days."

"How come?" Her forehead creases with concern. "Is he okay?"

"The old coot is *fine*, I promise." It's me with all the issues. "My apartment has a loft bed and my doctor doesn't want me climbing stairs. I'm sick of my pull-out sofa."

"Oh. I'm sorry. Of course I'll drop you at your father's place. He lives in the West 70s, right?"

"Yeah, thanks." We step into the elevator and I clear my throat. "No news tonight?"

Alex pulls her phone out and unlocks it. "Here. I got a call a few minutes ago but I didn't look. Tell me who it's from."

I take the phone. "Uh oh. I'm sorry to say that your ex called again. No voice message." I notice her caller ID reads: *Asshole Tatum*. "I'm afraid to ask how my number displays on your phone?"

"Well, you're not in there at all."

"Let's fix that." I open her contacts list and add my number myself. I title it *Eric Babe-yer*. Then I hand it back.

"Subtle." She gives me a smile leave the elevator and head for the exit. "I can see the car waiting right outside."

"Dude!" the young bodyguard says as he holds open the back

door of a glossy BMW 5 Series. "It's an honor, man."

"Thanks." I swear he makes me feel about a hundred years old. "I'm headed to Seventy-ninth and Broadway, if you wouldn't mind. The Apthorp."

"No way?" He squints at me. "Say, you're not related to—"

"Carl Bayer? He's my dad. Max is my brother."

"Shut the front door! I knew you were cool."

"Uh, thanks. I think."

Luckily for my grumpy ass, Alex's car has a partition between the driver and our seat. "Now tell me," I ask as soon as we're in motion. "How are you feeling?"

"Busy. Large. It's a strange moment for me."

"How so?"

"I have so much on the line at work. My whole career rides on this expensive project launch. But I also have a baby to plan for. I'm usually *all* about work. I feel guilty when my mind is on other things."

"Ah." I dig my fingers into the muscles at the sides of my knee again. "I've been all about work for just as long as you have. But it isn't going that well right now, and I don't know where that leaves me."

"What's the worst that can happen?" Alex asks. "I mean that literally."

"My contract isn't renewed in the spring, and nobody picks me up. I'll be teamless. This isn't my favorite subject."

"Ouch," Alex says. "I'm in the same boat, really."

"What? You run the place."

"For now. If my new product fails, the board could fire me. Dad's vote isn't enough to save me. That would be extreme, but my general counsel would love to make it happen," she says.

"Whitbread, right?" I remember that dude from Hawaii.

"Nice memory. That's the guy. He's been plotting my destruction since the day I took over the C-Suite."

We sit in silence for a moment. I reach a hand across the leather and take her smoother one in it. She lets me. Her hand feels so smooth against mine. "Listen, Engels. You'll outmaneuver him. I have no doubt."

"I probably will," she says quietly. "But that isn't even my biggest problem. What will I do if Tatum won't relinquish? I can't make him sign away his rights."

"You'll still be okay," I promise. "Max and my dad are pretty resourceful. They won't let you or your daughter feel unsafe."

"I trust them. And I know better than to complain. I have nearly unlimited resources. Can you *imagine* what most women go through if they need to steer clear of a man?"

I shake my head. Because I can't. I'm used to feeling strong and pretty much in control of everything around me. "I'm just glad you don't have to find out."

Her fingers close around mine. "Me too."

We sit quietly while the car glides over the East River and into Manhattan. "Do me a favor?" I ask as the car approaches my dad's neighborhood. "Return my call this time? I need to know what happens."

"Okay. Absolutely," Alex says.

I give her a sideways glance.

"No, I mean it this time." She smiles at me in the glow of the streetlamps. The she pulls her hand from mine and places it on her belly, between the halves of her coat. "Good grief, kid. Take a break already."

"There's kicking?"

"So much kicking. Always at night, if I'm sitting down."

Curious, I move my hand up to her belly. And sure enough, something—some*body*—nudges my palm a moment later. I let out a hoot of surprise. "Okay, that's wild. The baby could only be the size of a kitten, right?"

"The books always compare them to fruits and vegetables. I believe we've reached the butternut squash stage."

She. A very small little girl just kicked me. "Did you paint her room pink?"

"No! Cornflower."

"What's cornflower? Is that yellow?"

Alex laughs. "It's a shade of purply blue."

"If you say so." My hand is still on Alex's belly. We turn at the same time and look into each other's eyes.

The silence thickens. I need to kiss her. So badly. And she doesn't hate the idea, either. I see it in her eyes. So I lean down and brush my lips against hers, asking permission.

Her chin tilts upward.

"Excuse me!" The glass partition descends as we jerk apart. "I'm gonna have to pass your corner, man. It's not a good time to stop." Duff's voice sounds a little tight.

"Why's that?" I ask.

"Got someone following us on a motorcycle since the stadium. At first, I thought it could be a coincidence. I don't like sounding paranoid, but he's *still* back there."

I turn around and squint out of the window. The glass is darkly tinted, but I can just make out a Triumph riding two cars back. "From where in Brooklyn?"

"Right outside the stadium. Then I lost him for a while, but he reappeared on my tail on the bridge. Three cars back."

At least the kid is observant. "You call it in?"

"Yeah. Five minutes ago. They're sending backup, but you might be in for a bumpy ride."

I reach over Alex's head for her seatbelt and stretch it low, under her belly, clicking it into place. Then I take care of my own. Then I pull out my phone and text my dad. *911 You home?*

Duff turns sharply onto seventy-ninth, heading for the West Side Highway. That's a good impulse, since New York City stoplights make us vulnerable.

No. Why? Dad replies immediately.

Bummer. If he were home, he might've extracted Alex from this car himself. *I'm in a Company car with Alex on your block. We might have a tail. Young driver is trying to figure out how to play it.*

Head downtown. I'm calling Max.

Roger.

"Go south to headquarters," I tell Duff. "That comes from Carl."

"Okay," Duff says. "Light's turning red. Damn it."

The car in front of us decelerates, leaving Duff no choice but to stop. I tuck Alex against my body and slide down a few inches, taking her with me. There's probably no reason to panic. But there's no reason to be an easy target, either.

"He stopping?" I ask.

"Not sure," he says, voice calm as he watches the mirrors.

"Give me your piece. I want both your hands on the wheel."

He only hesitates for a second. Then he unholsters a Glock and passes it back to me.

Alex's eyes widen as I check the gun and then stash it in the seat pocket, the handle where I can reach it. "Hey now, we're just being paranoid."

But the red light seems to last all year. I hear the motorcycle rev. And then the sound begins to edge closer, as if the bike is idling forward past the other stopped cars. In two seconds he'll be right here beside the car…

Duff jerks the car out into the empty oncoming lane, shoots past the car in front of us and brings us across West End Avenue before the bike manages to overtake us.

"Jesus Christ and mother Mary," Alex gasps as the acceleration pushes us back against the seat.

But I'm strangely exhilarated. Duff wouldn't have done that if he didn't have a clear path. And the kid happens to handle this car with the finesse of a racetrack veteran.

Nice hire, Max.

The car leaps forward the short distance to Riverside, where Duff runs a yellow light to beat feet onto the West Side Highway onramp.

Then we're flying. "Is he still with us?" I ask.

"I don't see him. Yet."

The radio squawks. "Duff—your backup is Scout in a black Mercedes. Two minutes until she's on your six."

"Copy." At this hour, the West Side Highway is clear. He keeps us at high speed until he sees Scout on our tail. Unfortunately, the highway slows down as we approach the midtown traffic lights.

"You hanging in there?" I ask Alex, who's pasted to my chest.

"Sure. But I've had easier days."

I chuckle as Duff brings the car through a traffic light, scanning for trouble. "ETA five minutes."

"We're good back here," I say, lifting Alex's hand and bringing it to my lips.

Duff rolls along at a speed that's calibrated to hit each light when it's green. Scout's voice crackles through the radio. "I have a motorcycle at seven o'clock. Black helmet. Black jacket. Triumph. That your guy?"

"Sounds like him," Duff says.

"Okay. Falling back."

Now this I have to see. I straighten up and turn around just as Scout executes a plodding lane change. She drives the Mercedes like a pokey elephant. So the motorcycle has to slow down momentarily. Then, anticipating his next move, Scout does a snappy lane change back in the other direction, boxing the guy again.

To free himself, he pulls up beside her. But now he's stuck behind a minivan. So he reverses his plan, falling back and moving in behind her.

She brakes. Then jumps forward. And then anticipates his next lane change.

Scout is a badass. She slowly maneuvers him toward the far right lane, and then Duff peels off to the left, leaving Twelfth Avenue and the motorcycle behind.

"That was fun to watch," I say, turning around again.

"I am sorry I couldn't watch," Duff says, turning sharply down Twentieth Street.

"You both have a strange idea of fun," Alex murmurs.

Duff makes a succession of quick turns as we head for the secret rear entrance to my brother's building.

"The van behind you is also friendly," someone says into the radio.

"Copy."

"We're ready for you at the back door."

And then we're there. A metal door rolls open just before Duff can pull inside. I hear it rolling closed again immediately behind us.

The car stops. Someone knocks on the window, and Duff disengages the locks.

The side door opens, revealing my brother's smiling face. "Didn't know you'd be dropping by tonight. Come on upstairs."

23

ALEX

MY HEART IS in my mouth. And it isn't until I have to get out of the car that I realize I've plastered myself to Eric.

Hastily, I peel myself off his comforting body, allowing Max to take my hand.

"Let's all get on the elevator together," he's saying. "I don't want to fuck around with security badges at this hour."

"Okay," I say, voice shaky. We're moving through the garage, and my senses are reeling. I'm vaguely aware that the collection of vehicles around me is extraordinary. In addition to a few ordinary cars and SUVs, there's a Maserati, a Con Ed repair van, a Jeep Wrangler, a jacked-up minivan, and an armored car.

There's even a small yellow school bus. I can't imagine what that's for.

On shaky knees, I allow myself to be shuttled into a modern brass elevator. A wide, steadying hand lands on my lower back, and I lean back into Eric's protective embrace without even thinking.

Max presses his hand against a sensor, and the elevator glides smoothly upward for a while. When the doors slide open, I don't see offices, though. Instead there's a beautiful loft apartment with brick walls and tall windows, the lower portions of which are hidden by velvet curtains in the color of smoke. City lights filter in through their arched tops, illuminating a suite of funky furniture and thick rugs covering the wood floors.

I've heard my bodyguards gossiping about Max's private lair before, but I wasn't sure it was real. "He could survive the zombie apocalypse up there," they whisper. "It's a fucking bunker. Even the windows are bomb proof."

I hope some part of that is true, because I am *freaked out* right now.

"Sit down," Eric says, gently steering me toward the sofa. "That's it." I'm eased onto a deep, velvet sofa with a high, curving back. The style is a cross between Sumptuous Men's Club and Alice in Wonderland. Eric props my feet onto a leather foot stool and covers me with a thick throw of ivory-colored wool.

But then Eric walks away from me, and I'm not okay. I force myself to breathe deeply. It's possible that I've been holding my breath since Broadway and Seventy-ninth streets. I glance around the room and notice how solid this place really is. The beams crossing the distant ceiling must be a foot thick.

I'm at the top of one of the most fortified buildings in Manhattan, I remind myself. *I'm fine*. Although the hockey game feels like it happened a month ago.

I close my eyes and try to relax.

The sofa depresses under someone's weight a few minutes later. "I made this for you," Eric says. "But you don't need to drink it."

I open my eyes. "What is it?"

"Apple cinnamon herbal tea."

The spicy scent reaches me, and it's almost as comforting as this sofa. "Thank you," I say, sitting up a little straighter. He passes the mug into my hands, which already feel steadier. "Thank you," I say again, pulling myself together. I take a tiny sip, because the tea is too hot to drink yet. But the heat is bracing and just what I need.

Max prowls around his space, turning on some music. Ella Fitzgerald's crooning starts up from speakers hidden somewhere nearby. He pours a bit of whiskey from a crystal decanter into two glasses. He crosses the room and hands one to Eric, who is seated beside me. "Just a nip. The night isn't over yet."

"Whatever you say." He takes the glass and inhales deeply. "How many decades old is this one?" He sips carefully.

"Four," Max says, settling into a leather chair. "Life is short, so I only drink the good shit."

"Oh, I've noticed."

There's a low chime from the direction of the elevator. Max sets down his drink on a dark wood table and crosses to a small control panel. He glances at the screen, then places his palm onto it before walking back to his seat again.

A moment later the doors slide open. Scout strides out in leather pants and a form-fitting sweater. She marches over to where Max sits and slaps a piece of paper down onto the table beside him. "Here's his license plate number."

"Nice work, as always." Max lifts his chin and takes her in, a smile playing at his lips. "Feel free to reward yourself with a nip of this Glen Keith. Not too much, though. You'll be driving again tonight."

She doesn't cross to the decanter like I expect her to, though. Instead, she takes Max's glass right out of his hand and gives it a sniff.

"Hey, I'm drinking that."

Scout takes a sip, as if he hadn't spoken. "Nice." She hands it back to him, and then disappears toward the sleek kitchen in the corner. I wouldn't actually be able to tell that it's a kitchen except for the tea kettle sitting on one of the sleek surfaces. And because when Scout tugs on a panel, it opens to reveal a refrigerator. She pulls out a bottle of Mexican soda and opens it with a tool that's hanging off the set of keys on her belt.

She is riveting, honestly. She reminds me of a black cat—quick and graceful and wholly at ease in her body. If I ever felt like that, I can't even remember it now.

Whale mode is my new normal.

Max taps his watch and speaks to someone. "Trace this Jersey license plate: 2 Alpha Lima Quebec 3."

Ella Fitzgerald sings on as Scout joins us in the main seating area, taking the leather chair beside Max's, tossing her short legs over the arm of it and swigging her soda.

"Okay, debrief," Max says. "Where did the motorcycle find you?"

I explain Duff's Brooklyn sighting, and the subsequent events. "The kid can drive."

"His dad is a NASCAR champion. And he has the best eyesight of anyone on my team. I talked him out of becoming a Navy SEAL." Max sips his whiskey. "So what do we know?"

"Motorcycle man has a trimmed black beard and a small stature," Scout says. "He wasn't Jared Tatum."

"I could have told you that," I hear myself offer. "I never heard him mention a motorcycle. Golf is more his speed."

"He's at home watching golf right now, as a matter of fact," Max says. "It's the first thing I checked."

"But wouldn't Tatum hire someone to intimidate Alex?" Eric asks. "Cowards outsource."

"Maybe," Max says, and his tone makes me think he isn't a believer. "It's not as easy to pull off as the movies would have you think, though. You can't go to goons.com and order up a guy in creepy black motorcycle goggles. And it's only been ten hours since Alex's lawyers dropped their bombshell on him."

"Maybe he has a crazy little brother, too," Eric says.

Max shakes his head. "Only child. Besides, I've been monitoring his phone. The first person he called after the lawyers left was his mom."

"Oh," I say quietly. He called his mom for advice. "That's not what a deranged man does."

"Not generally, no," Max says quietly.

We all sit with that idea for a second. And then I ask the obvious question. "If Jared Tatum isn't trying to scare me, then who is?"

"I don't know, but I intend to find out," Max says. "What if this has more to do with your factory fire than with your baby?"

"But…" A factory burns down in China. What does that have to do with me? "I still don't follow the logic. Intimidation would be a ridiculous idea. I'm never doing business with anyone who tries to frighten me."

Max drains his scotch. "It doesn't all add up yet. But I'm going to figure it out."

I hope he does.

"So what's the plan for getting Alex home?" Scout asks. "It's already midnight."

"She'll have two guards tonight, not just one," Max says. "I've already woken Pieter to send him home with Alex and Duff."

"I'll go," Eric says beside me. And I throw him a quick, grateful glance. I don't know why I associate Eric with safety. But I just do.

"No," Max says. "I got other plans for you. We're going to pull a classic maneuver. You're driving Alex's BMW out of the garage. But Alex won't be in it. I'll put Scout on your tail, so it *looks* like the same caravan the biker followed earlier. Then I'll depart in a third car and then Duff, then Pieter and Alex in a fourth car. Nobody takes a direct route."

Max really is a smart man. "So, if that motorcyclist is still out there, he won't know who to follow."

"Right," Max agrees, tucking his hands behind his head. "It's a classic for a reason. We'll leave in fifteen?"

"Sure. Thank you."

"Just doing my job, ma'am." Max gets up and makes a call, peeking out of the heavy curtains as he talks.

"How's that appetite of yours?" Eric asks. "Want a snack before we leave?"

"No thank you." Now that my hands have stopped shaking, I could totally use a snack, but I've had enough of being the helpless pregnant lady tonight. Except for one thing. "If you could point me toward the bathroom, though?"

"Sure." He stands up and takes my hand. When we walk around behind the sofa, I see a doorway I'd missed. It's a hallway, and the first door opens into a powder room. "You okay?" he asks me before I can slip inside.

"Yes. Really," I promise. I give him a smile just to make the point.

The smile I get back makes me all squishy inside.

It isn't until after I close the door on Max's beautiful bathroom

—with glass subway tiles and bamboo towels—that I remember what happened right before our car chase unfolded.

Eric was just about to kiss me. And I was just about to let him.

And now I'm really enraged at whichever psycho stopped that from happening. Kissing Eric would have been a bad idea. But I would have enjoyed the heck out of it.

I'M FEELING calm again by the time Max assembles us on the garage level again. He hands my car key to Eric. "Good thing the surgery was on your left knee," he says.

"Good thing," Eric grunts.

"You want a vest? The car is armored, though."

He shakes his head. "If our stalker tonight had wanted to fire some shots, he would have already done so."

"My thoughts exactly," Max agrees. "Drive over to the east side, okay? Cruise past Alex's place on Park Avenue. Take your time. Then cut across the park and leave her car in Dad's garage. With the key in it. I'll have Duff get the car tomorrow."

"Sure thing."

"If you're followed, call it in." He gives Eric a back slap and turns away to make sure everyone is ready for our mission.

Eric gets into my car looking as serene as a man who's out for a Sunday drive. I don't even get a chance to say goodnight to him. I'm shown to the back of an armored van. I hear the garage doors open, allowing Eric to drive out. And I have no idea when I'll see him again.

The ride home is completely uneventful. I'm yawning up a storm by the time Duff and Pieter open the door to the van and escort me through my own building's parking garage and upstairs to my apartment.

Before they leave, Pieter does a walk-through of my apartment, checking to make sure there's nobody here except us. I don't know if they're actually concerned, or if they're just trying to make me feel safe.

"Looks good," he says after a few minutes of peering into bathrooms and closets. "We'll be right outside in the hallway if you need us."

"Get some rest," Duff adds. "And I hope you have a really boring day tomorrow."

"Will do," I promise

AFTER ALL THAT EXCITEMENT, I sleep like the dead. When I open my eyes on Saturday morning, it's bright in my room. Too bright.

I sit up fast. Well, as fast as a girl who has to use both arms to push her bulk off the mattress can.

The clock on my bedside table says 9:45. *Holy hell*. I haven't woken this late since college. I must have slept through my weekend alarm. Which means I've missed whale yoga, which is a shame because the preggo class is only offered at nine a.m.

Damn. It.

After a trip to the bathroom, I put on a bathrobe and take stock of myself. I've been an early riser my whole life. Waking up at 9:45 feels like half the day is gone already. Also, I'm starving. So I guess it's time for brunch.

In the kitchen, I pull an omelet pan out of a drawer, and then eggs out of the fridge. And also the feta cheese. I'm out of onions though, which is a bummer.

"Bingley," I call, because my Butler keeps my shopping list current.

Or he's supposed to. But right now he's silent.

"Bingley. Hello?"

Silence.

What's worse than technology failing you? Being failed by your own technology.

Leaving my brunch fixings behind, I walk over to the main unit. The power light is off. When I pick up the Butler unit, I realize why. Bingley is unplugged.

Okay, that's weird. I would never do that. But maybe Duff or

Pieter tripped on the cord while checking out my home last night. I plug the butler back in, and the light winks on.

I go back to my meal prep while counting under my breath. "One one thousand. Two one thousand." I get to sixteen before Bingley speaks up. "Hullo, Alex! How can I help you on this fine evening... Whoops! Fine *morning*. I'm just buttoning my jacket. One more moment, please."

"No problem, you slacker." I wish the plug-in lag were shorter, and I make a mental note to ask the development team about it. "So you're sleeping on the job, Bingley?"

"Apologies, my queen! I pray you have mercy on me. My power source was disconnected at 11:05 p.m. by an unknown person."

Back at the counter I crack an egg into a bowl. Unfortunately, 11:05 can't be right. I wasn't home for more than an hour and a half after that.

So something in the software is buggy. *Lovely.*

"Bingley, when was the last time we interacted?"

"You spoke directly to me at 6:15 p.m. The last time I heard your voice was at 7:05 p.m."

That sounds about right. "Play that back, please. The last two minutes."

There's a brief pause, and then I hear the audio of my own apartment just before Duff and I left for the hockey game. I hear the door open, and my own voice saying thank you as Duff holds it for me. And then the door closes again.

Okay, nothing weird there.

"Bingley. Now play the last two minutes before you were powered down."

"Yes, my liege! Playback from 11:03 p.m.

At first, there's just silence. And I hear a thump, and a bump. For some reason, I get goose bumps. I don't hear the sound of the door, though. And I don't hear voices.

Hmm.

I strain to hear anything more, my whisk poised above the eggs in the bowl so I don't miss anything. Not that the three of us were very quiet when we returned last night.

And then another bump, followed by a man's whisper. "I'm in." Then? Nothing.

My heart begins to thud like a kick drum. Because there was a *stranger here in my apartment*. Holy shit.

"That is all Miss Alex!" Bingley says cheerfully.

But I feel bile rise in my throat. I set the whisk down silently, as if someone might still be here listening. And I tiptoe slowly through my empty space to the front door. My apartment door has a peephole in it. And when I peer through it, I can see the chair where the bodyguard sits.

It's empty.

My body flashes cold, and I quietly back away from the door without touching it. Where is my phone? I tiptoe through my own living room like a thief in the night. Back in my bedroom, my cell phone sits right where I plugged it in before I went to sleep. I lift it and tap the screen to unlock it.

But nothing happens. And I notice that the lock screen shows only the time—not the photograph I took of New York from the window of the jet. With a sweaty hand, I tap the phone again. And when it refuses to unlock again, I try the pass code, instead.

PASS CODE INCORRECT.

I reach for the land line, which luckily, I still have, because I own a cable company that packages all these services together. I hit the talk button.

No dial tone.

That's when I scream.

24

ERIC

"GOOD WORK TODAY," Chip says.

"Thanks," I grunt at the therapist, accepting the towel he hands me. I'm starving, and all my muscles are screaming. I swear Chip is trying to kill me.

Rehab is the worst. Ask any athlete. It's all pain without much gain. It didn't help that I was up late last night driving around the city like one of my brother's operatives.

And now I have to hustle to make my lunch date. Although "hustle" is a relative term on a knee you're trying to rebuild. I walk slowly down the Brooklyn sidewalk, taking care to use a measured gait that would make Chip proud.

I pass myself in the plate glass window of a Brooklyn cookie Shop. My reflection shows a guy in the prime of his years, looking fit and healthy after a morning workout. I only *feel* old, I suppose. And did I mention that rehab sucks?

My phone buzzes with a text from my agent. *Eric, I hope you're almost here because I ordered two hot appetizers. We're starting with the Thai wings and the avocado tacos.*

Thank God for Bess Beringer. She knows exactly how to cheer a guy up. *I'm so in. Order me the pulled pork sandwich with fries. I'm two minutes away.*

When I finally walk into the bustling restaurant, she waves me down from a table in the corner that's already loaded down with a bread basket so appealing that I nearly let out an unmanly whimper.

"Hey, Bessie," I say as she stands up to receive a kiss on the cheek.

"Sit down, sit down! The focaccia is barking our names."

I take my seat and we dig in. "Good to see you in New York," I say after my first bite. "What's the big occasion?" Bess is based in Detroit, so I don't see her on my home turf very often.

"Get used to it. I plan to spend more time here," she says. "I need to see more of my brother and his family. I'm not getting any younger."

"Same," I grumble. "And that makes your job harder. This spring you need to convince the Bruisers to hang on to my geezer ass. And you're probably renegotiating Dave at the same time, right?" Bess's brother is my teammate, Dave Beringer. I expected him to sign an early extension over the summer, but then it didn't happen. I wonder if the team is balking at resigning two of its older players.

Bess can't tell me. She would never reveal the confidential negotiations of another player. But I'm sure hoping she says something to put my mind at ease. Anything really.

I'm reaching for the breadbasket again when she grabs my hand to give it a squeeze. "Eric, if you rehab like a trooper these next few months, Brooklyn *will* offer you an extension."

"Did you hear something that I didn't?"

"No. But I don't need anyone to tell me how valuable you are to your team. You bring so much more to the room than your score tally. Without you, they'd have a really young forward lineup. You have wisdom that the younger guys need time to develop. And your temperament is rock solid. Coach Worthington knows better than to staff himself with a bunch of young hotheads. So it's not all about points."

"Yeah, sure." This sounds like something an agent says to a client who's in a perilous position. "It's only, like, ninety percent about points." Luckily, I've got months to prove that I can come back.

"You don't have to listen." She shrugs. "The rehab is the same either way. At least until the moment you have to decide whether to have that other knee surgery, or to wait."

"I haven't made any decisions."

"Uh huh. You forget that I know you. You're going to avoid that other surgery and try to skate on your right knee. You're going to do the macho thing and play through the pain. And that's your choice. But promise me you won't hurt yourself just because you're worried about your contract extension. That's not the most important thing."

"Of course it's the most important thing. What else is there?"

She sets down her butter knife and gives me a green-eyed glare. "Your *life*, dumbass."

But hockey is my life.

"Look." She goes back to buttering a piece of bread rather violently. "You told me after your 2012 season that you regretted putting off that shoulder surgery. That you never wanted to play another entire season in pain. You said, 'I got the stats I wanted, but I was miserable from December to May.'"

"Good memory," I mutter. Because that does sound familiar.

"Yeah, well I hope my memory isn't better than yours. If you put off the meniscal repair because you're so desperate for a contract extension, it might be 2012 all over again."

"Except for the part where I'm seven years older."

"Except for that." She shoves a piece of bread in her mouth and then waves over a waiter who's holding our platter of wings.

"I need that contract extension," I remind her. "And so do you." Fifteen percent of nothing is nothing.

"Not if you're miserable, Eric. Not if you regret it."

This is why I trust Bess. This is why I signed with her when she was just a green agent at a big shop. And this is why I followed her to the boutique firm she runs now.

Just as I'm picking up a chicken wing, she points her phone at me and takes a photo. "Say cheese and thank you!"

"What's that for? Social media?"

"Well, you're wearing a tight Brooklyn shirt and dining in a local restaurant. The fans will eat that up. So thanks for the suggestion. But I really took it to send to you later."

"For what?"

"Someday soon, you'll find this photo in your inbox. And you'll say—'oh yeah, I remember eating avocado tacos with Bess on a day when I thought avocado tacos were all I had going for me. She was right. I have so much to celebrate. Actually Bess is a genius.'"

"That doesn't sound like something I'd say. And what the hell is an avocado taco anyway?"

Even as I say it, another plate lands on the table, laden with tiny little taco shells stuffed with bright green guacamole. And my mouth waters on command.

I pick one up and bite into the creamy, spicy goodness. And, wow. Avocado tacos might actually be the best thing in my life.

"Take another one," Bess says. "If I eat all those, my ass will be as wide as the F train. Besides—rehab takes energy."

She's not wrong. So I reach for another one.

AFTER LUNCH AND A NAP, I'm feeling almost human again. So I do some stretches in the practice facility gym and wait for my workout buddy to show up.

"Drake, you're late!" I call from the mats when the rookie finally walks in.

"Dude, I didn't know you were coming!" He removes his backward baseball cap and grins at me.

"What do you mean? It's Saturday, right?"

"Yeah, but…" he drops his gym bag. "With your knee, I thought you'd skip."

"Skip chest day? Who's going to motivate you? Who's going to teach you about nineties grunge music? Put some plates on the bar." I clap my hands together. "Let's go."

"Wait. Isn't it my turn to pick the music?" Drake asks.

"I guess." Last time I put on Soundgarden, and the rookie claimed he'd never heard "Black Hole Sun" in his short little life.

Kids these days.

Drake fires up some Twenty-One Pilots, which I can live with.

And I slide onto the bench for the warmup set. The music is already pumping when I push the bar overhead for the first time.

"So it's chest day!" the new trainer says, strutting into the room like a muscle-bound peacock. His name is Gino, and he enters bodybuilding competitions when he's not training hockey players. "Anybody need a spot?"

I sit up after my set. "Drake will need you in about ten minutes. I'm not allowed to spot him on this knee yet."

"No problem. I'm here for you guys."

We rotate through some sets, and Gino spots Drake when the weight starts to climb. And when Drake steps out to refill his water bottle, he spots me, too.

"How's your knee?" he asks between sets.

"It'll get there. I have daily PT with Chip."

"No, I meant your other knee. The stiff one."

"Oh. The same, I guess."

"You gonna have the surgery?" he asks. "I wouldn't."

My first reaction is a grumpy one. *Who asked you?* But I'm curious anyway. "Why wouldn't you?"

"If you let them tidy up your meniscus, that's a big, destabilizing surgery. Guys never really come back from that. Not at the same level."

He's not a doctor, I remind myself. "I'll take that under advisement," I grunt.

"But there's a lot we can do to make you more comfortable. You could have some injections in the right knee and play like a champ just as soon as your left knee is ready."

Now he's got my attention. "What kind of injections?"

"Hyaluronic acid. Or corticosteroids. I know a doctor you can see for that. He trains at my gym. He can take care of your pain, and the swelling, too. You could finish the season."

"What's his name?" I hear myself asking. Nobody mentioned this option to me, and now I wonder why.

"Ivanov. I have his card in my locker."

"Yeah, okay. Do that." A little research wouldn't hurt, right?

Drake comes back. "Ready to switch it up?"

"Sure. Leverage decline press?"

"Let's go!" the youngster says. Then he shakes his hips. "This is the music, geezer. This right here."

I squirt him with my water bottle, and he lets out a howl. "That's for calling me a geezer."

To think that I get paid for this job. It's like summer camp every day.

WHEN FIVE O'CLOCK COMES, I shower and then check my phone. The screen lights up with texts from teammates who are trying to decide between poker and clubbing. I don't feel like weighing in, because I haven't decided if I'm going out.

First, I'll need to call Alex to see how she's holding up.

But just as I'm putting my gym shoes back into my locker, the phone rings. It's a number I don't recognize. But there's an icon of a skeleton key beside it, meaning that the call is coming from someone inside The Company.

I answer immediately. "Hello?"

"Eric! This is Duff. The bodyguard from last night?"

"Sure, man. What's up? Is there a problem?"

"Sort of." He drops his voice. "Alex is in a bad way. There was a break-in last night. A real pro job."

"A break in… where?"

"Dude—her apartment. These guys repelled off the roof of her building and came in through the kitchen window. There was nothing on the hallway security video."

My heart leaps into my mouth. "Jesus Christ. Was she *home?*"

"No! It was earlier. While we were busy evading that motorcycle, they broke in and planted a device that stole the data off her phone."

"Back up," I grunt. "So the motorcycle was a diversion?"

"Exactly. Kept us busy, right? It was quite the caper—they shut off her internet to prevent any security devices from functioning. Then they swapped out her phone charger for a fake. She plugged in her phone, unlocked it and *boom*. The phone gets a lobotomy. She couldn't tell anything was wrong until this morning when it was too late."

"Oh, fuck."

"Yeah. I mean, she's perfectly safe. These guys were after her data, not her person. But she's shaken up. She's in the baby's room trying to build something with, like, hammers. And she won't let me help. I was wondering if…" He pauses.

"If what?"

"If you could, like, calm her down."

I let out a snort. "You're sending me into the lion's den?"

"Something like that."

But of course I'm going over there. "How about I pick up some dinner and come by in an hour?"

"Would you? Thank fuck."

"What do you think she'd want to eat?"

"Dunno," the kid says. "Just get a lot of it. She was too freaked out to eat lunch. And when that appetite kicks in…" I can almost hear him shiver.

"Roger. See you soon, man."

WHEN I SHOW my ID in the lobby of Alex's building, the guy behind the desk waves me inside. "They're expecting you." He peers over the edge of the desk at the bags in my hands. "What did you bring her?"

"This and that." I basically cleaned out and entire aisle of prepared foods at Eli's. There are meatballs and pasta salads and olives and pickles. And dumplings. Samosas and some tandoori chicken. Cheeses and charcuterie. I picked up some bagels (plus toppings) and fresh juices and sparkling water. Also cookies.

And a cherry pie.

"Godspeed." The doorman points at the elevator bank. "You want the penthouse level."

When the elevator doors open up, I find a small lobby leading to only one door. Alex clearly has the entire floor to herself.

Duff rises from a chair parked just outside her door. "Dude. I thought you'd *never* get here. I've been fired three times tonight just for offering to help her. But it's hard to watch her with that hammer. I've got 911 on speed dial just in case."

I hand him the smaller of the take-out bags I brought. "Here. For you. It's a bunch of samosas and some chicken. Thanks for looking out for my girl."

Duff blinks. "You didn't have to do that."

"Consider it hazard pay. Now let me in so I can assess the threat level."

He leaps to the door and places his palm on a sensor. The light winks green. "I could probably be fired for this. But that would be the fourth time tonight, so I'm kinda used to it already."

"Have some dinner and take a load off. I've got this."

Duff, looking grateful, closes the door behind me.

I'm standing in the entryway of the most beautiful apartment I've ever seen. The foyer is larger than some New York apartments. There's a painting by Jasper Johns on the wall in front of me.

I give myself a mental high five for knowing who'd painted it. And then I walk on, finding myself in a chic but comfortable living space with floor to ceiling windows and big comfortable sofas. *Nice pad, Alex.*

There's a ridiculously fancy kitchen off to my left. It's sleek but approachable. The cabinets are made of a shiny red material, and upholstered stools line the broad marble counter. I set my bag on the island and leave the kitchen in search of Alex.

I pass a den with a giant TV on one wall and a desk on another. No Alex.

But then, from deeper inside the apartment, I hear the sound of banging. And then cursing. "Goddammit!"

Hastening my steps down a thickly carpeted hallway, I move toward the sound of a frustrated female. I find Alex in a room that's painted a cheery purple-blue color. She has her back to me, but I can see that she's using the claw end of a hammer to try to pull a nail out of the wall.

She's dressed in sweatpants, mismatched socks, and a giant T-shirt that reads *MIT Summer Nerd Patrol 2008* across the back. Her hair is half falling out of a messy ponytail.

And I have never seen anyone so beautiful in my life as this creature who's tugging on a nail, cheeks flushed, belly bumping against the wall.

"Alex," I say softly.

She whirls around, hammer out, ready to strike. And when she spots me, she only relaxes part way. "Where did you come from?"

"Duff let me in. Actually, he called to tell me that you might need some dinner and a hug."

Her expression softens. "Did he mention that I'd fired him?"

"That might have come up." I'm still parked against the door-frame because if I leave this spot, I'm probably going to take that hammer out of her hand and kiss her senseless.

"I was having a moment," she says, pulling herself up to full height. "But I'm fine now. I'm not losing my mind, I swear."

"Nobody said you were," I lie.

"Maybe I was a little tense. But I'm not actually in danger. I just accidentally handed ten years of corporate secrets over to an unknown thief. It could happen to anyone."

"It could," I agree.

"But everything is fine now. So I'm finishing the day with something productive."

"Uh huh. Want to take a break from…" I look around the room. There are wooden pieces in two different colors, plus hardware scattered everywhere. "What are you doing, exactly?"

"Putting up some shelves. It's nice of you to come all the way over here, but I need to get this done. Isn't it cute?" She moves a flap of packing paper and shows me a wooden bookshelf that's framed in the shape of a crescent moon. And there's another one in the shape of a star.

"Fancy. Want some help?" I ask, in spite of Duff's warning. "Maybe you could use an extra set of hands?"

"No!" Her eyes go a little wild. "I need to do this myself." She squats awkwardly toward the floor, reaching for a molly. But her belly is in the way. Every particle of my being wants to grab it for her. But I resist, because I think she'd just fire me, too.

Eventually her fingers close around the plastic part, and then she heaves herself up again.

Now I understand Duff's pain. "Listen," I say gently. "At least take a five-minute breather to help me with all this food I brought from Eli's. It's in your kitchen right now. I could bring you a plate."

"Food?" She perks up a little. "What kind?"

"Oh, all kinds. They had those Korean meatballs. And spicy samosas. Tandoori chicken. Bagels with smoked salmon."

She swallows. "Maybe I could take a short break. Thank you."

"Right this way," I say, turning around so that the victory won't show on my face. "There's also a cherry pie."

I'm only about three paces down the hall when Alex passes me, galloping toward her kitchen.

TEN MINUTES LATER, every surface of that marble kitchen is covered with open food containers. I've filled my own plate twice already. But Alex is like the Tasmanian devil of gourmet food, doing laps around the kitchen island, sampling everything again with each pass.

"I need to get a grip," she says, shoving a meatball in her mouth. "But my life is a dumpster fire. Did Max tell you? Someone stole the data off my phone."

"Yeah," I say slowly. "I heard that."

She shoves an olive in her mouth and sighs. "Someone broke into my apartment, Eric. He *repelled off the roof* into my kitchen window. Then he swapped my phone charger for a spy device. And did I even notice? *Nope!* I just plugged in my phone last night. And when it asked me if I wanted to install a new peripheral, I just *clicked right on through*. Then I went to sleep."

"Okay, wow," I say softly. "Must have been creepy to realize that someone invaded your space."

Her cheeks are bright pink. "I screamed like a horror movie cheerleader. The guard wasn't in his chair where I could see him, and the phone was unplugged. I was positive that the zombie apocalypse had begun without me."

"That sounds like a fun morning."

She nods, chewing. "And how was your day?"

The samosa I'm holding pauses on the way to my mouth. It's weird, but I haven't thought about my own dumpster fire since I picked up Duff's call. "My day was okay, I guess." I clear my throat. Alex waits for me to answer, one hand on her rounded belly. And I just want to take her straight to bed. Is it weird that her pregnant body is making me crazy? "I have some big decisions to make pretty soon," I admit.

"Oh." Her face falls. "Want to talk about it?"

"Not even a little bit."

She regards me for a moment. Then she sets her plate down with a contented sigh. "I ate a lot. Even for me. Thank you for being a good friend."

Ouch. Back in the friend zone again. "I did it for Duff, honestly. He's polishing up his résumé out in the hall right now."

She rubs that belly. "I'll apologize to him. I apologize a lot lately." She carries her plate to the sink and rinses it off.

I start closing up all the packages we opened. "I hope this all fits in your fridge. Where is your fridge, by the way?" Every gleaming red panel looks the same.

"Here." She touches a panel and it slides open to reveal a giant refrigerator.

"Huh. No problem, then. Want to watch a movie or something?"

Alex dries her hands on a dish towel. "I wasn't kidding when I said I had to hang those shelves. It's harder than it looks, though. The nails didn't want to stay in the walls. So I had to use screws, and a thing called…a micky?"

"A molly?"

"Right! That. But you need a drill, which I borrowed from the super. And then I drilled two holes that weren't level." She throws the dish towel onto the counter. "But now I think I'm on the right track. It might take me another half hour. And then maybe I could watch a movie?"

"Okay," I say easily. She still looks strung out to me. But maybe the food will help.

"There might be beer in my fridge. I usually have some in there for when my dad stops by. Help yourself?" She pads out of the kitchen and heads back toward the baby's room.

I go to the foyer and open the front door.

Duff looks up. He's holding an empty take-out container. "Hey! How's it going in there?"

"Good," I say, taking the container from his hands. "Why don't you take the night off? Go to the gym. Go out for a beer. I'll hold down the fort."

"Really?" His eyes widen. "I've worked a lot of hours this weekend because Max is a little freaked, too."

"Is he now?" I don't know why I like hearing that my brother is capable of panic. It makes him more human, I guess.

"You know. For *him*." Duff shrugs. "I'll call in and see if they would mind if I went home for a nap."

"Good plan. I promise not to leave until you're back."

"I knew you were my favorite hockey player." Duff pulls out his phone.

"Thanks, man."

I go back inside and finish tidying up Alex's kitchen. I brought enough food for six people and half of it is gone. It makes me weirdly happy to feed her, and I have no idea why.

Afterward, I get a beer and then take a tour of her den, turning on the TV and then looking at the magazines spread out on the coffee table. *The Economist. Barron's.* I flip one of them open. The first article is "The Upcoming Currency Crisis."

Nope. I flip it closed again.

And then there's a loud crash in the bedroom.

"FUCK!" I shriek, clutching the star-shaped unit before it can fall all the way to the floor.

Eric hurries into the room, stopping when he sees that I'm unharmed, but surrounded by chaos.

"Everything is fine!" I say in a voice betraying more hysteria than light home repair usually calls for. "All it takes is a couple of simple steps, and I can't even get it right on the fourth try!"

"Hey, Alex," Eric says in the sort of calm voice you're supposed to use on crazy people. He eases the unit out of my hands. "Can I ask how much shelving you've hung before?"

"None. Obviously."

"Then why the hell wouldn't you let me just help you for a second?"

I take a deep breath of air all the way into my diaphragm. "Please take your manly self into the next room and watch some television. I need to do this myself."

"Because?" His pretty eyes are stormy.

"Because I just do."

"Are you trying to make me crazy, here? Or does it just come naturally?"

"Hey, guess what? This isn't about you. This isn't even a little bit about you. I just want to build my own freaking shelf."

"Is it the pregnancy hormones? You live in a fucking gorgeous apartment. But I would bet my left nut that there isn't a single thing in this place that you built yourself. Why start today?"

"I'm having a child."

"I noticed that."

"I was once a child, as were you. However, I lived in a house where everything was done by the help. My parents never did a thing for me with their own hands. That summer you spent with us on the Vineyard — do you remember my father ever making us a sandwich?

"No."

"That's not the kind of parent I want to be. So I am hanging my child's bookshelves. Even if they are the *worst bookshelves ever seen* in New York City. Perfection is not the point. I'm doing it because I care, and I want my child to know that."

"Oh," he says quietly. "I see."

"You know that expression: born with a silver spoon in your mouth? My kid's spoon is from freaking Cartier. Money is not our issue. But we are going to have plenty of issues."

"Okay."

"You think I'm crazy."

"No." He shakes his head vigorously.

"You're still looking at me like I might flip out at any moment."

"Only because you're swinging a screwdriver around while you talk. I'm just trying to make sure I stay out of the way. I've had enough injuries already this year."

"Oh." I look down at my hand where there is, indeed, a rather large screwdriver. "Sorry. Thank you for listening."

"Anytime." The corners of his beautiful gray eyes crinkle, as if he's trying not to smile. "I'll be in the other room, with the world's worst magazines."

He leaves, and I go back to work. I drill a new hole for the molly, and then I tap the plastic anchor into the wall with my hammer. But it doesn't really want to go in. Part of it hangs out even when I've hammered at it for quite a while.

Whatever. This part will be hidden, right? I take one of the screws and fit it against the ugly molly, then I screw it in about halfway, until I can't get it to go in any further.

The last step is to lift the star once again, and then line up the hole in the back with the screw. Clearly the manufacturer expects me to have x-ray vision. I wiggle the star back and forth, trying to hit the hole. But I can't seem to find it.

Honestly this would be easier with a little help, but I can't ask now. I've already scared off all my help. I wiggle and wiggle until finally the screw engages with the hole. Then I ease the shelf onto the screw before stepping back to admire my work.

It looks amazing. For about two seconds. And then it leaps off the wall and lands with a crash at my feet. I look down and see wreckage. There's a big scrape on the fresh paint, too, where it nicked the wall on the way down.

And I burst into tears.

Then Eric is back again, pulling me into his arms.

"For fuck's sake!" I sob into his shoulder. He feels so good, though, and I'm just *done* with this day. "All I wanted to do was hang a damn shelf for my baby girl! Idiots can do this!"

"You're not an idiot, though," he says, patting my back. "That must be the problem."

"That's…" I hiccup. "You're too nice to me."

"Nah," he says. And then he bends down and actually *picks me up off the floor*. Which is amazing, given my size. But there's a lot of junk on the floor, and he has trouble maneuvering.

"Eric, your knees," I whisper.

"Yeah." He sighs and eases me to the floor again. "Can we get out of here, though?"

"Yes." I take him by the hand and lead him out of the baby's room and down the hall to my bedroom, where my tissue box is. I sit down on the bed and grab a tissue, wiping my eyes.

Eric sits down beside me. Then he wraps both arms around me and pulls me down onto the bed, holding me tightly. "Everything is going to be okay. You know that, right?"

"Yup." But it's a lie. There's no proof that *anything* will be okay. My eyes leak a little more, just to prove that they can.

"Oh, honey," he says, pushing the hair out of my face. "Max will figure it out."

"Will he? I doubt it was Jared Tatum who had us followed."

"Shh." He rubs my cheekbone with his thumb.

"It's someone else. We don't know what they want. My poor kid! It's bad enough that half her DNA comes from an asshole. But now I have to try to keep industrial spies out of her nursery."

"Mmm hmm," Eric says sweetly. "But we will."

I take a deep breath and lean into the sturdiness of his body. I rest my forehead against his, and he blinks at close range, those gorgeous gray eyes looking into mine.

And, wow. I'm horizontal on a bed with Eric. How did this happen?

The kiss happens in slow motion. He lifts a hand to cup my cheek. But it isn't a casual gesture. His touch is hot, and his eyes challenge me not to ruin the moment.

As if I even could. My whole being just waits for him, anticipating his mouth on mine.

And he doesn't disappoint. He tips my chin upward and then quietly fits his lips against mine. The slide of his kiss, and his masculine scent are all I need right now. His arms close around me, and I lean into the kiss. His whiskers are scratchy against my face. But his lips are soft.

For a moment, though, I try to hold back my heart. I've spent the whole day vibrating between strength and despair. If I let myself go—if I let Eric hold me and take away my fear—I honestly might not find the dignity to pull myself together again afterward.

But his kiss is slow and convincing. It asks all the questions and then answers them at the same time. *See how much you need this? Yes.*

Don't we understand each other? Yes.

Are you going to let me taste you one more time?

Yes, I really am. The second I part my lips, we're making out like teenagers in the middle of my bed, his hands in my hair. No matter that my giant belly keeps bumping up against the hard planes of his abs. I strain to move even closer to the heat of his mouth, and the eager slide of his tongue against mine.

And even though we don't line up exactly the same way as we did in Hawaii, I can feel his body beckoning to mine. Our legs intertwine. My face is flushed, and my nipples are hard, and my lips are bitten from his kisses.

But this is not Hawaii. "What are we doing, Eric?" I gasp.

"Stress relief," he grunts as his hand moves temptingly along my ass.

"But we're not a couple." The effect of my argument is muted somewhat by the whimper I let out as he kisses me again.

"So you say," he says between kisses. "And yet you're stroking my cock."

Oh hell, I am! My palm goes still. Even through the fabric of his jeans, I can feel how hard he is. And now I'm clenching my thighs against the desire that's already pooling there.

"Well, sure," I stammer. "I really miss your cock. But on the other hand, I'm so—" It's just dawning on me that getting naked in front of Eric might be embarrassing. The sports bra I'm wearing could shelter a small village. "I'm a bloated *whale*."

"Maybe I have a thing for oversized marine life." He kisses me again. Then his hand dips into my yoga pants, coasting over my ass.

And I stop worrying, at least temporarily, because I lose my train of thought. Eric kisses the way he does everything else—with understated skill and intelligence. And great reflexes. His hands mold and press. His fingers tease my skin, while his tongue stokes me toward heat and heaven.

"You're a crazy man," I moan between kisses.

"Where I come from that's a compliment. Unzip me, Engels. You know you want to."

He isn't wrong. And after considering the idea for at least a half second, I fumble for the button on his jeans. If Eric Bayer wants to give this pregnant lady one more fun night, who am I to argue?

It's awfully bright in here, though. There's still a part of me who worries that he'll get one look at my round body and run for the door. "This might be awkward," I warn him.

"Why? Do you have a cat who likes to watch?"

"What? No!" I let out a nervous giggle. "But...I can't be on my stomach. And I'm not supposed to lie on my back. And up against the door is a nonstarter..." I wiggle away from him and shut off the bedside lamp, plunging us into relative darkness.

"You are thinking way too hard," he says, grasping my T-shirt and lifting it over my head. "But thank you for wearing elastic pants." He grabs those and tugs them off, too.

His next kiss shuts me up, which is a relief to both of us. I *am* thinking way too hard. It's my superpower.

But not for long. My hands are too busy pushing down his jeans and boxers. And then my palm finds his erection, with his hard, hot shaft against my hand.

"Now we're talking." His voice is a rough scrape. He sheds his T-shirt, tossing it to the floor.

And now I'm just a little bit sorry I turned out the light, because I'm becoming reacquainted with his impressive abs. I'm on all fours now, tracing my lips across his tight stomach, inhaling the scent of his skin.

Eric kicks off his shoes and pushes his jeans all the way off. *Yes.* And when I dip my chin and take his cockhead into my mouth, he lets out a happy grunt.

"Fuck yes." His hands are in my hair. "Take more."

I moan my assent, and then try to do just that. The truth is that I never enjoyed this before I did it for Eric. It was a part of sex that was expected rather than enjoyed.

But Eric makes me feel like a sex queen as he groans and shifts his hips. I relax my throat and take him as deeply as I dare, and the noises he makes are everything to me.

"Jesus fuck. Yes. Hell," he babbles as I hollow out my cheeks and suck. It's the sexiest thing I ever heard. I don't know why he wants me so badly. It's not because of my money, or connections. It's sure as hell not for my giant, pregnant body.

But God it's nice to be desired like this. To be *craved*. I'm having some cravings of my own. It's not clear to me how they're going be fulfilled. It won't be easy, but I'm already having fun.

"Better stop that soon," Eric rasps.

I release him with a wet pop, because I can't wait to see what he'll do next.

"Come here," he says, slapping my ass. "Lose these panties. And that bra."

"Not the bra," I say quickly. My breasts are too heavy and tender.

"Suit yourself. Just get over here. I need to touch you." He punctuates this statement by running a hand between my legs, over the fabric of my panties.

And my breath hitches as the damp silk brushes against my overheated body.

"You're soaked," he groans. "Get over here."

I step onto the floor to shed the panties. "Better brace yourself," I joke. "Just like you'd do on the ice before a dangerous hit."

"Oh, please. Bracing is a bad strategy. It's better to absorb the impact. Like this." He tugs my hips until I join him on the mattress again. And then I'm straddling him. He lowers me down until I'm crouching over his thighs. "Oh hell yes. *God*," he adds as his fingers make contact with my pussy, which is already ripe and wet.

I moan shamelessly. Even this light touch makes me want to yell his name. "I...I don't know how you're going to pull this off," I gasp. "But I need it so badly."

He clicks his tongue. "I know you do. Is it okay for the baby?"

"It must be," I say quickly. "The baby is already acquainted with my vibrator."

His hand goes still on my body. "Alex," he rasps. "Do you fuck yourself and think of me?"

I brace my hands on his shoulders and lean my achy body into his palm. "Sometimes," I hedge. "Okay. Definitely." I'm glad it's dark in here so he can't see my face turn red.

But Eric doesn't laugh. He's too busy sitting up, grabbing his cock, and lining it up beneath me. And I lower my hungry body down, welcoming him inside for the first time in months. I feel my muscles clench around him.

His moan is long and loud. "Yes," he whispers. "Finally." He tugs my hips down, until I'm taking him so deeply that I gasp. And then he's kissing my neck, and cupping my breasts over the bra, and tracing his lips all over my skin.

Then he takes my mouth, and the kiss is shockingly tender. I feel goose bumps rise on my arms as his tongue greets mine with a slow slide.

My heart gives a kick. I like this man way too much. He has no idea what he's doing to me right now. Tonight he's the perfect imitation of an expectant father—bringing food home to his ravenous, pregnant wife. Offering to help out in the nursery.

Making love to her carefully after she erupts in a hormonal snit.

But it's *not* real. None of this is really my life. I can only pretend that it is.

Pretending has its merits, though. I can rise slowly up on his cock and grind my hips against his as he groans. I can lower my pussy again and again while our kisses bleed onward toward infinity. I can grip his biceps while he kneads my ass and ride him until he makes a more desperate sound with each thrust.

It's a gorgeous, mind-melting imitation of everything I want in the world. And when I finally come, moaning against his tongue, it feels real enough. His strong arms hold me tightly as he buries his face in my neck and clenches through his own groaning, shuddering climax.

But it's over too soon. I come to a halt, still pinned against his big, sturdy body, with hot tears springing into my eyes.

I am not really sure if they are happy tears or sad ones.

GOOD. Lord. If you'd told me six months ago that I'd be having steamy hot sex with a very pregnant friend, I'd have laughed my ass off.

But nobody is laughing now. I'm too busy catching my breath, and then easing us down onto the pillow together. Eyes closed, I tuck Alex's head under my chin. I can feel the rise and fall of her chest as she floats down from the same high I'm on.

And I'm more at peace right now than I have been in weeks. Maybe ever. Maybe it makes me a sap, but none of the bad shit matters quite so much when you're curled up around a woman who makes you smile.

I won't lie—I'm a little startled by how much I've missed Alex. How badly I want her. And by how easy it is for me to picture spending a lot of time with her. I'm invested. I don't know how it happened, but it doesn't seem to be going away.

"Eric," she whispers.

"Mmm?"

"What are you thinking about right now?"

"Umm…" *That I might be falling for someone for the first time in my adult life.* "Sleepy thoughts," I answer, because it's not entirely a lie.

"How's the knee?"

"Fine," I croak. "The same."

"Are you ready to tell me what's bothering you?"

"No."

She pokes me in the side. "Eric."

"Don't kill my buzz, woman. It doesn't get any better than this." I open my eyes and find her blue ones looking at me. "I mean that. It really doesn't."

She falls silent. And if she doesn't outright agree with me, at least she's not arguing. I'll take it.

"I'm staying over tonight," I inform her. "I already told Duff he could leave."

"Okay," she says, burrowing closer. "But I have one unrelated question."

"Mmm?" I could seriously fall asleep right now. That's how deeply relaxed I am.

"Earlier, did you say something about cherry pie?"

I grin without opening my eyes. "I did. You want some?"

But she's already pulling herself up and heading for the kitchen.

I TAKE a quick shower in the posh oasis otherwise known as Alex's spa bathroom. Then we eat giant slices of pie in her bed. When we turn out the light at midnight, I sleep like a dead man.

When morning finally comes, I wake up slowly. And I'm already happy. In the first place, I'm stretched out in Alex's wonderful king-sized bed.

In the second place, her lips are skimming my cock. A groan comes from deep in my soul to erupt as she licks me and then takes me deep.

And to think I was having a shitty week before now.

"Baby," I grunt as she works me over. "You better stop that before it's too late."

She doesn't stop, though. Instead she just looks up and makes eye contact as she gives me a good, hard suck.

"Oh, Jesus. You are really good at this."

She makes a happy sound and bobs up and down on my dick. The view is killing me. Red lips. Flushed cheeks. Satisfaction curls through my chest, down my spine and tightens my balls.

"Okay," I gasp. "You've been warned." With a happy sigh, I lift my hips off the bed and begin to fuck her mouth in short thrusts.

Alex moans around my cock, and that's when I start to lose control.

Most mornings I wake up to a stiff knee, and yet I can't even feel that fucker right now. Because Alex is sucking half of my IQ out through my cock.

I take a deep breath and let myself be pushed over the sweet edge of orgasm. The sound I make is half roar, half gasp. And then I'm spilling myself onto her willing tongue.

Afterward, she rests her head on my thigh with a sigh.

"Baby," I rasp. "I'm trying really hard here not to fall too deeply in love with you, but you don't make it easy."

Alex buries her face against the messy sheets and laughs. "You are such a romantic."

"I know, right?" I flop a careless hand onto her soft hair. But even if my sentiment lacks finesse, it's still true.

Alex's smile says she doesn't believe me, though. And when she waddles off to the shower a few minutes later, I stare up at the ceiling for a moment and wonder what it all means.

The ceiling doesn't answer.

Meanwhile, there's only a few minutes until she'll be back. So I hop into my boxers and T-shirt, and then scoot into the baby's room while I have the chance.

At the risk of making Alex angry, I hang both shelves. It takes less than ten minutes. All I need to do is change the drill bit and enlarge the holes to the proper size. Once the mollys fit correctly, it's a snap to screw in the supports and then hang the star and the moon where Alex had begun them.

I'm just admiring my work when Alex makes a startled sound from the doorway.

Turning around, I brace myself for her displeasure.

But it doesn't come. Instead, her voice is sheepish. "Thank you."

"Sure, baby." I clear my throat. "It still counts, you know."

"What does?"

"Hanging the shelves. You're still using your own hands to make this room ready. Even if I helped you a little."

"I guess. My mom used to cater my birthday parties. But then she made sure to light the candles herself." She rolls her eyes. "I can probably bake a cake, right? Although decorating them sounds hard. If I keep up this stubborn streak, my daughter is going to have some scary looking birthday cakes."

I'll still eat it. The idea just leaps into my brain. As if I'd ever be invited to her daughter's birthday.

You never know, though. Alex thinks she'll be rid of me as soon as this latest craziness blows over. But I'm starting to think that it won't. Craziness seems to hang on to Alex and me with both hands.

And I'm not sure I mind.

She crosses the room and wraps her arms around my waist. "You're very patient with me," she says quietly. "I don't think I deserve you."

Her belly is stretching her shirt out to a preposterous degree, so I absently place a palm on it and rub gently.

Alex's expression goes soft. She stands on her tiptoes and kisses my jaw. I palm the back of her head with my free hand and kiss her forehead. "You hungry? I bet you are."

"Oh definitely." She gives me a shy smile.

I can't stop staring into her eyes. This feels so different to me than I often feel with women. I mean—I love women, and fun is fun. But I usually have one foot out the door. Right now I just want to scramble some eggs and ask her where she keeps the coffee.

And the look she's giving me right back wants all those same things.

"Hey, Engels," I say, just to break the tension. "Stop looking at me that way."

"What way?"

"Like I just hung the moon." I jerk my thumb toward the new shelves.

"Oh, Eric." She lets out a peal of laughter. "That is a seriously bad joke."

"I know. But that's why I snuck in here to do this. 'Cause I was saving that one up. And you haven't fired me."

"Yet," she laughs. "But it's early in the day."

"True."

We're both smiling at each other like crazy people when I hear a knock on the door.

Alex looks down at her bathrobe. "Can you get that? I need real clothes."

"Sure." I'm still in my boxers, but as usual I don't give a crap. So we part ways, and I walk to the front door and open it.

My brother blinks back at me with a sour expression. "Seriously? Again?"

I shrug. "Is there something you need?"

"I need Alex." He holds up her phone—the one that was hacked yesterday. "She and I need to talk."

28

ALEX

EVEN IF ERIC BAYER has just treated me to a twelve-hour break from reality, his brother's appearance does the opposite. First, he searches my apartment for a second time just to make sure there aren't any bugs or other detection devices.

That alone is enough to freak me out. But now he wants to talk.

After I make myself presentable, I sit down on the sofa beside Eric, who reaches for my knee to give it a comforting squeeze. "What did you learn?" I ask.

"First things first." Max sets a shiny K-Tech phone down on the table.

I eye it the same way you'd watch a venomous snake. "Is that mine?"

"It is now. It's a new one, Alex. Nate's team didn't have time to entirely reverse engineer the hack. So—just to be safe—Nate kept your old one and sent you this one. The passcode is 911, but you should change it immediately."

"Thanks." I take the phone with a sigh. "I want to catch this asshole."

"Trust me, we will. And there's some good news, okay? Nate's operating system has some unadvertised security functions. And when the hacking software began copying all your files, it got spooked and locked the phone."

"Wait. I thought the *hacker* locked me out."

Max shakes his head. "No, that was a safety mechanism. These guys only got about twenty percent of the data on your phone."

My heart leaps. "Do we know *which* twenty percent?"

"Mostly recent emails from your ECM account."

I groan.

"But no texts were compromised before the shutdown," Max says. "So that's something."

"Who did this, Max? Could it be Jared Tatum?"

"We'll rule him out today," Max says. "But my suspicions lie in another direction." He sits back in his chair, absently tapping one knee. "I'm working on an espionage theory."

"Oh goody. How much danger am I in?" My hand is already rubbing my belly. I'm already apologizing to my baby and she isn't even here yet.

"The good news is that nobody wants you dead. Probably."

"*Max*," barks Eric as a chill runs through me.

"I'm only being honest," Max says. "But my gut says the culprit is after a financial gain. That said, his methods so far are risky. So we're maintaining extra vigilance."

"Of *course* you are," says Eric through clenched teeth. The two brothers have a brief stare down. "What about those license plates from the other night? Did you get anything?"

Max shakes his head. "They were both faked. Neither plate is registered to a real person."

"That's slick," Eric says.

"Everything these guys have done is slick," Max agrees. "The phone charger in Alex's bedroom was a nice piece of engineering."

"Made where?" Eric asks, getting up from the sofa.

"Probably China. But the software has Ukrainian origins."

Eric makes a noise of displeasure. Then he gets up and leaves the room, and I miss him already.

"So I have a grand theory for why you're suddenly a target," Max says. "And it's the Butler's fault."

"Wait, what? Why?"

"Did someone address me?" Bingley chimes in. "Can I be of assistance?"

"No, Bingley," Eric calls from the kitchen. "Not unless you can make coffee."

Max leans forward in his chair. "Humor me for a second with this exercise. If you could spy on any ten thousand people in the world, who would you pick?"

"Heads of state? CEOs? This isn't a tricky question."

"Right," Max agrees. "Though heads of state typically don't buy and install their own internet hardware. So I'm with you on the CEOs. And if you couldn't pick and choose your ten thousand people, but you had to pick a geographic region, what would it be?"

"Washington, DC? New York City. The Bay Area. London. Hong Kong…"

"Exactly. Alex, this is your problem. New York was second on your list. You have a monopoly over cable internet access in the tristate area. You control the internet connections of some of the wealthiest and most powerful people in the world. And now you're launching an expensive hardware that promises utter security and privacy."

"But…" I don't like where this conversation is headed. "The Butler is not an easy hack, Max. You'd need to hack each device *individually*. Or hack the entire network and find the encrypted node belonging to the home you wanted to breech…"

Max holds up a hand to silence me. "Your software is as secure as anything on the market," he says by way of agreement. "And the Butler's privacy safeguards are exquisitely designed. But what if the hack weren't a question of *software*."

I blink. "That leaves hardware. But nobody could hack the hardware unless they do it during—" I gulp. And now I understand where he's going with this.

"Manufacturing," Max says quietly. "It was that fire at the motherboard factory that got me thinking."

"But—" And now my mind is bounding along after Max's. "So you think someone wants to take over the manufacture of my motherboards. So they can change the design and modify my hardware?"

"With a tracking device," Max says.

"But we'd *notice*," I argue. "We have rigorous quality control."

His eyebrows lift. "Do you? Can you honestly say that your current workflow inspects each motherboard before it's installed in the device?"

Damn it. I flop back against the sofa. "No. You're right. The testing happens when the unit is complete. If the device boots up normally, there'd be no cause for suspicion." Which Max knows. "But *still*. This is the craziest idea I've ever heard. The Butler is smaller than a salad plate. The motherboard is the size of my hand. How would you hide all the electronics you'd need to control the unit?"

"Easily. And I can prove that it works, because somebody has already done it. Do you remember a news item about a major hardware hack of a server manufacturer?"

"Sure. Crazy story." I must have read it a year or so ago. "But that story didn't pan out. Nobody would go on record, and both companies denied that it ever happened. Besides—those servers are big." I spread my hands to indicate the size of a server. "You could hide a forest creature in there."

Max grins. "A forest creature?"

"You're the one here with the crazy tales," I grumble. This conversation is terrifying. If someone—or some nation state—is trying to hack my products, there will be no end to this war. There'd be far more disruption than a simple factory fire.

Max reaches in his pocket and pulls up a small box—the size that might hold an engagement ring. But when he opens it, there's no ring sitting in the velvet crevice. Instead, there's a silicon object the same size as a pencil eraser.

"What is that?" I ask. As if I even want to know.

"This was removed from one of the hacked servers."

"And you have it because…?"

Max grins. "I bought it for my collection. And my guys verified that it's all you'd need to perform a rudimentary takeover of the privacy functions of a server. Or, say, a modem."

"You're *kidding* me." I'm a computer programmer, not an electrical engineer, so this isn't my area of expertise. But that thing is *tiny*.

"No, it's true. The only good news is that you can't just plop it in there anywhere. It needs to be integrated in just the right spot to do its job."

I sink a little further into my sofa as my anxiety meter approaches the red zone. "Shit, Max. I believe you. But why are you so sure I'm the next target? It's a big leap from factory fire to zombie hardware."

"It is," he says. "But you're making a device which promises to have robust privacy features. And rich dudes in New York are going to scoop them up. If I were a hardware hacker, I'd choose you. And furthermore, the hacked servers carrying these—" He picks up the chip from its special box and balances it on his fingertip. "—Were manufactured in a factory controlled by Xian Smith."

"Oh, shit." *Oh, shit. Oh shit.*

He nods. "If it helps, you're probably not his only target. You're merely his favorite."

"How do you know that?"

"I'm sorry, but I can't say. You're eventually going to have to explain this scenario to your board of directors. And I have to protect my source."

Board of directors. My poor, overwhelmed brain hadn't even reached that grizzly conclusion yet. But I'm already sorry I got up this morning.

That's when Eric walks back into the room with a coffee mug and a plate, setting both down on the coffee table. The plate bears both halves of a toasted bagel that's been smeared with cream cheese and decorated with smoked salmon, onions, capers, and cherry tomato halves.

"Please tell me that half of that is for me," I squeak.

"It's all for you," Eric says, laying a hand on my head. "Do you want coffee? Or are we saving the daily caffeine boost for later."

"No thank you. If I have coffee right now, I'll probably start firing people again."

"I'd take coffee," Max says.

Wordlessly, Eric points toward the kitchen.

With a disgruntled look at his brother, Max gets up and heads that direction. "Mugs are over the pot!" Eric calls, sipping his cup.

I pick up the plate and take a big bite of bagel. "You are a prince among men and please let me know how I can return the favor."

"Oh, you're already in my good graces," he says in a sultry voice. He skims a hand down my hair and gives me a sexy wink.

I just want to climb into his lap and be somebody else for a day. I really do.

But Max is already back with a cup of coffee and a determined expression. "Let's talk about your options," he says.

"Who is Xian Smith, anyway?" Eric asks.

"I wish I knew," Max says. "It's probably an alias. I can't find anyone with that legal name anywhere in the world. He seems to have popped up in 2013, selling cheap cameras to drone manufacturers."

"What passport does he hold?" I ask through a mouth full of cream cheese.

Max shakes his head. "I can't find anyone who knows."

"Let's invite him to a meeting and frisk him," I say, shoving a tomato in my mouth. God, espionage makes me hungry.

"I like a good caper as much as the next guy. But he's so slick you wouldn't find anything," Max says. "So let's talk about your options. I can think of three, in order of easiest to hardest."

"Let's hear 'em."

"First one is obvious—pretend we never had this conversation."

"God, it's tempting."

"I'm sure it is. But you and I are the good guys. We don't just let the bastards win." Max sips his coffee and gives me a rare smile. He looks more like Eric when he smiles.

"And the second option?"

"You drop a lot of extra money into manufacturing. Send a team of your most trusted engineers to stand around in the factory while the motherboards are made. Compare the results to your blueprint every few hours. And send more trusted people to watch the shipping container all the way home. You'll blow your budget, but at least you'll know you have clean hardware."

Even as he's speaking, the difficulties are multiplying like mushrooms. I'd have to convince my board to spend a lot of money on a problem that I can't prove we actually have.

"I could manufacture my own product," I say slowly. That's only slightly more palatable though. "But that would cost just as much and take twice as long."

"Yeah, that's why I left that solution off the list."

"What's behind door number three?" I have to ask. "Please tell me it's cheaper."

"Well…" Max chuckles. "I love door number three. It's my personal favorite. And it will possibly save you money. You'd agree to buy motherboards from Xian Smith, while buying them from someone else at the same time. You'd order twice the number you reasonably need. And then we nail his ass when he delivers something dirty."

"It's only cheaper if I can decline to pay," I point out.

Max shrugs, because he doesn't think about these things. He doesn't have to. His business has no cranky board members, and no hungry shareholders. Max runs a fiefdom. And I'm envious.

"Remind me why you like this option?" I ask.

"Because I like to make people pay for their indiscretions. And because he may be backed by a sovereign nation. If we let him get away with this, the bad guys just won. They could use their tools to shut down the whole financial system. Or shut down our legal system. Shut down our power grid. Shut down—"

"Okay, I get it. Jesus. If you had to guess, is Xian Smith a spy? For who?"

Max shakes his head. "I can't guess. China is the obvious answer, given his factory connections there. But it could be anyone. You can no longer say 'China wants this' or 'Russia wants that.' The world is now run by a bunch of billionaire plutocrats with too much money and power, pulling everyone else's puppet strings in the name of national defense. Xian Smith might be working only for himself. At his whim, he might sell information to China, Russia, Iran…"

I rub my temples. "Okay. I get it. I need to think."

"I'll bet you do."

"And I need to think fast. I only have a few days to order the parts I need. Maybe I'll use the guy in Thailand. Nobody is expecting me to do that."

"Send me everything you have on the manufacturers you're vetting. And when Xian Smith contacts you again, wave him over."

The last bite of bagel pauses on its way to my mouth as I realize I'll have to meet with him again. I wonder if he does his own dirty work. That man might have rappelled into my kitchen window the other night. He might have searched my bedroom.

I have never felt such loathing for a stranger in my life. And I'm not even sure that he's guilty.

"Alex, I know this is a lot to take in," Max tells me. "And there's a small chance I'm wrong. Very small."

Eric lets out a bark of laughter.

"It's a crazy thing," I babble. "To hack an entire factory design. Too many things could go wrong. Too many people might notice."

"That is all true," Max agrees. "But you have to weigh the difficulty of a crime against the potential payoff. How much would it be worth to someone to eavesdrop on New York's richest people?"

"You wouldn't be able to control the targets," I point out.

"So? Once the spy chips are in place, you could switch on the whole mess and then search their communications for keywords. *Merger. Acquisition. Prototype.* You could spy on their Slack channels. You could read emails and texts at will. You could eavesdrop…"

"Okay!" I yelp. "I get it. Three years ago all I had to worry about was cord-cutters shrinking my subscriber base. Now I'm at the epicenter of the best hacking operation to ever grace a major American city?"

Nobody argues this point.

I put the plate down and put my head in my hands. "Max, tell me the truth. What does your gut say about my personal safety? And my team's?" *And my baby's.* The timing could not be worse.

He sets down his coffee cup. "It's all about money, Alex. And harming you or your executives just doesn't seem like a great strategy. The only thing that gives me caution is that I'm having trouble calculating the value of the hack."

"Why?"

Max's grey eyes bore into me. They're so much colder than his brother's. "Because the payoff is infinite. Secrets beget money, which begets power. Whomever can pull off the ultimate hack can have whatever he wishes. The price is so high that I can't rule anything out."

It's so quiet now that all I can hear is the wall clock ticking. "We have to nail him," I whisper. "It's the only way to stay on top of this."

Slowly, Max smiles. "You're right. I can do it alone, but it's easier if you help."

"Okay," I say, because I'm not sure I have a choice.

"It won't be fast," he cautions. "The trap we're setting is going to take months."

"And it won't be cheap," I grumble. "We'll have to order the motherboards twice. I'm going to have a fun time explaining this to the board."

"You can't. Not yet."

"Right." My mind is full of strategies and problems. The baby kicks, and I rub my stomach.

It's going to be a really tricky couple of months.

29

ERIC

"WALK ME OUT?" my brother says when he's ready to leave Alex's place. "There's a favor I need to ask."

"Of me?" I gasp. "What could possibly go wrong."

"Come on. It will take an hour, tops. And then I'll drive you home."

His expression is so serious that for once I don't even argue. "Fine. Let me just say goodbye to Alex. Wait here."

I find her rinsing her plate in the kitchen. "Another cup of coffee?" she asks me.

"No thanks. I'm going to head out with Max."

"Oh." Disappointment flashes across her face for a hot second. Then she straightens her spine. "Thank you for feeding me."

"Well, I can't solve many of your problems, but that one was easy. Are you going to be okay here?"

"Of course." She sighs. "But it won't be an easy week. I've put years of my life into that company. I learned it from the bottom up. Did you know I started out in the sales department selling advertising minutes?"

"That sounds like I job I don't want." I move closer to give her a hug. Not that it's easy with that belly in the way.

She wraps her arms around me. "A hundred and seventy-five bucks got you a thirty second spot during daytime TV in the suburbs, on a low rent channel. I sold so many the price went up to two-twenty-five."

"You shark." I kiss her on the nose.

"My father wanted me to understand how the money was made. So it was three years until I had a management job. Every time I began to outperform the old timers, he'd just move me to a different department where I'd start learning all over again. And when I took the helm three years ago, the business media still screamed nepotism."

"You probably saw that coming, though." There's a lot of trash talk in journalism. Ask any hockey player.

"Of course. They're warmer to me now. Or at least until my company sells a device that exposes every Engels Cable Media customer to international identity theft."

"You won't let it come to that."

"No." She shakes her head. "But I hate the thought that one man can lob a grenade at my life's work. God knows how much this will cost us. I hope your brother is wrong. How often is Max wrong, by the way?" She puts a hand on her swollen belly and rubs.

"Well…" That's a tricky question. "He's wrong about me all the time. About matters of security? Not so much."

"I was afraid you'd say that."

"Geniuses are frustrating people," I point out. "That's why you want to stick with a dumb jock, baby. It's my *body* that's talented."

"I noticed that." She reaches up and puts her hand on the back of my neck. "Thank you for sharing your talents with me last night."

Last night has a certain finality to it. I'm pretty sure she's giving me the brush off. "It was my pleasure," I whisper. And then I duck my head and kiss her neck very softly, but very thoroughly, until I feel her shiver.

"Geez, Eric. Your mouth is probably illegal in several states."

"Yours is pretty talented," I point out, kissing my way into the collar of her shirt. When I walk out that door in a few minutes, I want her to remember I was here. "What time is it, anyway?"

She glanced up at a clock on the wall. "Eleven-thirty. That

means I can call Rolf and give him the bad news that we're working on a Sunday."

"Poor Rolf." I kiss her neck, wondering how soon I can visit again.

"He's..." Her body melts against mine. "W-well compensated for the inconvenience of being my assistant."

"Mmm hmm." *Kiss.* "I'd better go." *Kiss.* "And let you get to work, then." Because I'm evil, I suck her earlobe into my mouth until she shivers.

Alex gives my chest a shove. "Go already. I can't think when you do that. And right now, I really need to think."

I give her one more kiss—a real one—and then I leave the kitchen behind.

In the hallway, Duff is seated in the guard's chair. "She doing okay, man?"

"She's doing great," I say. "Your job is safe for another day."

"You're a miracle worker. What's your secret?"

"Don't answer that," Max says under his breath.

"Bagels with all the fixings," I say, giving Duff a wave as the elevator arrives.

Max presses the button for the parking garage beneath Alex's building. We get into his new favorite ride—a Maserati GT. I can't even keep track of all my brother's toys.

His finger hovers over the ignition, but he doesn't start the engine. "Before I take you downtown, I need to know. Are you ready to go to war for her?"

"War," I repeat slowly. "Against whom?"

"Does it matter?" he asks, squinting at me from the driver's seat. "Are you all in for Alex. You need to decide before we walk in there."

And now I understand. "We're going to Tatum's place."

"I am. And you can come with me if you are ready to do what needs to be done."

I lean back in the leather seat and fasten my seatbelt. I know what Max is asking. He told Alex he'd "rule out" Tatum's involvement. But he doesn't mean to use email surveillance this time. "I'm in."

"Even if it gets messy?"

Fifteen floors above us, I picture Alex curled up on her couch, a protective hand over her stomach. And I just know. I'd do anything for her.

"Even then," I agree.

MAX PICKS a parking spot around the corner from Tatum's building. "Don't get out yet," he says, poking at his watch. "We need to give Scout a few minutes to let us into the building."

"What's her plan?" I ask, forever intrigued by my brother's strange job.

"Pork bun delivery," he says. "She has a label maker in the car. Takes her a few minutes to print out a fake patch for a cap or her jacket. They already know that the man eats a lot of pork buns, so they won't question her if she gives them a pretty smile."

"Nice."

Scout is very good at her job because she knows when to let people's expectations do the hard work for her. She's five-foot-two, with a pixie haircut and an easy smile. If she says, "I'm here to deliver pork buns," there are few on the planet who'd disbelieve her.

"Listen, I need to show you something." My brother unfolds a paper from his pocket and hands it to me. "It's an affidavit that Tatum is supposed to sign, admitting to hitting her. It ensures that he can't turn around and easily petition for custody."

I, Jared Tatum, confess to the following behavior... I read it. But when I turn over the paper, I am not prepared for what I see. It's a photo of Alex looking straight into the camera.

With a hugely swollen eye, and a large bruise covering a quarter of her face.

"*Holy* fuck." I suddenly understand what it means to see red. My body flashes with adrenaline, and I swear my vision goes wonky for a moment. Because all I can see right now is my own fist colliding with Jared Tatum's face. "I'm going to *kill* him."

"Eric," Max says softly. "You're not."

And now I am full of rage. "Why the fuck did you show that to me, then? What man could do that? There is not one fucking thing she could ever say to me that would make me hit her. That eye. Jesus."

My brother lays a steadying hand on my forearm. "A stupid man," he says quietly. "But not a habitual abuser."

"What?" I gasp, my hand twitching for the door handle. Just let me at him.

"Listen carefully," Max says in his iciest tone. "I didn't show you that photo to get you riled up. I showed it to you so that you'd understand. A serial abuser doesn't punch a woman in the eye. It's too obvious. Alex had to call in sick for three days until she could cover it up with makeup. This guy lost it when he hit her."

"Who cares? You still can't do that."

"No," Max agrees. "He can't. But there are two things you need to understand before we go upstairs. The first is that if you lose control, you'll be just like him—another asshole with no moral standing. He punched Alex in the face, and he lost her trust forever. You punch him and you could fuck this up for Alex, and complicate your own life, too."

I take a deep breath and try to calm down. I know he's right.

"The other thing is harder to accept. That man will always be that baby's father. Legal documents can put the law on Alex's side. But they can't change biology. And if this man decides someday that seeing his child is his only priority, he may be successful."

"He'll have to go through me," I sputter.

"And you can say that. You can scare him off—but only up to a point. You want to end this. You want to make him disappear. But you can't. Not completely. Not without ruining your own life, too."

I hate that he's right. I hate it so much.

Max checks his watch. "Scout says—*back door at 12:19*. That's my girl! Let's go."

We get out of the car and walk slowly down the block. "How do you want to play this?"

"You'll be out of sight while I get him to open the door. And then—surprise. The jealous boyfriend with the violent day job is back to stare him down. He'll remember you, right?"

"Hell yes. Although I'm slightly less menacing than I was in Hawaii. Good thing I'm not carrying my cane."

"A cane can be very menacing. I have one that is actually a four-way camera. And I have another that's a dart gun."

"Of course you do."

"Admit it," Max says, stopping on the sidewalk. "You love this. The joyride last night was fun. And now you get to scare the bejesus out of Jared Tatum."

"It's not unappealing."

"There's always an open position waiting for you." Max checks his watch. "Give her another minute."

"Max, I don't want a job. I'm only here for Alex. Menacing strangers for pay isn't my style. Unless I'm wearing skates."

"But I wouldn't make you a goon," my brother argues. He waves me forward. "The fun part isn't even the fast cars, or tricking doormen. The fun part is having the drop on how people think. You're smart, Eric. With great reflexes. You could be amazing."

"I'm already amazing," I remind him. And I really don't appreciate the hard sell. But it comes to a natural end, because it's now 12:19 and we're strolling up to the rear door of an apartment high rise.

Casually, Max flashes his wallet for the benefit of the security cameras. He pulls out a card with a shiny mylar finish.

Somewhere inside, the building's security guy may or may not be eyeing the camera that's right above this door. If he is watching, he sees Max wave this card past the scanner. And since the card is so reflective, the security man won't notice that it isn't the right color and style for the building.

And now the door swings open right on cue. Scout, wearing a cap that says Ben's Buns, exits to the street without a glance at us. It will look like pure coincidence to the security guy's eye.

Max pockets his card casually, touching me on the shoulder as if we're deep in conversation. "Sixth floor," he says mildly as we stroll past a bank of mailboxes. We reach the elevators without anyone glancing our way.

Nobody stops us on the way to Tatum's door. I step out of sight while Max knocks.

Max doesn't even have to sweet talk him, because the idiot opens the door without a question. "Yes?" He's wearing a Duke T-shirt and flannel pants. I can hear the TV in the background.

My brother pushes the door open with a cool authority that he's possessed since, oh, the age of four. "Tatum. Let's talk."

"Excuse me? And you would be…?"

I step into the room, and Tatum's face drops.

"Remember me?"

"Well…"

I grab him and push him roughly against the wall. "Do you remember me? Because I remember you. You're the asswipe who gave her a black eye. Every time I punch the heavy bag, I picture your face. Did you know that?"

Tatum gapes at me just in time for me to slam him against the wall a second time. I hear his teeth click hard together from the impact.

"Eric," Max says in a low voice. "Make your point nicely."

"Are you scared right now?" I spit. "Because I need you to remember this feeling. Did you punch her face right here by the front door? Is this the spot?"

His eyes are wide with terror, and it only feeds my anger. Tatum's face is bright red, and his eyes are begging. But I want him to feel pain, too. I want it so badly.

If you lose control, you'll be just like him.

It almost kills me to release him. But I do it suddenly, and he sags against the wall. My heart thumps, and my fists still clench. But I make myself step back. "Every time she hears your name, that's what she remembers," I tell him. "Every time your name pops up on her cell phone, she sees your fist."

Tatum slides out of my reach and sort of staggers over to his leather couch, where he sits down heavily. "I've made a lot of mistakes, okay? I know it."

"How many, exactly?" Max asks, as calm as ever. "Was one of them sending people to intimidate Alex last night?"

Tatum's chin jerks upward. "What? *No!* Is she okay?"

Max is stock still, watching our guy's reaction carefully. "She's fine," he says eventually. "We took care of it."

"Jesus, I hope so." He flops back against the sofa. "Why are you really here? Just to scare me? Like it's not enough to make me sign that affidavit? If that thing ever leaks…"

The fact that his reputation is his biggest concern says a lot.

"We're here," I tell him, "to make sure you understand how serious we are about protecting Alex and her child. It's his full-time job," I point to my brother. "And it's also my personal hobby."

Tatum eyes me with a blend of fear and distaste. Not that I blame him. "Alex has nothing to fear from me."

"Yet the evidence suggests otherwise," Max clips.

"I lost my shit that *one* time." He shakes his head. "Tell me what to do, okay? How can apologize to her? I want to meet my kid someday."

"You have two choices," Max says. "Take her to court. She'll tell a room full of people what you did, and show them the photo of her eye swelled shut. You'll probably lose, though."

Tatum puts his head in his hands.

"Or you can sign the papers, so that Alex feels safe. And you can get therapy and accept what an asshole you've been. And try to make your case to Alex, through her lawyers."

Tatum rises off the sofa, a beaten man. "You want both documents signed? Fine." He brushes past Max, slouching over to a desk in a corner. There's a folder on it, which he flips open. He grabs a pen out of a polished brass pencil cup and hastily signs his name on two different pages. "Here." He shoves the paper back into the folder. In three paces he's thrusting it at Max. "Take it. Full custody. You win. But she can keep her fucking money."

"Wasn't that the whole point of dating Alex?" Max asks. "To get your company funded?"

"No! And fuck you for saying so. We were supposed to be a team. A power couple. Sure, I wanted her family's support. But not like this." He shoves the folder into Max's abs. "I don't want her blood money. But I do want to meet my kid. You tell her that."

"This says you can't." I reach over and take the folder from him, flipping it open to make sure he signed the affidavit, too. "Hey, it's supposed to be notarized."

"I'm a notary," Max says. "I got it."

"A rubber stamp doesn't mean shit anyway," Tatum snarls. "Just like signing that thing doesn't mean I'll forget my kid exists. I will *always* be that baby's father. You can't change that with money or visits from the goon squad."

I wish he weren't right. "Stay away from Alex."

"You call her lawyer if there's something you want to say," Max adds.

He deflates. "Message received. You got what you wanted. So now you can get the hell out of my apartment."

"Don't call," I say quietly. "If you do, I'm the one who's going to answer."

Tatum just gives me the kind of glare that would be fatal if laser eyes were a real thing.

Max takes the folder out of my hands. "All right. Thank you for this. Alex appreciates your cooperation. Just out of curiosity, where were you last night?"

"At a restaurant in the east twenties," he says. "NoMad on twenty-eighth."

"What time did you leave?"

"Ten?" he shrugs. "Then I came home."

"Okay," Max says quietly. "I hope for your sake that's true."

And that's the last thing anybody says until Max and I show ourselves out.

We leave by the back door of the building, walking toward Max's sports car. "Good job in there," Max says. "Do you believe him about last night?"

"Yup," I say tightly. "So who the fuck was on that motorcycle? And who broke in?"

Max just shakes his head.

30

ERIC

"GREAT WORK TODAY," Chip says, as always. He's setting up the stationary bike for our last exercise. "The left knee has good extension. Good flexion. I told you this was going well."

"Yeah you did." Although I'm still weeks away from competing. But it's late November, and—God willing—my team will still be skating into June.

And then there's my other knee. "Hey, Chip? Can I ask you something?"

"Always."

"What do you know about injections for arthritis?" If Gino's right about pain relief, it's something I might want to try.

"Injections?" He adjusts the stationary bike we're using next. "Who's trying to sell you on that?"

"Nobody," I say quickly. "But I heard they can reduce pain and swelling."

"They can," he says, and my heart actually leaps. "But corticosteroids can mimic some banned substances. So you might need a waiver for that treatment."

That sound you hear is my hopes being dashed again. Nobody wants to mess around with the banned substances list.

"But—more importantly—pain is a signal that something is wrong. An injection could mask your pain while you actually break down more cartilage. It would be short sighted to shoot up your knee with a harmful substance just to get a few more months of playing time."

"Gotcha," I say glumly.

Chip puts a hand on my shoulder and gives it a squeeze. "Nobody wants a knee replacement before age forty. There aren't any shortcuts, man. I'm sorry."

"Right." But God I wish there were.

"Feet on the pedals, Eric. Let's finish up. Then you can go home."

HOME SOUNDS PRETTY GOOD. My dad's place is great, but I miss my own bed. So I head back to my own apartment after the session.

During the short walk home, I check my messages. There's a bunch from my dad. *Hey buddy guess what? I …*

I scroll right past, because—for the first time ever—a message from Alex awaits me.

HE SIGNED!!!! He signed the papers! I have them right here! I'm so happy with your brother I could hug him.

Oh man. I wish I could have seen her face when Max handed over that folder. I told my brother I didn't want any credit. Alex doesn't need to know what I did to get that fucker's signature. I don't want to describe how close I came to smashing Tatum's face in.

I'm so happy for her, though. At least something is going right for her. *Don't hug Max! You're supposed to save those for me.*

"Whatcha smiling about?"

I look up to find my teammate Dave Beringer holding the elevator for me. "Oh, nothing." Even if I felt like explaining what's happening between Alex and me, I'm not sure I really know. "I saw your sister for lunch the other day. Is Bess staying with you?"

"She was, until one of her players got a suspension, and she had to fly back to Detroit."

"Fun times."

"Yeah." He presses the elevator button. "I wouldn't want her job. Trying to keep players out of trouble."

"Right?"

The conversation stalls for a moment because Beringer and I aren't very close, in spite of having names that some people confuse with each other's. And even though we're nearly the same age. But Dave is a d-man and I'm a forward. So we run in different circles.

"Look, I've got some news," he says suddenly.

"Yeah?" The elevator rises.

"I decided not to renew after this year."

"Renew…?" A magazine subscription? I try to figure out what he means, and I come up blank.

"My contract. I'm retiring at the end of the season. They're going to announce it in the next couple weeks. But I wanted to tell you first."

"Why?" I blurt, and it comes out sounding rude. "I mean, why retire?"

"Everyone retires eventually," he says. "A year ago the idea gave me the cold sweats. Hockey was literally my entire life. Well, hockey and my sister. That's all I had."

"Uh huh. Not like there's anything wrong with that."

He gives me a quick smile. "Not until it ends."

"But it doesn't have to end for you." He was injured at the end of last season. But he seems perfectly heathy now.

"Yeah, but I want to pick the date," he says. "This way it's my choice. And now I have a family who needs me, so…" He shrugs.

An actual shrug! Like this isn't the biggest decision he'll ever make. "So…" I try to wrap my brain around this development. "You're moving to Vermont?" That's where his girlfriend and his baby live.

"That's the plan." He smiles, and I kind of want to smack him. We have the best job in the whole goddamn world. And you do not just walk away from that lightly.

"Okay," I say. "Thanks for telling me."

The elevator opens on the third floor, and we both get out. "Later, man," he says, heading toward the rear of the building.

"Yeah. See you." I turn in the opposite direction, feeling strangely angry.

Dave is quitting hockey? He's thirty-two. Younger than me, and healthy. I'd give anything to be as healthy as he is right now. And he's just going to throw it away?

I'm so distracted that I almost don't notice the music emanating from behind the apartment door. But just as I'm ready to swipe my key card, I realize that the pulsing beat is coming from inside.

I actually check the apartment number, just to make sure I'm not standing in front of the wrong door. But no, it's mine. I have an intruder. And he's blasting Panic at The Disco on my speaker system.

Can't I get through one day without some kind of bonkers security issue?

I set my gym bag down on the floor. Then I get out my key card and cross my hands on the door handle. I swipe and then unlatch as quickly as possible, throwing open the door and scanning the big room.

Not like it's hard, though. My cousin Anton is perched in the center of my coffee table. And he's dancing to "Hey Look Ma I Made It."

What the fuck?

I grab my bag out of the hall and shut the door. "Hey! Anton!" I call.

He can't hear me. He's busy gyrating in the other direction.

I put two fingers in my mouth and whistle.

That does the trick. Anton finally hears me. His body jerks around toward the door.

Then he falls off the coffee table, landing half on my pull-out couch and half on the floor. "Ouch, fuck! Cousin Eric!" the younger man yells. "You are not going to *believe* where I just got traded!" He beams at me like he's just won the lottery.

And maybe he has. "Is it Brooklyn?" I ask cautiously. He is wearing a purple shirt, and in my apartment no less.

"Dude! You're a genius! This is so rad. We're gonna be team-mates now!"

"No way!" *No fucking way*. I make my way over to the speakers and turn the music down, like the old fart I've become.

"I just got the call this morning!" he babbles. "After I called my dad, I called yours! And then I got on a plane."

"That's amazing, man." I clear my throat. "So, if you don't mind my asking, how did you get into my apartment?"

"Uncle Carl sent me!" he says cheerfully. "He called you first, but you weren't answering your phone."

"Oh. Well, I was at the—"

"I didn't even have to spend a single night in the hotel!" Anton yawps. "Your dad says I can crash here, because you're not supposed to climb into that loft bed right now. Bummer about your injury dude!"

"Thanks," I grunt.

"Carl didn't think you'd mind if I stayed a couple of weeks."

Weeks? "Well, it's a studio, though. Plus that loft," I say, trying to find the right words to express my horror.

I'm sure my young cousin is a great guy. But a couple of weeks with a twenty-two-year-old roommate sounds hellish. I've watched rookies settling in before. Hell, I've *been* that rookie. You just got promoted from the minors to the big leagues. It's time to celebrate. *I've arrived, New York! Hear me roar*.

I wonder how quickly we can find this kid his own apartment.

"It's gonna be epic!" He climbs off the floor. "I need you to introduce me around."

"Okay, sure." I agree. "We'll go to the Tavern on Hicks. The guys are always there. When do you have to sign paperwork?" *Please say right now*.

"Already done! I got the Katt phone, too. Is it weird that I'm almost more excited about the phone?"

"A little," I admit. When Nate Kattenberger bought the team, he gave every player a custom phone to carry.

"Does it really glow with a gold star when we win?" A big smile breaks across his big face.

"That part is true." I don't worship technology the way some people do. But I have to admit that I love the gold star. Not that I've gotten one in a while.

"Awesome!" He jumps up and down in a way that people can do when they don't have knee pain. "So let's get drinkin'! It's early, Eric. We could do some serious damage. I am so high on life right now I could just burst."

Something goes a little wrong inside my chest when he says that, because I used to feel that way, too. I don't carry that kind of optimism anymore. The kind that feels like anything is possible.

Anton does, though. This is his night. And I'm going to do my best to show him a good time.

And then tomorrow? I'll find him somewhere else to stay.

TWO HOURS later I'm on my second beer, my second burger, and my second dose of ibuprofen.

"You okay?" asks Heidi the intern as I chase the pills with water. "I haven't seen much of you since the week I brought you home from the surgical clinic."

"I'm doing great. But I worked out hard at PT." Rehab is harder than playing a game into double overtime. Because you can never have the satisfaction of winning. The only gold star in rehab is being allowed back on the ice.

"I can't believe we've got two Bayers on one team!" Georgia says, eyeing my cousin, who's playing darts with Drake. The two rookies hit it off like puppies at the dog park. "The press is going to eat this up with a spoon."

"It's the coolest," I say, trying to chase away the superstition that we won't actually end up skating together. I should be ecstatic for Anton. But I can't shake the feeling that fate has plunked him down in Brooklyn to take my place.

"One forward, one defenseman," Georgia says. "A Bayer for every need. But the kid needs a nickname, stat. How about Bayer the Younger?"

"I like 'Care Bayer,'" Heidi says, and Georgia giggles.

"Nah," I argue. "He's Baby Bayer all the way."

"Yes!" Heidi shrieks. "*Baby Bayer*. And when he's hungover tomorrow we'll call him Baby Aspirin."

She and Georgia high five each other.

"I'm not drunk enough to be hungover. Yet," Anton yells, a dart in his hand. He lets the dart fly, and it embeds in the wall about two inches shy of the dartboard.

"We have to work on our accuracy," Drake complains. "I think you're a little overexcited."

"Alcohol to the rescue!" Anton yells. "Let's break out the tequila shots."

"Oh man." I shake my head. "It's going to get ugly."

Heidi puts a hand on my shoulder. "Should you drink? Aren't you worried about stability?"

"No!" I snort. "Of course I can drink."

I AM VERY good at drinking.

Yup. I'm a champ tonight. Anton has his big break and we're made of tequila and by… Okay, I have no idea what time it is. But the whole world is a big limey hug.

It might be late, though, because I just looked up to see that all the women are gone. That's a clue. When the respectable people have turned in for the night, it means something.

I forgot what, though.

"Will you take a photo of me in the jersey?" Anton asks.

"Of course," I promise.

"Gotta send it to my girlfriend."

"Send her a jersey," I suggest, because I'm brilliant. Especially tonight. "Put 'cher name right on the back and mail it to her. Then tell her to wear only the jersey and call you."

"Dude, you have it all figured out!" Anton shouts. He shouts a lot. All the time, maybe. "How many goals I gotta score before they make a jersey with my name on it?"

"Dunno," I say, shaking my head. The room is spinning just a bit. "For a defenseman? Five? Ten?"

"Ten! She'll forget my name before that. You got a girlfriend?"

"Hey—I want to know, too," Drake chimes in. He sounds less drunk than I do. "Weren't you dating Alex Engels?"

"Yes no," I say, because I'm drunk, and it best describes the situation. "I have a thing for Alex Engels. But we aren't a couple. I mean, we do all the things that couples do. Really good things. And I want her to be happy, but…" I scrub my forehead. "I don't think she's taking it seriously."

"Bummer," Drake says. "When is her baby due, anyway?"

"*Dude!*" Anton shouts. "You have a pregnant girlfriend? Shut the front door. Nobody tells me anything."

"She is—" I let out a giant belch "—pregnant for sure. But she is not my girlfriend and I am not the father's baby. I mean…" I have to think about it for a second. "I am not the baby's father."

"*Really*," my cousin says. "But then what? After the baby comes, are you two still getting it on?"

"I don't think they can," Drake points out. "After my brother's kid was born, they weren't allowed to."

"Ever?" I gasp.

"Not for like six weeks."

Oh. That doesn't sound so bad.

"So how pregnant is she?" Anton prods. "Like, a little bump in the middle, pregnant? Or, like, dump truck sized?"

"Not a truck!" I insist. "More like a whale. Her word."

Anton's eyes bulge. "And that turns you on?"

"Everything about her turns me on. She's just so…Alex." I sigh.

"Holy fuck. I-I can't believe this," Drake sputters.

"What?"

"Dude, you're in *love*."

"Nah," I say, laughing.

"But you *are*. If you're hoisting the flag for a super preggo, you're already a goner. Does she know?"

"She definitely notices when my flag is hoisted. I mean—it's hard to hide this kickstand when the bike is in gear."

"No, man." Anton slaps the table. "Does she know you *love* her?"

I love her. Jesus. The bar does a slow rotation while I think that over. But God damn. He's right! "She doesn't know!" I yelp. "Because I just found out myself."

"Then you have to tell her," Anton insists. "It could make all the difference."

"Okay?"

"Where does she live?"

"Manhattan."

"Then let's go!" He leaps off his stool, then grabs the table to steady himself.

"Right now?"

"Yeah, man! You gotta tell your girl. Either that, or we could drink more tequila."

More tequila sounds like a bad idea, so I follow him out of the bar.

MONDAY HAS ALREADY LASTED about a hundred years. By midnight, I'm pacing my apartment in a nightgown, reviewing the whole disaster, wondering what I could have done differently.

First, Rolf and I worked a twelve-hour day. Then I presided over a business dinner I planned for my chief technology officer and my corporate treasurer.

The conversation needed secrecy, so I booked the tiny private dining room at En on Hudson Street. And there—over exquisite Japanese food—I described the scenario that Max had laid out. Then I presented my plan to double down on motherboards, ordering half from an untested Thai producer and half from a man I suspected would embed them with malicious hardware.

And they balked.

"I don't understand why we have to play this game," my CTO said.

"What if we end up with twice as many perfectly good parts?" the CFO wanted to know.

"So Max Bayer is telepathic? Does he have a crystal ball? How could he possibly know?"

And so on and so on. It only got worse when someone asked, "What does counsel think?" Because I'm not telling Whitbread about this crisis until I absolutely have to.

They didn't like that either.

"Listen, I spent all of yesterday reeling from this news," I tried to reassure them. "I know it sounds crazy. But this is the hand we've been dealt. No good deed goes unpunished. We made a great product, and someone else wants to use it to his advantage. We can't let that happen."

I'd estimate that I left them—hours later—eighty percent convinced.

It's that last twenty percent that's bothering me now. It occurs to me that I should have asked Max to explain it. He could whip out his top-secret hacker chip and weave the tale. Max is very convincing. He has those flinty gray eyes and the air of craftiness that comes with spending all your time thinking like a thief.

He also has a penis. And in my experience, executives with penises are ninety percent more likely to accept bad news from a person who also has a penis.

Or maybe that's just the panic talking.

I march over to my new, unhacked phone and dial the person I try never to turn to. But I need him right now. And it's only nine o'clock in California.

"Darling girl!" my father booms from the line. "What's got you up so late?"

"There's a problem with my rollout. It's confidential. And it's weird as hell."

"Let's hear it," he says.

"Sit down," I begin. "It's not a short story."

"Motherfucker," my father says when I've explained the whole thing. "Do you really think you can keep this secret?"

"I have to. I can use Max's people for some of the extra legwork."

"Can you do the final assembly in this country?"

"Maybe. There's a recently shuttered cabinet factory in Pennsylvania that might work. Nine hundred employees are jobless."

"Sawdust, though," my father grumbles.

"I hired an environmental company to fly down and check it out."

He's quiet for a moment. "You'll have the technical issues

handled, Alexandra. You're an ace at that. But your credibility might take a hit."

"It might," I agree.

"I can't decide if it will be worse in the press, or worse in the boardroom. If institutional investors get jumpy, they'll be calling for your head."

"That's why I need secrecy."

"That comes with a cost, too," Dad says. "You're relying on Max Bayer's intuition. Not like that's bad. I trust those guys with my life. But when this leaks to the board, you'll be saying a lot of 'Max says this and Max says that.' Without much proof."

"Without *any* proof," I grumble.

"They're going to say Max runs your company."

"Dad!" I gripe, sounding like a pissed-off teenager. "I already understand how that works. Half of them already think that you run my company. The other half thinks that Nate Kattenberger does. That rumor started when I licensed his AI software."

He chuckles. "I know you're just trying to save the world, honey. But so many people will be ungrateful. Especially when they realize they've been kept out of the loop."

"You're preaching to the choir. But I can't let anyone in on this until after the trap's been set. I need a month at least."

He clicks his tongue. "Be careful with the optics. Don't let Max hire out anything you can do yourself. And for God's sake, squash those rumors about you and the other Bayer kid. The athlete."

"What? He has nothing to do with this."

"Gossip forms in a vacuum. I've heard so many rumors about the father of your child. First I heard Nate; then I heard Max. Now Eric."

I close my eyes and take a deep breath. I have over a thousand employees. I knew people would gossip. But the fact that my own father hears these rumors? That makes me ill.

"Hang in there, honey. Don't give them any extra reasons to doubt you. When the baby comes, you won't be around to defend yourself, either. The timing is terrible."

"You think?"

"Deep breaths. You need me to fly out for a visit?"

"No," I say quickly. "Not until the holidays. I don't want people saying that daddy had to come and rescue me."

I don't need *anyone* to rescue me. This problem is big, but it will not break me.

"Okay. Call me tomorrow? I know you hate asking for help, Alexandra. But everyone needs a springboard sometimes. And there aren't many people you can trust."

"Thank you," I say softly, because he's right. "I'll fill you in tomorrow."

"Sleep well, honey. I can't wait to meet my granddaughter."

My stupid eyes fill. "Night dad."

We hang up, and I shut out the light. Then I curl up in the center of my giant bed. I take one of my many pillows and tuck it between my knees. Then I grab another and hug it in my arms. Sleeping while eight months pregnant is hard. It requires props. Or the hard body of a man—

No. It does not require that.

I close my eyes.

"ALEXXXXX!" someone bellows.

My eyes fly open in the dark, and my heart is already pounding.

I hear a muted thud. Like a body falling against my front door. "Alex, baby! I need to speak to you!"

As I wake up quickly, I realize that's Eric's voice. Eric's very drunk voice. And he seems to be outside my apartment.

With a groan, I throw my pillows out of the way and heave myself off the bed. As I approach the front door, I hear Duff out there trying to reason with him.

"Eric, buddy, I can see that you have a few things on your mind. But maybe sleep on it? You can come back tomorrow."

"Alex! It can't wait!"

"Cut it out," Duff complains. "I like you, and I don't want to pull rank, here. But if you keep yelling, I'll put you in a headlock and stuff you into that elevator. It's, like, literally my job."

I'm right outside the door now, and Eric switches to a stage whisper. "Alex! Open the door!"

I yank it open. "This better be good. I was *sleeping*. After the longest day of my career, I was out cold."

"Dude," says a man I've never seen before. "Rough start. But you can turn this around. I believe in you. When you know, you know."

"When you know, you know!" crows a drunken Eric. His beautiful gray eyes are a little unfocused, but he's grinning at me. "Alex, baby, let me in. We gotta talk."

"Who's that?" I demand, pointing at the stranger.

"My cousin," Eric slurs. "He's the newest Bayer on the Bruisers. That's what twenty-two and optimistic looks like."

"I'll show them both the door," Duff says. "So sorry about this."

But I have a feeling that hurricane Eric won't leave quietly. My quickest path back to bed is just to hear the man out. "You have five minutes," I say with a sigh, widening the door. "Start talking."

"You got this, buddy!" says the cousin in the Bruisers T-shirt. "You're right. She *is* a hot whale."

"*What* did you just call me?" I yelp.

"He said *fox tail*," Duff says quickly. "They've been, um, drinking."

"Gosh, really?" I wave Eric inside, and then close the door. "I was sleeping, and I'd like to do that again soon. So what did you need to say?"

Eric paces into my darkened foyer and stands in the middle of the marble floor. "You know how people say I was just in the neighborhood?"

"Yeah?" I tap my foot.

"Well, I was just nowhere near yours, but there's always Lyft, you know? And I realized I had something to say to you, Alex. In my whole life, I thought I never would say these words."

That's some build up. I just cross my arms over my giant tummy and wait.

He throws his hands out to the sides. "I love you, and I think we should get married."

At first I'm distracted by a muffled cheer from the other side of the door. But then the words sink in. "Wait. *What?*" I yelp. "You're crazy. Eric, you did not just get wasted and ride into Manhattan to stand here and say that."

"Oh, shit. I am standing!" Eric slaps himself in the forehead. "I'm doing it all wrong. All the jewelry stores are closed. I checked. But I guess I could kneel—" He starts to slide toward the floor.

"Stop!" I shriek, thinking of his injured knees. "It's marble!"

He catches himself with his hands. "Shit. My knees. I can't even kneel right. And I don't have a ring."

"It's not about that!" I can't believe this is happening. The only marriage proposal I'm *ever* going to hear is from a drunk man who probably won't remember this in the morning. "This visit isn't about me at all. It's about too much scotch and not enough hockey."

He lifts a finger in the air. "Tequila, actually."

"Whatever! Eric, go home. We had a lot of fun." So, so much fun. "But it can't last. I'm in deep with a problem that I might not be able to solve before I give birth to a tiny, needy human…"

"I could help you with that!" Eric crows. "Not the, uh, birth-giving but I could hold it." He burps. "The baby, I mean."

And, damn it, I can almost picture it. Not this drunk version of Eric, of course. But the kind one who shows up here to kiss me and feed me bagels. That Eric—the sober one—never once said anything about babies, though. And I clearly remember that first day when I told him I was pregnant, when utter horror crossed his rugged features.

Right. Eric loves hockey and beaches and sexy-times. I don't blame him one bit. But I'm pissed off that drunk Eric showed up to mockingly *propose* to me at one in the morning.

"Here's what's going to happen," I say in a cool voice. "You're going to go home and sleep it off. And I hope for both our sakes that you don't remember this conversation in the morning. I'm going back to bed. And tomorrow I'm going to keep fighting for my company and for New York City's cybersecurity until this baby shows up. At which time I'll take at least a nine week maternity leave—or I'll pretend to—because if I don't, then I'm sending the wrong message. I'll be telling the women who work at Engels

Cable Media that they can't have a personal life. Even if that seems utterly, horribly true in my case."

"No way," Eric says, shaking his head so hard that he sways. "I'm your personal life. I'm a person!" He thinks that over a second. "*Your* person. Yeah. That. We're supposed to be a team. All of us."

He looks as sincere as a babbling, heavy-lidded hottie can. But that's just the Jose Cuervo talking. "You're the one who told me I can't," I remind him. "Remember? You can do anything, but you can't do everything."

Eric gives a slow blink. "What if I was wrong about that?"

"You called it the best advice you've ever been given *in your life*, Eric. So forgive me if I'm skeptical when you're marinated. Now take your midlife crisis and your twenty-two year-old cousin home."

The door pops open. "Time's up, big man," Duff says. "You heard the lady."

Eric turns, giving me puppy dog eyes. That's how I know he's not himself. He doesn't ever look at me like that. He takes one of my hands and lifts it, kissing the back of it. "Take care, honey. I'm sorry I interrupted your sleep."

Then he goes.

Duff gives me a pitying look before he closes the door again.

I go back to bed, arranging my pillows just-so. And I try not to imagine what it would be like to hear sober words of love from Eric Bayer.

32

ERIC

I WAKE up to the sound of my phone ringing. It's my brother Max's ring tone, which is a full orchestra version of "Hall of the Mountain King." I ignore it. Eventually it stops.

And, wow. My head is killing me. I must have gotten very drunk last night.

When I force my eyes open, I recognize the sun streaming in my windows. But it's coming from a weird angle. Because I'm lying on the floor of my apartment.

Another thing in my field of vision is someone's hairy toe. That might be alarming, except it's starting to come back to me. That's Anton's hairy toe. And it's his groan that I'm hearing now. "Why am I on this floor," he grunts.

"Um…" I don't remember lying down on the floor. Except there's a bottle of Scotch just out of his reach. And it's empty. We broke out the Scotch because I was sad about something.

But what?

Anton sits up. "Shit. What time is it?"

"How would I know?" I haven't reached a vertical position yet. Both my knees are so stiff that I have to work up the courage first.

He fumbles for his phone. "Nine-thirty."

"Morning skate is at ten," I point out.

"Fuck!" He leaps to his feet with the agility that twenty-two-year-old professional athletes possess. "We gotta get going!"

"*You* gotta," I correct. "I have physical therapy at noon." At least I managed to have my drinking spree the night before a nice, late start. That's the luckiest thing that's happened to me in a while.

Something unlucky happened last night, I think. I just can't remember what. "Where did we go after the tavern?" I ask, heaving my aching torso off the floor, and sitting up.

Anton is already galloping toward my bathroom. "Manhattan!" Now I hear water running. "We didn't stay long, though. Your girl threw you out."

My girl.

Alex.

Alex in a nightgown.

Alex in a nightgown with a pissed-off expression.

Alex yelling at me not to kneel down on the marble floor.

Kneel down?

Dread settles over me like a cold fog. I have vague memories of talking to Alex in her foyer. But there's still a chance that was all some kind of drunken dream.

"Anton?" I slowly ease my body into a standing position. "Why did we drink Scotch when we came home?"

He sticks his face out of the bathroom door. It's still half covered with shaving cream. "You were sad she said no."

"She said no," I repeat with mounting horror. To what? I was talking about Alex last night. That part I remember. I said I loved her. Even if my blood was fifty percent alcohol, it's still true. I love her.

That's something you *tell*, though. Not ask.

So what did I ask her? I suppose it could have been…

Nah. Even at my drunkest, I wouldn't be *that* stupid. Or that boorish.

Anton comes out of the bathroom, naked as a jay bird. "Do you know where my suitcase went?"

"I think it's under the coffee table. What did Alex say no to? Did I want to stay overnight?" *Please say yes.*

He grabs his suitcase and then gives me a pitying look. "No, dude. That's not it. But this ain't over. You can go to Tiffany later and buy a ring. I swear it will make all the difference."

"A ring." I almost choke on the word. "What kind of ring?"

"Oh buddy." He shakes his head. "And here I thought you were the smarter one. It's a diamond, man. Always propose with a diamond."

"Anton." My heart stops. "Why did you get me loaded and tell me to *propose?*"

"I didn't know you were going *there*," he says with a shrug. "You just wanted to tell her you loved her. I think the marriage thing mighta just popped out."

"It just popped out."

"Yeah, man. And you went with it. Balls to the wall!" He pumps his fist. "You miss a hundred percent of the shots you don't take."

I'm never drinking again.

My phone starts playing The Hall of the Mountain King again, at a head-splitting volume. I ignore it.

"Look, I gotta bounce," Anton says. "Want to go out again tonight?"

"No!" *Jesus*.

"Even for dinner?" My young cousin looks insulted. "Drake said I gotta try Brooklyn pizza."

"Sure, maybe. After I spend the day trying to figure out how to apologize to Alex." No woman deserves a slurred marriage proposal from a drunken buffoon.

I really do love Alex. I want to be with her. And I think I just fucked that up. I pick my phone up off the floor to find that it has a cracked screen. There's no telling when that happened.

It does not, however, have any texts from Alex. I was hoping for something along the lines of: *Morning sunshine. You sure were funny last night! Talk later?*

But no.

There are several texts from my brother, though. And every one of them makes me grumpy. *Answer your phone. Eric. Come on, it's almost ten. I need to talk to you.*

And, finally: *Don't text Alex. I doubt she wants to hear from you. Just call me back instead.*

"No fucking way!" I yell, as if he could hear me.

Anton gives me a wary look, waves, and then runs out my apartment door.

I'm just pouring myself a glass of orange juice when my phone rings again. But it's not Max, so I have to peer at the cracked screen to identify the caller.

DUFF it says.

"Hi," I say into the phone. "Whatever you were going to say, can it wait until after I've metabolized some painkillers?"

"No man," he says, chuckling. "I'm downstairs in the car. Get down here."

"Why? Did I agree to go somewhere?"

"Nope. But I brought you two egg sandwiches from Lenwich, and a cup of coffee."

Ooh, Lenwich. My mouth waters. "With bacon?"

"And double cheese."

I frown. "Fuck, only Max knows I like double cheese. He sent you?"

"Yeah. He needs to show you something. Down at his office."

"Don't you ever sleep?" I grumble.

"Not for long. I was off from two until eight."

"That is probably against the law," I point out.

"I'm aware. But we are really understaffed right now. Listen, man. These sandwiches smell really good. I'm going to eat one of them if you're not down here in five minutes."

"You are not the person I thought you were, Duff. That is just cruel."

"Four minutes ten seconds…"

"I need ten," I bark. "You do not want me there until I've showered."

That offer of sandwiches better not be a ruse.

IT WASN'T.

By the time I eat two egg sandwiches and slurp down the coffee, we are almost all the way to my brother's building on West Eighteenth Street. And I am feeling almost human.

I pull out my phone and text Alex. *Honey, I'm sorry I showed up to see you when I was in no condition to communicate. Can we talk? Are you free later?*

She responds immediately, but only with one word. *No.*

Well, fuck. I tap her number anyway, and let it ring. It rolls to voicemail immediately. And then her clear voice says: "You're reached the personal voicemail of Alex Engels. If this is a business call, kindly dial my office number instead. If this is Eric Bayer, please lose my number."

I let out a groan.

"Tummy bothering you?" Duff asks as he turns onto Eighteenth.

"No. But Alex hates me."

"Hate is a strong word," he says soothingly. "The word she actually used was *loathe*."

I groan again as the garage door lifts on my brother's garage. Duff parks next to the Maserati. "Hang in there. I'm sure you'll find a way to apologize."

"But then what?" If I tell her I really do love her, she won't believe me.

"Baby steps," he says. "Obviously you can't repeat the proposal for a while. Until she trusts that you mean it. But you'll get it done."

"Wait." I stare at him, shocked. "You think Alex and I will really end up married?"

I don't know why it's such a tricky concept when I'm sober. It's just that I've never pictured myself as a married guy. With half a bottle of tequila up me, it seemed rational, though. Maybe my drunken subconscious knows things.

"What I'm saying is this—I look great in a tux, and I like to dance. So don't give up."

That makes about as much sense as anything else this morning. "Thanks for the sandwiches!"

"Anytime. Tell Max I'm headed to the off-duty room to crash out."

THAT'S the first thing I tell my brother when I find him bent over a project in the middle of the open office space. And the second thing is, "I need more coffee."

"In a minute," he says without looking up. "You have to see this."

It's hard to say what "this" is, though. There's a beehive of activity around my brother. A large worktable has been moved into the center of the testing area. On the table are two workspaces, with a track stretching above them. The thing on the track might or might not be a camera.

On the other end of the table are parked several computer monitors, complete with a handful of my brother's hired nerds peering at them.

"Test number twenty-seven starts…now!" someone says.

The camera glides to a location over one workspace, which seems to contain a blueprint for something inscrutably technical. I see a flash of light. And then the camera is on the move, gliding to the other workspace. That one has the guts of some kind of computing device lying open, its circuits and chips exposed. The light flashes again.

"Now watch this," Max says, towing me by the elbow over to a computer monitor, where a whole lot of code is scrolling past the screen. There's a status bar across the top. *SCANNING*, it says. Then it changes to ANALYZING as the bar crawls from the left to the right.

As it reaches the point of conclusion, everyone cheers. "Five point two seconds!"

It's a match, the screen declares in red text.

"What's our accuracy?" Max asks.

"Eighty percent and climbing."

Max turns to me with a smirk. "Not bad for forty-eight hours work. We should reach full potential on this thing by the weekend."

"What is it?" I ask, glancing around to try to spot my father's assistant. Maybe she'd be willing to find me some coffee. My head still throbs.

"Well, I realized that manufacturers will need a quick, reliable way to verify the accuracy of their designs. I'm building a device that can screen electronics for unwanted extra hardware. Every single internet device should be checked before it ships. Every smart speaker. Every computer. Every smart doorbell. Every internet-connected microwave…"

"I get it," I grunt.

"It has to fast and accurate, and at least semi-portable."

"Okay. So you'll sell these things and make another fortune."

"Not sell them," my brother gasps. "This will be a service company. Hire us to come in and verify your products. This is actually where you come in…"

"Not really," I argue. "I was just in it for the egg sandwiches and coffee. Have you seen Shelby anywhere?"

"Eric, listen. I have a proposition for you."

"No," I say immediately.

"You haven't heard it yet!"

"I'm just saving us both the time. I'm going to say no. Unless this proposition lets me scare Tatum again." Max shakes his head. "See? Then I don't care."

"Max!" Call the nerds at the table. "We need a new testing configuration. How about a phone this time?"

"Sure," Max agrees. "Eric, hand me your phone."

"No way!" I put a protective hand on my back pocket.

"It's just for a minute, I'll put it back together when we're done."

"That's *exactly* what you said about my Operation game," I argue.

"I was nine years old!" Max yelps. "I didn't have access to the right tools. It's not the same at all. Besides, I'll make you an espresso."

"Use your own damn phone."

"I can't. I can't get a blueprint for mine, because I've altered it myself."

Of course he has. "Where are you getting these blueprints anyway?" I pull out my phone. "That can't be public information."

"Oh, the dark web." He shrugs. "And I called in a couple of favors. That's why I need your Katt phone. Nate sent over the plans." Max tries to grab the phone out of my hands, but first I have to see whether I have any new messages from Alex.

Nope.

"Bummer about the cracked screen." Max clicks his tongue. "Heads up, Kyler!" He takes it from me and throws it to his guy at the other end of the table.

"Why am I really here, Max? Aside from letting you perform surgery on my phone."

He grabs my arm and steers me over to the kitchenette on one wall.

The heavens are merciful. There's an espresso machine here. Max grabs four pods out of the overhead cabinet and shoves two of them into the machine. He puts two cups underneath and pushes the button.

"This is a big deal," he says. "Not just for me, but for the future. A year from now, hardware hacks will be all over the front page of the *Times* and the *Post*. Everything is in play. Privacy, industrial espionage, and national security. I need someone I trust to shepherd this project along. I can't be everywhere at once."

It's not that I don't believe him. My brother's big ideas are exciting, but they're just not me. "I already have a job," I remind him.

"Do you?" He takes the cups out from under the espresso machine and hands me one. "What if you can't go back to hockey?"

"I can if I want to." It's just a matter of how much pain, surgery and rehab I'm willing to endure.

"But for how much longer, Eric? Be honest."

Sulking, I take a sip of espresso. Does Max know how terrifying this question really is? I think he does, and he just doesn't care. "One season, tops," I admit.

"Then do this for me. Now, or in 18 months. It will help Alex."

And this is exactly why I hate discussing my inevitable retirement. I don't have a fucking clue what I'm going to do with myself afterward. But it will not be this. "I want Alex to get all the help she needs. But not like this, Max."

"Look, I know an office job would be an adjustment—"

I stop him right there. "It's not the office. It's your world view. I don't want to spend eighty hours a week thinking of all the ways the world is about to end. Even if it's true. That's not how my mind works."

My brother sighs. "You're smart enough for security work. But you're just not cynical enough. It's a problem." My brother drains his coffee, then puts the cup beneath the machine again.

"Look," I say as he grabs two more pods to make himself a double. "Duff told me he's worked a lot of overtime this week."

"Yeah, and I haven't slept since I last saw you."

"That was forty-eight hours ago."

"I noticed." He hits the button and espresso begins to stream into his cup.

"There's a way I can help you guys. I want to."

"Really?" He glances my way, and then he frowns. "Wait. No. You cannot be serious."

But I totally am.

33

ALEX

"I DON'T UNDERSTAND," Whitbread grumbles into my ear. "Why are we vetting two contracts for the same manufacturing job?"

"I'm spreading the risk around," I explain for the third time. "The factory fire was a wake-up call. Two manufacturers will insure a steady supply."

"But this is the only part you're buying two of?" he asks. "That makes no sense."

Honestly, he's right. But Whitbread brings out my self-righteous side. "It makes sense to *me*," I argue. "The Butler will sell out during Christmas, and I'm not taking any chances."

"There are things I don't like about the contract from the Thai company," he grumbles.

"Then mark it up like you always do. And let me get on with my day." *You grumpy old turd*.

"When will I see this second contract?"

"After lunch, I hope. Tomorrow at the latest. Is there anything else?"

He's silent for a moment, probably because he's tossing another dart at the photo of me I imagine he keeps on his office wall. "Send it over when you can," he says, before hanging up.

And just like that, another fun call with Whitbread ends. When we send out the employee satisfaction survey at the end of the year, I hope he doesn't fill his out.

"Bingley?" I ask the Butler on my desk. "Have I received any more calls?"

"No, my queen! You are free to go to lunch. Your dining companion is a Mr. Xian Smith, and you will lunch together at The Modern on East Fifty-Third Street." I know all that already. Until Bingley adds: "Table for three."

"Three?" I ask. "Who's the third person?"

"Apologies, oh great one. That information is not on your calendar. The reservation was altered just two hours ago by Rolf."

"Rolf?" I shout.

But he can't hear me, because my office door is closed. And a glance at the phone shows me his line is lit up. That means I have to heave this very pregnant body out of the chair to go figure it out myself.

I put both hands on the desk and rock forward until my feet reach the rug. There should be a tool for this. I'm picturing a crane-like device, suspended from the ceiling. The *Pregnant Power-Assist*. A woman could rent one for her third trimester.

Take my money.

Waddling out of my private office, I spot Rolf on the phone. "She has no availability that week," he says, my calendar up on the screen in front of him. "No availability at *all*," he repeats. "You can email her if you'd like to communicate directly. Thank you." He punches the button to disconnect the call.

"Who's trying to see me?" I ask.

"The CEO and lead programmer for *Maximum*. That channel you—"

"Canceled. I remember."

"They want to plead their case." He shrugs. "I suppose I could fit them in if you want me to."

"Nope. I already told them we don't want their sexist crap that nobody watches."

"So," Rolf frowns. "If they made sexist crap that people watched, you'd still carry their channel?"

"Perhaps," I admit. "It would depend on their numbers, and

how far up the barf meter I found their content. Hey, Rolf? Why did you change my lunch to three people?"

"Oh. Your security team emailed to ask for that."

I feel a frisson of fear. "Do you know why?" Usually my guard sits at the bar or waits just outside.

Rolf shrugs. "I figured you'd know. The car is downstairs, by the way."

"Okay." I go back into my office for my coat and bag. Up until now I haven't let myself get nervous about meeting Xian Smith again.

When I emailed him on Sunday, asking if his offer to manufacture still stands, he'd replied immediately. He offered to fly in for lunch. And, sure, it's a little unusual to sit down to a $138 tasting menu with a man I suspect is trying to hijack my company and all of New York's elite.

But my job is confrontational even on the best days. I have competitors. I have detractors. Business is a battlefield, and I'm accustomed to the clashing of swords. My security team never asks for a seat at the lunch table, though. That's a little nerve wracking.

I refresh my lipstick and then head out again. "Hold down the fort, Rolf. I'll be back in time for the finance meeting at two-thirty."

"Feel free to bring back leftovers," he grumbles. "I'm trapped here taking calls from all the people who want your attention."

"Poor baby," I tease. "What a shame that none of the hundred restaurants within a two-mile radius will deliver. Oh wait…"

The phone rings again. He gives me a sour look as he answers it. Everyone is a grump today. Except for me, of course, the one who has to dine with her alleged enemy.

I'm still feeling rock solid as I descend the elevator and arrive at the side door, where the head of building security greets me with a smile. "G'day, Ms. Alex," he says. "Your car is waiting to the right." He points through the window and then holds the door for me.

"Thank you, Mr. Mendes!" As I march outside, Duff gets out of the car to open the rear door for me.

And then I do a double take. Because that's not Duff at all. It's Eric Bayer. He's wearing a gorgeous charcoal suit with a crisp white shirt and a blue silk tie with puffins on it.

I already know I'm in trouble. It's hard to hate a man in a puffin tie. I don't know why. It just is.

"Good afternoon, Ms. Engels," he says primly. "The drive to the restaurant should be less than fifteen minutes."

I come to a halt in front of the open door. "Eric, what are you doing?"

"Taking you to lunch."

"Why?"

"Would you get into the car, please? This is not a secure location."

Grumbling, I get into the back seat of my own car. "Is this some kind of joke? Are you the third seat at lunch?"

"It's not a joke at all," he says, hopping into the front and slamming the driver's side door. "You're sitting down with someone we believe to be a dangerous cybercrime lord. Since he'll remember me from Hawaii, he'll just assume that you take me everywhere you go."

"You're trying to pass yourself off as my employee?"

"I know I'm too ruggedly handsome for that. But I can make this play, coach. Besides, I'll be wearing a recording device, so that Max can review it later."

"Fine," I grumble. "If Max wants to browbeat you into escorting me around, I'm not getting in the middle of it."

"He didn't browbeat me," Eric says, pulling into the stream of midtown traffic. "I volunteered."

"Oh." I study the back of Eric's handsome, kissable neck. "Thank you," I grumble. But how am I supposed to focus now?

"Do you have a moment to hear my apology?" he asks, stopping for a traffic light.

"I suppose." Seeing as I'm trapped here.

"I am sorry about my ridiculous behavior. I wasn't myself the other night."

"You sure weren't." *I love you and I think we should get married.* That did not sound like the Eric I know.

"If I recall, though, you said the same thing to me after that party in Florida. You weren't yourself."

"I wasn't," I admit with a sigh. "Fine. It's the same. We're even."

"Not really," he says, turning onto Sixth Avenue. "It's not the same at all. You were telling me to get lost, and I was only professing my love for you. So you should probably be less insulted than I was back in April."

"But I didn't hope you'd get lost," I point out. "I just didn't really deserve you at that moment. So I lied. And since you don't actually love me, it really is the same."

Unfortunately, he has to stop for another light. With his foot on the brake, he turns to look me right in the eye. "I do love you, though. That was true. Still is."

My stomach flips over as his warm gray eyes crinkle at the edges.

The light turns green, and someone behind us leans on his horn. Eric turns around again and drives through the intersection. "I meant a lot of what I said, Engels. I can't give you a precise figure because I, uh, don't remember all of it. But I didn't show up there to hurt you or make fun of you. I don't have a lot of lightbulb moments. Except in hockey. So I think I just needed to get that off my chest."

"You always said that hockey was your true love," I point out. "You never sang a different tune until your cousin showed up and passed you the tequila."

"I know," he says, following the traffic up sixth. "And that's unfortunate. But the young pup helped me realize a few things, so it's hard to hold it against him." The car glides to a stop on Fifty-Third Street. "But now we have to concentrate on Xian Smith."

"No kidding?" I give him an eye roll. "You're the one who wanted to go off topic."

"Thank you for indulging me," he says, handing his keys to a valet. "Now let's go run up your expense account." He offers me his arm. "Can I begin recording now?"

"Of course."

He pulls out his phone and opens some kind of app. His finger hovers over the screen. "It's not switched on yet. If you wanted to say anything filthy, you should get that out of your system right now. Like—your ass looks *spectacular* in that suit."

I snort. "No thanks, I'm good."

"Suit yourself. But I'd like to say that you look especially ravishing today. And I'm going to spend the whole lunch thinking about kissing you." He taps the screen, turning on the recorder. "*Everywhere*."

I feel myself blush, and he gives me an evil grin. "Could you focus on my personal safety now, please?" I say.

"Oh, always." He opens the restaurant door for me. "Mr. Smith is thirty feet away at the hostess stand, and he's looking out into the garden."

"Thank you," I say, straightening my spine. "Let's go buy some motherboards."

"I love it when you get feisty," he whispers.

I can't even glare at him because Xian Smith has turned around, and he's watching us approach. So I put on my business face.

"Hello, Mr. Smith. I'm sure you remember Eric." I don't plan on explaining why he's here. "Thank you for flying in from California to meet with us."

"Ms. Engels, it was my pleasure," he says silkily. "I'm glad you were feeling well enough to suggest lunch."

"Oh, I feel just fine, thank you. And lunch is a big priority for me lately."

I'm tired of people commenting on my pregnancy. But I've also reached a point where I feel like it's never going to end. That I'll always be this size. That I'll never bend over again.

"Follow me, please," the maître d' says, and I waddle toward a perfect table for three.

Eric pulls out my chair with a flourish. "Thank you." Now that he's had thirty-six hours to sober up, he's a perfect gentleman.

I'm seated directly across from Xian Smith. Now that Max has shared his suspicions, I'd wondered if Mr. Smith would seem even more sinister to me than he did before.

If I'm honest, he's too beautiful to be truly terrifying. He has the smoothest, most flawless skin that I've ever seen on a man, and intelligent dark eyes. But his gaze is too knowing to make me comfortable, as if he can see more of me than I can see of him.

"Do you come to New York often?" I ask.

"Four or six times a year," he says with that unblinking stare. "I prefer New York to California, but I have more West Coast clients than East Coast."

"I'll bet," I say easily.

"Where did you grow up?" Eric asks, picking up his menu at the same time, as if the question isn't truly interesting.

"Oh, where didn't I?" He laughs. "Military brat."

"Mmm," Eric says noncommittally.

"Have you eaten here before?" Xian asks.

"A few times." *But never with a hacker who was trying to ruin me.* "The scallops are wonderful."

AFTER EVERYONE ORDERS, I feel I can finally dispense with small talk. "Before the food arrives, I need to ask if you can still help me with my motherboard situation. We've had a rough go of it."

He nods stoically. "I heard about the fire. So unfortunate."

"Yes," I say as goose bumps rise on my arms. *Were you the cause of it?* "Back in August, you offered to help me produce motherboards at a seventeen percent savings. And I should have taken you up on it."

"Yes, you should have." He gives me a small smile that only increases the size of my goose bumps.

"Mea culpa," I say. Although I'd rather kick him under the table. "Could you help me shore up my production now?"

"I can," he says quietly. "Although I'm afraid the seventeen percent discount was for a three-month lead time."

"At this point I only have a six-week lead time. That's when I run out of inventory."

Another stoic nod. "The shorter time frame is still possible. But the discount will only be eight percent."

I make my mouth into a tight line, which is not difficult to do, considering how fed up I am with the whole problem. "If that's the best you can do, I will have to accept that."

"We'll need a signed contract immediately," he says.

"My legal team is ready when you are," I reply, picturing Whitbread's jowly face. If that man knew what I was doing right now, he'd have a litter of kittens.

"Bread?" asks Eric, passing me the basket. "Ooh, herbed butter."

At least one of us is happy.

34

ERIC

"C'MON, Eric. Give me three more."

Slowly, I straighten my knees, my legs shaking with effort. The weight on the leg press is about half my usual. But I'm sweating like a pig in a sauna. And every muscle in both knees is screaming.

This is rehab. It hurts. It's exhausting. And the results are depressing.

"Two more!" Chip calls. "You're doing great."

I bear down and bend my knees again. The shaking is worse this time.

"Breathe," Chip coaches. "One more."

I finish the set, but it's ugly. The plates clang back into place when I'm through. And I'm panting like I just went seven rounds with a grizzly bear.

"How you feeling?" Chip has the balls to ask.

"How does it look like I'm feeling?" I snarl.

But the man is not offended. He's used to pushing people further than they think they can go. "You look like a man who wants to kill me. That's how I know we're done here. Good work today, Eric. Nobody works harder than you." He tosses a clean towel at me.

I catch it and wipe the sweat out of my eyes.

"Go stretch out one more time. I'll see you Friday."

"Thanks," I grunt.

I limp into the warmup room with all the mats, tossing down my towel and then easing my body down onto it. This is the low point, right? It had better be. I need a shower and some food. Maybe a nap.

Everything seems impossible today. I should be scheduling my other knee surgery right about now. But the idea of doing all this again on the other side makes me want to howl.

I'm asking my hamstrings for a little more stretch when I hear the trainer's voice just outside the door. "You ever try injectables? They can make you stronger real fast."

"Yeah? Like, how, man?" And, hell, that's Anton's voice.

"Injections right into the muscle. I know a guy. You'll be unstoppable."

"Dude, really? What's in it?"

The young trainer drops his voice, so I miss whatever he says next.

But I've heard enough. I struggle to my feet and walk out into the hallway. "Hey."

"Hey, man," Gino says. "Need something?"

"Yeah. I need you to stop selling bullshit to a healthy twenty-two-year old. The last thing he needs is injectables."

"Dude," Gino says with a nervous chuckle. "We were just chewing the fat."

"Really?" I challenge. I'm pissed off, now. I'm pissed at my knees. And I'm pissed at the universe. And I'm pissed off that this jacked up muscle head would try to push supplements and drugs on a youngster who's willing to do whatever he's told to start his first NHL game.

"Henry!" I call down the hallway. "Are you around?"

The head trainer appears at the far end of the hallway, a roll of tape in his hands. "Right here, Eric. Problem?"

"Are injectable supplements part of your healthy player protocol?"

"No," the older man shakes his head. "'Course not. Who said that?"

"Gino. He referred me to a friend of his – a doctor – that's not on your referral list. And now he wants Anton to look into some kind of supplement."

Henry's eyes narrow. "My office, Gino. Now."

I'M WORKING with Anton on the mats when Henry appears in the doorway.

He doesn't say anything for a moment, because I'm in the middle of trying to get my cousin to stretch his sartorius properly. "The muscle wraps around, see? You have to lengthen the whole thing so you can avoid a strain. Be kind to your groin."

"Cool, man," my dopey cousin says. "Speaking of my groin, Drake and I are headed to the Coco Club tonight. He says the women are *fine*. Want to come?"

"No thanks. I got plans."

"Is your lady over her snit?"

"Not yet. But soon. What's up, Henry?"

"Will you drop by my office before you go? I want to ask you something."

"Sure. Be there in fifteen. We're done here, anyway."

After I'm showered and dressed, I retrieve the business card that Gino gave me from my locker, in case Henry wants a look at it.

"Hey," I say, entering the trainer's office. "Am I interrupting?" Coach Worthington is in there, too.

"Not at all," Coach says. "Come in, will ya? Close the door."

I do, and then I lay the business card on Henry's desk. "I assume you wanted to see this?"

"Nice catch on that guy," Coach says. "Who knows what's in those supplements? Some kids will do anything the trainer tells them. Next thing you know, they're testing positive for banned substances. And their only crime is trusting some asshole."

"Yeah." He's got it exactly right. "A kid like Anton will do literally anything to make it on this team. Hell, so would I. I know better than to think that injections would magically improve my knee. But the idea is really seductive."

Coach and Henry share a glance. Henry picks up the card on his desk, makes a face, and then tosses it down again. "Obviously

Gino isn't going to work out for the long term. I told him that spotting, stretching, and taping are the only things he's allowed to do. I'm going to have to fire him as soon as I can find someone else."

"Good plan."

"But, listen. Have you ever thought about training?"

"Training?" I repeat. I train all the time.

"As a career," Henry says.

"What? No." *I have a career*, my subconscious argues. Although Henry's serious expression prevents me from brushing the question aside. "No. I hadn't ever thought of that."

"Look," he says, waving me into a chair. "I know you don't want my advice. You've made it very clear that rehabbing your way back onto the roster is your goal. I respect that. But everyone's career ends eventually."

"I know that," I say. Although, to be fair, I do my best to forget it.

"You have a lot to offer, Eric," Coach says. "Any G.M. would be thrilled to have you as a scout. Any program would hire you as a trainer."

"You'd have to certify," Henry adds. "But you're so smart that it'd be a walk in the park for you."

"Thank you," I say, my face heating. "I'm not ready to think about that yet."

"We know," Coach says. "You're not done with hockey. But hockey isn't done with you, either. So when you're ready to figure out your second act, we'll be here to discuss it with you."

"Thanks." I clear my throat, which is suddenly tight. "I'll remember that." I glance at the clock on Henry's desk. "I'd better run. There's somewhere I need to be."

"Run carefully," Coach jokes. "Wear your knee brace."

"You know it."

A FEW HOURS later I'm doing leg lifts outside Alex's apartment, when the door jerks open. "Hey, Duff? You want anything from Hunan Garden?"

After her head pokes out of the door, it still takes her a second to find me, since I'm not in the chair, but rather on a yoga mat on the floor. She lets out a surprised little yelp when our gazes collide.

"No thanks, I already ate," I answer, sitting up.

"You're not Duff," she says, leaning against the door frame. She's wearing yoga pants and a pink maternity T-shirt that says "Loading…" on the belly, with a half-filled status bar running beneath the word.

"I'm not Duff," I agree with a smile. Her hair is in a messy bun with a pencil holding it together, and I just want to take her in my arms and kiss her.

Which I will, just as soon as she gives me the chance.

"Really, Eric? Don't you have better things to do than hang around in the hallway in place of my body man?"

"Not at all," I tell her. "This is the highest use of my time. I can rehab while I look after you. And those are the only two things I enjoy, so…" I shrug.

Her eyes narrow. "It won't work."

"What won't?" I rise from the floor and casually stretch my right quad.

"This little game you're playing. I'm *not* going to invite you inside. And then, you know…" She clears her throat.

"Invite me *inside?*" I clarify in a sultry voice.

"Eric!"

"That's okay," I say mildly. "I wasn't expecting you to."

"I'm working."

"You and me both, honey. Let me know when you order that food, so I can intercept the delivery man for you and make sure he didn't short your order. I take my work very seriously."

"You're teasing me." She tries to cross her arms over that giant, wonderful belly.

"Not at all. Now go and order one of everything and I'll get back to strengthening my muscles and keeping the bad guys away."

She gives me one more grumpy look and then shuts the door.

I chuckle.

"I heard that!" she says from the other side of the door.

"Must not be working very hard, then." She doesn't reply. I've worked my way up to my hip flexors when the door opens again. "Back so soon? Did you miss me?"

"I placed my order. It will be here in thirty minutes."

"Good to know." I lift my T-shirt over my head and toss it onto the chair.

Her eyes widen, and then stray down my torso. "Is there a problem with the heating system out here?"

"No problem. I'm just more comfortable this way. Go back to work now, okay?" I bend down and pick up the dumbbell I've stashed against the wall, beginning a set of curls. "I'm not afraid to fight dirty, you know."

"I don't have the first idea what you're talking about."

"Then you'll soon find out. Run along. You're interrupting the concentration of the security personnel."

Alex swallows. Then she closes the door and disappears. But I swear it's not even ten minutes later when that door opens again. "Eric?"

"You *do* miss me! Just admit it." I'm on my fourth set of curls.

"I have a problem. I need to go downtown."

That gets my attention. I set down the weight and grab my shirt. "What kind of problem?"

She waves me inside, where I follow her into the kitchen. She turns on the kitchen faucet, which is what paranoid people do if they are worried about bugs. I'm sure my brother taught her that trick. "Earlier today, I pushed through a contract with a Thai manufacturer who will supply my next shipment of motherboards."

"Right," I agree. "The other half of your double order."

"Well, that manufacturer's representative just called to say they will be unable to fulfill the contract. Then he said he would like to explain why, but it has to be in person. And would I meet him downtown near his hotel?"

"So you said yes?" I don't like the sound of this at all. A random nighttime meetup?

"The whole thing is weird, but I really need to know why he'd bail on me. I really liked these guys. Maybe I can still change his mind."

"Does this sound creepy to you?" I ask.

"Well, it's weird. But he wants to meet me at The Dutch in SOHO. There's nothing creepy about that. Nothing bad ever happens at a cute bistro..."

"So you want to go?"

"Of course. Let me just change. Would you warn the doorman that my dinner order is going to show up without me? It's prepaid. Thanks." She's gone again.

I pull out my phone and connect to The Company's personal security dispatch. "Hey, this is Eric Bayer. Who've I got tonight?"

"Your old man," my father says into my ear. "Got a problem at the Engels place?"

"I'm really not sure."

35

ALEX

"CAN'T I SIT UP FRONT?" I ask Eric as he opens the rear door.

"No. The back is safer," he says. "It's standard operating procedure, Alex. You know this."

He's right, and The Company makes my father sit in back, too. So I slide into my seat. But still, I feel the need to resist Eric's little game. "I don't like being guarded. It's infantilizing."

"Uh huh." He snickers. "Does the quarterback feel infantilized by the offensive line?"

I guess the man has a point. "How long are you going to play at bodyguard?"

"As long as it takes," he says before shutting the door.

"As long as it takes, for what?"

"To prove my point."

"But—"

Before I can continue this exchange, Eric begins speaking to dispatch. "ETA is twenty-five minutes," he says, pulling out of the underground garage. "I'm taking the FDR."

I can't hear the other side of their conversation, though, because it's in his earpiece.

So I settle back in the seat and watch New York City go by. The Upper East Side is decorated for the holidays, with pine boughs, red bows, and fairy lights.

Last Christmas I had no idea what was coming my way. I

hadn't yet complicated my friendship with Nate. I hadn't hooked up with Jared Tatum. And the Butler was still a big idea in development.

I took on too much this year. And now I'm paying the price.

Though next Christmas could be amazing. My baby might already be walking or saying her first words. I'll be shopping for age-appropriate toys and board books. I'll be worrying about bedtimes and solid foods and the transition to sippy cups.

But first, I have to save my product launch, shore up my career, and give birth.

And, seriously, what does a girl have to do to buy ten thousand motherboards? An hour ago I had a signed contract. Now I've got cold Chinese food delivered to my apartment building and a date with a manufacturer who's trying to back out of a job that I need badly.

"Stay where you are, please," Eric says when we pull up in front of the bistro.

"Yessir."

Pieter materializes beside the car, tapping once on the glass. Eric gets out, hands off the keys and then opens my door.

"Two guards for a restaurant visit?" I ask. "Isn't that overkill?"

"Probably," Eric admits, taking my arm and walking me toward the entrance. He glances up and down the street then holds the door open for me. "Do you see him?"

"No," I say, scanning the tables.

"Good evening. Do you have a reservation?" asks a tall man behind the podium.

"I do not," I say. "There will be three of us."

"I'm afraid there's a bit of a wait. Perhaps forty minutes."

"Forty minutes!" I gasp as the scent of rack of lamb with home-made frites washes over me. "On a Tuesday at nine p.m.? This is why people move out of New York."

The host looks unapologetic. It's literally his job to turn hungry people away all evening. "It's a bit crowded at the bar. Perhaps you could stand over—"

I shed my coat quickly, revealing my big, pregnant belly.

"Uh…" He falters. "Let me find you a table. Excuse me one moment." He hurries off.

"That's handy," Eric says under his breath.

"He knows I might chew his arm off," I point out. "It happens."

Eric puts a protective arm around me as he scans the busy room, ever vigilant. "Isn't there a quieter restaurant where you could meet this guy?"

"Probably. But it was his choice."

"Miss? I can seat you right here by the windows." The host puts a third chair at a tiny table, but size doesn't matter, not in this case, anyway. It's a table, and it's all mine.

I've already darted over to seat myself when I catch Eric's frown. "Window seats aren't very secure."

"Look on the bright side. They have food here. And I'll be able to spot Mr. Khun on his way in."

Eric sits down with a sigh. "There are postage stamps larger than this table."

"As long as the steak fits right here," I frame out a space in front of me. "And we'll need a bread basket, of course."

"And soon." He stops looking worried long enough to smile at me. "Wouldn't want you to chew anyone's limbs off."

His gaze warms me, and his smile hits me low in my belly. Or maybe that's just the hunger pains. I turn my attention out onto Sullivan Street. I love the low brick buildings of Soho. It's been dark for hours, but the streetlights and storefronts light the sidewalk.

That's how I spot Mr. Khun approaching from half a block away. He's striding down the sidewalk, glancing around in much the same way that Eric did as we left the car. I see him turn to look over his shoulder.

Then he breaks into a dead run.

"Eric—" The word barely leaves my mouth before I hear a loud *bang*.

Someone screams, but not me. I am already airborne, Eric's arms clamped around me. The lights of the restaurant blur as he sweeps me deeper into the room, away from the window.

Bang. Bang.

Breaking glass. More screams. And they don't stop.

"*Get down*," Eric says as my feet touch the floor again.

My knees give way, and I sink below a counter, my back against a dark wooden panel. *Wainscoting*, my brain offers up, trying to make sense of something. Anything.

"Taking cover," Eric says to dispatch. "Total of three shots fired."

We're so close together that I can hear the reply from his earbud. "Standby for instructions. One man on the ground. Emergency services notified and responding. Pieter is in pursuit of the shooter."

"Eric!" I gasp. "We should help that man. Is it Mr. Khun? Did they—" I gulp.

"We're staying put," he says.

"Just tell me. Did they hurt him?"

The chaos of the restaurant has evolved from the high pitch of terror to the low murmurs of shock. Eric rises, putting a hand on my head as a reminder not to move. He stands there for a long moment, not saying anything.

"What do you see?" I squeak.

"Don't look," is all he says. "Do *not* look."

LATER, I'll barely remember the ride home. Pieter drove. Eric sat in back, where I pasted myself to his body, still unable to understand what just happened.

Mr. Khun invites me to dinner to explain why he's going to break our signed contract, but on his way down the block, someone shoots him.

Eric and I left by the back door, but I heard Pieter say under his breath, "…brains all over the sidewalk."

Why? No matter that Max's grand theory looks more true by the minute. What prize could possibly be worth a gunned-down tech manufacturer?

I have never shied away from a challenge. I never expected my job to be easy. But this? I did *not* sign up for this.

And I'm terrified that I'm to blame. What if I hadn't chosen him? Or what if I'd told Mr. Khun that it was late, and I didn't want to come to Soho?

I spend the rest of the trip literally trying to rewrite the last two hours. It's illogical to the extreme. But I do it anyway, answering his call again, telling him that tonight isn't a good night to meet. Suggesting an alternate date…

We arrive at my building without incident. When we reach the penthouse floor, I don't wait outside the apartment while Pieter and Eric check the rooms. I just march inside and head straight for my bathroom, where I close and lock the door. I turn on the cold water and pour myself a large glass, and then drink it all.

It takes a while until I can pull myself together. I change into a tent-shaped nightie and waddle out to my bed, getting in. But I don't turn out the lights. I'm not ready to plunge into darkness with my thoughts.

Eric arrives a couple of minutes later, carrying a tray.

No, my stomach says immediately. It's the first time I haven't been hungry in…

Okay, I don't remember the last time I wasn't hungry.

Since my lap is gone, Eric puts the tray over my knees. I look down and see a bowl of egg drop soup that I ordered a lifetime ago. Eric has heated it to steaming hot.

"I know you're upset," he says quietly. "But you should eat this."

I pick up the spoon and find that my body knows what to do. Before long, I'm scraping an empty dish and Eric is trading the bowl for a small plate of rice and chicken.

That's all I can handle, though. After I eat a little, I slide off the bed and carry the tray into the kitchen by myself, abandoning it on the counter.

Eric sits on a kitchen stool, texting madly, an untouched beer in front of him.

"I'm not on the job," he says when he sees me looking at it. "Pieter and Duff are outside."

"Drink all you want," I say in a deadened voice. "I'd join you if

I could. Being careful doesn't seem to help very much, does it?"
And now tears are threatening.

"Hey," he says, gathering me up. "You're okay."

"I know," I rasp. But I don't, really. *Nothing* is okay tonight.

"Come on," he says, steering me out of the kitchen. "Lie down, okay?"

"I have to b-brush my teeth," I stutter, discovering that those same teeth are now chattering.

"All right." Eric actually follows me into the bathroom and leans against the counter while I hastily clean up. Then he watches me get into bed, sitting down on the edge afterward. He shuts off the lamp, and then runs a hand down my hair. "Sleep now," he says.

"Okay."

"You're safe here. You know, that right?"

"I d-do." My teeth click. I'm shivering. "D-don't go."

"Okay." He pets my hair.

But it isn't close enough. "P-please come over here with me."

"Careful, Engels," he whispers. "You might accidentally convince yourself that you like having me around."

"I've always liked having you around," I say, and then shiver again. "I like it way too much."

He stands up and unbuttons his pants, kicking them off. Then his shirt, too. I feel the covers shift as he climbs in. He moves over until he can wrap an arm around my great girth.

But it's not even enough. I shift back into the warmth of his body. I force myself to take a deep, slow breath, and then let it out again. If Eric Bayer's strong body pressed against mine isn't enough to make me stop shivering? Then nothing is.

Roughened fingers move slowly up and down my forearm. "Shh," he whispers. "I've got you."

He does. His lips find the place where my neck meets my shoulder. And I get a series of soft kisses.

I breathe deeply a few more times. And finally I stop shaking. "Will you stay the night?"

"Anytime, honey," he says. "Anytime."

WE DON'T TALK. And I'm no longer shaking. But we don't sleep, either. "I'm going to have to talk to the police," I whisper eventually.

"Yeah," he agrees, stroking my hair. "Tomorrow. Dad will call them and tell them you were at that restaurant to meet the victim."

"I don't know anything," I realize. "It's going to be a short conversation."

"The shorter the better," Eric agrees. "It's not a great time to bring up Max's conspiracy theories."

"I guess it isn't." I think about that for a moment. "Fucking Max."

Eric barks out a laugh. "I say that all the time."

"No, really. I don't want to know some of the things I know."

"Yeah, but even if Max didn't share his theories, nothing would change. Someone is targeting The Butler's manufacture. You didn't choose this problem. It chose you."

"Really?" That may not be true. "I got up in front of a tech crowd in Hawaii and told the whole room that I was going to make the smartest product in the world. The most secure. I basically implied that I was a beacon of light in a dark sea of bullshit."

Eric tucks his face against the back of my head and laughs. "You're funny when you're in shock."

"Seriously—I waved a red flag in front of a bull. 'My product will be purchased by rich people who value their privacy and security! Please step right over here and shit on my lawn!'"

I can feel Eric's body shaking with laughter.

"It isn't funny."

"No." He snorts. "But you're funny. And smart. You're all the good things, Engels. And I love you, even if you don't want to hear it."

Oh, Eric. I screw my eyes shut, because I don't have the mental energy to resist those words tonight. I want to hear them more than I care to admit.

"I had a bad feeling about tonight," he says in a low voice. "I can't even explain it. But when you got out of that car, I just wanted to put you back inside it and drive away. And when I heard that gunshot, I couldn't get you away fast enough. And not because it was sort of my job. Because I need you, honey. And I won't stop trying to convince you that it's true."

I need you, too. The words are on the tip of my tongue.

But Eric isn't listening, anyway. He's already kissing my shoulder. And after he sweeps my hair out of the way, my neck.

I roll imperceptibly closer, granting him access. Chills break out all over my skin as he drops lazy kisses anywhere he can reach.

My body and my mind are so exhausted. But I let his kisses and ministrations roll across my consciousness, washing away the fear. I doze on a cloud of kisses. I'm so relaxed that when he slides a hand into my panties, I gasp in surprise.

"No?" he asks, pausing.

"Yes," I breathe, waking to all the possibilities. "Yes, please." I kick off the panties, and he lifts my gown over my head.

He's so gentle as he takes my heavy breasts in his hands, and fits our bodies together, the way they're meant to fit.

"Need you," he sighs as he thrusts slowly.

"I need—" I gasp as my pleasure mounts. "—You, too."

And I get more of those beautiful neck kisses just for admitting it.

O——

WHEN MY ALARM music starts playing in the morning, I wake to find myself wrapped around Eric. I'm clutching him the way I used to hold my teddy bear.

"Make it stop," he mutters, grabbing my phone off the bedside table. "What do I tap?"

"That's not how it works," I say, pressing my cheek against his shoulder. "You have to ask Bingley nicely."

"Bingley!" Eric bellows. "Shut that off!"

The music is silenced immediately. "Of course, my lord. Would you like to snooze?"

"Yes," Eric grunts.

"Until when, sire?"

"Next Tuesday."

"Tuesday at what time?"

"Oh, for fuck's sake."

I hug Eric even more tightly. "We have to get up anyway."

"No." He rolls over and wraps his arms around my great girth. "Don't we *deserve* a day off?" One gray eye opens. "Are you okay? Did you sleep?"

"Mostly." Although my subconscious poked me a few times in the night. My eyes flew open in the dark as I remembered the sound of gunfire, and people's screams. I lay awake for a while, listening to Eric breathe, before eventually falling asleep again. "I'll be okay," I decide. Because I'm the lucky one. "Mr. Khun won't be."

"I know, baby. Did you know him well?"

"Not at all. I met him exactly once before, in my office. But still…" I swallow.

Eric runs a comforting hand up my bare back. "It's not your fault. You were just trying to pay him a lot of money."

"I know that. It's possible he was killed for reasons that have nothing to do with me." Possible, but not likely. "And where do I go from here? I can't just ring up the next manufacturer on my list and offer them the job. Too dangerous."

Eric makes a disgruntled noise. "Max better punish this fucker, then. Xian Smith or whoever. He's like a cloud over your life."

I curl up a little closer to Eric. "Listen, can I take you out to lunch later?"

"In a restaurant?" he asks sleepily. "Really?"

"Yes, that's the whole point. Maybe not the window seat. But life is short, and I'd like to spend more of mine sitting across from you."

His eyes spring open. "Engels, are you asking me out on a date?"

"Yeah," I say softly. "It's going to be a long day. But it would be better if I could see you in the middle of it."

Those gray eyes soften. "Now she gets it."

Yep. I totally do.

Eric pulls me close and kisses my temple. Then his hand finds my bare belly, rubbing it sweetly. "I know we have to get up. But I sure as hell don't want to."

"You make me want to stay in bed too, sir." His eyes flare as I run a hand down his muscular chest.

"Excuse me, queen," Bingley says. "I have a message from Max."

"I do *not* like that guy," Eric mumbles, kissing my shoulder.

"Which guy? Bingley or Max?" I tease.

"I'm afraid to answer that question," Eric whispers. "I don't want to turn the robot against me."

"I can hear you perfectly well, sire," Bingley says.

"Oh Engels," Eric complains. "I thought you said your home speaker wasn't creepy."

"He will never share your data," I assure him. "But that doesn't mean he understands tact."

"Tact!" Bingley announces. "A noun, meaning: a keen sense of how to deal with others. Would you like to hear the message from Max?"

"No," Eric says at the same time I say "yes."

"Dear me, that is confusing," Bingley fusses. "But my queen is the admin, therefore I obey her wishes above all others. Ergo: Max would like you to know that he's on his way over. He'll escort you to the office, where police officers will interview you about last night's events."

Well, that's a sobering start to my day.

"I'm going to physical therapy this morning," Eric says. "And then we'll see about lunch, okay? I'll come back into Manhattan either way, to see how you're doing."

"It's a date," I promise him.

36

ERIC

IT'S ANOTHER SWEATY, painful morning with Chip the therapist. But I take my punishment like a man.

"Good effort!" he says when I'm about three quarters dead, his voice as cheerful as always.

"Thanks," I gasp, rolling up off the mats.

"Did you hear we're getting a bunch of snow?"

"Really?" It rarely snows in Manhattan. Not more than a dusting, anyway. And never in December.

"Yeah. Like, eight inches. Might have to cancel our session tomorrow if the subways are shut down."

"What a shame," I say as sweat drips into my eyes.

Chip laughs as he walks away. "You sound really broken up about it. Come on, man. Go reward yourself with a shower and a protein shake."

But my real reward is a trip into midtown to have lunch with Alex. After my shower I put on a nice shirt and slacks. *On my way into the city*, I text her. *Still have time for lunch?*

By the time I reach Manhattan, I have a reply. *Your dad and brother are here to rehash the situation. But I'll kick everyone out of my office as soon as I can.*

When I reach the front desk of her building, I have to wait in line for a visitor's pass. This is a theme in my life, although Alex is worth it.

"ID, please," says the young woman behind the desk. "Who are you here to visit?" She gives me an appreciative once-over.

"Alex Engels." I set the ID down on the countertop.

"Do you have an appointment?"

"She's expecting me for lunch. Do you want me to call upstairs and ask her to approve the pass?"

"Hang on…" Her shiny nails make a clickety sound on the keyboard. "She added you to her approved list. I'm printing your pass now."

"Thanks."

A moment later I'm passing through the turnstile and then riding the elevator to the top floor. It's easy to find Alex's suite, because Rolf is parked at a desk right outside.

"You again," he says with a scowl.

"I told you I was the boyfriend."

He rolls his eyes. "Big security meeting, though." He hooks a thumb toward Alex's door. "They're not finished."

"That's okay. Those people all like me." I can see a flash of my dad's gray hair through the slats in the blinds that shield the office from curious eyes.

When I open the door, conversation stops.

"Eric," my brother says. He's standing in front of a whiteboard, a marker in his hand. "After last night, I can't put you back on Alex's detail. I need to use my pros."

"I'm not here for that," I say, crossing to Alex where she sits behind her desk. As soon as I reach her, Alex beams up at me, ready to receive my kiss, which I give her. "I'm here because I was invited to lunch. But please carry on. I'll just sit here and look pretty." I park my ass in a chair against the wall.

"Okay," my brother says with a sigh. "We're writing down everything we've learned about Xian Smith."

"Because we're trying to decide," Alex echoes, "whether it's even ethical for me to reach out to yet another supplier with an order. So far we've got one factory fire and one shooting death."

"Unless it's just a shitty coincidence," my father ventures.

Max slowly shakes his head. "This was not a coincidence. Eric —is there anything you can add to this timeline?" He points at the word *July* on the whiteboard. "He stopped you two in Hawaii to ask for a meeting. Did he say why?"

Hell, did he?

Alex and I glance at each other. "That encounter lasted two minutes, tops. And I don't think he said a word about his mission."

"Right," Alex agrees. "He wanted a meeting, but he didn't say why. Not until he showed up in August."

"August?" I ask.

"The…" Alex checks her phone. "Nineteenth. He turned up here in front of Rolf's desk, asking to meet with me. I gave him five minutes, tops. That time he said that changes were coming to Shenzhen, and that the old providers would become less reliable. Rolf was there, too."

Max crosses the office to open the door. "Hey, Rolf? Come here a sec?"

"What's up?" the young man says when he comes in.

"Remember in August, when Xian Smith just showed up one night?" Alex says. "Do you still have your notes? We're trying to remember exactly what he said."

"I dunno?" he says with a shrug. "I can check."

"Would you?" Alex says.

"And how'd the guy get in?" I ask, holding up my own visitor's pass. "Couldn't have been easy."

"Oh," Alex says softly. "I wondered that, too. Rolf! Didn't you call downstairs and ask about his security pass?"

"Sure I did," Rolf calls back from his desk. "But they never got back to me."

"Follow up, would you? The date in question was August nineteenth."

Alex and Max and my father go back to making notes about Xian Smith. But I'm getting hungry. Which means Alex must be starved. "Should I run out for tacos?" I offer.

"No!" Alex yelps. "I invited you to have a nice lunch, and we will have a nice lunch. Three courses. Linen napkins. No gunfire."

"We're almost done here," my father says. "Just as soon as your assistant gets that name from building security."

Impatient now, I get up and walk out of Alex's office. Rolf is tidying up his desk. He takes a framed photo of an elderly woman and slips it into his jacket pocket. "Can I help you?" he asks in a tone of voice that manages to convey that he'd really rather not.

"Any word from building security? I could go downstairs and ask them for you."

"They're calling me right back," he grumbles. "Give it a minute."

"Fine. And then where am I taking Alex for lunch?"

"Hillstone on Third Avenue," he says. "Table for two in back, nowhere near the window."

"Okay. Let us know when you've got that other information."

"Christ, I wouldn't want to hold up your reservation. Let me call 'em back." He grabs the phone and begins stabbing the buttons.

I leave his grumpy ass and go back into Alex's office.

"Exactly how many people knew about your lunch with Xian Smith?" my father is asking Alex.

"I told my security team. And I told the same two executives I named before—my chief technology officer and my CFO."

"That's all," Max says slowly.

"That's all," Alex agrees.

There's a tap on the door frame, and then Rolf pops his head in. "I have a name." He swallows visibly. "On August nineteenth, a visitor's pass for Xian Smith was authorized by Peter Whitbread."

"*Whitbread*," Alex breathes. "You have got to be shitting me."

"Your general counsel?" my dad asks. "That makes no sense."

"Sure it does," Max argues. "Whitbread wants Alex gone. And Xian Smith wants a foot in the door. If I were Smith, I'd ask Whitbread for help, too."

Nobody says anything for a minute. We're all busy thinking.

"Is that all?" Rolf asks finally.

"Yeah," Alex croaks. "Thank you."

More silence, while everyone works through the ramifications.

"He had the Thai contract," Alex says slowly. "He knew we were using Mr. Khun as a supplier."

"You're saying he passed that information to Smith?" my father asks. "If Whitbread is your mole, then nothing is safe."

"I have to confront him," Alex says.

"Or you could keep him around, but feed him misinformation," Max says.

"No," Alex shakes her head. "He's the leak that endangers anyone else I hire. Even if I try to misdirect him, someone else could get hurt."

"She's right," Carl agrees. "Let's walk into his office right now, before he gets a whiff that we're onto him."

"Is he in today?" my brother asks. "He'd be on this floor, right?"

"Yes, at the other end of the hall." Alex lifts her phone's handset. "Should I call him and check?"

"Do it," my father says. "I'll step out to make sure he doesn't leave."

As soon as the door closes behind him, Alex dials. "Everyone stay quiet a second."

The three of us listen to the phone ring through Alex's speaker. He answers on the second ring. "Whitbread."

"It's Alex. Listen, Peter. There's been some more trouble with a supplier. And I suspect that one of our manufacturers is up to no good. Can I come down to your office and fill you in?"

"Of course," he says. "If there's trouble, I'll need to know about it right away."

"Wonderful," she says smoothly. "I'll be there in five." She ends the call.

"Well," Max chuckles. "That will terrify him whether he's your leak or not."

She pushes back her chair. "Let's go. We'll start by asking him why the hell he gave Xian Smith a visitor's pass. I can't think of a single legitimate reason for Whitbread to meet with him."

My brother and Alex advance toward the door, looking tense.

"I suppose I shouldn't complain about my lost lunch plans?" I joke as Max opens the door for her. "Can I go buy us all takeout?"

Alex cups my cheek before she steps out. "You're always feeding me."

"Someone has to."

We all pass Rolf's desk. "Off to the restaurant?" the assistant asks.

"Not yet," Alex says, her voice tense. "Rolf, this might be another late night."

"Color me surprised. So I'm taking a lunch break now, okay?"

Alex doesn't answer. She's already on the move.

My father is waiting a ways off, in view of the elevators. He gives his head a shake to let her know that our man has not come by. Then he falls in with my brother and Alex on their way to Whitbread's office.

I bring up the rear, keeping my distance. Although I'm curious, this really has nothing to do with me. So I wait in the hallway outside the lawyer's office, my shoes sinking into the plush carpet runner underfoot.

The C-suite of a big corporation is always plushly furnished. At the end of the hall I can see a handsome boardroom with a giant oak table surrounded by more than a dozen leather chairs. I hear only the murmurs of executives on the phone, and the quiet tapping of keystrokes.

Something moves in my peripheral vision. But it's only Rolf heading out to lunch, his gym bag over his shoulder.

Rolf is a weird one. But aren't we all.

Although I don't take my gym bag out to lunch. Or bring along the photos from my desk.

Hold on.

I walk into the office where she and my family just disappeared. Whitbread is saying, "John Smith? Who?"

At my entrance, all four heads whip toward me, including Whitbread's jowly one.

"What?" Max demands.

"Alex—does Rolf visit the gym at lunch?"

Alex frowns. "No? Never."

"Shit!" I turn on my heel and head for the elevators.

Max is at my back about five paces later. "You think it's Rolf?"

"He fingered Whitbread," I say as we both race for the elevator bank. Rolf has already disappeared. I slap the button. "We just assumed he was telling the truth."

"Goddamn it!" Max taps his phone. "Dispatch, call building security at the Engels Tower. Lobby security needs to stop Alex's assistant Rolf…" Max falters because he doesn't know the kid's last name.

"Donhauser!" Alex says, pulling up the rear. "He's 5-11, twenty-six years old. Slender. Glasses. Caucasian. God, was it really him?"

"Yes," Max answers with more certainty than I feel. "Did he know you were meeting with Khun last night?"

"He could have," Alex says. "I logged the reservation into my calendar when I was on the phone with Khun. God *damn* it. Rolf never occurred to me!"

We all pile into the elevator, my dad and Whitbread bringing up the rear. "What is happening?" Whitbread asks. "Did he steal from us?"

"It's not clear," Max says, studying the elevator panel. "But we have to find him. Any chance he skipped the lobby for the basement?"

"Maybe," Alex says.

"I'll go to the basement," I offer. "We'll split up."

When the doors open at the lobby, everyone gets off except for me. And Alex. "Go with them," I urge.

She shakes her head. "I want to help."

I jam my finger onto the button so that the doors close again. "Dear God, let him not be in the basement," I grumble as we descend again.

"Why? He's not actually dangerous."

"Everyone is dangerous when he's cornered, Alex." The doors part in the basement. We're in a wide, utilitarian hallway stretching in both directions. "Do you know where the loading dock is?"

"This way." Alex takes off toward the left.

"Would Rolf know, too?"

"Absolutely." The corridor gets more interesting as we go along. There's a copy center, a mail room, and a boiler room. Then it branches off to the left and right. Alex takes a right-hand turn, and I follow her toward double doors marked *loading dock*. She waves her security pass at the scanner.

Nothing happens.

"What? No!" she yelps. "How do I not have access?"

I study the doors. "There's a fire alarm override."

"But the alarm isn't going off," she points out.

"True." So Rolf probably didn't go out this way. I pull out my phone. There's a text from Max. *He's not in the lobby. Nobody saw him. Reviewing elevator tape next. Got anything?*

Not yet, I reply. Which means he might be in this goddamn basement somewhere. Unless he got off on another floor? "Alex, are there exits on other floors? A mezzanine level, maybe?"

She shakes her head.

"Why don't I poke around down here, while you go up to the lobby? Max needs your help in the surveillance room." *In the nice, safe security office.*

"Okay." We walk back the way we came, but this time Alex stops to peek into every door along the way.

"Move along, now," I whisper as she lingers in front of a door marked *brooms*. I give her ass a little swat.

She turns around, and I assume she means to tell me to keep my hands off her backside. But she beckons me closer instead. I lean down so she can whisper in my ear. "The light just went out under the door."

Hell. He could be right there. I'm about to mouth: "Stay out here in the hall," when Alex grabs the door handle and flings it open. Light from the hallway spills into the dark space, illuminating the tiny room just enough to show us the shadowed figure of Rolf.

And the pistol he's aiming at Alex.

"Here's what's going to happen," Rolf says in a trembling voice. "Both of you are going to step forward. Put your phones on the floor. Slowly. And then Alex and I are going out the loading dock door. Together."

Shit. My eyes are fixed on that gun. It's pointed right at Alex's belly. "The alarm will go off," I say, watching that gun.

"Yeah, that can't be helped. Alex is going to walk with me to the Subway entrance. Once I get there, she's free to go."

"O-okay," she breathes.

"You won't hurt her," I snarl.

"Not if I make it down into the station." He lifts his pointy little chin. "Move forward. Both of you. And Eric doesn't leave this room until after the fire alarm stops."

"Okay," I grunt.

"Come on. Tick tock. Put your phone on the floor and kick it to me."

"I don't even have mine," Alex says tightly. "It's upstairs on my desk."

"Whatever. I want the jock's. What's your pass code?"

I raise one hand in the air and slowly reach for my phone with the other. "My passcode is my father's birthday. April 20, 1943." I put it on the floor and kick it toward him.

Holding my gaze, he begins to reach for it.

"But the phone is traceable, man. Just saying. They might be listening to us right now."

Rolf blinks. He's a man who's making this shit up as he goes along, and this bit of information throws him off.

And that's the hesitation I'd been waiting for. The point of the gun dips, so that now it's aimed at Alex's thigh.

That's the opening I've been waiting for.

My right hand closes around one of the brooms hanging on the wall beside me. With a snap of my wrist, the handle slices through the space between Rolf and Alex, catching Rolf's gun hand and bouncing it off the nearby wall.

The pistol falls right to the floor before Alex even has time to scream.

I lunge forward, grabbing Rolf and shoving him chest-first into the wall. His hands are behind his back a microsecond later. "You stupid fuck. You point a gun at my girl, and I'll break you in half."

He lets out an angry cry. "It's not loaded!"

"You are still a stupid—" I bounce his face off the wall. "—Fuck."

He lets out a sob. "He gave me money. I put my grandma in a nicer nursing home."

"Who did?" I demand, tightening my grip on his arms.

"Xian Smith!"

"Did you know he was going to *kill* people?"

"No! I swear. He just said he wanted to get closer to Alex. For business. He wanted to curry favor."

"What did you give him?" Max asks from the doorway. "How much does he have?"

"The visitor's pass. And the schedule," Rolf stammers. "Her home address. He said he wanted to send flowers."

"Flowers!" Alex shrieks. "He broke into my apartment to hack my phone."

"I didn't know! And when I told him I was done, he threatened me."

"Of course he did," Max says with a sigh. "You really *are* a stupid fuck. Eric, don't break his arms."

"Here's a zip tie!" my father says, pulling one out of his pocket. Some families carry tissues and gum. We carry restraints.

"Are we handing him to the police?" I ask.

"I haven't decided," Max says, fitting the tie around Rolf's wrists. "Got him."

As soon as I can step back, I duck out of the room to find Alex in the hallway. She's leaning back against the wall, breathing deeply. Like a person trying to get a grip. "Eric," she says breathily.

"Yeah, baby?"

"I'm sorry I opened the door when you were going to tell me not to."

"It's okay now, baby." I fold her into my arms.

"I can't believe Rolf is a traitor. Good assistants are hard to find. This is a disaster."

I laugh against her cheek. "One thing at a time, honey."

"There was a gun." She swallows hard.

"I'll bet he doesn't even own the bullets. That thing looked like a stage prop."

"Still. Is it awful that I could be hungry right after someone points a gun at me?"

"That's just biology, honey. Could you maybe knock off early? Let me take you home and feed you."

"I was going to take you out to lunch."

"Another time. We have time, right? I'm not going anywhere."

"True." She shifts, looking me dead in the eye. "I love you, Eric Bayer."

"Aw. That's just the adrenaline talking," I tease her. "It's only real if you say it when you're not drunk on fear."

"No, really." She leans her forehead against mine. "I love you. Thank you for rescuing me from my hundred-pound assistant and his unloaded gun."

"Now you're just fucking with me." I kiss her quickly.

We're nose to nose and smiling at each other when my brother drags Rolf out of the broom closet and hauls him past us.

"Good luck without me," the little twerp spits. "Ten bucks says you can't get through the day without someone to bring your coffee and fetch your dry cleaning."

"That's what I'm for," I say. "Told you I was really the boyfriend."

He makes an angry noise before they drag him out of sight.

Alex sighs. "That was pretty hot what you did with the broomstick."

"Hockey, baby. And my family thinks stickhandling is not a useful skill."

"They're wrong," she whispers. "Dead wrong."

37

ALEX

DUFF SHOWS up to take us home. "Guys," he says from behind the wheel. "It's going to snow. Like, snowpacalypse. So if your big fridge is empty, Alex, you might want to stop somewhere on the way home."

I look out the car window at the steely sky and find that I like this idea. New York shuts down whenever there's any accumulation. And I need a day of quiet just to stop my mind from spinning.

"S'posed to start around five and keep going for two days," Duff adds.

"I'll go out shopping," Eric says. "I might want to pick up a couple of things if I'm going to be snowed in at your place."

"I like that idea," I say, squeezing his hand. "We might get that day off after all."

And that's what happens. Eric buys out Eli's again, stuffing the fridge with prepared foods. He makes a quick trip to the Gap for a change of clothes, too.

By the time he returns, fat flakes are already falling from the sky. And I've cued up three different movies to watch with him.

We pass a quiet evening together on the sofa. When we wake up the next morning, New York lies under a thick layer of snow. And it's still coming down.

I spend an hour or two returning email, even though Engels Cable Media is staffed only by telecommuters for the day. My first task is writing a brief but apologetic email to Whitbread for bursting into his office to accuse him of leaking sensitive information.

He still hates me, and he'll probably assume that all our new troubles are my fault. And if I'm unable to buy parts for the Butler by mid-February, I'll finally be the failure he's always hoped I'd be.

But no matter. I have a fresh pot of decaf and warm slippers. Eric has left the apartment for an hour to work out in my building's basement gym. And even that is too far away. It's such a comfort to have him with me right now. There aren't even words to describe it.

Whenever he walks into a room where I am, I just feel happier. And when he smiles at me, I light up inside. I really do love him. And I'm going to repeat it until he believes me.

He probably already does, though. He's pretty smart.

I can't show him the way I'd like. I'm so pregnant that sex sounds like more work than fun. My back aches intermittently today, too. It's hard to believe that I'm going to be pregnant for at least two more weeks. If I get any larger, I'll burst.

When Eric returns from the gym, he takes a shower and joins me on the bed, where I'm propped up with my book. "It's still snowing," he reports. "But it's supposed to stop around midnight. The subways are all down, the airports are shut, and no cars can cross any of the major bridges."

"That sounds ghastly," I say.

"All the hotels are full because nobody can leave." Eric grabs a book off my bedside table and opens it. *What to Expect from Childbirth*.

"You are not reading that!" I gasp.

"Why not? You did."

"I give you five minutes, tops. Ten if you read the introduction."

He opens the book then peers at me over the top of it. "You think I'm not man enough to read about childbirth? Like I can't handle it?"

"You'll see," I promise.

I go back to my own book. But a few minutes later he makes a small gagging sound.

"Uh huh," I say. "What was it that got to you?"

"*Mucus plug.*"

"Keep reading, big boy. You haven't gotten to placentas yet."

"I can take it," he says, sounding a little smug.

"There's a chapter about eating your own placenta."

"*What?*" he yelps. "You're just fucking with me now."

"You wish, tough guy."

"Do you have a birth plan?" he asks.

"No."

"It says here you need one."

"I have eighteen days," I point out. "And I haven't figured out if I want an epidural. That's chapter three."

"Hmm," he says, flipping pages.

We go back to reading, but my back is killing me. I spend an inordinate amount of time adjusting my pillows.

"You okay?" Eric asks.

"Sure. My back just aches. I've been spending a lot of time on my feet."

He looks at me over the top of the book. "That's a sign of early labor."

"Really? You're on page fifty, and you're an expert now?" Just like a man.

"Hey, Bingley?" he says.

"Yes, my liege!"

"For a pregnant woman, what are the signs of early labor?"

Oh, this is rich. He's using my own butler against me?

"My lord, some signs of early labor include: fluid leaking from the vagina, cramping, and lower back pain."

"Thank you, Bingley." He closes the book. "Is it your lower back?"

"Well, sure," I grumble. "But doesn't your lower back ache sometimes?"

Eric shakes his head slowly.

"Mine does."

"Fine," he says quietly. "But if you think you might be in labor, raise your hand, okay? The snow might be an issue."

"I'm *not* in labor!" I can't be. "It's too early."

He gives me a sideways glance. "Okay. You're the expert."

I try to keep reading, but it's no good. I can't follow the story because now I'm panicking a little. "The, uh, backaches come and go."

Eric closes the childbirth book. "How often do they do that?"

"I'm not sure. It aches right now."

"Bingley!" Eric says. "Time this. Starting now."

"Yessir."

He rolls toward me. "Come here." When I adjust my giant body, he reaches around and starts rubbing my lower back.

"Ohhhhhh…yes. Yes yes yes. Keep doing that. Please." It feels so good, I want to weep. After a couple minutes I exhale, and the pain leaves.

"Better?"

"Yeah." We lie together in silence for a while. Until I say, "Uh oh."

"It hurts again?"

"Yep. Bingley, how much time has passed?"

"Nine minutes, my queen."

"Okay," Eric says softly. "Nine minutes is no big deal. The book says you could have contractions for twenty-four hours before it's even time to go to the hospital."

"Right." I blow out a breath. "I'm nervous. I'm not ready."

"I'll bet nobody is ever really ready," he says kindly. "But you'll be fine."

"You don't scare easily."

"No." He shakes his head. "I don't. Not much scares me. Not even a *mucus plug*."

I giggle. "Most men would be running for the door right now."

"Not me." He kisses me on the nose. "I told you. I'm here for this."

"Okay." I take a deep breath and try to calm my nerves. "Would it be a bad time to tell you that my mother had me on the back seat of the car? She didn't make it to the hospital."

He stops smiling. "Why not?"

"I showed up really fast."

"Is that…" He clears his throat. "A hereditary thing, you think?"

"Probably not, right?" We blink at each other for a long moment. "What time did you say it was going to stop snowing?"

"Midnight."

"And what time is it now?"

"Six forty-seven p.m.!" Bingley announces. "It is five hours and thirteen minutes until midnight."

"Thank you, Bingley," Eric says with a sigh.

"You just thanked a computer program," I point out.

"I'll thank all kinds of inanimate objects if the baby can just sit tight for one more night."

SHE DOESN'T.

By nine p.m., my back pains turn into front pains, and the space between them narrows from nine minutes down to four.

Eric spends half the time rubbing my aching back, and half of it staring out at the fat snowflakes falling past the window. When he calls down to the front desk to ask about road conditions, the doormen are not optimistic. "We don't plan on making it home tonight," they tell him. "The plows have been doing their best, but they're running out of places to put the snow. Madison Avenue has at least two fresh inches on it already. Nothing is getting through."

And when I come out of the bathroom, I overhear a whispered conversation between Eric and Duff, who's on shift again out in the hallway. "No way," Duff says. "The Mercedes has rear wheel drive and performance tires. We wouldn't make it two blocks."

"Can Max get an SUV up here? He must have a Jeep or a Hummer somewhere in that collection of his."

"I'll call it in. But he's all the way downtown."

Oh God. Eric told me not to panic. But I'm now starting to panic.

"Alex," Eric says in a calm voice when he returns to the bedroom. "New plan. We're not going to NYU. Mount Sinai is only eighteen blocks away. We can walk it."

"Walk it?" I squeak. And before I get a chance to voice my objections to this plan, another contraction hits me. I sit down on the edge of the bed and rub my lower stomach. It's tight, like a giant rubber band.

"Breathe," Eric reminds me.

"It's—really starting to hurt," I pant.

"Okay. Okay. Okay," he says in a voice that's a lot less calm than it was a few minutes ago. "We're going to put some boots on you, and a coat. And we're going to go outside and see if we can get a taxi. If we can't get that, I'll call 911 and see what they want us to do."

"Okay," I agree. Eric has a plan. Plans are good.

I stand up. And that's when I feel a popping sensation, followed by a flooding sensation. "Oh!" I gasp. "Water. Broke."

Then things begin to move very fast. And by "things," I mean Eric. First, he brings me a dry pair of yoga pants. Then he brings me a coat and a pair of hiking boots I'd forgotten I owned. Those must have come from the back of my closet. He even laces up the boots while I breathe through another contraction.

And, wow, I thought I knew pain before. "These aren't fooling around," I gasp.

"I know," he says, bundling me into my coat.

"My b-bag for the hospital is in the front hall closet."

"Bag?" he asks. "Okay. Sure. Let's go."

And then I'm in the elevator with Eric and a freaked-out Duff. "What happens if we can't get to the hospital?" the young man asks.

"We're getting there," Eric says.

"But what happens if—"

"Shut it!" I gasp as another contraction digs in.

Eric glances at his phone. "Three minutes? Shit."

The moment the elevator doors open, Duff shoots out, running for the street like a man on fire. "Taxi!"

Eric and I exchange a glance. "Just don't say *mucus plug*. I don't think he can take it."

"Gotcha," I wheeze.

Outside, there are no taxis. There aren't any cars, period. We see people out walking ecstatic dogs and giggling children. There are even diners inside the restaurants on Madison.

But the only cars are buried in snowbanks.

Duff gives a low whistle. "I've never seen anything like it."

"Let's walk," Eric says. "We'll go slow. And if you can't make it, I'll carry you."

There's no way I can let him do that. Not on bad knees, and not for fifteen blocks. "I can make it," I say.

"Eric, change shoes with me," Duff says.

We all look down at Eric's Vans. Duff is right. His work boots are better suited to the snow.

"Okay, thanks."

They swap right there in the snow, while I try to imagine walking to Madison and a Hundredth Street in eight inches of snow.

"This will be a story we'll tell her," Eric says, wrapping an arm around me and gently leading me up the street. "It was snowing when you decided to be born. There were no busses. No taxis. The subway stopped running. But you decided to come to us, anyway."

"Okay. Yes." Tears spring to my eyes. I can picture Eric walking down a snowy street, holding a little girl's hand, telling her this story.

"One foot in front of the other," he says. "You've got this."

And I do. At least until the next contraction. And then I'm standing there with snow soaking my shoes, whimpering in pain as my body squeezes the air out of me.

"Lean on me," Eric coaches. "That's it."

"Eric," I wheeze. "I decided it's a yes on that epidural."

"Right. Soon," he says. As soon as I catch my breath, we're walking again. We cross Eighty-ninth street, and Eric helps me over the snowbank that's blocking the corner.

The sidewalk here is thick with snow. "We should walk in the street," I point out.

"Next block," he agrees.

We're almost to Ninetieth when Eric yells suddenly. "Hey, kids!"

The group ahead of us halts in their tracks. "What?"

"I need that sled!" He lets go of my hand and jogs a few paces toward them. "It's an emergency."

"I just got this out of our storage unit!" a boy's voice argues. "We're going to the park!"

"Give you fifty bucks for it," Eric says. "The lady needs to go to the hospital."

The kid is eight or ten years old. He looks wary. "A hundred," he says.

"Jesus Christ." Eric is pulling out his wallet. "I got eighty. Come on."

The transaction goes through, and I can hear Duff laughing as he catches up to us, still lugging my hospital bag.

Eric trots back to me, a drugstore plastic sled in tow. "Climb aboard, Engels."

I climb gratefully onto the sled, and Eric takes off at a trot. Madison Avenue glides by, its shops advertising last minute holiday ideas and drink specials.

But the next contraction takes my breath away. I must have screamed because the sled stops, and Eric and Duff both peer down at me.

"Keep going," I pant.

And we do. Eric maneuvers the sled into the center of Madison Avenue, with Duff bringing up the rear to watch for cars that never pass by.

I lose track of our progress, though, because I have a new problem. "I-I want to p-push," I wheeze. "Really, a lot."

"Don't push," Eric barks. "No pushing."

"What does that mean?" Duff asks.

"Nothing good," Eric says, moving faster.

"Lemme take a turn?" Duff offers. "Your knee must hate this."

"Nope. I braced it." Eric pushes on. "This is easier than a bag skate. Hockey is an endurance sport."

"Labor is an endurance sport," I wheeze. My back is on fire, and my pelvis is as tight as a drum. "I need to push."

"There will be no pushing," Eric says as we fly toward the big red EMERGENCY sign on the west side of the street.

But the urge is so strong, I find I'm holding my breath. And when the contraction peaks, I scream.

That's how I enter the emergency room at Mount Sinai—screaming on a plastic sled. Coincidentally, they put me onto a gurney and get me into an exam room faster than you can say *ten centimeters dilated*.

Someone approaches with a pair of shears, which are used to cut off my yoga pants, and all I have to say is, "I need to push." Then I burst into tears.

"She's crowning!" a voice calls out.

"Page OB! Page peds," another voice demands.

Eric wipes my face and pets my hair. "You're okay," he whispers. "This is a great story, remember?"

"On the next contraction, you can push," someone says. My vision swims. The lights are so bright, and the doctor is completely swathed in blue scrubs, and with the cap and mask. I can't see anything but a pair of eyes.

"Arrrghhh!" someone screams. And that someone is me. I bear down, and the pain is extreme. I might rip right in half on this table.

And then something just gives way, and I feel the greatest relief I have ever felt in my *entire life*.

"Your baby's head has arrived," the doctor says. It's a woman. Through the blur, I focus on her very dark brown eyes. "One more push and you're there."

One more push. I'm so tired. "Can I have an epidural?"

The doctor laughs. So, I guess that's a no. "Daddy, come down here. You can help me deliver your baby."

"What? I don't know how to do that," he says.

"I've never delivered a baby before, either," the doctor says with a shrug. "But this one is coming either way."

Eric moves to the end of the table. He shed his jacket at some point. He's wearing a gray T-shirt with GAP in purple letters stretched across the chest, along with two days' worth of whiskers. I already know everything will be okay, and that I would follow him *anywhere*.

I take a deep breath. I can feel the next contraction coming, like a big swell in the ocean, ready to suck me under.

"Showtime!" the doctor says. "Push!"

I let out a roar as I bear down.

"There you are," Eric croons. "Hello, baby girl."

"Oh yeah, the umbilical cord," the doctor says. "Clamp?"

"Here."

And then I hear the best sound—a thin little wail. It's the sound of victory. I flop back onto the gurney, sweating from every pore.

When I look up, Eric is there, holding a slimy, wet baby in two big hands. A nurse sweeps a towel underneath that tiny body, gathering her up and easing her into Eric's arms.

"Oh, don't cry," Eric says, rocking her against his chest. "So— this is the world. It's a little bright, and a little loud. But we got you. And you really won big in the mama lottery."

Suddenly my eyes are fountains.

"Time of birth, eleven forty-two," someone says. "Where's the peds consult?"

"How much does she weigh?" I sob, hoping it's enough.

"Who knows? We don't have a baby scale in here. But God, that was fun!" the doctor says. "I should have been an OB. Come back any time."

This is pure chaos, and I don't even care. My baby girl is here. Eric has her in his arms.

We made it.

38

JANURARY

ERIC

I'M JUST FINISHING my coffee when I hear Rosie begin to mewl from the crib. I set my mug down on Alex's coffee table and go, because Alex is still in the shower.

"Hello, baby girl!" I say, entering the tidy nursery. Rosie's early arrival caught us off-guard, of course. But now this room is ready, with a soft flannel sheet on the crib mattress and tiny diapers stocked beside the changing table.

When I reach the edge of the crib, she looks up at me, blue eyes blinking, little hands opening and closing rapidly. *Pick me up, man,* she's saying. *This nap is over.*

I lean over the crib and lift her little body onto my forearm. "Look who's getting heavy! Did you put on another ounce in your sleep?"

Rose looks up at me without comment. But that's how it is with us. I do all the talking.

I lay her down on the changing table and unzip her pink sleeper. I trade the wet diaper for a dry one. But just as I'm about to zip her up again, I notice that Alex has laid out another outfit. It's like a whole-body sweater in pink and gray stripes.

"Looks like you're getting dolled up for company," I say, grabbing the garment and holding it up. I have socks larger than this thing. There are snaps around the crotch and legs, so I carefully undo those. And there's a single snap on the shoulder to widen the neck hole.

Hmm. I'm pretty good at the zip-up sleepers now. But this thing goes over her head?

"Okay, kid," I say, easing her soft little arms out of the sleeper. "This would be easier if you could sit up." I sort of prop her up with my left hand and then ease the sweater over her with my right.

She makes a noise of displeasure.

"Yup, just another second." I tug the garment over her round little head.

When her face pops through, her expression is mildly accusatory.

"Don't look at me, this was all Mommy's idea." I lay her down again and snap the crotch closed. But then I realize her arms are still at her sides, so I open it up again and poke around until I can ease those little hands down through the armholes. "Yes!" I say when she's wearing the thing properly. "Did it."

Rose is unimpressed, though. She's hungry, and I've burned through all her goodwill with the sweater. She opens her mouth and howls.

"Okay, lady. No need to shout." I grab the baby sling off the doorknob and drop it over my head, then I tuck her in and head for the kitchen.

"Someone needs a bottle," says Tara, the young woman that Alex hired to come in and cook a few days a week.

Alex chose to hire help in the kitchen instead of hiring a baby nurse. "There will be nannies," she had said. "But so long as I'm home, I want to do it all myself." I would never question Alex's choices for Rosie. But after I tasted Tara's cooking, the wisdom of this decision truly became clear.

Tara lifts the bottle out of a bowl of warm water and dries it with a towel just as Rose begins wailing in earnest. "There you go."

"Excellent timing, thank you." I grab it and hustle to the living room, where I make us comfortable on the sofa. And after testing the temperature of the milk, I touch the nipple to Rose's tiny lips.

And—this part always kills me—after she opens her little

mouth and takes the nipple, she gives her little head a shake as she begins to suck, just to make sure she's on there good and tight.

"There you go. This bottle doesn't stand a chance."

Blue eyes look up at me, satisfied now. I find her tiny hand with my finger, which she grabs tightly. Her hands fascinate me. I didn't know they made hands that small. She has short little fingers, each knuckle articulated in miniature, and fingernails no bigger than the head of a pin.

When she's about half done, there's a tap on the door.

"Come in!" The sling allows me to stand up and walk to the foyer while Rose keeps on slurping.

"Oh my God," are Rebecca's first words when she enters the apartment. "That is the cutest thing I have ever seen. I'm dead." She puts a hand over her forehead. "Oh, and the baby is pretty cute, too."

"What? Jeez. Come in already." I wave her through.

Nate Kattenberger follows his fiancée. He stops to smirk at me. "I need a photo. I'm thinking of a before and after picture. You with a whiskey bottle, then you with a baby bottle."

"Get your licks in now. Your day will come."

He laughs. "I don't doubt it."

"Hold up," Duff says instead of closing the door. "You have two more guests arriving."

I poke my head out into the hallway and spot Coach Worthington getting off the elevator with Georgia, his daughter. "Hey, guys! Come on in."

Georgia lets out a squeal. "Now I've seen everything."

"Yeah, yeah. In you go." I step aside to let her through. "Hey, coach. I'd shake your hand, but the little miss doesn't like it when I take away the bottle."

"Oh, I remember how that goes." Coach thwacks me on the shoulder as he passes me.

"Thanks, Duff. Just send people in, okay? There will be more."

"Sure thing. How's everyone sleeping this weekend?" Duff asks.

"We're sleeping well, but not often enough. Come in for a plate later, okay? Tara is cooking up some good party food."

"I'll do that."

Duff is the one who drove us home from the hospital last week. It was hilarious, honestly. With a newborn on board, Race-car Duff never topped ten miles per hour. And the plastic sled rode home with us in the passenger's seat.

"You're keeping that thing?" Alex had asked.

"Are you kidding? I paid eighty bucks for this. And when it snows next year, we can go sledding in Central Park." It's somewhere in her coat closet now.

Back in the living room, Alex has appeared in lipstick and a sweater dress. She's accepting kisses and presents from her guests.

"You look amazing!" Rebecca says. "Not at all like the sleep-deprived raccoon that most women turn into."

"It's all a facade," she says. "Concealer has been deployed. I don't even remember what a full night's sleep feels like."

It's true. Rosie likes to nurse every three or four hours. I'm usually in bed with both of them, but Alex doesn't use bottles at night, so I can just roll over and fall back to sleep.

My main job is making coffee in the morning and taking trips to the grocery store at regular intervals. And—this is educational—I have never received so much female attention as the time I wore Rosie in a sling to the deli. Forget professional hockey. The women of New York find nothing sexier than a man buying milk and bread with a baby sleeping on his chest.

Go figure.

I sit on the couch and remove the empty bottle from Rosie's mouth, then I lift her from the sling to a chorus of coos from the women.

"I'll burp her," Alex says, reaching over.

"Really? In that dress?" I wave her off and face Little Miss Spit-up toward my Bruisers T-shirt. "You can have her back in a second, I swear." I begin my patented series of rapid back pats until Rosie lets out a nice, locker-room-worthy belch.

The women are all watching with giant hearts in their eyes. And, sure enough, there's a little blob of milky goo on my shoulder.

"Who gets to hold her first?" Becca asks.

"Me!" Nate says. "Show me how this works."

I stand up, and Alex reaches for the baby. "Oh, you put on her sweater! I was going to put a cotton onesie on under this, though."

"You go ahead and try."

"That tricky, huh?" Alex asks with a big smile.

"You'll see."

I head for the bedroom to change my shirt, but Coach is on my heels. "Can I talk to you for a second?"

"Of course. Come on back." I've made myself at home in Alex's apartment.

After a week of my running home to shower and change, Alex invited me to store whatever I needed in her closet. "I really love having you here," she said as we held each other after a midnight feeding. "I hope you know that."

"I really love being here."

That was all the discussion we've had about it, so far. But I know Alex is it for me, and she's no longer fighting me on that question. We have time later to discuss it. Lots of time.

I toss my T-shirt into the hamper and grab another one out of the dresser drawer I've been allotted. "What's on your mind, Coach?"

"You," he says. "Doc says the surgery on your right knee is a certainty now. How are you not limping?"

"This is how." I lift the leg of my jeans and show the giant brace I've been wearing.

"I see. Does Alex know?"

"Not really." I shake my head. "I mean—when I tell her I need another surgery, it won't come as a shock. But she doesn't know how I reinjured it."

It happened the night Rosie was born. I don't know exactly when I got the brand-new meniscal tear. The pain began some-where on Madison Avenue, when I was focused entirely on getting Alex to the hospital, and on bringing our baby girl into the world.

It doesn't matter. I have no regrets at all. It would have happened at the rink if it didn't happen in the snow.

Life happens. And much of it is beautiful.

Coach sits backward on the chair in front of Alex's dressing table. "So, what does this mean for you?"

"Ah, so today's the day, huh? You're going to make me say it out loud."

He holds both hands outstretched. "Why not today?"

Why not today? The truth has been staring me in the face for a long time. "I'm out. I'm done. Even if I had the surgery tomorrow, I can't get back for playoffs. And even if everything goes exactly right, I probably won't play at the same level again. Not unless I want to have knee replacements before I'm forty."

"All right," Coach says quietly. "I'm sure you know best."

"Honestly I'll never know," I admit, sitting on the edge of the bed to button my clean shirt. "Hell, it's not easy to give up."

"You're not giving up," he assures me. "Unless we all are. I'm going to retire someday too, Eric. Do you think that's giving up?"

"No way." I laugh.

"Sometimes a man just needs to move on. I don't know what you're going to do next. But I'm sure it's something great."

"Thanks," I say, my throat suddenly tight. "This hasn't been an easy year."

"They never are," Coach says, getting up. "You have coffee somewhere in this fancy pad?"

"You bet. Let's pour you a cup."

I'VE HOSTED millions of parties, all of them bigger than this one. But I have never felt so much pride as I do right now, showing off my baby girl to friends and family. My heart might burst in front of fifteen guests.

My father is here, accompanied by his new girlfriend. There are three Bayers as well: Anton, Max, and Carl. Aside from family, my oldest friends make an interesting mix with the hockey people.

Eric's teammates have quietly embraced his strange and sudden transition to quasi-fatherhood by bringing a collection of beers and baby gifts, including a teddy bear wearing a Brooklyn Bruisers T-shirt.

"Something for everyone," Silas says, slapping Eric on the back. "Is that story about the sled true?"

"Which version?" he asks with a laugh. Apparently, our snowy trip to the hospital is making the rounds in the locker room. "Yes, I paid off a kid for it. Yes, I dragged it all the way into the emergency room. But the part about the cop giving me a speeding ticket? That's just bullshit. Anton invented it."

They all crack up.

"Happy New Year, dude," Castro says. "It's not the same without you around the gym."

"Oh, I'll be back in the gym."

"Come by tomorrow," the Coach says, putting Eric on the spot. "Team meeting."

"Sure, why not," he says. "But it's time to grab a plate, guys. Tara has put up a terrific spread."

After he points his friends toward the buffet, Eric comes over to see me. "Hey, pretty lady."

"Hey yourself." I kiss him on the jaw.

"I meant this one." Eric slides Rosie from my arms and holds her up. "Come with me, so your mama can eat something."

I swear—every time I see them together, my ovaries dance a jig. There is nothing like the sight of a man talking sweetly to a baby. It's all I need in the world.

"Grab a plate for yourself," Eric says. "I've got this."

But I have other plans to put into motion.

When everyone has a plate, I pick a spot in the center of the room and then tap a spoon against my mimosa glass. "Friends! I just want to thank you for coming to see us. It's hard to take a newborn out in the snow. I didn't plan that very well. Heck, I didn't plan much of anything very well this year."

A few people laugh, but not Eric. His warm eyes hold mine for a beat. He and I are both still trying to process all the ways that our lives have been reshaped.

It wasn't that long ago that I thought of Eric as a nice little break from reality. But that was so shortsighted. Once I stopped fighting it, I realized he could *be* my reality. I love him. He's here to stay. And the rest of it is really just noise.

I still have to fight for my company, and eventually catch a hacker. But first I get to spend another few weeks at home with the people who mean everything to me. And right now, I get to give them both a gift.

"While I have you," I say to the small crowd in my living room, "I want to show you all the hand-painted sign my father made for Rosie's room. He made it himself."

"I did!" my dad crows. "With these two hands. So if it's ugly, I don't want to know."

It isn't ugly. But that wouldn't matter. Dad stunned me by offering to make the sign, so of course I said yes right away.

"Okay, Dad. Let's do the big reveal. Ladies and gentlemen, the sign that will help Rosie learn to write her name—"

My father reaches behind his chair and pulls out a wide canvas on which he's lettered, in three shades of yellow, surrounded by daisies: ROSEMARIE ERICA ENGELS.

"Oh, perfect!" Rebecca squeals.

There are murmurs of approval. But only one person's opinion interests me right now. My gaze swings toward Eric because I purposefully hadn't told him Rosie's middle name yet.

He bursts out laughing. "You didn't."

"I did," I say, crossing the room to me. "It's legal. Right on her birth certificate. You campaigned hard, my love. And I can't think of anyone who deserves it more."

And right there, in front of the whole wide world—including both our families—I give him a big, juicy kiss on the lips. When I'm done, he's still laughing.

AFTER EVERYONE IS GONE, and while Rosie and I are nursing in the rocking chair, Eric hangs the new sign over Rosie's changing table. "Are you sure you don't need to do this yourself?" he teases, tapping in the molly.

"Nope. You go ahead. I'm retired from carpentry. I breastfeed, and I diaper, and I plan to read her the entire Harry Potter series, all four thousand pages."

"You know…" He picks up the screwdriver next. "I retired from something today, too."

"What's that?" I rock the chair gently as Rosie sucks.

"Hockey."

My chair abruptly stops rocking. He did not just say that. "Eric. Tell me you're joking?"

He shakes his head and then calmly screws in the hardware. "It's time, Alex. It always was. I just didn't want to believe it. I need another knee surgery, but this way I can put it off until spring instead of hurrying in there to become useless again."

"Wait," I sputter. "You're not putting it off on my account, are you? Eric—I love all the help you've given me. But I do not want to be the reason that you cut your career short."

"It's not like that," he says, lifting the painted sign into place on the wall. The wire catches the screw on the first try.

Of course it does.

"I'm happy to be here with you guys. It's a privilege." He turns around to face me. "I mean that literally. Most men can't spend time with the people they love whenever they want to. But I have money, time, and choices. Feeling sorry for myself would be a fucking crime."

Rosie picks that moment to pop off my breast and look up at him. I hope her first word won't be an f-bomb.

I tuck my breast away, my head still spinning as I lift Rosie to my shoulder to burp her. "I need a minute to get used to this idea."

"I needed about three months. So take your time." He straightens the painting. It looks really nice up there.

"You still need surgery," I say slowly. "Is that why you're wearing that giant brace all the time?"

"Yep. It's just to keep things stable."

"Will you move in with me before it happens? I don't want you to be alone in that studio with the stairs. I want to take care of you."

"Slow down, there." He chuckles. "It's not a hovel. It's a nice apartment. But the stairs are an issue."

"So is the location," I add. "If I ask you to move in, will you believe that it's because I love you and not just because you buy the groceries?"

"Oh, Engels," he laughs. "Tara made the last grocery run. Did you ask her to move in, too?"

"She's not my type."

He grins, and then he comes over to kiss me. "I believe you. I'd love to move in with you both. But you don't need to take care of me."

"I said I *wanted* to. You've taken such good care of me. If you have the surgery while I'm still home on maternity leave, I can take care of you both at once."

"Let me think about it." I get one more kiss before he stands up again.

"Here." I lift Rosie toward him. "Hold her for a moment?"

"Anytime." He perches the baby on his muscular shoulder. Then he catches me around the waist before I can get away. "Hey, I love you."

"I love you, too. And I know you don't like to accept help. We're the same that way."

"Yeah, we are. But thank you."

"For what?" I rest my cheek against his other shoulder.

"For everything. For making this transition bearable for me. For reminding me that hockey isn't everything."

"You're right, it isn't." I pat his ass. "But does that mean we aren't watching the game tonight?"

"Oh, we're watching it," he says. "It's time to introduce Rosie to hockey. I wonder how small they make skates?"

I can't wait to find out.

40

ERIC

IT ISN'T easy to walk into the big meeting room at the practice facility the next day. Because I'm pretty sure I'm doing it for the last time. As a team member anyway.

So I dawdle a little and walk in at the last second, hoping to slip into a chair in the back row.

But Coach isn't having that. "Eric Bayer!" he calls from the front. "Come down here, will you? There's something I need to know."

I hope he doesn't make a big deal out of this. I know that retiring is the right move for me, but I don't really want a lot of attention.

"Gentlemen!" he barks. "You recognize this guy?"

There are chuckles around the room.

"I do. I recognize him as somebody who spent last season keeping a cool head while the rest of us were losing our minds. But look—I've been your coach for less than a year. I've missed a lot of what this man did for the franchise these last ten years. So I'm going to need you to fill me in."

It's very quiet in the room now. I stand beside Coach, hands in my pockets, wondering what he means.

"Do me a favor," Coach says. "If Eric Bayer has given you a casual tip in the gym that changed your whole workout routine for the better, then please stand up."

Drake pops out of his seat, saying, "Every damn week!" And four or five more of my teammates rise, too.

My neck heats.

"Now stand up if Eric has ever stepped in to spot you when you needed an extra pair of hands in the gym. Or if he's lent you a piece of equipment, or if he offered to meet you for a run, so you didn't have to work out alone."

Half the room stands up now. My neck is on fire.

"That's what I thought," Coach says. "Now stand up if you've ever taken the seat next to Bayer's on the jet, or in the bar, because you knew that he wasn't going to poke you about some dumbass thing you did. Or because you knew he wasn't going to bring you drama. Stand up if you ever looked at Eric and said—that guy is solid. If I have to be trapped in an elevator, I hope it's with him."

Every single person in the room is on his feet, now. Including the coaches and support staff. I'm pretty sure I haven't cried in twenty-five years. I don't plan to start today.

But it sure is tempting.

"Yeah, that's what I thought," Coach says. "Guys, Eric will be hanging up his skates for a while. But I don't think we can get along without him. I can't tell you how it's going to work, or exactly what Eric will do with us going forward. But I will figure it out, because you don't lose a man like Eric Bayer. Not without a fight. So please put your hands together for our teammate, Eric Bayer."

The cheering, the applause, and the whistles are deafening.

RED-FACED NOW, I slip out the back of the room as soon as I can. Coach doesn't need me to stay for the meeting, so I go into the locker room alone to remove my skates and my personal items.

It doesn't take long, honestly. I don't want to linger, and I don't need to wallow. So I'm just zipping up my gym bag when my phone buzzes with a message from Bess. *How was it? Did he offer you a job?*

Basically, is all I say.

At the risk of being an asshole, take a look at this.

The next thing to light up my phone is a photo—it's me sitting with Bess at the restaurant, eating an avocado taco.

I like tacos, I tell her. *So I guess you're an asshole for making me hungry?*

Nah, she replies. *It's an I-told-you-so. I told you that this photo would remind you that you have a lot going for you.*

Okay, you win. She's right. I do have a lot going for me.

Don't take the job with Coach, she texts next.

Bess, I love you. But can I have an hour to myself before I plan my life?

Sure thing.

I shoulder my gym bag and walk out of the room, purposely not looking back as I go. I don't know when I'll be back. But I will be. As a coach, maybe. As a therapist? Or maybe a commentator.

Nah, not that.

I walk down the quiet hallway. Everyone is still in the meeting. But now Bess's message has piqued my curiosity, and I text her a question.

Who do you want me to work for if it's not Coach?

My phone rings immediately. I answer it.

"For me, dummy," Bess says. "I've been toying with the idea of taking on a partner. And you'd be an amazing agent. You're smart. You're easy to talk to. You know the sport so well."

And I'm speechless. *An agent.* Working with players and talking to management? I could do that. I'd *love* doing that. "You are messing with my head right now."

"I know," she says cheerfully. "And guess what? I'm sitting at the avocado taco restaurant right now. Think of it as our office. I just ordered the appetizers. Get down here, okay? I can feed you while I blow your mind."

"Okay," I say, because when a woman offers you food, you say yes.

And then I walk out of the practice facility. Into the sunshine, and into the next chapter of my life.

The End

ACKNOWLEDGMENTS AND FURTHER READING

Thank You!

Thank you Dr. Mark Kraus for explaining various knee surgeries! (It's not your fault that every time you mentioned ligaments and tendons, I wanted to dry heave.) You were super helpful! And all mistakes are my own.

Thank you to Jo Pettibone and Claudia Fosca Stahl for solving my proofreading emergency! I'm so grateful and I'm so impressed with both of you. I'd say "I owe you my firstborn" except my firstborn is a teenage boy who eats a lot. So it's better if I owe you something else instead.

Thank you to Hang Le for putting up with my last minute cover change, and with me in general! Your work always amazes me.

What's Real and What's Not?

Well, there's some creepy tech in this book, and unfortunately most of it is real!

The *least* realistic things in this book are: 1. Handing your keys to a valet for a lunch at The Modern on East 5rd and 2. Bingley's impressive sense of humor.

However, the hardware hack that Max describes to Alex is not a figment of my imagination! I wish it were. The potentially true story about the server hack was reported here in Bloomberg Magazine. You can draw your own conclusions. It's a good read.

As for Max's pork bun discount app that allowed him to read Tatum's emails? That's barely stretching the truth. In July 2018 it was reported in the *Wall Street Journal* that some app developers on a major phone platform had read thousands of user emails without their explicit permission. But their Terms of Service (that thing you click through without reading?) gave them that right. So they say.

Be safe out there! And stay tuned for more craziness from The Company!

Made in the
USA
Monee, IL

15567541R00181